Rob Gorthy lives with his partner, Heather, in the Cotswolds, where he writes, enjoys theatre, going for walks in the countryside, and birdwatching. He has an abiding interest in philosophy, US politics, reading good literature, and listening to music (Amadeus through to Zappa).

Dedication

To Heather, who has been patiently, and enthusiastically, supportive throughout.

Alistair Robin Gorthy

PARICHE

AUSTIN MACAULEY PUBLISHERS™

LONDON • CAMBRIDGE • NEW YORK • SHARJAH

A CIP catalogue record for this title is available from the British Library.

ISBN 9781787105652 (Paperback)
ISBN 9781787105669 (E-Book)

www.austinmacauley.com

First Published (2018)
Austin Macauley Publishers Ltd.
25 Canada Square
Canary Wharf
London
E14 5LQ

Acknowledgments

Joy for her encouragement and unstinting proof reading, Helen and Elaine for their friendly encouragement and advice, Steven for his patient reading, Jo, Paul and Lindsey, and of course, Heather, without whose help this book would not have been possible.

1

Berkeley, California

Jedemiah Pariche had been provoked. Provoked beyond measure. What else was he supposed to do, when such an example of an East Bay low-life gatecrashes The Project he and his good friend, Professor Soren Karlsson, had been working on for all these years? The nerve of it! Just what had Charlie Wilson been thinking? Why had the (acting) dean of faculty been so derelict as to have brought along Flaxel Boateng Mohamed, an associate of known crooks and a dealer in narcotics, to *their* groundbreaking ceremony? Of course Pariche could have handled things differently: threatening the two of them with the ceremonial spade he'd been using to break the soil, well that had not been the best of ideas.

Perhaps it was a bit rich of Pariche to think of The Project as *their* creation, for it had been his friend, Professor Karlsson, who'd put in all the legwork, writing the proposals and pitching them to committee. He'd been the one who'd fought for the funding and had won over the sponsors. He would, of course, have been the first to attest to Pariche's finer points; that he was good company and the provider of sometimes excellent counsel. But, with Jedemiah Pariche, this always came with an irascibility that would often have people running for the hills. A cantankerous cussedness that drove him to wreak a profound havoc, especially with those he contemptuously referred to as the 'committee people'.

Ah, yes, the 'committee people'. The harlots and charlatans who were plotting against his good friend and blackening his name whilst he was away. Wilson and his

9

cronies were exemplars of these and already they were at it; spreading rumours about how Soren Karlsson was no longer up to the job. Karlsson, they would say, had lost the confidence of those in authority over at the Chancellor's Office. How he was running away. Hadn't the fool only gone ahead and appointed an Asian teaching assistant to look after the store while he was away? 'A Chinaman,' Flaxel had scoffed, 'teaching about the Great Diaspora! Teaching Black History! Just what had the prof been thinking?' So now they were going after his teaching as well.

This was why Pariche had been there at the groundbreaking ceremony, looking out for his good friend's back; protecting him from this unholy alliance. Pariche, a cussed old fool whose faults, for some reason, the good professor had always been prepared to overlook. And there was indeed much to overlook.

Pariche, a biochemist at Berkeley, and highly regarded in his field, had a reputation for being difficult. He'd go back to his home in the Eastern Sierras, clambering up and down the hills around June and Mammoth Lakes, barking at strangers and getting himself re-tooled for the fight against the demons he found in and around the Bay area. He was good at giving the impression of being the everyman drifter, regaling anyone who cared to listen with stories of how, from his lair, high up in the mountains, he could see just what an amazing freak of nature California really was. How anyone, with a scintilla of good sense, could gaze across the Owens and Death Valleys and see just how pityingly insignificant human interests really were. It beggared belief that one of them had already been drained and leeched dry in California's increasingly desperate search for water; proof, writ large, of man's egregious folly in thinking he could improve upon the Promised Land. One day the Gods would bear down from the mountains and reclaim their due.

Some people found it hard to believe that this really was the distinguished university-wide professor at the University of California, Berkeley. For here was a man with a temperament born of an honest brilliance, that might, in any other place or time, be accommodated as a somewhat cussed eccentricity. But in Berkeley there had to be an attitude; an attitude more attuned to the political sensitivities of the times. It was something Pariche could never have attended to. That he was tolerated, even lauded by some, was down to past deeds and, whenever the charm was turned on, a persuasive and winning personality. A string of university Chancellors had, over the years, proved a cinch to carouse and entertain. Even to this day, the current occupant, Ira Heyman, very much against the wishes of those in charge of his timetable, would carry on the tradition of submitting to an annual meeting with Pariche, where, over drinks, they would shoot the breeze and talk about old times. It was something Wilson, the current (acting) dean, very much resented.

2

The Berkshires, western Massachusetts

Professor Soren Karlsson had just left his mother's house in western New England, blissfully unaware of what Pariche had been up to on his behalf, on the other side of the continent. He was presently gazing up at Porter's Mount, one of his favourite childhood haunts, invigorated and enthused by that penetratingly fresh autumnal air he'd come to miss in the balmy atmosphere of Northern California. For just the briefest of moments, there was an all too fleeting sensation of sweet freedom; that exhilarating sense of release and wellbeing so often associated with the anticipation of new beginnings.

Starting along an old valley footpath, moss laden and shielded from the sunlight, he sensed that once again his beloved Berkshires were conspiring to prevent him from making this damned fool journey. Ah, doubt! This was something of which Pariche would most definitely approve; just enough to challenge the sweetness of the moment and deter what so easily could become a descent into the otiose ghastliness of sentiment. Something that was only for the sheltered and the unprovoked. Doubt, and its twin, scepticism, may have been welcome, but Pariche would not have countenanced the lack of resolve that so often accompanied them. In his mind, there would be the need for his friend to dig deep and draw upon all the resources he could muster in the good fight that was to come. He would need to shield himself against the evils of this world, masquerading as the good life and the sublimely content. For things were about to happen to Soren Karlsson, who, for the moment, was far too content in his discovery of old haunts to be unduly worried by such matters.

Apart from the need for that rejuvenated – if illusory – taste of sweet freedom, another reason for being on Porter's Mount had been the much more mundane need of having to get away from the calamity that was his mother, Christina, returning home to the sweet herbal smells of Marrakesh. It had caused her to launch straightaway into an attack on his oldest friend, Brad Hemlin, an attending physician at San Francisco General, for violating just about every professional and ethical statute she could imagine. More woundingly she'd held her son responsible, upbraiding him further for what she perceived to be his uncaring attitude.

'You really have been beastly, Soren,' she'd said, pounding the cushion upon which she sat, as she looked around for further objects to assault. 'Why was I not informed of this ill-conceived folly? This trip to Mississippi? I even had to break off an important meeting!'

And all her son could find, by way of response, was a rather immature and feeble, 'Plotting again, Mother?' Then the explosions came, as the pent-up energies of two closely conjoined and repressed irreconcilables finally blew. So Soren had retired hurt to the surrogacy of the wilderness he loved, knowing a temporary distance would serve them both well.

His pace quickened as he passed through the first beech plantation, driving deeper into the shaded basin of a valley floor. When he had last been here, in the summer, the woods had been alive to the sound of birdsong, when he'd recognised the call of chickadees, warblers and thrushes. Now there was silence, save for the creaking of branches and the rustle of leaves, blowing in the fall breeze, and the occasional distant honking of migrating geese. As he walked, he continued to dwell on what his mother had said. How, over the past six months, she, as a senior Senator in the Massachusetts state legislature, had managed to exchange more words with the Mafioso hoodlum her committee had been investigating, than with her own son. Just another thing to occupy his thoughts. He also remembered the patrol car waiting patiently on the driveway outside the house. It was his mother's protection detail and a reminder that she'd been dealing with a malignancy that held grudges. One that could prove deadly if provoked.

'She wouldn't be in any danger now, would she?' he'd asked of his friends.

'Of course not,' they'd all replied, shaking their heads in disbelief. 'Of course not.'

3

At the same time Soren was reflecting on the safety of his mother, she was also occupying the thoughts of two gentlemen sitting in a black Oldsmobile, parked down the lane from the house where she was holding court. The word 'gentlemen' is used advisedly, as this was a description rarely applied to the likes of Tank and his associate, Felix. It was never applied to their boss, Albert Constanze. He'd been in one of his rages and this had driven these two foot soldiers all the way to this rustic outpost. A payphone, across the street from the pizza parlour he often frequented, in Boston's North End, would normally have served as a vehicle for one of Albert's tirades, as some poor sap quaked at the end of the line. But not this time. Had the officers in Christina's protection detail got out of their patrol car, and had they been minded to take a stroll around the property, they would have noticed the pair. They could have then run a check on the car and found it was registered in the name of a well-known racketeer who was himself under investigation by the owner of the property they were protecting. But the checks were not made and the two 'gentlemen' continued their observations uninterrupted. There they sat, just fifty yards away from a large and imposing three-gabled house, whose occupants continued to go about their business, unaware of the scrutiny and the danger so close to home.

Tank, the more senior of the two men, gave the impression he could break, and had probably broken, necks with his bare hands. Like his boss, he thought of himself as a moral being; something confirmed in his own mind by his regular attendance at confession. Before he'd set out he'd dutifully listened as his boss had held forth. How he'd like to see her hog-tied, with various bits chopped off of her and fed to the fishes. Yes, foul words, from a foul man. A man who'd been reduced to mouthing derogatory imprecations as he sat accused before the Senator's hearings. The humiliation of having to prostrate himself before this hick politician, from this hick town, somewhere in the Berkshires, had been galling. Who the hell did she think she was? Women weren't supposed to be like this. And the house that Tank and Felix were presently gazing at, would only have added to his sense of outrage.

'How does anyone afford a place like this?' asked Felix, a man with shockingly white hair.

'She steals, just like everyone else,' was Tank's reply.

'She could have married into it.'

Had Albert been with them, he would have told them that this wasn't the case. Senator Karlsson had never married, a fact that had puzzled him ever since she'd started prying into his affairs. He would often counsel his minions as to what a woman needed, and, in his somewhat earthy delivery, would tell them how this would always involve a firm hand delivered by a man. And if the woman protested, well, she was obviously a dyke or a whore, as the frigid, ugly ones nearly always were. But this didn't seem to be the case with her. A dame like that should have guys queuing around the block. But no, not this one. No men, no relatives, no family or folks. No one to put the squeeze on, save for the bitch herself. As yet, he didn't know she had a son.

'I'm sure I know this place,' Felix continued, biting into a pastrami sandwich that oozed red sauce down his chin. 'One of Messina's boys had a joint like this. Used it as a weekend place during the fifties. Some of the parties I hear were kinda wild.'

Yes, Albert would have been able to tell them a yarn or two about the parties, and the women. Although he was short and squat, he once had a physique that he fancied women found attractive. Years ago, when not working his way through the grisly task of disposing of dead bodies, making his way up through the ranks of his prospective trade, Albert could be seen trying out his platforms at the Boston-Boston.

There he would let off steam and impress those around him with the extravagance of his spending and his ability to peddle influence. But this woman was different; there was just no way of getting through to her. That Christina, like most women today, would have found him singly unattractive, appeared never to have crossed his mind.

On Christina's part there had been the avoidance of anything that could be construed as personable engagement, their only eye contact being on the occasions when he was squirming and struggling to be something more than he was: a dapper-dressed, wise-cracking hood, out of his depth. He'd hopes of breaking her down, but her iron grip on proceedings had precluded anything that would signal an accommodation with this bogus personification of Italian-American charm. She was thorough, meticulously even handed, always with a look of scepticism as to what she was witnessing and maddeningly impervious to any of his blandishments. Each compliment, insult, threat or guffaw was met with the same aloof detachment. Sometimes there would be a flash of irritation; but never one of shared insight or appreciation. And on top of this, along with all the indignities she'd heaped upon him, he'd had to endure the increasingly attentive gaze of the Boston police, the FBI and the IRS. Albert was now fearful they were going to put him away for good. And the paranoid in him knew that *she'd* been responsible, using her position to goad the authorities into taking further action. 'What did the police think they were doing?' he'd heard her trumpet from the steps of the State House. 'Allowing such a man as this his continued liberty! Could they not remove this cancer?'

'Cancer? Cancer!!' Albert had screamed, as he heard the sirens beginning to wail in his head. How had it come to this? All he'd wanted, at this stage in life, was to retire under the increasingly beneficent eye of a Boston public, conveniently forgetful of his hoodlum past. He'd even gone legit with some of the charities and organisations he supported. But then along came the Karlsson Committee.

Christina had just wanted to look into the misbehaviour of a certain priest, someone who'd become a local celebrity and darling of the media, but no big shakes. He was shown to be connected to a couple of two-bit hoodlums involved in loan sharking and child prostitution. There had also been dealings with a corrupt police precinct captain and a crooked city councilman, all of which had somehow led to the door of Albert Constanze. And, with this, the Boston Globe and the local radio and TV networks all got in on the act, righteous in their indignation that once again their fair and noble city was laying itself open to graft and corruption. There had even been talk of a Grand Jury. Albert had been justifiably alarmed and had quickly sought to distance himself from it all, especially when the priest in question had charges brought against him relating to underage prostitution.

'Me?' Albert had protested with wide-eyed innocence, 'Doing stuff like that?' If only the committee were to name a date, he'd be happy to appear as a friendly witness.

But this had not been enough. Not enough for *her*. The bitch had just kept coming, no doubt on a mission to nail his vitals to the State House doors. She wanted the good folks of Boston to know that Albert Constanze and his ilk were being dealt with. And it was working. She was getting too many of the witnesses to talk before Albert could get to them. It was an indignity that couldn't be allowed to stand. Her committee had real power. When people appeared before it, they were reminded of the fact that they were under oath. Albert had seen how this had unnerved many. It led to a loosening of tongues. Witnesses suddenly had the habit of becoming upright citizens. Hell, some even developed the habit of telling the truth. It had to stop. But how? How could you get to all these people? The answer was simple. Go to the top. Go after the bitch herself.

Tank could see the logic of such a course of action, but was unsure of the wisdom of such a move.

'Can we do that, Boss?' He'd asked at the time. 'You know; whack her?'

'Hell, I didn't mean that, Tank!' Albert was horrified his lieutenant could be so indiscreet. 'Perhaps we could put Felix onto it. Scare her a little.'

'That would be difficult. She's got a lot of protection.'

'Yes, to do it here would bring down too much heat. Maybe there's someone she's got working for her. Is there anyone on her payroll? There's got to be somebody, Tank. Jesus, I'm drowning here!'

'Leave it with me, Boss,' said Tank, his doleful expression masking a picture of murderous intent.

'But remember, nothing silly.'

'Sure, Boss, nothing silly.'

4

Jedemiah Joshua Pariche was born high up on the Coconino Plateau in Northern Arizona just over three score years ago. His parents, of Anglo-Scottish stock, lived and worked amongst the Havasupai, Hualapai and Kaibab Indians, passing on to their son a tradition of self-help and the importance of the struggle for civil rights. Later, they moved to the town of Bishop, in the foothills of the High Sierras, in California, where Pariche set about busying himself in the family tradition. A youthful Pariche, during the years of the Second World War, could be found pounding the roads in and around Bishop, fighting the good fight. There had been a time when, still in high school, Pariche had agitated for the admission of black members to a local Mormon church, although the one family living in the area had shown no such interest in wanting to do so. A newsletter had been produced and duly distributed by the boy Pariche to all the local churches, urging everyone to join in the campaign. It sold for a nickel (free to black residents, and any descendants of the local Paiute and Shoshone tribes). Locals would still talk of the lanky, gawky kid who'd spent the summer of '44 cycling the district, earnestly engaged upon the mission of 'improving the lot of the Native American, the negro, and one's soul.' Later, Pariche, with the assistance of some Inyo County school friends, led forays into Modesto, where there had been the challenge of a whole school district to desegregate. Dare one say, it went down a bomb.

The fifties and sixties were to prove the most fertile of times for the cultivation of the issues and indignities that would feed Pariche's sense of radical injustice. After a somewhat curtailed experience in the army, following attempts to introduce his notion of social equality to that organisation, Pariche leant his support to the department store boycotts in Berkeley and the efforts to get more black workers employed front-of-house. Then there were his first forays into the Deep South, followed by the Free Speech and Anti-Vietnam War campaigns being fought closer to home. It was only natural therefore that Pariche should attempt to encourage Soren down a similar path, when the latter had shown increasing signs of restlessness. Two years ago they'd been on one of their annual treks in Pariche's old stomping ground, high up in the Kaibab Forest, in Northern Arizona. Pariche had taken one look at his friend and concluded that here was someone in serious need of a break. What better than to take advantage of an invitation from an old friend and sparring partner, Basil Doleson, who needed help with a project he was planning down in Mississippi; something he referred to as 'The Institute'. So later, over whiskies and blues music, at a Western Division Conference in Denver, the two of them set about convincing Soren of how a trip to Mississippi might do him the world of good. It would also get him away from the clutches of Charlie Wilson. Drunk and somewhat maudlin, Soren had taken the bait and this was why he was presently contemplating this forthcoming journey to Mississippi. A journey that would begin in two days' time.

Now, though, as he continued his enjoyment of Porter's Mount, Soren could feel the doubts beginning to mount, not least those regarding his motives for embarking on this journey in the first place. The venture seemed nothing more than a desperately futile gesture. Already he could sense that original declaration of sweet freedom he'd felt earlier being subjected to anxious interrogation and doubt. He thought of Pariche and muttered to himself, 'God save us from those who would seek to save our souls.'

5

Soren's gait was now more purposeful, in tune with his reinvigorated resolve. Of course he was blissfully ignorant of what Albert Constanze and his foot soldiers had resolved to do, and completely unaware of what Pariche had been up to on his behalf back in Berkeley. Soon he was at the wood's edge, before a badly weathered limestone wall. Beyond lay an open expanse of hillside, with its mottled specks of white and gold set amidst rolling banks of green. As he stepped into the light, he let forth a rejuvenated sigh. This was indeed an old and valued friend. He marched on, clambering higher and higher, until presently he was perched aloft Porter's mount. From here he was able to gaze westwards, towards the Hudson River. The fading evening light appeared to lift the river's serpentine meanders from the plain they bisected. Beyond could just be discerned the darkened contours of the Catskills as they made their gentle descent into the Mohawk Valley.

For Soren it had always been the hills. Here there were memories of wide-eyed and free-wheeling madness. A young fool with his head filled with the tunes of the day and scarcely a care in the world. He remembered sunny days spent playing games with the other kids from the village, and lying in the long grass, gazing up at the wispy vapour trails of Stratojets, those emblems of Cold War potency and threat, as they made their silent progress, beyond the Adirondacks, towards Plattsburgh. There had been those summer electric storms that would light up the escarpment and the walks along the back roads and lanes he knew so well. The times he'd hitched a ride on the back of a local tractor or come across the quick-striding Tod Beecher, off to give the Star

Inn one more trashing, before a return to the hills and recuperation. And, of course, there were memories of Virginia. Distant, almost ghostly, memories, and the wonder of innocent discovery. That first kiss. The warmth of her embrace. Her lithe figure walking the path before him. And their lying together in Harper's Meadow.

He was gazing upon a scene that was both familiar and wonderfully ordinary. He'd forgotten how human the scale of life was, here in Western Massachusetts. Intimate, ghostly still and agreeably bland. The evening sun cast long vespertine shadows across the valley floor, raising and lowering silhouetted forms. In the distance, lights could be seen coming from the sleepy hamlet of East Brunswick, a village that had served, for most of Soren's upbringing, as an enjoyable, if somewhat anaesthetising, backdrop. The place had escaped what he'd come to regard as the more insidious encroachments of modern corporate America, with its wall-to-wall advertising, fast food outlets and ready-to-wear leisure. Here there were no TV evangelists exhorting the masses to find spiritual salvation at the touch of a TV screen and the nearest any citizen came by way of worldly anxiety, was whenever they deigned to visit Pittsfield, just down the road, with its intimation of the possible mayhem that might exist in the world beyond. In such matters East Brunswick held a courteous silence, with just a hint of pained disbelief. Yes, the scene before him was wonderfully familiar and Episcopal, and it served only to hasten the question; why was he still so set on persevering with this trip to Toshoba County, Mississippi?

The weight of the question seemed almost unbearable. To paraphrase an Englishwoman and novelist of the Georgian era, it is a truth universally acknowledged that there can be few more attractive propositions than that of a young man, unattached, and in possession of academic tenure from one of the world's most prestigious universities. It was the position in which Soren Karlsson had found himself. But now, along with some friends from the Bay area, he was seeking to get away from what he'd increasingly come to see as a fraught existence, too much within the clutches of a highly manipulative, and unforgiving, acting dean of faculty.

6

Back in Mountain View, California, Pariche was standing before a large office facility that was the Zenotech HQ, where besuited and frisbee-playing men-children were engaged in a project to genetically recalibrate a new world. These were going to be the masters of the next millennium. Forget the big city slickers, the financiers and the bankers, these people wanted to change the very essence of what it is to be human. Some of them were Pariche's old students, but the knowledge base they possessed now, and what they were overseeing in the building's 'reflection rooms' and research labs, had long passed him by. The basic science hadn't changed; it was what they were doing to it that had become a mystery and perhaps something to dread. He entered a reception area whose bright and breezy atmosphere belied the gravity of the science carried out here. He was there to atone; to make amends for that little misunderstanding that had taken place earlier at the groundbreaking. Pariche was going to prostrate himself before those who had the power to pass sentence on the project he and his good friend, Soren Karlsson, had been working on. Had the latter known what he was up to, it would have added to the already considerable apprehension and anxiety he was feeling.

It had been Pariche's idea to go to Mississippi, informing the younger man that he would be in a much healthier place if he just got shot of Wilson, the acting dean, and the 'committee people'. In providing such counsel, Pariche could not have known that such a venture would end in murder. Had he known, of course, then he would never have urged his good friend to go. But all the old fool could see was an increasingly restless and listless soul, driving himself to despair, in a department overseen by crooks. Pariche had just the antidote; something that would get his friend away from those who were doing their best to bring him down. So Soren had found himself agreeing to put some time in, down there, in Mississippi; just like Pariche had done some twenty-five years earlier. And while Soren was away, Pariche would take it upon himself to look after 'the farm', as he called it, back in Berkeley.

So why was Pariche so, well, Pariche? There were many theories. Those who know him, if it can ever be said that anyone could truly know the man, say that he never really got over the disappearance of his wife, Mildred, some ten years ago. The cantankerousness had been there all along, of course, latching onto whatever issue was waiting to be championed, but it had grown worse with the passing of his wife.

Mildred Hildegaarth Neuman had been a woman any man worth his salt would have killed for; not least, Professor Maynard Sentor, then the prospective Chair of the Chemistry Department, and the man Pariche had taken her away from some thirty years ago. Mildred, a woman of slight build, had a stoic forbearance that had been a must for anyone bent upon living an eternity with Pariche. At the time, Pariche had perceived a woman who'd been dreadfully wronged by a philandering, abusive and no good husband. The resulting scandal had almost ended Pariche's fledgling career, but it had been Mildred who'd been the rock. She had been the one who'd provided the platform by which Pariche was able to execute his assault upon the man who had so wronged this 'treasure'. And to this aim Pariche had made use of his old contacts in the Governor's Mansion in Sacramento to put pressure on the Chancellor's Office. At the same time his newly tenured, but non-sinecure, voice, could be heard railing against the evils of allowing such a pre-eminent university department to fall into the hands of such a debaser of moral virtues. The prospective Chemistry Chair didn't stand a chance.

Subsequently, through all the mishaps and hardships, Pariche had come to rely upon the support of this woman who'd been so endowed with a ruggedness of spirit that had suited the Sierra landscape she'd come to love. She was a medical doctor, trained in her native Chicago, who, for the best part of the next twenty years, could regularly be seen doing the rounds and administering to the local populace. A tough, no-nonsense woman, who'd soon become used to the long Sierra winters and basic living. It was a thing that came as something of a surprise to some of the old hands at Berkeley, who remembered her as Maynard Sentor's flighty, and somewhat precious, wife.

Five years his junior, with small green eyes that peered through tiny moon-shaped glasses, Mildred had a mannered countenance that complemented the volatility of Pariche; knowing exactly the best moments when the old fool had needed to be reined in and put back in his box. From the stories he'd heard, Soren had been able to get a glimpse into their life together, such as the annual New Year celebrations they would hold for the amusement of the local kids. With Pariche as Master of Ceremonies, and accompanied by Mildred at the piano, this 'assembly', as Pariche termed these occasions, would be composed of a series of 'happenings', frenetically enacted to the strains of The Mothers of Invention's 'Invocation and Ritual Dance of the Young Pumpkin.' Someone, on witnessing them, had once described it as a cross between an absurdist production of the Muppets and Bertold Brecht. Needless to say, the kids loved it.

But Pariche had lost Mildred, and in the most appalling of circumstances. Police had called at their home, after finding Mildred's car abandoned on one of the back roads, just above the town of Bishop. There had been blood on the seats – tests were to prove beyond doubt that it was hers – but a body had never been found. For Pariche, it was the lack of a body that was most soul destroying. He could have coped had there been one. Then the pain would have been bearable, the loss complete. But this limbo was far worse; as if the heavens had joined forces with a jealous and perniciously sadistic Satanist. Part of the therapy had been for Pariche to deny that Mildred had really gone. For as long as Soren had known him, Pariche had spoken of her as if she was still alive. It was an unacknowledged pact between the two men that this pretence, along with their budding friendship, had probably prevented the older man's decline and descent into madness.

Pariche would often talk about the fortuitousness of their friendship, coming as it did at a time when he was having to deal with such a grievous loss. The two men had first met at a homeless shelter in the Tenderloin district of San Francisco, where they were both doing voluntary work. At the time, Soren had needed a scientist to teach on the program he was setting up, and Pariche more than fitted the bill. Thus was started a process whereby a deep and lasting well of affection for the younger man was to be instilled. Somewhere in this bear of man's psyche, Soren had scored a direct hit; an affection that would have kept a Freudian analyst in fees for years. Pariche could see that Soren needed help himself. How the younger man appeared to be increasingly imprisoned by what the older man perceived to be the dark forces gathering around him. Someone who needed mentoring and taken in hand. And this would now be Pariche's calling; well this, and the continuing need to fight the good fight against the 'committee people' of course. But first, the younger man would have to be prised away from the grasp of the Great Satan, the current acting dean of faculty.

7

Before making the first of his journeys out west, Soren Karlsson had chosen to study at Columbia University, amidst the sleaze and seemingly terminal decline of Mayor Lindsey's New York. His choice, in no small part, had been due to the new love of his life, Geraldine Cassandra Stark. She was a dreamy Patti Smith lookalike he'd first met a year earlier at a party here in the Berkshires. It would be fair to say that most of the more influential figures in Soren's life had been women. There was his mother, of course, her close friend, Elizabeth Van Buren, Professor Genevieve Rosen, Soren's old mentor at Columbia, and Virginia. The one mistake was to have allowed Geraldine to insinuate herself into this august assemble. Part of the attraction had been that Gerry, as she liked to be called, hailed from nearby Lenox. Unfortunately, this also meant that she was one short drive or train ride away from her mother, Melissa. As Christina had been quick to point out at the time, she was also known to be as mad as the proverbial hatter. But Soren was hooked; Geraldine seemed to possess the same original spirit of counter culture that Soren had fallen in love with whilst still a junior at Exeter Phillips in New Hampshire. Then he'd been mesmerised by distant, flickering images, beaming in from the West Coast, of Mario Savio and the Free Speech Movement, protesting antiquated university statutes and the war in Vietnam. Closer to home, in New York, there was the emergence of a new alternative cultural scene and the protests at Columbia. He should have known better. By the time he'd enrolled there, the Mark Rudd era of protest had come and gone, and all of those Warhol 'Factories' now produced nothing but commercial tat, aided and abetted by a

Village Voice that had lost its soul. He'd attempted to engage with the usual left suspects, such as the remnants of the old SDS and the anti-apartheid movement, but those close to him perceived a deep seated scepticism about much of what he saw. It kept him from being too closely identified with the more extreme elements on campus; anyway, he found much of their ritual and rhetoric too embarrassing and hilarious to contemplate. With Geraldine, and his friend, Brad, he was more likely to be seen scouring the city's clubs and dives, attempting to score that elusive cultural hit. But there were limits. Harlem was out of bounds; only on rare occasions would they venture there for a bit of R&B music, or a live night at the Apollo. Far more likely would be the taking in of a rock show at the Palladium or whatever was playing down in the village. As Flaxel Boateng, the character who'd just been bearing the brunt of Pariche's displeasure at the groundbreaking ceremony, would have observed, this was someone in serious need of being reminded he was black.

After he'd completed his studies at Columbia, and in pursuit of Geraldine, Soren moved to Berkeley for a year. The whole experience proved to be painfully disappointing and, in the face of this disillusionment, Soren chose to act upon a call from Rosen and return to New York. By this time his tortuous relationship with Geraldine had come to a spluttering end and it was left to Rosen to salvage what she could. In this she appeared to have some success, for within no time at all, Soren was off to Europe, having completed a doctorate, investigating the aporias and stark beauty of the Theodore Adorno's work. The years spent there, in London and Uppsala, were to prove the most creative and productive of times, with the publication of two critically acclaimed texts within as many years. These were moments of intense insight and clarity, when ideas had presented themselves in all their sublimity at all times of the day and night. When authorship had meant a true loss of control. But then came the mistakes. The first was to move back to New York at the behest of his mother, who'd urged him to take advantage of the old contacts he had at Columbia and 'do the law.' This brought him back into contact with Geraldine who'd just moved back from California. Already a fragile and unbalanced girl, Geraldine had a malevolence quite alien to the probity and veracity of someone like Virginia. And now she was in cahoots again with her mother. With Melissa more unhinged than ever, they proceeded to hound Soren mercilessly. They wanted the world to know that Soren Karlsson was a fraud? That everything he'd ever done was stolen from the women he'd abused? The memory of that year still filled him with dread; the time when both women had turned up at one of Professor Rosen's seminars, shouting and screaming, and the times he'd had to call the police. There had been threats, and the increasingly fearful feeling that he'd been in physical, as well as psychological, danger. The upshot was for him to take flight back to California and a wonderfully gauche dead-end posting at a state college in Sonoma.

At first the whole Northern Californian experience proved to be a most agreeable contrast to the horrors he'd left behind in New York, as he made a reconnection with the great outdoors, assiduously cultivated those wine tasting and barbecue contacts that appeared to be so much the norm for this neck of the woods. But what followed, upon reflection, now promised to be an even bigger calamity. Charlie Wilson, yet to be installed as (acting) dean of faculty, made a call urging him to forsake Rohnert Park for the more rarefied heights of life in his department at Berkeley. Wilson had been after new blood, all the better to impress his masters over in the Chancellor's Office. On hearing that there was this young teacher in the vicinity with an already impressive body of published work, and flabbergasted at the nature of his employment, it had been Wilson who'd done the pursuing. He'd promised Soren the earth, a ladder appointment and tenure, which, after a couple of years, he'd delivered, in the shape of a shared associate post between Berkeley and UCSF. It had been typical Wilson, pulling strings, making threats and delivering upon promises. Of course it helped having such an excellent candidate in the first place; on his arrival at Berkeley, Soren had set up a very popular ethics program, something that was not lost on the bean counters over at the medical centre. Pariche, though, had been less certain and at the time had warned his friend that there would be consequences to pay; anything involving Wilson would involve the selling of one's soul.

8

A price had indeed been exacted, in the form of a growing awareness, by Soren, of being totally beholden to Wilson. Of not being his own man. It fed in him a need to get away from Wilson's malign and controlling influence. At being at Wilson's beck and call, and having to endure those petty, and always dispiriting, departmental squabbles. He had that awful feeling that things were being done to, and through, him. That, as far as Wilson was concerned, he was nothing more than a cypher. Pariche had been right; the perceived wisdom within the department was of Soren as being Wilson's man on committee, put there to do his bidding. And, with this, Soren came to see himself as something incomplete, even fraudulent.

The atmosphere within the department was one of contented stuffiness, reeking of puffed-up pomposity. Where many of the more senior staff were all too keen to foment the fears and anxieties held by those with a more tenuous foothold. A place where the wise and learned would call younger minds and firmer bodies to account. Where less august souls would have their ambitions curbed by constant reminders of their relative worthlessness, compounded by the fear of failure. Wrong choices would be made – and they were always the wrong choices – that led to old Committee men, inveighed with the trappings of power, making career-ending decisions; men, whose measured and knowingly mocking dispositions would be more usually engaged in attempts to lighten the tedium of those life-sapping faculty oversight and departmental meetings. All of which went some way to induce within Soren an almost intolerable strain. Life at Berkeley was not supposed to be like this. Now he would spend much of his time over at his office at the medical centre on Parnassus, away from the claustrophobic and paranoid world that characterised a Wilson-controlled department. But Wilson would have none of it. More committees and less teaching was the way to go. Leave the post-grads to your assistants and free up more time for those books you'd agreed to write for the University Press. Of course that last pass was a fake. Committees were the real deal. Don't discuss and engage, just see to it that the agreed line was executed at the next meeting you chaired. Sitting on and chairing committees was the way to get on at Berkeley. Pariche would never have allowed things to get this far. He would have been in their faces, fists flailing, barking and howling.

And it was Pariche who had come to Soren's aid, even sitting in for him on some of the meetings he'd needed to chair. Of course, the older man thoroughly enjoyed giving those stuffed shirts a taste of what was considered the norm over in Genetics. And with the passage of time, Soren started to reassess his own needs, especially those regarding the possibility of any academic preferment. 'Just let go, Solly,' Pariche had said at the time. 'It's all a crapshoot. Don't let Wilson have you jumping at shadows.'

Added to Soren's unease was the more vital anguish of what was being done to the students. Here they appeared to be a species of animal life whose intellect the system appeared to be hell bent on preventing any form of creative engagement. Instead, they were being turned into grade chasers; people who would do their utmost to get the edge on the opposition. Undergraduate life here didn't appear to have those essential characteristics of student life Soren had enjoyed at Columbia and Exeter. And the Harkness method of teaching he'd enjoyed at the latter, with its emphasis on discussion, tempered by disciplined and collaborative enquiry, well, that might as well have been a different world.

'Poppycock!'

Already he could hear the protesting tones of Pariche, raging against the sentimentality of it all. But it was something that Soren had been adamant about and one of the reasons he'd originally chosen to study at Columbia. He remembered the original interview he had with Professor Rosen and how it bespoke the promise of a future – intimate – involvement of like minds. It was an experience he feared would never be visited upon undergraduate life at Berkeley. As a colleague from the English department had once observed, only half-jokingly; 'They'll be giving out multiple-choice questions on Joyce next.' So now he was finally getting away from the embarrassing pomposity and bombast of it all. Away from colleagues who would still attempt to convince themselves that this really was a Cambridge, a Princeton or, heaven forbid, a Stanford.

Egged on by Pariche, Soren began to distance himself from the (acting) dean and the coterie of staffers he surrounded himself with. Colleagues noted how his focus increasingly appeared to be directed towards those friendships he'd forged back east. How, given half the chance, he would be on the late afternoon Pan Am flight, out of SFO, back to New York. It was something Soren himself had often reflected upon; he'd spent the best part of two decades striving to get to the Golden State, only to find that, after just five years of working for Wilson, he was doing his damnedest to get away.

A break from the academic treadmill was what was required; a decision rendered all the more urgent, now that Cindi, the latest in a long line of romantic disasters, had walked out of his life. He'd written to Rosen, who replied in even more emphatic tones. 'Get the hell out,' she'd demanded. 'Drop everything and come back to New York. We'll work something out.' But still he resisted. Something kept telling him that he needed a greater challenge. And this is where that ill-fated drunken tryst with Pariche and Doleson came into play. Perhaps a spell in Mississippi would provide some answers to what was ailing him. But now the date of departure loomed, casting an all-consuming shadow over his thoughts.

9

Soren had done his research. Almost everything about Toshoba County, Mississippi seemed awful. Had it only been a few score years ago that folks down there had wantonly raped, mutilated and lynched black people? The place even had its own Rosa Parks, a woman by the name of Hattie Mawlby, who'd also refused to give up her seat on a bus to a white man. Hattie, a civil rights volunteer from Ohio, had, by the time she'd crossed into Tennessee, become just a little tired of being made to sit at the back, in the 'coloured' seats. The bus driver decided to let this go, but he'd not made allowances for 'Scooter', Toshoba's own personification of the Ku Klux Klan. Scooter had boarded the bus at Memphis and immediately began remonstrating with this black woman, who'd the temerity to challenge his notion of what should be the racial order of things. When this didn't work, he became more forceful, almost dragging Hattie from her seat. But Hattie had fought back – oh, how she'd fought back. She had no idea from where it had all come from, but within seconds she was beating Scooter about the head with a commandeered umbrella, chasing the bloodied assailant off the bus. It earned her a week in the cells at the next stop, which just happened to be in Toshoba County, Mississippi. News of Hattie's predicament soon leaked out, threatening to draw folks from far afield; civil rights agitators from Jackson and Atlanta, and local elements of the Klan. Toshoba's Sheriff at the time, a certain Hollis White, then made one of the few intelligent decisions of his long inglorious career and put Hattie on the next bus out. Later, armed with a lawyer, a federal warrant, and the testimony of several witnesses, Hattie returned, determined to prosecute Scooter, the Greyhound bus line, and the authorities of Toshoba county, for assault, wrongful arrest, and the denial of interstate trade. It got nowhere, of course, but the furore it created forced many of the locals to take note; a subtle shift in the wind that spelt out the unmistakable message that times had changed. But how far? Soren still imagined Mississippi to be a place still haunted by its past, where everything would be shut on Sunday, with preciously few of the delights he'd come to regard as *de rigueur* in California. There would be no discussions on the merits of the 'Beautiful Soul', or debating the Kleistian account of Marionette Theatre. Even the parochial and narcissistic reporting of the San Francisco Chronicle was beginning to hold a certain charm. Sure, the city had been left in a sixties time warp, and Los Angeles had a much better music and cultural scene, but had he really resented the cramped conditions of his West Portal apartment? He'd miss those extended writing sessions into the small hours, while listening to jazz on KCSM, followed by a stroll through the early morning fog on Ulloa and a coffee at the Manor. He feared there would be no Mississippi equivalent of Symphony Hall and, of course, there was always Berkeley, about which it was so easy to feel shamelessly chauvinistic. There would certainly be no Kent Nagano conducting the Berkeley Symphony, dropping in on a seminar with Leo Lowenthal, or chairing a debate between Czeslaw Milosz and those relics of the old Free Speech Movement. Mississippi, he feared, would hold no such rapture.

10

He would also miss the work. Already he was beginning to regret putting off the book project he'd planned with Trudy Matterson over in English. She would think him unreliable and dilettante. And could Pariche and his teaching assistant, Denis Tsui, be trusted with the supervision of his post-grads? Soren had seen through the first couple of months of the semester, but the handover hadn't been the smoothest of operations, with Donat, a born-again Christian, particularly vexed by his impending departure. Her faith had been severely tested by her studies at Berkeley and Soren wondered if either Denis or Pariche would be so inclined to coax her along to the weekly seminars, as he'd had to do all last year? Teaching and research supervision were things Soren did particularly well and Pariche for one knew that this would be a difficult thing to replicate. He would help Denis out as much as he could, but he had hardly the expertise to pontificate on subjects as disparate as the *antebellum* South, medical ethics and neo-Kantian philosophy. There was also Chumley, the curvaceous drag queen from Austria, who did a cracking impersonation of Jackie Kennedy. He was a very gifted Post Doc, currently researching the work of Walter Benjamin, but his flirtatious manner was a disaster just waiting to happen. More worryingly, he was someone who could always be relied upon to browbeat the hardiest of souls into submission. Would Denis be capable of resisting the barrage that Chumley would most certainly manufacture? He was also someone who was just as likely to tell a certain (acting) dean exactly what he thought of him.

And, of course, there was Pariche! Soren could live with most of the things Pariche had chosen to adopt, of which the defence of Salmon Rushdie, against the fatwa issued by Ayatollah Khomeini, was only the latest. But there were times when Pariche sailed close to the wind, such as when he'd insisted on defending the rights of one of his students - one with neo-Nazi survivalist tendencies - to pursue a line of enquiry that most people at Berkeley would never have touched with a barge pole. 'Free enquiry!' Pariche had protested, as the case was passed on up, up to the University Regents. And he'd got his way. In the end, though, the student had still insisted on adding his ill-advised and prejudicial ramblings to the thesis he'd produced, so Pariche failed him anyway. It was the only time Pariche had ever had a less than one hundred percent completion rate and, in the process, had also managed to earn the undying hatred of some of the Bay Area's more unhinged and bigoted elements.

Wilson, the (acting) dean, was a different proposition altogether. He was a known quantity who'd be intent on inflicting the maximum amount of distress. He was someone who'd never taught in his life and had very little interest in so doing. In Wilson's view teaching tended to detract from the need to keep those research dollars rolling in. Not one to be trusted, he had lately been behind a whispering campaign, within the Department, aimed primarily at Pariche and Denis and, ultimately, at Soren himself. Pariche was seen as an interloper from the Genetics Department and Denis Tsui, as an assistant, just didn't count. So they were to be played, by Wilson and his cronies, so that people in the Department began to see them as a nuisance, perhaps even a threat. Soren knew that Kurst, an old friend and Harvard lag, would be OK, but there were others in the Department who would pull rank. There would be fights. So there it was, a host of anxieties, eating away, forcing Soren to reassess what he was doing with his life. There were other more mundane worries, of course, such as whether it would be safe to leave his apartment unattended over the coming year? Colleagues had urged him to let it out, but he was having none of it; the thought of strangers rattling around in his home for the best part of six months, and having to put a couple of thousand books into storage, filled him with dread. Hell, he was even beginning to think winsomely of enduring yet another Giants' failure. Yes, it was going to be a very long year.

11

For some time Soren remained seated aloft Porter's Mount, consumed in thought. But then came the gloom and with it a certain chill to match his mood. He was also beginning to feel hungry and he knew the others would have left it to him to rustle up something to eat. It was time to descend. Keeping to the path he'd clambered up, his descent was swift, carrying him past a disused limestone quarry that cut a disfiguring, if familiar, gash in the hillside. Despite the enveloping darkness, his stride was assured, the ground beneath him well known. Through the trees below could just be discerned the winding emptiness of Route 22, as it rambled its way beyond Hillsdale, towards Canada. Soon he would be home.

Within moments he was breaking from the cover of Harper's Meadow. Beyond a tall limestone wall, he could see lights coming from Ashleighs, the family home. He stepped onto a track that followed a wall round to the front of the house. He didn't notice the car, in which the two gentlemen from Boston's North End were sitting. But they noticed him. They were puzzled as to who he was, but, as was the North End way, they immediately settled for the likelihood of him being the family help or driver. What else would a black man be doing in these parts?

Soren made his way through a gate that barred the main entrance and walked up a short drive towards the house. There were a couple of parked cars – expensive foreign imports – and the police patrol car he'd passed earlier. He gave its occupants a nod of recognition and asked if they wanted anything to eat or drink. No, was the reply, Senator Karlsson had just brought them some coffee. Rather than entering the front of the house, Soren went to the source of the light he'd seen earlier. It was coming from a ground floor window and he could just make out the framed and silhouetted form of a woman. It was Christina, his mother, who, by her animated demeanour, appeared to be still very much exercised by Brad's imbibing of exotic herbal substances.

'Ah, there you are, Soren. Did you hear that?' Her voice was assured and deliberate and of the kind that expected no contradiction. They embraced.

'Yes, Mother. I'm sure the police would find the smell highly disconcerting,' he replied, shooting an exasperated look at his friend as he did so.

Christina Margaret Karlsson was an elegant self-possessed woman who appeared to carry few neuroses, save for an obsession with her weight, a loathing for Richard Milhous Nixon, and a compulsion to clean the house whenever she was stressed. Now in her late fifties, she was wearing a dark suit and a lemon-coloured blouse. Simple, no fuss. This was still an attractive-looking woman, but her pallor troubled her son. His mother had always had a fragile-looking quality about her; something that was so easily the undoing of the predatory or the confidently unwary. But Soren had not expected her to have aged so much. Momentarily, this appalled him. Her hands had always been thin and a little knotted, her arms a freckled stain, but this had always hinted at a healthy outdoor robustness. Now, there were the first portents of frailty and old age, and his reaction to this betrayed his discomfort.

'I'm sorry, is there something wrong?' she asked.

'No, definitely not,' he gushed, striving to reassure. He beckoned, and they embraced again; something that was just a little forced, as if they were unsure of each other and what the occasion called for. Ah, there it was: that quizzical, slightly untrusting look she always gave him after long separations. He was aware of that brooding intelligence again and a mind that was steeled and razor sharp and constantly probing. This did reassure. She was still in there, alert to deceit. Just how it should be, he thought; good to be home.

'I mean, when I saw that police car on the drive, I almost died,' she said, as she busied herself in tidying up the mess she obviously construed as being the fault of the room's present occupants.

Soren was confused; 'But I thought those people out there were your protection detail?'

'No, no, this was earlier, whilst you were out. An Officer Briand, from the local police, made a call.' She let out a derisive snort, shrugged her shoulders, and looked to the heavens. 'You couldn't make it up. Ask them!' she cried, gesturing towards Brad and Craig, the two other occupants in the room. The latter, who was tinkering with the insides of a Walkman, looked across and pointed a finger in the shape of a gun at Brad's head. Soren got the message; Brad was having one of his turns.

The object of their concern was sprawled out upon a blue patterned sofa. Although he gave the impression of being semi-comatose, Brad was in fact keeping half an eye on the flickering images of Peter Jennings delivering the nightly newscast. A feisty and pugnacious soul, Brad had been a friend of Soren's since the days they'd boarded together at Exeter. Now an attending physician at San Francisco General, much of his time was spent being reminded of his seeming irrelevance and impotence in the fight against AIDS. The condition had devastated much of the neighbourhood in which he lived and had gone some way towards hardening an already cynical disposition. His present listlessness also owed much to the glass of wine in his hand; probably the most recent of a veritable procession.

What only his partner, Martin, and Soren knew, was that he'd also become heavily reliant upon the considerable amounts of cocaine he snorted. Initially Soren hadn't been too alarmed, its recreational use seemed par for the course for much of what passed for professional life out on the West Coast. But then Brad's behaviour had taken on a more furtive and agitated – dare one say, wired – form. So there had been words; strident and unfriendly words. After a long

43

enough period of calm had elapsed, Soren – taking a leaf out of Pariche's book – had persuaded Brad on the merits of joining him on this trip to Mississippi. A brief spell down there, away from all the grief and stress of working at the General, would do him the world of good. Brad's partner though, had been less enthusiastic; being queer and strung out on coke was not the best comportment for someone intent on a visit to the Magnolia State.

'You had a call from the local police?' Soren could hardly believe his ears.

Brad looked up, momentarily speechless, his gaze vacant. Then his senses kicked in, something that was confirmed by a pained expression and the awful realisation that he was back in the land of the living. He pointed to his watch and, ignoring the question, asked: 'What time do you think this is? Just what have you been doing up there all this time?' His tone wasn't so much accusatory, more a mannered rebuke for leaving him to deal with the hell that was Christina, to who Soren now turned imploringly.

'Don't ask,' she said, desperately attempting not to notice the unlit cigarette Brad was toying with.

'Honestly, Christina,' Brad replied, struggling to sit himself upright, 'on the way out here I'm sure I saw somebody whacking something by the roadside with a baseball bat. You don't get too many baby seals around these parts.' His accent betrayed more than just a hint of Brooklyn, something that was a further source of irritation for Christina, who was certain that he'd never been anywhere near the place. He was, after all, an Exeter boy, just like her son.

Brad was medium height, with the muscular build of someone who regularly worked out. He distinguished himself by wearing a horseshoe style moustache and on his head was set something that looked to be a cross between an old scoutmaster's hat and a Homburg. The oval shaped glasses, through which he peered, had a pink tinge to them, leading Christina to wonder what the patients of this smiling Gerry Garcia lookalike must make of their attending physician? He looked agitated and Soren sensed, in his friend's troubled unease, a return of some of the drug-fuelled nervousness he'd witnessed back in San Francisco. It was something that Christina could also see, as she now gave her son that interested, 'what have we here?' look. Anyone with a wit could see that Brad was a mess. What had driven Brad to this was hard to say. There had always been the good fight to be fought against societal intolerance, but Soren suspected that the true cause of his friend's troubles were the grueling hours demanded of his work and the experience of watching so many of his friends die. Cocaine now appeared to be the only thing holding him together. The result had seen a downward spiral and the avoidance of too intimate an involvement with anyone, save for his partner, Martin. And now he appeared to be running away from him too. Attempting to hide a habit that would, if it ever became public, bring not just an end to his medical career, but possible jail time too.

The damage to his friendship with Soren had been substantial, as if a spell had been broken. Soren now saw in Brad what Christina had always professed to see; an affected, laid-back attitude and laconic turn of phrase, revealed as languid deceit. The perturbed agitations of a revealed inner sickness. Yes, it was clear that Christina did not like Brad; someone she'd always seen as being parasitic on her son. She was prepared to stomach his presence only as long as his friendship with her son remained close. Initially Brad had been seen as a rival, even a threat. Someone who exercised a claim to Soren that was beyond Christina's grasp and control and she couldn't abide that. She knew that her feelings of jealousy at the time had been foolish, but it had been the first impression that Brad had made on her, and it had stuck. Subsequently she had become – as she was now – ever alert to everything Brad said and did, paying attention to every perceived slight; always seeing in his actions and words attempts to drive a wedge, deeper and deeper, between herself and her son. It was something compounded by Christina's certain knowledge that she, herself, was seen by Brad, through her involvement in politics and law, as someone compromised and party to a profession whose sole raison d'être seemed to be the manufacture of malpractice suits and the suing of doctors. She also believed that Brad had been the one behind some of the more fractious episodes between herself and her son. That he'd been the one providing the ammunition. Ah, that madness again. Now, though, as she watched him unravel, she felt a perverse enjoyment in what she was witnessing; Brad's distress and its pointing towards a possible dissolution of his friendship with Soren. It could only be positive for the relationship she wished to forge with him herself.

12

The other person present in the room was, for Christina, an altogether different proposition. Tall, and with long blonde hair tied at the back, Craig Ginsberg had an easy-going charm, wedded to a rather wholesome urbanity. It was a quality that ran somewhat counter to the cowboy stereotypes one usually associates with the state of Montana. He was one of those plainsman boy-wonders who appear to tumble out of the womb with their geniuses fully formed. A brilliant mathematician, Craig had won accolades at Cornell and MIT, before moving on to the Lawrence Berkeley Lab, where, as a computer physicist, he was engaged in developing computer software that could simulate chemical reactions. Craig had first come to Christina's attention when the Montanan had come to her son's aid during a bar-room brawl in Oakland. Fighting for lost causes had long been a Ginsberg tradition, ever since their descendants had sought refuge from the Czarist anti-Jewish pogroms in Russia at the end of the last century. Active with the Wobblies up near Butte, a Ginsberg had been killed by mine militiamen, a wound that had been borne as a standard for future generations of the family. These were facts that fascinated the politician in Christina, always quick to point out the many party fundraisers she'd attended with Mike Mansfield, the former Senior Senator from the state, and how she'd once taken pride in a colleague's observation about her uncanny likeness to another Montanan, and Democratic Party stalwart, the actress, Myrna Loy.

Craig had immediately volunteered his services when Soren had first ventured the possibility of going to Mississippi, certain that such a venture would need a

47

scientific component. He'd had to run it past his wife, Alice, first, and their eight-year-old daughter Hazel, but they were soon won over. Presently he was engaged in the less hazardous exercise of baiting Christina about the use of illicit chemical substances and the reputation of a local law enforcement officer.

'Oh, don't be silly,' cried Christina, her gaze settling upon Craig's disbelieving expression. 'I don't believe you. Of course Officer Briand would disapprove...' Tilting his head to one side, he let out a chuckle, but Christina was having none of it; she had other, more pressing, fish to fry. 'It was extremely thoughtless,' she continued, turning her attention to Soren. 'You obviously had no intention of calling me before you went. Mississippi of all places! Goodness knows why you would even think of going to such a godforsaken place?'

'Honestly, we were going to tell you. That's why we're here.'

Eyes were beginning to roll heavenward, when, much to the relief of all concerned, Christina, on the pretext of going to fetch some more refreshments, made a rather theatrical exit, leaving the remaining occupants in various degrees of exasperation and tickled humour. Smiling nervously, Soren looked to the others.

'Does she seem all right to you?' he asked. That first appearance of his mother still haunted him.

'I suppose those hearings have taken their toll,' replied Craig, immediately sensing the concern in his voice.

'Yes,' Soren sighed, with a somewhat apprehensive and wistful look in the direction of the door through which Christina had just exited. He still wasn't sure. 'How the hell did it all turn into an enquiry about the mafia? I didn't expect it to get so bruising. And now she seems to be turning it into something like a Grand Jury!'

'She'll be OK. She always is!' Brad's tone was brusque, even dismissive. He could see Soren beginning to bridle just a little, his expression souring at the sight of that – still twitching – cigarette. 'I guess this isn't helping.' Brad put the offending item away. Then he appeared to remember something. 'Oh yes, there was a call whilst you were out. Kurst, I think his name was. Sounded British. Called about the groundbreaking ceremony. There's been some complications. And Denis left a message.'

13

Before Brad could say anything further, Christina returned from the kitchen, clutching glasses and a bottle of wine. It was clear to all that her original upset with Brad had not been forgotten. 'Surely you won't be going now,' she said, looking at him, 'what with your good news.'

'Good news?' Soren was intrigued. He shot his friend, who was now looking just a little self-conscious, a quizzical look.

'Yes,' Christina continued. 'They've only gone and made him a full professor. Can't help but wonder what they were thinking!'

Although Christina's remarks were intended to be light hearted, the knowing looks shared between her and her son hinted at something darker and more substantive. Both knew that in his present condition it would be expecting a lot of Brad to carry out the simplest of patient consultations, let alone be entrusted with a full professorship at one of the world's pre-eminent medical centres. Soren knew the deal. The system was looking after its own. Added to which, an influential member of the Appointments Committee just happened to be an old Exeter hand.

'Well, that's wonderful news.' Soren's reply betrayed a certain anxiety; the trip to Mississippi was becoming more impossible by the minute. Christina, though, was obviously enjoying the mischief.

'Yes, you'd be foolish to pass up such a golden opportunity, Brad,' she said, with a smile. 'Besides, you deserve it. From what Soren's been saying, you were doing the job already anyway.'

Yes, Mother, very good, thought Soren. She was in her element now, disingenuous in her concern for his friend's career, reveling in the idea that yet another thing was joining in the conspiracy to derail the 'voyage'. 'So, let's drink to Brad's good news shall we?' she said, triumphant, raising a glass in one hand and a bottle of Gold Seal in the other. 'I take it you won't be going now?'

'I don't see why not.' As always she could rely upon Brad being less than helpful. 'I'm sure I could get a few months in. Commencement won't be until next year anyway.'

'Really? But surely you'll have things to tie up first? And what will Martin be thinking?' The mention of Brad's partner brought forth a sharp intake of breath from Soren and a wry smile from Craig, who now spoke up.

'Come on, Christina, give him a break! As you've already said, he's doing the job already!' For Christina, Craig's intervention was as unexpected as it was unwelcome. Feeling just a little betrayed, she let it go; for now. Handing a drink to her son, she, rather sniffily, expressed the sentiment that life was far too short to waste time on such idle banter. After all, they had the prospect of another four years of continued Republican occupation of the White House to contend with.

'Yes,' she continued, speaking to no one in particular. 'I can see that it was all a foregone conclusion now. But four more years! I just can't believe that people could be so gullible. Are you all quite mad out there in California? At least we look to be holding our own here.' She sat herself down, next to Craig and opposite Brad.

'Well, we have managed to claw a few things back, especially in LA and the Bay area...' Soren said, before his attempts at further engagement were cut short by Brad.

'You can be sure as hell that the Vigueries and the Pearles of this world will be looking to give those Kennedy arse-kissers a bit of a kicking.'

'Brad!' Christina's complaint was more about his bar-room delivery, rather than for the assault upon a political friend. 'I trust I'm not to be included in that statement?'

'Of course not, Christina, sorry, of course not!'

'Anyway, just what is it? This thing you all have against the Kennedys?'

'Well, nothing I guess,' replied Soren, 'apart from their propensity to let the more primeval aspects of their personality run riot. You know, dead secretaries...'

'Oh, not that old chestnut again!' She was almost shouting now, as she sensed the old axis of Brad and her son reasserting itself.

'...cheating, double-dealing, lying, a bit of racial bigotry...'

'Racial bigotry? Now hold on a moment.'

'Look at the deal he did with those people in Southie.'

'We live in the real world here, laddie, the real world! The situation down there demanded tact and diplomacy. It was a very delicate situation.'

'What, worried about the natives shaking a few trees?' Brad immediately sensed that he'd gone too far; the withering aspect of Christina's stare and the disbelieving looks of Soren and Craig, were confirmation of this. He sheepishly retreated further into himself.

'A rather unfortunate choice of expression don't you think?' Christina was as much triumphant in Brad's discomfiture, as she was overjoyed at seeing how appalled the other two were. Not content to let such a good opportunity pass, she again rolled her eyes heavenward and pressed home her advantage. 'Oh boy, the Californians really are back in town! Are you all airheads out there?' The look she gave was at first beseeching, but soon turned to one of arched dismissal when there was no response. 'I get it; it's something they put in the water out there right?' Now her remarks were partially being directed towards her son. 'Hell, you can be such a disappointment sometimes, when I hear drivel like this. It just confirms my suspicions about whether we really do need all those schools out there, filling your heads with mush!' There was now a slow dismissive quality to her voice and its impact upon Soren was keenly felt. 'It's so easy for you, isn't it? No need to think before engaging your tongues. And just what is it about you and the

Kennedys? Is it an Irish thing? Perhaps you could all do with a little guidance about the nature of bigotry and perhaps desist from telling the Kennedys what to do about theirs!'

Time and distance had caused Soren to forget the power and awfulness of his mother's disapprobation, even if the main force of it had been aimed at someone else. It hinted of a force that had had her political and legal foes in Boston ducking for cover for years. It was only a glimpse, but Soren was left marvelling at how it could still catch him off-guard. He watched as Brad, almost childlike, gave a nod of complete capitulation and muttered, 'I suppose you know best.' Christina's taut facial muscles and fixed glare screamed 'you bet I do, Buster, you bet I do!'

14

The tension was heightened further by Christina's desire to force other uncomfortable issues home. And this time Soren *was* the object of her interest.

'So this departure, Soren, you thought you'd make it easier for yourself if you were to get your retaliation in first?' There was a harshness in her voice now. 'Thought you'd give the old girl a good going over, did ya? It's always the case with you, isn't it? If you can't sneak out the back, you purge your guilt by staging a full-scale frontal assault. Well this time it isn't going to work. There are a few things we need to discuss, not least the call I received earlier from Ginny.'

'Ginny? You got a call from Virginia?' Soren's initial shock of having the tables turned on him was transformed into one of unfolding and interested intrigue.

'She was concerned about her blessed car. Of course I told her we'd pay. That's money she can ill afford.'

'Hold on, Mother! I've already paid for the repairs, plus the transportation back east.'

The object of their discussion was a Saab 900 Convertible that Soren had shipped back from Sweden, following a trip there with his mother. The purchase had been at Virginia's instigation; an answer to a prayer she'd been harbouring for years. But, for some reason, physical possession had never taken place. One of the reasons for this had a lot to do with a certain gentleman from Mono County, California. Christina had questioned whether they had need for such a car in San Francisco, but Soren, egged on by Pariche, had taken little notice. The older man had drooled his appreciation of the car from the off, insisting they prove how much it had been made for the hills in and around the Bay area. They would be able to go up and down them just like Steve McQueen had in the film *Bullet*.

Even as he handed Pariche the car keys, so that the old fool could 'tweak' the engine a little, Soren knew that he was making a terrible mistake. On giving the car back, two weeks later, Pariche insisted they go down to the Valley and give it the kind of workout that such a beauty deserved. He'd heard the stories of how Saabs were supposed to be able to go on regardless, at top speed, for weeks at a time; why not go on down to the Mohave and give it a whirl?

For most people, California means Hollywood, golden beaches and golden suntans, with San Francisco, the Golden Gate Bridge, and a few Redwood groves thrown in for good measure. To be sure, Soren had briefly been seduced by the beauty of the Mendocino coast, when he'd been teaching at Rohnert Park, but, now, whenever he needed a break, there was always the cabin out at Bass Lake. For that's what California had always been about; the High Sierras and the valleys and deserts they tumbled into. There were memories of the first time he'd seen images of Death Valley as a child, alone, in the study at Ashleighs, leafing through old editions of *Time Life* and *National Geographic*. He remembered the fifties and sixties monochrome pictures of New York, with its foreshortened streets, billowing steam vents and big city scenes, and how this had sat so incongruously alongside the bright and breezy images of Pacific naval power, Death Valley lightness and blue Nevada luminescence. Then America had been at its zenith, its imperial and cultural dominance unchallenged; when men composed of the 'Right Stuff' had been launched heavenward, their confidence high about rising to any of the challenges the gods might deign to throw at them. So he and Pariche had driven down Route 395, in Pariche's backyard, passed the polluted backwater of Owens Lake, onto Mohave, Edwards Air Force Base and Willow Springs. There the car had stood, in all its Swedish, Social Democratic glory; a 900 SPG special, blood red, turbo charged and ready to go. And what a marvel that product of Swedish engineering had been. For seven hours, under the white, whisky cirrus clouds of the Mohave, cheered on by Pariche, Soren had driven it over that dried-up alluvial plain. He should have known better. After five hundred miles, disaster struck. The car had hit something, either a boulder, or an uneven piece of ground, but it had put the vehicle's sub-frame out of whack. Six thousand dollars it had cost to get it fixed. Six thousand hard-earned bucks!

'And while we're talking responsibilities,' Christina continued, 'what the blazes do you mean by buying this place on the Upper West Side?'

Now a veritable hell was being visited upon Soren's head. 'You know about that?' He paused for a moment, speechless, then it began to dawn on him. 'Ah, of course, the bank!'

'You bet your bottom dollar. Did you really think the bank wouldn't bother to get in touch? I could hardly believe my ears when Barny Strictland told me you'd used Ashleighs to raise a deposit. This is damnable Soren!'

'But I thought you'd be pleased. It would be a real investment!'

'Would you be so kind as to explain the logic behind that statement?'

'Well, apart from the money, it means that I still have thoughts of moving back east.' This placatory attempt, like the others, fell on stony ground.

'You already have the Morningside apartment! So what the hell do you think you're doing violating every state and federal statute by raising money on a place you don't own?'

He smiled nervously. 'But I'm selling it, I'm selling Morningside. I need to do that to raise the cash.'

'This is fucking damnable, Soren. The first thought I had when I heard about what you'd done was, God... this is theft! Why the sheer bloody nerve of it!'

'It was only a facility, Mother. I told the people at the bank that I'd be talking to you first. That's why I'm here.

'Well, if you are going to treat this place as your own, then perhaps you'd better buy it as well! I do happen to be spending more and more time down in Cohasset, so buying

Ashleighs would make a whole load of sense. Add to that portfolio of yours.'

There were smiles of sorts, but all Soren could think about was escape. It would serve his interests well by collecting what libations there were to hand and making a quick exit. He had calls to make and there was still the cooking to do. As he made his getaway, his mother called after him. 'Running away from responsibilities again, Soren? You and Ginny have to talk!'

15

The relationship between Christina and her son was one of warmth and relaxed co-existence that would periodically be punctuated by moments that, at times, required a certain amount of distance. This was something both recognised as being both painful and necessary. What could not be denied, though, was an obvious closeness between the two; an intimacy that had survived what could be considered the most unpromising of starts.

Soren's birth had been the last tremulous act of a desperately unhappy marriage to a Jewish physician, in Rochester, Minnesota, in the early 1950s. It was also a profound – albeit subconscious – defiance of Christina's austere Lutheran upbringing, though not of her faith. With her Canadian parents long dead, and shunned by other family, she had found herself alone, save for her bastard son. Toughened by this episode, Christina soon found employment as a personal assistant to a senior partner in a Chicago law firm. There she endeavoured in making herself indispensable, so that when her boss was head-hunted by a prestigious Wall Street firm, it seemed only natural that she should go with him to New York. Later, armed with a law degree from NYU and a wealth of experience gleaned from being at the centre of the firm's activities, Christina was given the task of reorganising the firm's Boston office, where the scions of Harvard and Tufts had seen it as their right to treat the place as a cosy backwater, charging exorbitant fees for a minimal amount of effort and success. Christina had set about them to such good effect that she was soon rewarded with the name of Karlsson joining those adorning the entrance of the firm's Wall Street headquarters.

Christina, though, had chosen to stay on in Boston; a city with a pedigree that appealed in ways that New York did not. It was a view not shared by her son. Her position afforded her the opportunity for much charitable work, hosting fundraising events for bodies such as the MFA and the Massachusetts General, where there were opportunities to score points off the depleted ranks of the old Brahmin elite along with the cementing of political ties with the Boston Irish. Soren's time in Boston was always limited to moments when he was in town for the odd conference, or there to look up old friends; yes, that insistence on keeping a safe distance again. His choice of Columbia as a place to study was a case in point. Outwardly Christina had lauded his winning a place there, but she also had the feeling that it was just another calculated snub, a cocked finger at her strenuous efforts to get him into Harvard. That compared to New York, Boston was seen as too parochial and too much within her sphere of influence.

So, once again, Soren found himself seeking to avoid the attentions of his mother. Still clutching his glass of wine, he passed along an alcoved landing that overlooked a large lounge area, to which he descended by way of a balustraded staircase. The room's focus centred upon a pair of large French windows, which opened onto a south-facing lawn, where, in the descending darkness, there could be discerned the feint reflections of a mill pond. The room's decor had been an ongoing homage to a time when Christina had endeavoured to keep her son 'on message'. This had been in the form of a pre-college summer project where Soren had been given free rein to decorate the place. On each of the lemon and isabelline-coloured walls were black and white faded decals of prominent cultural icons. Freud and Virginia Wolf were there, as were Paul Robeson and LBJ; all guaranteed to aid party conversation. He walked over to a table on which was set a CD player. He noticed the track listing hadn't moved on from the last time he'd been here in the summer. He pressed the play button and the strains of a Miles Davis number began to fill the room. Sitting himself down on one of the window seats, he took a prolonged sip of wine, and reflected upon those 'responsibilities' his mother had spoken of earlier. The phone call to Kurst and the cooking would have to wait.

16

For some time those 'responsibilities' had centred upon a
certain Virginia Leigh Bradley-Moore Van Buren. Yes, a bit
of a mouthful; the result of complications arising from
family merger and motherly ambitions. Anyway, she and
Soren had a mutual affection and regard that had been
through periodic bouts of renewal and abatement, lasting
from the time Virginia had been sent north by her parents to
be educated.

Virginia's father, Wendall Bradley, had initially wanted
to name her Leigh, but Virginia's mother, Elspeth, had
thoughts of impressing one of her aunts. Her insistence on
getting her own way should have been a harbinger of what
was in store. She was, after all, a Moore; old money and
much superior to the family of Nebraskan accountants she'd
the misfortune of marrying into. Long ago the Moores had
been joined to the Van Burens through marriage and it was
this connection that was to prove decisive in Soren and
Virginia's eventual union. The Moores were the epitome of
the old southern landowning plantocracy, dismissive of the
nouveau-riches of the northern half of the family, with its
banking and textile interests. The Van Burens, to be sure,
were equally contemptuous of the civilised veneer of the
southern branch of the family, built on what they saw as the
barbarity of slavery. With the onset of Civil War, the rupture
between the two families was complete. More recently,
though, there had been a rapprochement of sorts,
culminating in the decision by the Bradley-Moores to send
their only daughter north to be educated. It was true that
school at Lawrenceville, followed by Princeton, had given
generations of male heirs a good, solidly conservative

education, but for the New England Van Burens, this hardly constituted a good 'Yankee' experience. In New England there would be all those Pioneer Valley schools to choose from and, of course, there was always Harvard and Yale to seal the deal.

The Van Burens happened to live a few miles further up the valley from the Karlssons, in a large Byronic pile that had been in the family for well over one hundred and fifty years. When, during the time leading up to the Kennedy presidency, Peter Van Buren, the head of the family, had undergone a political transformation and renounced his ties to the Republican Party, it seemed only natural that Christina, recently elected to the Massachusetts state assembly and a neighbour, should be there to welcome him into the local Democratic Party fold. With Virginia now attending school in nearby Springfield, under the wardship of the Van Burens, it wasn't long before an introduction was made to Soren. Both had taken to each other immediately, although Soren had initially been embarrassed by the intensity of the attention given to him by this rather gangly child, three years his junior. To Christina, the young thing with the luxuriantly dark hair, immediately assumed the role of 'Pallas Athena' to her son's 'Odysseus'. She watched as the youngster worked her magic, forcing her son to take notice of the beauty that was unfolding before him. Christina saw their coming together as both fortuitous and providential. That it involved so much focused regard, on Virginia's part, towards her son, was something for which she was eternally grateful and, to some extent, mystified.

Their friendship – something the teenage Virginian referred to as 'a relationship' from the off – had, by the time Soren was due to go to Columbia, been going for some six years. For him, it was always innocently platonic; for her, it was anything but, imbued as it was with serious, and increasingly desperate, intent. It had always been impossible to hide the pleasure Virginia found in being in Soren's presence and as the time for his prospective departure for New York drew nearer, her desperation became increasingly evident. Firstly, there were the regular weekend visits to

New York during the first two years of his studies, followed by the giving up of a place at Radcliffe in the third, so that she could enroll at one of the city colleges. Then, after barely a year had elapsed, she'd upped sticks again, this time following him all the way to Berkeley, much to the displeasure of her parents, who watched with increasing alarm from their home in Charlottesville. That Soren's affections now appeared to be directed elsewhere, appeared not to matter, as Virginia was on a mission to save him from himself. It was a fixation not shared by her father, Wendell. The good fox hunting gentleman of Albermerle County, had already been greatly vexed by what he perceived to be his daughter's unnatural infatuation with the northerner and how the whole New England experience seemed to have unhinged her. There was talk of their daughter having been taken in by those northern scoundrels with their liberal ways. How she might had 'gone native'. But Berkeley! The place symbolised an entity that appeared to be somewhere between Sodom and Gomorra, with its lax morals, dubious scholarship, and odious notoriety. Egged on by Elspeth, Wendell had taken the hurt badly, believing it to be, at best, a dereliction of due guardianship, and, at worse, a monstrous northern plot.

His fears, though, were not to be realised, as an active and balanced upbringing, had indeed left its mark. His 'blessed Ginny', as he called her, soon revealed a healthy skepticism towards the activities and affected radical attitudes considered the norm at Berkeley. She had always been an excellent all-round athlete and it was to this that she once again turned, with rock climbing, tennis and field hockey all pursued to brutal effect. Added to this was an exceptional academic performance that resulted in straight distinctions on graduation. Friends and family in and around Charlottesville would still refer to her as that 'nice young Bradley girl', albeit one who might just be tempted, and led astray. That effusive placability though, in truth, hid an iron resolve and shrewd calculation. They were qualities that would be sorely needed, later, in her struggles with Geraldine.

17

Soren remembered how Virginia, on first meeting Geraldine, had reacted rather like a museum curator does when confronted with an exhibit whose provenance he or she isn't quite sure of. 'Interesting,' was all she said, in a tone that left Soren with the distinct impression that she was anything but impressed. But Soren had been dazzled by this graduate student at NYU, who appeared to be the perfect embodiment of post-Warhol cool. Virginia had observed at the time that Soren had given himself up, simpering and puppy-like, to a mother and daughter well versed in the art of animal cruelty. By the time of Virginia's arrival in New York, his and Geraldine's relationship had become well established. Virginia did not take this well. Although she'd initially hoped that Soren would come to his senses, she was soon forced to see Geraldine as a very formidable rival, a sentiment reciprocated by the older woman. Already a producer of various art installations on avant-garde and feminist themes, and favourably reviewed in the Village Post, Geraldine chose, at an 'engagement' party held at Soren's Morningside apartment, to announce that she had accepted a job with a radical press group out on the West Coast. What was more, Soren would be joining her. And she'd seen to it that the 'Southern Belle', as she dismissively referred to Virginia, would be there to hear the news. As for Soren, well he just fell into line; Geraldine had said jump and he did so.

Consequently Virginia had taken to her bed for a week, after which she'd resolved to harden herself and engage battle with this 'psycho-sexual harridan from hell'. She'd even upped sticks, and, as had so appalled her good parents, pursued the pair of them to Berkeley. In truth, though, as soon as she'd arrived, Virginia had felt the fight ebb from her; the eventual 'partnership' – not marriage – had seen to that. It had all happened so quickly and in a way that had both hurt and baffled the Southerner; not least by what she saw as Soren's hasty and insincere capitulation. The incompleteness of the pairing appeared to be confirmed by their decision to carry on living more or less separate lives, with Geraldine becoming ever more reliant on her therapist in San Francisco, and Soren returning to graduate study at Columbia. It was left to Christina to provide Virginia with good counsel, telling her it would be best to muster what dignity she could and walk away.

Separation from Geraldine served Soren well. Of course he should have known better than to move in with someone so given to fits of rage and threats of violence and, with a mother like Melissa calling the shots, they didn't stand a chance. She'd been on their case from day one, advising her daughter on how best to maximise Soren's pain, whilst at the same time minimising her own guilt. They were clearly the actions of someone bordering on the deranged, a woman who felt it her duty to protect her daughter from involvement with anyone. Soren's innocent and accommodating attitude appeared only to fan the flames of that particular malady. By hook or by crook Melissa had deliberately done all she could to sabotage and derail, and in the face of such formidable odds they called it a day. Afterwards Virginia had talked rather wickedly to Christina about how Melissa had made an excellent series of plays for the team.

For Soren, this had all been a somewhat salutary experience. The end had come at the time when he appeared to realise just what a fool he'd been. How, in Virginia, he had managed to throw away a true pearl. He knew he'd treated her appallingly and that there was no hope of reconciliation there. Besides, she'd found new friends and new loves. For both, it had been an awful twelve month's tutelage at the hands of a real live Clytemnestra figure, albeit one also steeped in the black arts of the Marquis De Sade. On Soren's part, there had been a series of rebounds, of which his relationship with Cindi had been but the latest manifestation. This had been the last, in a long line of disasters that had induced in Virginia, on hearing the news, a brief moment of levity.

'Oh Soren, you dear, dear fool' she'd said at the time to no one in particular. 'One should try to avoid entanglements with children who still skateboard to work.'

18

For Virginia there was more than just a hint of bitterness and betrayal. She'd always been of the view that Soren's relationship with Geraldine would fail, but, by the time it did, was too tired to care. She thus entered what she liked to refer to as her rehab phase. It signalled, that, for the first time, for as long as she could remember, she would no longer feel the need, nor the desire, to so obsessively subordinate her sense of place to something so dependent upon Soren. She knew him to be honest, albeit prone to be bounced from pillar to post, by whoever he was in a relationship with; but then, that had always been the problem. With Melissa and Geraldine pulling the strings, she and Soren had been put through a veritable hell and, for the moment, she hadn't the confidence to venture thoughts of any future rapprochement. She wouldn't do anything as drastic as retiring to the surrogacy of study, but would, as she informed Christina, 'get a life and party a little.' In the end though, study did win out, with her undergraduate work at Berkeley followed by a Stanford Law degree and, a few years later, an appointment at the University of Pittsburgh as an associate professor of Law and Criminology. After a suitable period of mourning had elapsed, though, there was a renewal of interest in Soren, albeit one that was hesitant and observed from a distance. It was very much welcomed by Christina.

Christina saw in Virginia qualities she fancifully claimed as her own. It gave the younger woman great power. Christina came to relish the moments when she and Virginia could find time to rendezvous, here in the Berkshires, or in New York. Ginny always held the promise of agreeable company that spoke of an agreed purpose between them both. In the face of such formidable odds, Christina would willingly bow to the inevitable and allow her thoughts of Virginia to become imbued with aspirations she herself held for her son. To that end she worked relentlessly to ensure that Virginia was kept appraised of her son's affairs, and, whenever it was at all possible, she would steer Virginia towards giving him a helping hand.

During that purple patch in Europe, when Soren had been at his most productive, Virginia had given him much-needed support in the form of an acuity of ear sensitive to the nuances of language that his research required. And when he returned to the States, they kept in touch; something that was made easier by the strict physical distance they were able to keep between themselves. It seemed to encourage an increasing confidence about the suggestions that could be proffered and the promises made, confident in the belief that there would be very little chance of such entreaties being taken up. But now the distance seemed to be breaking down. Had his mother not just spoken of their need to talk? That inquiry, by Virginia, about the damage done to the car, seemed to be sending the unmistakable message, that, at some time in the not too distant future, their paths might cross again. For Soren, the sensation was hardly disagreeable, although it was tempered by the thought that he was, once again, in danger of being found out. That he might just be deficient in some quality; something he construed as being passion. There had been times, increasingly of late, when he'd entertained thoughts about the traits he might fancifully possess, such as intellect and good humour, allied to a desire to meet the bloody awfulness of life with civility and a degree of discretion, and how these might indeed be bogus, both in their possession and as qualities in themselves. That without passion he was lost.

Virginia had a playful disregard, mixed with a mannered rectitude, that gave the impression to all of being in the presence of great intelligence. It was a thing that Soren had always found irresistible. That this was also wrapped in a figure that could do justice to someone wishing to enter the modelling profession, often had him believing that her continued interest in him, if it wasn't a hangover from juvenile infatuation, might just be the manifestation of something wantonly perverse. Thoughts that were confirmed by Virginia's actions, just a few years ago, when she'd decided upon a career change that both baffled and intrigued in equal measure.

While at the University of Pittsburgh, Virginia had begun to work closely with people over in the District Attorney's office. They soon came to appreciate her prescient understanding of how best to deal with crime. She also appeared to have an aptitude for solving it. It was something that was not lost on the folks down in the Criminal Investigations Branch of the Pittsburgh Bureau of Police, who began seeking her advice, most famously in regard to a particularly gruesome series of murders in which they appeared to be hopelessly at sea. Not only had Virginia helped to solve them, she'd also assisted in the compulsory retirement of a Commander, along with the re-assignment of a couple of MPOs, in the process. More importantly the Division decided to adopt a new rule book; one that seemed to have Virginia's imprimatur stamped all over it. And after all of this? Well, it seemed only natural that there should be a move by Virginia herself into the said bureau, followed by a fast-track rise through the uniformed ranks and, after a couple of years paying her dues, employment as a detective in the aforementioned Criminal Investigations Branch. Yes, very perverse indeed.

19

Soren was distracted and just a little agitated. A glass of wine in hand would usually lighten the mood, but not this time. The news about the trouble in Berkeley was far too worrying. He rose and walked over to the phone, his attention drawn to the flickering light of the answering machine. He pressed the message button and the disembodied voice of Denis Tsui, his teaching assistant, filled the room.

'Hi, Soren. Denis here. Trouble on the Genotech front.'

He sounded calm, still very much attempting to project the laid-back cool that was his trademark. Even so, Soren could detect a certain urgency in the message.

'Wilson has been playing up. I think it's manageable. Pariche fought our corner well, though. Think we need you back on the ground. Give us a call.'

It was typical Denis, short, abbreviated and to the point. Soren put the phone down and winced a little at the thought of what Pariche might have been doing on his behalf. Trust Denis to resist bad mouthing him. Then he remembered Kurst. Yes, Kurst would be the one to provide a take on what had happened; he was much more in tune with the politics of the department and, more importantly, resistant to the somewhat dubious charms of a certain (acting) dean. He dialled and within moments the voice of Lawrence Kurst came on the line.

'Ah, Soren, you got my message?' Brad had been right, his accent was unmistakenly English and just a little camp. From the muffled voices that could be heard in the background, Soren surmised that he'd interrupted an afternoon seminar.

'I hear there's been some trouble?'

'You could say that. It concerns one of our colleagues.' Kurst's language was guarded and his voice hushed; he obviously didn't want his students to overhear the conversation.

'I take it you mean Pariche?' asked Soren, helping him out.

'One and the same, old boy, one and the same.' The sound of moving furniture indicated that Kurst was getting up from his seat. Soren heard him making his apologies, along with the sound of a door opening. 'Just hold on a moment while I take this call outside.' Once in the corridor, in a place that sounded rather like an echo chamber, Kurst was able to talk more freely.

'It does help to have a phone with an extra bit of cord! Now, where was I? Yes, it seems Pariche got himself into a fight with our man Flaxel.'

'Flaxel? What the hell was *he* doing there?'

'Wilson invited him along. Got into a terrible fight with the Genotech chap over their equal opportunities policy.'

'Wilson invited Flaxel along?' Soren was still having trouble comprehending the idea of Wilson and Flaxel in consort.

'I know, old boy,' said Kurst, echoing his thoughts, 'I'm finding it difficult to get my head around that one myself.'

'An argument with Genotech, you said?' Soren was at last getting up to speed. 'An argument with Burdon? How did this all happen?'

'Yes, about their equal opps policy. It gets worse, old boy,' continued Kurst, pushing things along. 'Pariche and Flaxel then go head-to-head over that Moynihan thing; you know, about benign neglect.' Soren's heart began to sink. 'And the man, Flaxel, is saying that's what Pariche wanted to do to him. You know, treat him with a little of that old benign neglect. Wilson says he heard everything and that Pariche might have cost us a million bucks. The short of it is, he wants him out.'

'Larry, I'm not sure what to make of all this.' Soren was beginning to struggle. The stuff about benign neglect was just too awful to contemplate. It pointed to something that Moynihan, now the Senior Senator for the state of New York, was supposed to have written about the poor. How they – the mainly black poor masses – might, more profitably, be left to their own devices. Soren didn't believe, for one moment, that Pariche could even think such a thing, let alone give voice to it. Here was someone who, when not helping out at the local homeless centre, was a sustainer for the NAACP for Chrissake! No, Wilson would have deliberately misrepresented him.

'Look, Soren, I know that you and Pariche go way back, but do I have to spell it out? As far as Wilson is concerned, Pariche is bad news. He wants him gone!'

'But he can't do that, Larry! Jesus, this is Berkeley!' Soren found himself almost shouting down the phone. 'I'm not having that guy meddling with *my* program.'

'I know, old thing, I know, but in the end, Wilson could do a lot of mischief; he is the dean!'

Kurst was right; Wilson was in the position to do a hell lot of harm, if he so put his mind to it. He could prevent professors teaching and assessing their preferred courses and he was someone who revelled in the noise, the hurt and the pain that could be exacted during the university's arduous research productivity process. He could also play merry hell with lecture times and see to it that certain teaching halls suddenly became unavailable.

'If I know Pariche, he'll fight this tooth and nail,' countered Soren. 'He has friends too. You just can't go treating people like this! It could get very messy!'

'Already has, Soren, it already has. The last thing Wilson wants is people pointing the hand of bigotry at the department. He wants an end to it.'

'Okay, Larry, give me a moment and I'll get back to you.'

'Sure, Soren, but be quick. Wilson looks like someone in a hurry.' Before hanging up, almost as an afterthought, Kurst added an extra titbit calculated to stoke Soren's anxieties still further. 'Oh, by the way, there have been complaints made about Dr. Tsui.'

'Complaints? By who?'

'Wilson wouldn't say, but you can guess. Just more of the usual. Anyway, I've got to go. As I said, you need to be quick.'

'Ok, Larry, I'll speak to you soon.'

20

Soren slumped back in his chair. The last item about Denis Tsui was by far the most worrying. So they were going after him as well! This was how careers at Berkeley get stopped before they've even begun. The need to get back and give him support was now a paramount concern; Mississippi would have to wait. His mother would be delighted of course; the further the departure date for that trip was put back, the better.

Still wondering what the hand of bigotry might look like, Soren's thoughts turned to the Zenotech deal and who could possibly have said what to Burdon. Anything that suggested a problem with the Zenotech people was a worry; not only were they funding the Diaspora Project at Berkeley, but Soren also had hopes they might help with some of the work he had planned down in Mississippi. The Diaspora Project, and the teaching and the research at its heart, had been a eureka moment for Soren, and, against all the odds, it was one that, until yesterday, appeared to be coming to fruition. The project would be housed in a state-of-the-art research facility and would be closely connected to a teaching program that was already up and running. It was also bound to be a surefire hit with all the funding bodies, such as the Rockefeller and MacArthur Foundations. So a deal had been signed, with Burdon and the Zenotech Corporation he headed, releasing the monies promised, in tranches, as the project progressed. But now, all of this had been thrown into doubt. The groundbreaking ceremony that had been planned for the new build, along with a photo opportunity and champagne reception, 'icing on the cake' as Pariche had said, had been disrupted and thrown into turmoil. Soren buried his head in his hands at the thought of it. Already he was beginning to get a picture of what Flaxel probably had in mind. He would be wanting a piece of the action and promising dire consequences for anyone who had the temerity to get in his way; threatening to undo everything that Soren and Pariche had been working on for all these years. The potential fallout was too awful to contemplate. People such as Osterhagen and his colleagues, up at the Graduate Theological Union, would be fearful. It didn't take much to imagine how they would respond when faced with boycotts and threats and worse. But why was Wilson involved? Why was he doing this? The only thing that seemed to make any sense was that there must have been a deal. Something that involved money. With Flaxel Mohamed, it was always about money. There would be a fully staffed director's post to fill, plus funding for an administrator and all those researchers. Hell, Flaxel would be in pig heaven, with Wilson only too happy to have been able to dispense largesse to a grateful community. But hold on a minute; this was crazy. You just couldn't have a world-class facility – and at Berkeley they were always world class – run by crooks. And Flaxel would be pushing hard against a corruption that was equal to his own: academic ambition. At Berkeley, people took this very seriously indeed. What Soren couldn't have known, was how the arrangement between Wilson and Flaxel was driven by something much more personal and compelling and so much more corrupt.

What he did know was that he had a fight on his hands. Wilson now appeared to be extending his consummate skills, at working the university's committees, to the more lawless environment of the street. And he was someone who usually got his way. The forces he could muster were considerable. He had contacts all over the university campus, strategically worked into place. All could be called upon to smooth the process if push came to shove. Wilson could also be very ruthless; viciously so. The way that he'd dealt with poor Jimmy Beck was a case in point. Beck had once been foolish enough to question the cobbled together readings that Wilson had submitted as his published works for the first

NRC's doctoral research rankings exercise, at the time when Wilson was first beginning to manoeuvre himself towards the position of (acting) dean.

'Not one original piece,' Beck had truthfully, but somewhat rashly, declared. 'It would struggle to get itself recommended to the local trade school.'

Wilson responded, by using his powers, as Chair of the Department, to blow up a minor case of plagiarism into a full-scale investigation of Beck, resulting in the poor wretch's attempted suicide. And there were other ways that Wilson could get at staff. Grants could be withdrawn and academic preferment denied; something that Soren was only too keenly aware of. Getting on the wrong side of Wilson had probably meant the loss of any prospect of a full professorship, leaving him stuck on an associate professor's salary of $45,000.

Yes, Wilson was of a type to give Scottish Presbyterianism a bad name. Someone who liked to think of himself as a man of granite countenance, imbued with a sour severity and ruthlessness, but whose florid, rotund physique, and ingratiating disposition towards those in authority, in reality, conveyed more than just a hint of supine spinelessness and greed, of someone on the make. He might not have been the most imposing of figures, but Wilson was quick to learn his way around the committees and structures of Berkeley, making himself available to the powerful and the good. It had ensured that folks came to see him as the go-to person. A byproduct of all of this was a certain paranoia, on Wilson's part, about anyone else from the Department gaining the Chancellor's ear. Of course one such person at the top of the list – not of, but working in the Department – was a certain Jedemiah Pariche. And now, as he sat there gazing at the phone before him, Soren figured that he too was probably up there with him.

He was beginning to think more clearly now. Sure, it looked like the most god-awful mess, but there were glimmers of hope. Why, for example, had Wilson still not been made full dean of faculty? Someone in the Chancellor's Office must be holding out, and there were indeed many who'd expressed the view that something about Wilson just didn't sit right. Pariche would often suggest, not entirely mischievously, that there was the belief that Wilson might have got into Berkeley by mistake; that the appointments panel had really been looking for a senior clerk. Also, Soren's hunch about relations cooling between Wilson and the powers that be, was not too far off the mark. People in the Chancellor's Office did seem to have misgivings about the man. Wilson might have carried a degree of weight in his own department, but in the others that made up the school, there were varying degrees of hostility. On his way up the greasy pole, he'd obviously made enemies. So, at the moment, they were content to leave Wilson, as (acting) dean, twisting in the wind, unsure in their own mind whether to make the position permanent or not.

21

Soren took a few moments to compose himself before he made the next call, this time to Burdon.

'Hi, Soren, thanks for getting back to me so quickly. I take it you've heard about what happened yesterday?' Burdon's tone was urgent and his voice a staccato contrast to the camp elongated vowels of Kurst. He sounded like someone who did not suffer fools gladly.

'Yes, I'm extremely sorry.'

'Well, stuff happens. Anyway, we have to act fast! We've got a lot riding on this. It took a lot to convince folks here to get with the program. We here at Genotech take subjects like the Holocaust pretty seriously!' Soren bit his lip; just what did they think they got up to at Berkeley? Then he noticed a subtle change in tone. 'I also have people here I have to answer to, Soren. We're a little worried about the splits that seem to be appearing at your end.'

'There are no splits, Tom.'

'You could have fooled me! The dean seemed to think that you wouldn't be leading things.'

'Acting dean, Tom. He had no right saying such a thing. Hell, you've always known that I'd be taking a sabbatical this year.'

'I guess. But he did appear to echo some of the concerns we've been having here ourselves. How can you direct things from all the way down there in Mississippi? It might not have mattered, had this guy Wilson not made such a fuss about it.'

Exactly, thought Soren, exactly.

'But Tom, this year will just involve the build. Most things can be left to Jennings down at Estates.'

'I know, Soren, but my people need a name; a go to person who can give answers to any questions they might have. Someone who can nip any emerging problems in the bud.'

Once again, Soren found himself beginning to struggle. Burdon helped him out.

'I'll stonewall things here as long as I can, Soren, but you do need to get out here and sort this out. We're getting too many mixed signals. It's getting so we don't know who to trust.'

'Yes, Tom, I've been coming to that same conclusion myself. Leave Wilson to me. I'm getting a flight back in a few days. Before I go Mississippi.'

'Good, let's meet up and thrash this thing out. I'll be honest with you, Soren, our people like to be seen to have an interest in all things cultural, but this Flaxel guy! Please tell me he's not part of the picture?' Soren smiled to himself. He'd been wondering how long it would take before his name cropped up.

'Of course not, Tom. He should never have been there in the first place. Wilson had no right bringing him along.'

'That's exactly what your friend, Pariche, said, when he came out earlier.'

'Pariche! Pariche came out to see you?' Soren braced himself, but the assault he'd feared, didn't materialise. In fact, Burdon appeared to be quite taken with the man.

'You've got to keep him on board, Soren. He appeared to make a lot of sense.' There was a barely suppressed laugh from Soren's end of the line. 'He seems to know bullshit when he sees it. All those people crawling out of the woodwork when there's a buck to be had. He struck me as the type who'd give them short shrift. I'll leave the politics to you, Soren, but from where I'm standing the picture isn't all that great. My people are expecting results. Anyway, got to go; but Soren, be quick!'

Soren breathed deeply and let out a slow whistle. So Pariche had actually been out to see Burdon at Mountain View. And, lo and behold, he appeared to have made a favourable impression. Halfway between belief and disbelief, he put the phone down and wondered if he'd been making too much of the possible damage that had been done. After all, things did appear to be back on track. It took only a few moments though for the doubts to seep back in. A valued client and a million research dollars still appeared to be in jeopardy, and Charlie Wilson was still on the loose.

Soren was also beginning to resent the way events were conspiring to force him back to West Coast. Worse still, he had little or no idea as to what to say or do when he got there. He could see that a meeting with Wilson would have to happen, if only to mark the man's card. This would not be pleasant. As for that named 'go to person', as Burdon had called it, well, for some time Soren sat there thinking it through. Then, a thought, an idea, did indeed begin to form, but he figured that now would probably not be the right time to trouble Burdon with the outrageousness of it.

22

Further thoughts on the subject were interrupted by his mother calling from the study alcove above. She had obviously come to make amends.

'I thought I might find you here!'

Christina had watched her son spend the best part of his childhood hidden away in this room, reading magazines and books and listening to music spanning the decade between Elvis Presley's *Wooden Heart* and Crosby, Stills and Nash's *Wooden Ships*. Times spent in splendid isolation, during the dog days of summer, when windows would be thrown open to the smell of honeysuckle drifting in on the breeze. Thoughts of languid moments spent lolling beside the mill race, before venturing out for those solitary spells on the tennis court, perfecting that Roy Emerson serv. And there were memories of Virginia here too, on the other side of the net, returning those serves with interest, before taking in a ball game at Wahconah Park, down the road in Pittsfield. What there had not been, though, were many precious memories of his mother.

There were moments he fancied when he could remember early preschool times in Rochester, when the radio would crackle to the sound of fifties Doo Wop floating in across the plains. He could remember his mother then. Memories of her long slender hands, the warmth of her breath, and the moist softness of her lips pursed against his forehead. And memories of watching her weep.

'May I?'

Christina managed to kick off one of her shoes, before easing herself half onto his lap and into the seat beside him. The other shoe persistently clung on.

'Here, let me,' he said, coming to her aid and removing the offending item. For a while they sat together in silence, enacting a scene, increasingly irregular of late, that had become something of a Karlsson family ritual; making up for lost time. There was both a natural and forced quality about the arrangement. The two of them needed and enjoyed each other's company and there was a real, but somewhat restrained, affection between them. It was something that, on Christina's part, had always been compounded by guilt at the knowing impairment that had been caused by her absence.

'I hope I didn't drive you away earlier?' Her voice was soft and conciliatory, her body relaxed. Stretching, she leaned over and picked up his glass of wine from the side table and handed it to him.

'I have to go back to San Francisco,' he said.

'Really!' The relief in her voice was palpable, the shake of her body working itself into a chuckle. Her grey-blue eyes disappeared into a squint of a smile. 'I thought I heard Pariche's name being mentioned earlier! Has he been goading that man Wilson again?' Although Christina had never met Jedemiah Pariche, she had grown to like the man her son would often mention in various shades of exasperated despair. From day one she had trusted his judgement, especially as far as Wilson was concerned. She arched her back into a stretch and gazed around the room. 'I do remember the first time you set eyes on this place,' she said. 'Your face was such a picture.'

'Ah yes, the new Camelot!' His tone was playful, rather than dismissive. The reference was to a time not long after they'd arrived in Massachusetts, when Christina was first embarking upon the political trail. She'd discovered that, during the fifties, Ashleighs had once hosted a party graced by the newly elected junior Senator for the state, a certain John F. Kennedy. She had been much exercised by the prospect of emulating this; turning Ashleighs into a must-have invitation for the Tanglewood set, as well as providing a weekend sanctuary for her business and political friends from Boston. The somewhat faded Persian carpet in the centre of the room bore testimony to the weight of some of the nation's shakers and movers. Nelson Rockefeller, Silvio Conti and Elliot Richardson had all been here, as had the usual suspects from Christina's side of the aisle – Ted Kennedy, Tip O'Neil and Mayor Flynn. The lamp on the table that now illuminated them both was itself a gift from Pierre Salinger.

For Christina, though, reminiscences like these where something of a double-edged sword and she was always alert to the need to deflect any talk hinting of the times she'd been absent from her post. 'You have been a bitch,' she'd often said to herself, knowing that it had been left to her good friend, Elizabeth Van Buren, from across the valley, to provide Soren with some form of parental surrogacy for the many times she'd been away.

'Would it have hurt too much to have got in touch?' Her tone did not seek to accuse. 'Perhaps I was a little harsh earlier. It *is* good to see that you're still fond of this neck of the woods. That you might be thinking of moving back.' She gave him a playful nudge before – a little distractedly – looking up and fixing her gaze upon a bureau in the corner of the room. She struggled to her feet and walked over to it, returning with a large buff envelope.

'I thought this would have been the first thing you would have noticed,' she said, as she handed it to him. 'Ginny dropped it off earlier. She's been staying at the Van Burens.'

In the package was a small manuscript to which was attached a brief note, written upon University of Pittsburgh letter-headed paper. Soren let forth a nervous exhale and gave the note a quick scan.

'She's back at the university?' he asked.

Christina nodded. 'From what I can tell she's been doing the odd lecture. She's thinking of moving on from her job with the police.'

'She is?' Soren's question was purely rhetorical, his interest still very much directed towards finishing the note. It was indeed from Virginia, inviting him to comment on a piece she'd written for possible inclusion in the *New York Review of Books*. For a while he remained motionless, ensnared by that familiar hand. He shrugged and let forth a slow exhale. 'So they finally got in touch?' Once again his refrain was rhetorical. It had been a couple of years ago, at a party, that he'd let mention to Barbara Epstein that he knew of this criminologist – turned detective – who'd just been investigating a series of murders down in Pittsburgh. If ever she wanted an inside twist on the crime genre, and a feminist one to boot! A promise had been made, there and then, to put one of Bob Silver's assistants onto it.

Christina, who'd been studying her son's reactions carefully, interrupted his reverie.

'You will be replying, won't you?'

'So, she's been staying up at the Van Burens?' he asked, ignoring her question.

'Come on, Soren, don't play games with me. Why did you think I brought up the question of that blessed car? We were discussing the possibility of the two of you doing the circuit again.'

'We, Mother?'

'Yes, Ginny and myself were thinking of the times you'd go up to Saratoga together and the runs you used to make up to Lake Champaign; you could get the old Hacker out on the water again! Methinks 'tis time to put her out of her misery!'

23

Sitting upright, Christina arched her back again, extending her arms into a stretch. 'You know, I sometimes think we're more like a couple of old lovers.' She was coursing into one of her more irresistible moods; coquettish and utterly endearing. Often, when she was alone with Soren, Christina would employ a subversive playfulness that contrasted with her usual mannered demeanour. Soren would have to be on his guard. The pallor, that had so worried him earlier, had gone, revealing a woman of real beauty, with eyes that once again had a sparkle and youthful mischief about them.

The moment raised a question in Soren, similar to the one posed earlier by Albert Canstanze, albeit in a more benign fashion. Why had there been so few men in his mother's life? The most obvious answer was that over the past twenty years she'd been far too busy clambering up the corporate ladder, to give them much thought. A more nuanced view would have to take into account Christina's view of the species. It wasn't good. It's not that she disliked men; on the contrary, Christina had always enjoyed their company, whether it was being adept at mirroring their conceits or deferring to their supposedly better judgements. Rather, she saw them as beings that didn't quite add up. Rather like the sight that beholds you when you happen across a seeing eye dog. You wonder how the blessed creature does it, but rejoice in not having the need of one yourself. It therefore intrigued and baffled her why such a seemingly intelligent and beautiful lass as Virginia could become so swooningly intoxicated, so easily swayed, by such a creature, even if the beneficiary of this focused regard just happened to be her son. It was as if the poor girl had some kind of malady. Of course Christina reveled in the prospect of their union, but, on a rational level, could see no point to the emotion that drove it.

A photograph now caught his attention, brought to prominence by the increased luminescence of the Salinger lamp. It was of a young couple, arm in arm. The woman in the photograph was staring straight at the camera whilst her partner was lovingly gazing at her. The woman was Christina, and the man – one of the few who'd successful pursued and won her over – was Harold Bishop, Soren's father.

'Do you think you'll ever get back together again?' Even before the words had left his mouth, Soren found himself wishing he'd not given in to such a nervous and lazy impertinence.

'I think that one sailed a long time ago,' she replied, almost imperceptibly, but with a smile. Christina had wanted far more than Harold Bishop could ever possibly offer. He had the amiability, the charm and definitely the intelligence, but he lacked the ambition. Small towns and skilled trades had their attractions, but they were hardly enough to contain the ambitions of a woman like Christina. Besides, Harold had the look of a loser about him; someone who'd always be making the wrong choices. His decision to move to Utica, in the midst of one of the worst recessions a town could possibly have, appeared to be a continuance of that tradition. About twenty years ago, Christina had found out that Harold had moved there, only about a hundred miles away, up the Mohawk Valley. After much deliberation and soul searching, he agreed to have Soren stay with him for a trial period. Harold had just started work as a phone engineer and had managed to move into an apartment on the edge of town. Utica was small town, provincial and increasingly derelict. Soren had wanted to like the place, but some of the local Italian kids had been a terror. He remembered how he had to duck and weave as he raced past flailing fists and taunts, and how a few words, from his father to their parents, had managed to make it stop. Harold Bishop was like that: able to charm the birds down from the trees. Soren could also recall an apartment that had been homely and warm, its cramped conditions owing much to the regiment of women who seemed to be perpetually visiting the place. There was also the discovery of a half-sister. To this day, Soren would wonder just how his mother had managed to contrive this; how, by making that introduction and sending him there, she had managed to get it so right.

'And this trip to Mississippi, Soren,' his mother was back on track, 'you will be alright?'

He nodded. 'It's not exactly *Mississippi Burning*, Mother. Things have moved on.' She didn't look entirely convinced. 'Anyway,' he continued, turning the tables, 'all this concern about my well-being! What about yours? This Constanze guy; you really seem to be bent on humiliating him. And we've never had a police car parked outside before!'

'Par for the course, Soren, par for the course,' she sighed. 'They're just taking precautions.'

She had, of course, not been privy to the conversation that had taken place earlier between Felix and Tank, just down the road. Had she been so, she would have been mortified by the thought that her son might one day come to the attention of men with such a predilection for violence and the inflicting of pain.

24

Christina had sought to keep Soren safe from all manner of perceived slights and threats, real and imaginary. During his years at boarding school, he'd been cocooned in a world of *Exonion* ritual and tradition, away from much of the recurrent background noise that had made up the sixties. Those images of beautiful and otiose defiance; of black children being escorted past the incredulous hate-filled expressions of white men and women, the water cannon and the billy club, and the gleeful smiles of smug overweight Klansman, starring in yet another failed courtroom arraignment, somewhere in the South. All had been observed from a safe distance. What might have happened, had her son's upbringing been left to his father, scarcely needed thinking about. The despair of the ghetto and the big city riots, along with the rise of the Black Panthers and the establishment's response of the gun, had, for Christina, been a little too close to home for comfort.

At Exeter there had been the odd run-in with the authorities, something that had usually been the product of adventures co-manufactured with Brad, but these had been trifling affairs, even – *sotto voce* – a source of pride. As much as it might have been troubling at the time, whether it was skipping school to go on a protest, or breaking into the dorms of student proctors and swapping the furniture between them, it had always been the harbinger of something touchingly laudable, rather than being a source of worry or alarm. It comforted her to know that her son was a balanced child, with an affable countenance that she'd never known to be malign. It was a quality that had made Soren popular with most of those he'd come into contact with, from the nannies who'd doted on him in his pre St. Bernard days in New York, all the way up to his friends and acquaintances at Exeter and Columbia. Here was a person of a sociable outlook, once the initial reserve had been overcome, who was also the most consummate of listeners. Those who turned to him, and many did, would find their fears and concerns attended to by someone with a finely tuned ear. It was a thing that had had a considerable impact on Virginia.

For the moment, though, Soren was content to watch his mother's metronomic breathing as she drifted off into sleep. It was as if their presence together was a signal for her to let go of the worries she had, be it the investigation or the – at times – equally egregious concerns she had with the partners in her law practice. Soren loved moments like this, when he could feel that he was contributing towards her well-being and hence her sense of place.

With his mother asleep Soren was able to turn his attention again to the manuscript. He read it carefully. The writing was, of course, very good; Virginia obviously knew her audience. She'd started with references to the TV series *Hill Street Blues* and Fleischer's treatment of the *Boston Strangler*, before swiftly moving onto Freud and Camus, by way of Luce Iragary. He could see that she'd been out of academia perhaps a little too long, with some of her allusions revealing a tell-tale clumsiness, but she still managed to hold the tension between the science and the literary, almost perfectly. As he read further he felt a remorse for that lost counsel he'd come to rely upon during his time in Europe. Then it had been Virginia who'd filtered out the rubbish during those long transatlantic calls, when they'd talked through to the early hours. They were conversations that had been probingly intimate; moments he'd cherished. He knew that she would also have been able to provide a critical and positive counterpoint to the nonsense he'd had to endure with the likes of Wilson and Geraldine. He'd failed to appreciate it then; that much he now knew. He'd been too blind to see what was before him. Women of such beauty and cache as Virginia didn't wait around for long. Unless, that is, they were in some way flawed.

Having given the manuscript a quick flip through, Soren looked up and tilted his head backwards. In the distance he could see the silhouetted form of St Mary's Episcopal Church set against the night sky. It had been there that he'd first set eyes on her. He remembered how he'd exchanged fitful glances with this skinny slip of a girl wearing a short summer frock, her hair tied in a bun and her Cheshire cat grin honed to the maximum. And beyond St Mary's, just on the rise, he could see the lights of Brewster's Diner on Highway 22. He remembered the twilight get-togethers he'd had there with friends, before moving on to a party or dance at West Stockbridge or Great Barrington. How he and Virginia would do a spirited rendition of something that appeared to be a cross between the Lindy Hop and the Sailor's Horn Pipe, and always, for some unfathomable reason, to the accompaniment of Len Barry's *'1-2-3',* or was it Chris Montel's *'The More I See You'?* He could never remember. He did remember, though, the exquisiteness of her dance and her dextrous footwork, as if both mind and body were being sublimely worked by some ghostly puppeteer.

His mother was now beginning to stir. She stretched, smiled, and, looking at her watch, hurriedly rose to her feet.

'Is that the time?' She said huffily, smoothing the contours of her suit. 'We have a meeting to go to. You do know about the Fairford Hospital closure, don't you?' She knew perfectly well he didn't. 'I'll be helping out on the platform. It's vital that we all attend and show our support.'

Already, as she hastily climbed the stairs to the study landing above, Soren could hear himself agreeing to accompany her to East Brunswick's only hostelry, where the meeting was going to take place. She turned and peered down at him.

'You can forget about cooking tonight. We've been invited to the Van Burens. I know I'm supposed to be banished from the kitchen – small mercies – but Peter heard that you were in the neighborhood and has insisted on your presence. If you do feel up to making something, I promised the police detail outside some refreshments. You know, one of the specials in the fridge.'

Soren nodded, but this was not good. He could feel himself being knocked off balance yet again. His mother was calling the shots, taking charge. And there had been something about her demeanor that gave out the possibility that a night of extreme discomfort might be in store.

25

The Star Inn liked to think of itself as the gathering place for the surrounding countryside. An impertinence of course, but the bar that Soren's party now entered was busy enough. It was low ceilinged and split-levelled, with large amounts of exposed timber. On the walls were portraits of upper class revolutionary figures engaged in various country pursuits, with central focus given to a picture of Paul Revere's Midnight Ride. The hospital closure meeting was due to take place in one of the back rooms, towards which Soren ushered the others. Afterwards he presented himself to a small muscular figure standing behind the bar. The man's somewhat sombre expression broke into a smile of recognition.

'Soren, how good it is to see you. When was the last time?'

'July, Mario, for the jazz.'

They shook hands, then Mario bent down and pulled an already opened bottle from underneath the counter. 'I have something for you. *Spanner*, direct from the Piedmont!' he enthused. 'Have one on the house.' Soren watched contently as Mario poured him a glass, after which he pushed its oxblood-coloured contents towards him. Soren lifted the glass to his nose and sniffed, taking in the heavy aroma. He took a sip.

'Very smooth, Mario. Not what I was expecting.'

'Rewards being left to breathe for a while.'

Whilst Mario was taking care of the rest of the order, Soren took the opportunity to have a look round the bar. It was a scene both reassuringly familiar and depressingly predictable. In one corner, through a throng of people, he could see an elderly man sitting alone, drinking his coffee. He remembered he'd been connected in some way to people most locals were convinced were New York mobsters. Then there was Pretzel, still very much the hippy, albeit one very much steeped in the revolutionary thoughts of Chairman Mao. Soren wondered if he was still trying to convince the people over at Rensselaer of his plans to produce energy from fresh air, or if he was still capable of boring people to death about the exploits of General Wolf? He chose not to find out, giving him the politest of noncommittal waves. At the other end of the bar was a group of people who Soren judged to be teachers from the local academy. With them was a woman he thought he did recognise, listening intently to the others, hand on hip, head bobbing backwards and forwards like a hen. She turned and noticed him watching. Her expression, self-conscious at first, dissolved into a smile of recognition. She raised her glass in acknowledgment, before turning again to the conversation with her friends. His gaze moved on. There were the usual office workers, home after a day's toil in Great Barrington and Pittsfield, leaner and younger than he remembered. He knew the type; new arrivals to rural small-town exurbia, extending the time of their homeward commutes into the happy hour and putting off the moment they would have to report home to their respective spouses. Their bosses could usually be found standing drinks over at the golf club, rueing a missed opportunity of getting out onto the links at this time of year. Then he noticed her. A woman seated at the far end of the bar. She was partially hidden and all he could see was her back and a lot of highly toned and burnished thigh.

'One of the beautiful people,' he murmured to himself.

'Quite a lady, eh?' Mario had returned with the drinks order.

'Oh, was I that obvious?' Soren replied, a little embarrassed at his own indiscretion, but determined to continue in his study of her. This woman was somehow irresistibly familiar. Her blonde hair was cut short, extenuating the slimness of her neck. Part of the attraction was that she was with someone he knew; a certain Miss

Tyndale, product of Vassar College, with a background that included running with the horsey set of Hudson Valley. In her privileged and pampered upbringing, Miss Tyndale had, as Soren remembered, precious few qualities, other than at one time being a friend of Virginia's and an occasionally excellent conversational foil. She looked up and noticed him. Immediately she was on her feet, waving enthusiastically for him to come over.

'Why, Soren, how marvelous!' her voice had a creaking tone, as if it had been forced from the back of the throat. Soren made his way over to where the pair of them were seated and gazed heavenward.

'In the room the women come and go talking of Michelangelo.' He stooped to kiss her hand.

'Oh, Ginny,' she laughed, gazing down at her companion. 'Is he always like this?'

Soren froze in his stoop. What was that? Virginia! Looking around, his eyes met those he knew so well.

He was aware of suppressed giggles, interested scrutiny, and the swilling around of his brain inside his skull. He rose awkwardly, to be stopped by the warmth of a familiar embrace. Virginia, half rising to meet him, arched her back and tilted her head so that their lips would meet. The kiss was gentle, lingering. The softness of her form and the memory of her smell did much to offset his sense of disorientation.

'Come on, take a seat!' she said, motioning him to sit next to her. 'It has been quite a while. Still the incorrigible flirt I see.' Her voice was soft, her accent mid-Atlantic. Fighting for composure, Soren found himself looking at a beauty that appeared both familiar and other worldly. Soren always carried a memorably clear picture of Virginia in his head, but it was nothing compared to the real vibrancy of her presence before him now. There was that straight, almost perfect, nose and the high cheekbones. And, of course, there were those wide, smiling, almost tearful, big brown eyes. Ah, that Cheshire Cat grin again. It was a smile he knew so well, with its ability to bestow gracious beneficence upon those it favoured. As always her dress was immaculate; but it was not what he'd expected. She was wearing a beige and gold – almost mini – dress, brocaded out of a thin lightweight material, from which protruded those beautifully entwined legs, their muscular tone still hinting at their continued exposure to the possibility of breakage and fracture somewhere upon a distant hockey field. The sensible shoes, stylish slacks and plain shirts, worn for work, had obviously been dispensed with tonight. His raised eyebrow and disbelieving smirk conveyed un-alloyed surprise at her ensemble. More Beverley Hills, than her usual stomping ground of Walnut Street, in Pittsburgh or, dare one say, Madison Avenue. His surprise didn't go unnoticed.

'Oh, do forgive us, Soren, we've just come back from a bit of shopping.' She noticed him looking at her hair; short and cut to the jaw. 'Oh, don't worry, just revisiting a crush I once had on Amelia Earhart.'

For someone who so obviously didn't have to try, this was one hell of a statement. A few months ago Christina had been expressing worry as to how harried Virginia had looked, but not here, not now. Here was a woman sporting a healthy looking suntan as if she'd been away vacationing all summer long. Someone working for the Pittsburgh Bureau of Police wasn't supposed to look like this. Didn't they have airless interrogation rooms, tedious stakeouts, and long sessions burning the midnight oil writing up reports? Stunning was the only way to describe the way she looked and Soren couldn't help but think that this, and her renewed association with Miss Tyndale, presaged change. As if certain issues had been resolved and decisions made.

It was a sentiment that was duly returned, except she could also see in him a frustrated listlessness; she had, after all, been kept fully informed by his mother. She gave him a look that said she was still alert to finding in him things to fix. If there were any faults, and there were many, a lack of fashion sense would not be one of them. He might have put on a couple of pounds, but she could see that he was still probably making those regular forays back east to New York's garment district. There were the tanned derbies, the straight-legged, camel-coloured cords and the dark Italian jacket. Whatever was driving Soren's unsettled sense of anomie, it had yet to infect his sense of style; she imagined that hell would have to freeze over before he allowed that. When she spoke again there was a plaintiff accusatory tone to her voice.

'Why so long?'

Soren wanted to protest his innocence, but an arched eyebrow urged caution. His thoughts conjured up a picture of himself emerging, later that evening, limbless and broken.

'My eyes and the indigestible portions which the Leopards reject.'

He could feel the sweat pouring from him. Would she help? Surely she could sense his discomfiture!

'You do look very well,' he said, ignoring her question and throwing himself on her mercy.

'The effects of helping your mother out with the election.' Good, she was playing the game.

'Yes, I heard.'

'She works those committees damnably well. That district should have gone Republican years ago.'

'Perhaps the water's a little different up here!'

For a moment there was silence as they both strove to find each other and move the conversation on, under the interested gaze of Miss Tyndale. He was still very much stunned by Virginia's appearance: the suntan, the short hair, and the large radial sunglasses resting on her forehead. It had been an almost too perfect disguise.

26

What was Virginia doing here? It appeared not to be coincidental; the arrival of that manuscript, and her sitting here before him now, was proof of that. But he did delight in what he saw. Had he really been so resolute in his desire to keep a distance? Hardly. The 'marriage' to Geraldine had been the product of indolence and its subsequent breakdown inevitable. He could see that now. But his regard for Virginia was an entirely different proposition. Many of her letters had gone unanswered, but none unread. Now he could detect his resistance weakening once more and he felt panicky; something that was presently suffused with that old demon again, a compulsion to flee. Before he could make amends though, his rather incoherent and bumbling thoughts were bought to a halt by Craig, returning to make an enquiry about the drinks.

'Is that you, Ginny? Of course it is. So you're the reason for the drinks hold-up. Shame on you.' She rose to meet his embrace. 'We're in the back room.'

'Oh yes, for the hospital closure meeting.'

'You know about that?' asked Soren.

'Of course. Wouldn't miss it for the world. Lucy (Miss Tyndale) and myself were just talking about it.'

'All the way from Pittsburgh for the Fairfield Hospital closure?'

'Now, now, Soren, you seem to be forgetting that I do have family in this neck of the woods! In any case, I wouldn't want to pass up on one of Geraldine's invitations now, would I?'

'Geraldine? Here?' Soren was now beginning to panic.

'Well, not Geraldine exactly; it's her mother.'

'Melissa?' Soren's enquiry was met with a nod of confirmation from Craig.

'Aye, she's chairing the meeting.'

Virginia got to her feet. 'Oh, this is going to be great fun!' she said, visibly enjoying the moment. At five nine, she was shorter than Soren, although her willowy physique made her look taller; something that was presently extenuated by the mini heels she was wearing. Then she was off, leaving him floundering in her wake. With a pounding heart and a churning in his stomach, he raced after her, through a dimly lit passageway and up a small flight of stairs. Her carefully measured cadence ensured that their entrance into the back room was made together, under the approving gaze of Christina and the equally disapproving – almost glacial – glare of Melissa. As they passed, Christina gave out an exaggerated look of disbelief, surreptitiously pointing to the woman seated next to her. 'Sorry,' she appeared to mouth, 'I didn't know.' In response Soren smiled and shrugged his shoulders, before following Virginia to a space at the side of the hall. With no spare seats available, they would have to stand. Looking around, Soren recognised some faces, but most were unfamiliar. Many – both men and women – were having trouble averting their eyes away from the vision that was Virginia. Bathing under the redeeming glow of the room's attention, she turned and tugged at Soren's sleeve. 'We're definitely in for an 'oot' of an evening tonight,' she whispered, mischievously mimicking Melissa's north border accent. Soren watched with growing trepidation at just how quickly Virginia's bearing could be transformed by contact with either Melissa or Geraldine. In the past she would have become agitated and defensive, but not now. Now there was exhibited a certain controlled belligerence, as if, through some perverse form of cognitive therapy, she'd every intention of pursuing the cause of what had once been so hurtful for her.

The room was far too small for the number of people present. In contrast to the subdued light of the bar, the lighting here was bright and the atmosphere airless. The place resonated to the sound of conversations conducted in familiar New England and up-state New York accents. Soren was conscious of various shades of blue denim, long hair and full beards, mingling with business suits and loosened ties. What he hadn't anticipated was the abundance of figures straight out of central casting. These were players from the local dramatic society, who would later be finishing a run of the play *Murder in Peyton Place* with a themed '60s party backstage. The women in slacks and knee-length tight-fitting dresses, all boots and horizontal stripes, sat next to men wearing Harrington jackets, dark suits and dark glasses.

Soren looked around to see if Geraldine was present. No, thank heavens, she was nowhere to be seen. Perhaps the thought of having to share the limelight with her mother had proved too much. Ah yes, the mother, Melissa. There she sat, at the front, seated behind a trestle table, still wearing that expression of ill-disguised contempt. After a while the noise in the room began to subside, as people, amidst a clearing of throats and a patting down of dresses, looked towards the front. As if on cue, Melissa's features morphed into a smile. With half an eye still directed at the late arrivals, she spoke firmly, her accent betraying the northern New England burr that had so tested Virginia's attempt at mimicry earlier. She was of slight stature, in her early sixties, with a few grey streaks, highlighted against what was still a shock of black hair. She wore her usual attire of black boots, black jeans, and yes, black shirt, giving the platform the distinct impression that it had been visited by a cross between Cruella de Vil and something perhaps a little more sinister. Melissa loved to think of herself as the local heretic. Something that was reinforced by her being the guiding light of the local spiritualist church. In truth, it just made her look a little odd. Like her daughter, she had an almost neurotic need to be centre stage and she was now in her element. She turned to an elderly gentleman sitting on the platform next to her:

'May I introduce Mr McCormack. He's an old friend from the UTWA local in Lynn, who just happened to be addressing a dispute this week up in North Adams. I'm sure you'll agree with me that he's in a good position to shed some light on this battle we're having over the Fairford Hospital closure.'

The room settled down to listen. True to form, though, Melissa was not going to let the opportunity of addressing such a large audience pass quietly. Furthermore, the presence of Virginia and Soren seemed to act as a spur to greater agitation on her part. The assembled audience were informed about how the state and county health boards, along with an HMO called the Mintle Corporation, had declared war on the well-being of local women. As usual, she informed her audience, the predominantly male professions would be protected and redeployed to other centres and agencies, whilst the lower grade workers – mostly women – would lose their jobs. Soon she was berating the politicians and their actions as otiose misogyny and, amidst a growing chorus of coughs and the clearing of throats, began to direct her fire towards the men present. Things were just beginning to get a little out of hand; with the mutterings and objections becoming more strident. There were increasingly exasperated cries of – mainly male – distress as Melissa continued in her now impassioned soliloquy, until she was eventually brought to book by a lone voice from the side of the room. It was Virginia.

'Melissa!' she called out. 'I do believe you were about to introduce Mr McCormack!' The salvo struck amidships. Embarrassed, Melissa turned to the somewhat bemused union leader. 'Yes, of course,' she blustered. 'Peter, the platform's yours.' And with this, she collapsed into her seat, gazing despairingly up at the ceiling. The expression on Virginia's face was one of complete triumph. For his part, Soren was having none of it. He could feel his head pounding and his brain swimming again, jarring against the serrated insides of his skull. After a suitable time had passed, he quietly made his exit and retired to the bar. What had so distressed him at Berkeley was now being visited upon him here as well. Somebody, somewhere, appeared to be having a great deal of fun at his expense and things were just about to take a turn for the worse.

27

'It's the second time he's called in as many minutes,' said Mario, pointing towards a wall phone.

'What, Pariche has been calling here?' Soren's face was a picture of disbelief. He walked across to the phone and lifted the receiver.

'Solly, is that you? Thank God I've got hold of you.'

'Jed, what are you doing calling here?'

'You heard about yesterday? They're out to get me!' He sounded just a little drunk. 'You've got to get back out here, Solly, they've started already. I've been getting phone calls, bad ones...'

'Phone calls? Are you sure?'

'I know when someone's trying to put the squeeze on me!'

Soren found himself wincing a little as Pariche's outrage coursed into a howl. 'I'm sorry. You say you were threatened?'

'Well, not exactly, but I know when I'm being played.'

Soren thought for a moment. He knew that it was just as likely that Pariche would have been the one getting his threats in first.

'Let's just go through things one at a time, shall we. What exactly happened at the groundbreaking earlier? What did Burdon actually say?' He was beginning to find his feet.

'It wasn't down to me, Solly. It was this Flaxel guy.'

'You mean Flaxel Boateng? Yes, I heard he was there.'

'That's the guy. Minding my own business and he ambles over and says he's interested in joining our little old project. '*Our little old project!*' he repeated, his voice booming down the line. 'Can you imagine the nerve of the

101

guy? He was primed, Solly. Wilson invited him along, wound him up, and pointed him in my direction.'

For Soren, things were beginning to slot into place.

'Hell knows what Wilson was thinking,' Pariche continued, 'inviting the guy along in the first place. I thought the Zenotech thing was ours, a done deal; something we could link to the Holocaust centre they're planning up on Geary. And what do we get? This goon attempting to gatecrash things, sprouting off about the sun people. Already Wilson appears to be mobbed up with the very people we should be fighting against. He was primed, Solly, that Flaxel guy was primed.'

Soren's continued silence indicated that this was playing on his mind too. Once again, Pariche filled in the blanks.

'He's got Wilson convinced that I was having a go at black people, Solly. Hell, I was attempting to say the exact opposite. Something Bellow said about black culture and Dostoevsky. That's how the damn Moynihan thing came about. I was trying to tell that snake oil salesman, Friessan, that a history of abuse and slavery is bound to leave its mark and that's when he ratted me out. He and Wilson chose to get it all wrong. Just heard what they wanted to hear.'

Soren was having to stretch his imagination as to what Pariche might really have said, although he had an inkling that any topic embracing the names of Bellow, Dostoevsky and Moynihan, would surely have been lost on the likes of Flaxel.

'And what's this about a fight?' asked Soren.

'There was no fight. Just that punk Flaxel thinking he could do the groundbreaking. I disabused him of that idea.' He paused, before continuing, his tone just a little subdued. He was beginning to calm down. 'He called me a disgrace, Solly; Wilson called me a disgrace!'

'I can't believe he'd say such a thing.'

'You calling me a liar?' Ah, there it was again, that barely suppressed whimper. Soren could picture Pariche at the other end of the line, with wild imploring eyes, head shaking, building into another howl.

'Now hold on a minute, Jed, of course I'm not.'

There was a moment's silence before a more contrite Pariche continued. 'Solly, you and me, we've got to stand up to the bullies of this world. People like Wilson and these new friends he's got down on the flatlands.' Ah, there it was again; vintage Pariche, always finding angles to both hook and offend at one and the same time. 'That's what I said to Wilson when I rang him earlier. Told him that you and I were united on this score...'

'You phoned Wilson?' Now it was Soren's turn to yelp.

'Sure did,' Pariche replied. 'Gave him a piece of my mind!'

My God, thought Soren, as the blows fell, Pariche really was quite mad. He also had an inkling of what Wilson would be thinking. That he, Soren Karlsson, had put Pariche up to it.

'But Jed, why did you have to go and do that?'

'He wants me off the program,' Pariche replied, hurt, and ignoring the question.

'But you wouldn't have been in this position had you kept yourself to yourself.'

This brought a hardly suppressed squeal again from down the line.

'Have you been listening? I was set up. Wilson set me up!' The silence, this time at Soren's end of the line, gave Pariche cause to think that he'd gone too far. 'Sorry, Solly, got to call it as it is. You know I have your best interests at heart? We're a lot closer on this than you think.'

'I know, Jed, I know,' replied Soren, certain that, flattery or not, an accolade from Pariche was the last thing he needed right now. For one fleeting moment he even fancied the old fool might just be trying to start a cult. It wasn't too far off the mark. Ever since their first meeting, when they'd worked together at that homeless shelter in Tenderloin, Pariche had tended to view Soren as if he were one of God's chosen. It was something that hinted, to the younger man, of a certain derangement.

'Soren, this is your moment of redemption, I can sense it. Forces are afoot, mark my word...'

Ah, there it was again, that flow into Parichean eulogy. Soren tried to deflect it. 'Come on Jed, don't be such a fool!'

It was to no avail. Once again he could feel himself being drawn into something beyond his control. Now Pariche was telling him about Burdon, and what the CEO of Genotech had said at the groundbreaking ceremony. He'd talked of wanting to speed things up and how this had been manner from heaven to Flaxel, alive to the quick hustle. Flaxel would be finding ways to work the scams and play on the guilt of all those 'prissy white' execs over at Mountain View. And that's why Pariche had gone out there to see Burdon, his newfound 'buddy', who was beginning to see things in the same way he did. How only Pariche, his good friend, Soren Karlsson, and the CEO of Genotech, now stood in the way of the ruin these fiends wished to inflict.

After a while Soren noticed the bar around him beginning to fill; a sure sign the hospital closure meeting was breaking up. To his horror, he could also see Melissa, of all people, with billowing and swirling striped head of hair, fast bearing down upon him.

'Look Pariche,' he said, hurriedly, 'I've got to hang up now. Don't do anything rash, I'll be catching a flight back out to San Francisco in the next couple of days.'

'Excellent news, Solly, excellent news.'

'We'll speak later...'

'We will, Solly, we will!'

28

Soren put the phone down and turned to greet Melissa. His half-hearted attempt at an embrace was rebuffed. 'Sorry I couldn't stay,' he lied, 'I had an important call to make.'

'Yes, of course you did,' she replied. Before he could proffer further thoughts or apologies, Melissa had sat herself down at a nearby table and in one fluent movement of the hand, forcefully beseeched him to join her.

'Still at the beck and call of others I see,' she said, fixing him a stare that was as always interestedly suspicious. 'The meeting's all but finished now. I thought it would be best to leave the closing stages to your mother, while I popped out to see how you were coping.'

Soren felt himself recoiling from her presence.

'And what have you decided?' he asked.

'Oh, you're doing fine,' she replied, 'just fine.' His slightly harassed demeanor hadn't gone unnoticed.

'Bad call, eh?' she asked, pointing to the phone, obviously buoyed by the thought that all might not be well.

'I was very surprised to see you here!' he said, seeking to deflect attention away from any complications that might arise from a discussion about Pariche.

She ignored this and drew closer, presenting him with a ripple of furrowed lines etched into cadaverous skin. 'You do know that Geraldine has moved back home, don't you?'

'Has she?' he replied, defensively, not wanting to be drawn in.

'It is so good to have her home. She's been doing some work over at Amherst. It gives her time to think and engage in new excavations.'

'Excavations?' he raised an eyebrow.

'Then again, you probably wouldn't understand, would you? You do find us so terribly mystifying, don't you? It's so good that you cured her of all that sort of thing.'

And there it was: the hardly veiled insult, just like old times. Melissa's daughter, Geraldine, was an almost perfect clone of the woman sat before him now; that had been part of the madness, with the two of them together, mother and daughter, reveling in their own and others' misfortune. He imagined that Geraldine would now be in her early forties, a physical beauty still, although, like her mother, there would be an attempt to conceal this beneath a gothic-inspired mask. Frailer and somewhat shorter than Virginia, Geraldine was of a type that Soren had always found attractive. Slim, small breasted and, in some lights, almost skeletal. Like her mother, she had a pale complexion, with dark sockets that held small, impenetrable eyes. Would she, again, like her mother, still be dressing in all black? Her appearance had screamed warnings of fragility and danger, and, of course, he'd dived straight in.

Geraldine had always radiated instability. Whenever Soren had been with her, he'd felt that overwhelming sense of being in the presence of great intelligence, a quality she shared with Virginia. Soren wondered if the woman before him now could throw verbal brickbats and crockery as skillfully as her daughter. On waking up, would her partner be confronted with a knife held close to his or her throat? And what of the sex? Sex with Geraldine had been more like a warzone, where every manoeuvre had to be revisited, re-examined and tortuously assessed. And after the relationship had ended, as with the sex, Soren had felt like just another item on a checklist. Something to be ticked off, added to life's great narrative and discarded. Perversely it had been a quality that had made Geraldine more appealing.

Now, even after such a short re-acquaintance, both were becoming just a little irritated with each other. Melissa had been right about Soren's unsuitability; it was a thing that could be said for all of her daughter's suitors. All had emerged from the experience with a somewhat damaged frame of mind and Soren had fared no better than the rest.

106

He could never get to grips with the ambiguity of her daughter's disapprobation; always expectant and waiting, in dread of her next ministration. How the merest attention, on his part, would be interpreted as a slight, or subject to withering scorn. In the end, though, he'd become more resistant to the incessant abuse, finding the unfathomable mystery, that Geraldine and her friends would love to exude, both tiresome and pitiable. It was a sensation that was now being visited upon him again by Melissa.

'I'm sorry for what happened,' she continued. 'Raymond said that Geraldine had a great deal of hurt to work through. And her behaviour *was* beastly sometimes. You just happened to be in the way.' He winced at the mention of Geraldine's therapist and the clever, malevolent, employment of Melissa's remorse. Of course she then had to add: 'But what you did was far worse. You walked away from someone in desperate need.' Soren kept his counsel as he listened again to the charge of betrayal. The facts were indisputable. He had flown the coop. But then again, what sane person wouldn't have?

'I suspect you haven't been the same since.' Her tone was buoyant, hopeful even; but not concerned. Now she was leaning forward, peering into his eyes. Her left hand was dexterously employed, brushing some seemingly mysterious fluff from the sleeve of his jacket.

'You know she still asks after you?' He sensed danger, something heightened by that ambiguity of motive again. Was this an expression of remorse for her daughter's behaviour? Or regret for lost opportunities? More likely she was just bored?

'California obviously suits you. I hear you've been making quite a name for yourself out there.' Once again he found himself recoiling, this time from what he perceived to be her unwarranted prying, disingenuously wrapped up in malevolent concern. 'Poor Geraldine, she hasn't done anything worthwhile since that radical press job she had out in Berkeley.' What was this? Was she showing signs of disloyalty to her daughter? 'The studio deal fell through. That was about five years ago. She hasn't been right since.'

'I'm sorry to hear it.'

'And you? You're back with *her*?'

He shrugged, but did not answer. Now her tone was accusatory again. It had all been his fault

'She's trouble, that one,' she scowled, her face a grimace. 'Never was good enough for you!'

That was it. Soren had had enough.

'I think I'd better be going,' he said, rising to his feet. As he did so, he noticed that his unease was mirrored in the face of Melissa, who'd caught sight of something or someone over his shoulder. He turned to see the object of her concern. It was Virginia, fast bearing down upon them.

'Ah, there you are!' She had noted Melissa's earlier exit from the meeting and had anticipated its purpose. As soon as had been expediently possible, she too had slipped out and made after her. Her presence, for Soren, was most welcome.

'Sorry, but I have to drag him away.' Virginia's manner was brusque; not a smile in sight. 'Could you rescue Mr McCormick, Melissa? Christina said you wouldn't mind. We have to dash!'

'But we were having such a lovely chat!' Melissa's reply was accompanied by a somewhat over theatrical flounce.

Soren needed no excuse and was soon heading towards the exit. Virginia made to follow, but was stopped by Melissa's next retort. 'Be careful,' she said, 'he did great harm to my daughter.'

With a flourish, Virginia turned on her heels, and, with her coat swirling around her knees, walked back over to where Melissa was sitting. Her face was one of tickled intrigue; as if the object before her might require deliberate and careful disposal. Her close proximity forced Melissa to flinch. 'Oh,' she finally said, after a pause that, for Melissa, had felt like an eternity, 'I think we both know that any harm to your daughter had been completed way before Soren came on the scene.' Then, with a rather disdainful sniff and without so much as a backwards glance, she turned again on her heels and was off.

Once outside Virginia directed Soren towards the familiar, and expensively repaired, Saab, in the back of which were seated his mother and Miss Tyndale. As they climbed in, the patrol car that Soren had spotted earlier pulled up a discreet distance behind them. Inside, the two officers were discussing a call they'd received earlier, from an Officer Briand, about a car he'd flagged, driving along Route 7, towards the Massachusetts Turnpike. He'd run a check on it and it just happened to belong to a well-known associate of the Boston hoodlum, Albert Constanze.

29

Soren felt a certain frisson of excitement. He was up front, sitting alongside Virginia, as she drove her car along a secluded valley. Just a few days ago he'd been bereft of any hopes of being with her again, and yet, here she was, one elbow resting upon his shoulder, in a putative show of ownership. The feeling felt good. All too quickly, though, the journey came to an end, as she manoeuvred the car to halt in front of a large and imposing country mansion.

Barrington House lay at the heart of a Van Buren estate that ran to well over five hundred acres, consisting of a managed dairy farm, extensive meadow land, and a tree plantation composed of those aforementioned beech. The house stood at the head of a valley, on a slightly raised terrace that overlooked a helicopter landing pad and immaculately kept lawns. The last time Soren had been here, the latter had been festooned with marquees and stalls in preparation for one of the charity fetes or jazz concerts the Van Burens hosted during the summer months. Formerly a hunting lodge, the residence now spread to more than fifty rooms, centred on a large inner courtyard that visitors entered by passing beneath an archway. To the right was the old Court Room, where visiting magistrates had once presided. Over the years it had become the main banqueting hall, and it was here their hosts, Peter and Elizabeth Van Buren, now awaited them.

After negotiating an impressively fashioned staircase, the visitors entered a room that was windowless, its wood-panelled walls reflecting the flickering glow of strategically placed candles and the dyeing embers of an open fire. Soren remembered there had always been a healthy mistrust of all things electrical in the Van Buren household.

Apart from Brad and Craig and the new arrivals, there were two other guests present, both familiar to Soren. One was an ever so slightly batty Van Buren aunt from across the border in Dutchess, the other, an elderly man called Dyson, who had a head that looked as if it had been grafted directly onto his shoulders without recourse to anything resembling a neck. A lifelong Republican, albeit of the fast-fading liberal variety, Dyson had been an assistant attorney with the Justice Department, busily engaged, during the sixties, in executing Nicholas Katzenback and Ramsey Clark's attempts to desegregate the South. It had been at this time, whenever he'd been home on leave, he and Soren had the first of what would become regular bird-watching walks together on Porter's Mount.

With the arrival of her guests, Elizabeth immediately took charge, ushering Soren and Christina to pride of place at each end of the table, usurping Craig and Brad from their respective seats in the process; the former directed towards Aunt Dorothea and the latter towards Dyson.

'All the way from California,' Elizabeth said to the aunt, as she sat Craig next to her. 'One of those special people who see lots of numbers and equations where we mere mortals just see life.'

Poor Dyson, lumbered with a somewhat inebriated Brad, gave the resigned expression of someone who knew he'd drawn the short straw. At least Elizabeth and Christina would be close at hand if the conversation began to flag.

Her organising duties temporarily over, Elizabeth Harkness Van Buren resumed her seat at the top of the table. Possessed of a wickedly subversive sense of humour, nurtured on the proving grounds of Cheltenham Ladies College and Somerville College, Oxford, Elizabeth had moved onto the world of publishing, New York, and marriage to Peter. She and Christina were particularly close, with the latter especially appreciative of the way her friend would apply humour to all the absurdities her newly adopted country cared to throw at her. Her husband, Peter, tall and

111

patrician looking, was, along with Dyson, the nearest Soren had to a father figure during the middling years of his upbringing. He wore a world weary and slightly baffled expression, as if modern society was just a little too much and its manners too coarse. When he spoke, it was in an abbreviated, clipped fashion, often accompanied by a mordant turn of phrase that was always knowledgeable and to the point. It was something both respected and deferred to at the various board meetings he presided over on Wall Street. The Van Burens, with that slightly gone-to-seed old money feel, were very much the epitome of a fading East Coast establishment. They were extremely well connected, with Peter more inclined to retain links in and around New York, rather than with his wife's circle of friends in Boston. His upbringing, via Groton and Yale, had been one of extreme privilege. After a brief interregnum with the Navy in the fifties, flying Cougars from the USS Ranger, a Van Buren tradition of spirited public duty had ensued, something that had been accomplished with just a whiff of self-interest as he rose swiftly through naval intelligence and the diplomatic service. This was effortlessly conjoined with learning the ropes of what remained of the family's mercantile and commercial banking interests, culminating in his eventual appointment to the board. He was presently using that position to advise federal regulators on how best to combat the worrying amounts of leveraged buyouts that appeared to be the mainstay of Wall Street these days; something that was currently putting him at loggerheads with members of his own board.

'It is good to see you again, Soren,' he said, assuming a proprietorial air. 'Thought you'd given up on us, didn't we, Lizzy?'

Elizabeth looked up and smiled her agreement, before returning to the task of keeping the conversation between Dyson and Brad from getting too out of hand.

'Still the same old Lizzy, Soren. Dotes on you, as you well know. Do you remember those times when you used to take those rides around the estate? Does seem such a long time ago now.' His voice had a remorseful quality to it.

'Yes, I miss them greatly,' Soren replied, carelessly.

'That's good. I think you had Master James then. He's still with us. Just as reliable. Could get you fixed up if you like. You and Ginny could join us tomorrow.'

There were a few half-hearted attempts at resistance as Soren glanced apprehensively at Elizabeth first, and then his mother. He also noticed the smirk beginning to form on Virginia's face as she and Elizabeth exchanged conspiratorial and knowing looks; it told him that first thing tomorrow, at some ungodly hour, he would be joining the Van Burens for a canter around the estate. The conversation moved on to the forthcoming trip to Mississippi. Peter was the first to start the interrogation.

'I suppose you will be alright with this expedition of yours? It does sound a little adventurous?' His voice rose slightly as he attempted to speak above the increasingly loud shrieks emanating from Aunt Dorothea, delighting in the latest of a series of stories from Craig, about computers, and how it would be possible to commit murder down the phone with something called the Morris worm.

'I don't think it will be too much trouble,' Soren replied, somewhat defensively.

'I must say that Lizzie and myself were a little concerned. The ground down there is so unfamiliar.'

Once again Soren could see the hidden hand of his mother at work; her next contribution confirmed as much. 'Exactly what I was saying earlier,' she said. 'It's such a different part of the country. Anyway, it might not get off the ground; what with Brad's good news!'

'Ah yes, the professorship!' Peter raised his glass.

'You know about that?'

'Yes, we were speaking about it before you arrived.'

'My, my,' said Virginia, *sotto voce,* to Soren seated next to her, breaking what had been, up to then, a meticulously held silence. 'They do appear to be giving them away these days!' Hers was a smile studied with a look of disdain, followed by a speculative and hopeful afterthought. 'Surely you won't be going now?'

Soren shrugged his shoulders, smiled and looked to the others for help. Miss Tyndale, sitting opposite, duly obliged:

'Now, now, Ginny, I think it's really quite exciting. I'd love to hear what they have planned down there.'

Miss Tyndale was someone Soren hadn't given much thought to, but now, as they spoke together, could see why Virginia might value her company. This was someone both bright and engaging, who, in that horsey Hudson Valley way, also appeared to be a good egg. A few years ago Miss Tyndale had tried her hand as a writer of short stories, but it had come to naught. Now she complained of the inordinate amount of time she had to spend, travelling the world, as a buyer of art. She was quietly confident, in that understated upper-class way, and just a little wary of coming across as too accomplished at what she did. After all, it was just a hobby. She did, though, become especially attentive on hearing that Soren had attended the summer Degas Exhibition at the Met; it had, after all, been her job to act as liaison between New York and the Réunion des Musées Nationaux. As he studied her now, Soren began to regret being so quick to write her off. It was a sentiment that had once been mirrored by Miss Tyndale herself. Years ago she had been of the opinion that her old Choat classmate had been too intemperate in her infatuation as far as Soren was concerned, but, over time, she had been won over. Yes, there had been worries about whether Virginia was being led a merry dance, but what had never been an issue, was Soren's pedigree and character. Miss Tyndale had soon come to see in him those same qualities – intelligence, discretion and affability – that her friend had so admired. More importantly, he was seen as 'one of us'.

This was something their host would also have been in agreement with. That Peter Van Buren was still on speaking terms with Soren and his mother, said much for the high regard in which he held the Karlssons, as it had been his belief that it had been Soren who'd been responsible for much of the hurt Virginia had felt subsequent to their breakup. Eventually though he'd concluded that there'd been nothing malevolent in Soren's actions; just befuddled, immature, and innocent, confusion.

Soren relaxed back into his chair. The evening was beginning to take on the more familiar ambience he remembered of gatherings past, with each participant aware of the niceties that needed to be observed and the liberties that might be taken. All, that is, with the exception of Brad, who was now quite drunk. In answer to an enquiry, by Dyson, about the AIDS crisis, he couldn't resist the employment of some of his more vivid turns of phrase to describe what would be required to keep the epidemic under control. The drug therapies would come, but before this happened, a large number of people would be joining this 'voyage of the damned'. Then it was onto the incompetence of junior medics and the bad faith of hospital bureaucrats, malpractice suits and lawyers. Ah, the lawyers! Ever since the two of them had sat down together, Brad had been sizing Dyson up as one of them. All were crooks, determined to fleece anyone with the misfortune to come into contact with them. Dyson kept his counsel and Elizabeth, smiling, attempted to smooth things over, but the look on Christina's face was knowingly unforgiving. Sensing he'd gone too far, Brad apologised, but, within moments, he was off again, this time lecturing Dyson about the dangers posed by the food they were eating. Ever the consummate diplomat, Dyson nodded, outwardly lapping it up, whilst plotting his eventual escape to Soren's half of the table.

Dyson, the man to whom Brad was being so cavalier with his opinions, had been a good friend of Peter Van Buren's since the days they'd been in naval intelligence together. He was someone renowned for giving very little away and whose avuncular smile hid an iron resolve; one that had once faced down a howling mob of segregationists in Georgia. Old colleagues at the Justice Department knew Dyson to be 'a bit of a nut job' when his blood was up. Gazing at the two of them from across the table, Soren knew that Brad had better watch his step. He'd not been on the receiving end of one of Dyson's outbursts himself, but he'd seen it in action. It was a wonder to behold.

When the party did finally break up, amidst farewells and entreaties to visit in the not-too-distant future, Virginia was called to answer the phone.

'It's Pittsburgh,' she said to Soren, as she leant against a wall with the receiver pinned to one ear. She caught hold of his arm and pulled him towards her. 'No, don't go,' she beseeched.

Soren watched as she took the call, the expression on her face becoming ever more incredulous as she listened to what was being said. 'What!' She was almost laughing now. 'A jumper accidentally drops his lighter moments before he jumps and that's what kills our guy? And this happened a week ago? Did nobody bother to cross-file? Jesus, you couldn't make it up!' She gave Soren a smile and squeezed his hand before proceeding to give him a running commentary about a case that was being prepared for trial; a litany of questions concerning the presentation of evidence, the degree of progress made by forensics, a possible new line of enquiry, depositions that still needed to be obtained, and who might be of use at the DA's office. In between, she would give Soren a smile, or feign a look of disbelief, before diving back into the fray.

'He said that, did he? Get Eric to threaten him with a summons. He's definitely a John. He needs to go home and make a clean breast of things with his wife.'

Soren was transfixed. It was the first time he'd observed Virginia at work. In her world things seemed to get done. There appeared to be none of the disorder that someone like Wilson or, dare one say, Pariche, could bring. The seduction was in full spate.

30

Virginia and Soren found themselves wandering the corridors of the east wing alone. In keeping with the Van Buren tradition of frugality, especially when it comes to finding money for heating, the place was draughty and cold, and their linked arms soon became something more canoodling, embracing and warm. A little unsteady on their feet, owing to the amount of wine they'd imbibed, they happened across the east lounge, a large room with an assortment of Chippendale and Queen Anne chairs. Thankfully, it also had radiators that appeared to be emitting some heat.

'So, here we are again, darn chumps an' crazy brawds,' Virginia said, with a mimic that invoked memories of a shared regard for Judy Holliday. 'You do remember the last time we were here?' He did.

'I remember then that I posed you a question!' He smiled, but said nothing. 'It was just before *that* affair.' Her tone was dismissive, not bitter. 'I asked you then, how it was we'd let it come to this?' The conjunction of past and present, and the enveloping sense of shared responsibility, induced a wariness in him. 'And now you appear to be doing it all over again.'

'I'm a fool, Ginny.' It was an obvious, but not very imaginative, gambit on his part. Play dumb and own up to everything.

'You know that's not what I meant, Soren; not what I meant at all.' She smiled, but her words still came across as if she were addressing a favoured, if mildly infuriating, child. 'No, I meant this trip, Soren, this attempt at running away again. I suppose you'll have to see it through now, won't you? I only hope it doesn't mean that you're going to go and do something unhinged; you know, something that might be construed as heroic.' She paused awhile, seeking to capture his gaze. 'Perhaps it would be intriguing if you did, but no, that would hardly be you at all, would it?'

She could sense his unease and a clamouring for that distance again. No, Soren wasn't known for his heroism, but he was no coward either. Just confused. There was never anything shabby or cowardly about his dealings with Geraldine. But he didn't run away either, although he had every right to do so. Loyal to a fault; that was always the way with Soren. And it *was* wretched the way Geraldine had treated him. No wonder he was wary now. Virginia drew a little closer and told him how she'd regretted not doing anything all those years ago. She now had his full attention. 'I suppose I didn't spell things out properly.' She shot him a quizzical look, as if she didn't quite judge him worthy of what she was about to propose. 'Soren, have you thought of moving back east?'

He twigged immediately. 'What... with you?'

'You don't have to sound so enthusiastic!' she cried, her voice hovering between the jovial and the affronted. 'You *do* appear to be thrashing around a little, out there in California.'

'You've been talking a little too much to mother!'

'Yes, guilty,' she shrugged, 'we've talked. Obviously we have. But Soren, you don't appear to be all that happy with things at the moment. And you've always moaned about how anybody can get anything done in that kind of climate!'

'Guess I've gotten used to it. You don't have to worry too much about the sunny days you've missed. Another will soon be along tomorrow.'

Virginia smiled, but wasn't to be deflected. 'Well this trip to Mississippi; it does seem to smack a little of desperation.' She leant forward again and, peering into his eyes, gave him a little pinch. 'Come on, let's give it a try. I think we could really make a go of it!'

And of course he wanted to. He wanted to submit there and then, but something held him back. The approach had been too direct. There had been that intensity of purpose again that both unnerved and embarrassed him. As always, whenever he felt that drowning sensation, his first impulse was to flee. The loosened embrace and his silence indicated to Virginia that this was what he was now contemplating. What would be required was quiescence and perhaps a change of tack.

'I'm sorry,' she said, quickly trying to think of other subjects to broach. 'Are you still in that cramped apartment?'

He nodded.

'I guess properties are still quite expensive out there?' She could hear herself digging deeper and deeper.

'Unbelievably so,' he replied, marvelling at her ability to move from one anxiety-producing subject to another. If there was one thing guaranteed to have such an impact, it was the thought of attempting to play the property market in San Francisco on an associate professor's salary.

'I can understand why you might want to spend a year doing research in Germany,' she said, piling on the pressure, 'but Mississippi! Why?'

'New challenges, I guess, and perhaps the need to give something back.'

At this, she almost laughed.

The following morning, Virginia's presence in the bed beside him, and the somewhat knowing glance that Elizabeth gave as she greeted Soren, on his arrival at the breakfast table, indicated that Virginia's ploy, if that's what it was, had met with a certain degree of success. It wasn't long before he was somewhat gingerly following Elizabeth into the harsh light of a crisp autumnal morn. They were alone, as Virginia had chosen to lie in and Peter Van Buren had business to deal with. Soren took a sharp intake of breath as he looked at his prospective mount, bigger and feistier than he remembered, all those years ago. In return, it looked at him with barely concealed suspicion, if not outright alarm.

'Ah, you're up at last.'

He turned to be greeted by the sight of Miss Tyndale; all jodhpurs and a jolly smile. 'We thought you'd never make it!'

Nursing a particularly bad hangover and feeling the after-effects of a conversation that had coursed into the early hours, Soren felt particularly vulnerable. The frozen ground and unsure footing added to his sense of disorientation and unease, something that was compounded by the sensation of awakening in an unfamiliar bed, with Virginia at his side. Now he was making a rather ungainly attempt at clambering aboard his mount, under what were certainly the judgmental gazes of the two women. They must surely think him fickle and weak willed, even louche. So, in the early morning fog, amidst the clatter of hooves and the uneasy sway of his mount, he was given the full Elizabeth treatment, aided and abetted by Miss Tyndale. It was an examination that probed here and coaxed there, but was relentless. And with this, he proceeded to willingly spill out his conscience and his guts to the two women. Their replies were short and their approach direct. He found himself nodding in agreement to Elizabeth's injunction to do something while the clock was still ticking. 'Stop being a bastard, Soren,' she said. 'Stop abusing and living off the attention of that lovely young lass and show some commitment. It would be so easy to let things drift and slip away.'

31

Boston's North End, Massachusetts

As soon as Felix and Tank returned from their surveillance activities in the Berkshires, the latter was dispatched to one of the many payphones in Boston's North End, to make a connect call to the gambling outpost of Reno, Nevada. The man at the end of the line sounded defensive. In the background could be heard the clatter of chips, the clinking of glasses and the playing of Muzak.

'Now, now, Harry,' said Tank, attempting to reassure, 'we've no beef this time, no complaint. We're just looking for a little assistance on your part. We need help in locating a certain professor of your parish. Just his whereabouts and his plans for the future would do fine. Nothing else.' He then proceeded to give details about their quarry, distilled from information provided by a very obliging federal agent.

Two days later, Tank, glowing with relished pride, placed a cassette recorder in front of his boss, Albert Constanze.

'Marty called the bitch this morning,' he said. 'Really had her squirming.'

He pressed a button and a disembodied voice, gleefully threatening in tone, came over the air. It was the sound of one of their associates delivering a message, over the phone, to a woman, who abruptly called proceedings to a halt. The message was unmistakably clear: they knew where her son was and how to get to him.

32

Wilson had been a model of courtesy when Soren called ahead to fix up a time and date for a meeting. He'd been in the office at the time and had insisted on taking the call. He told Soren he wanted action on what he referred to as 'the Pariche incident', and, from his tone, it was obvious that this would be best served by having Pariche's head served up on a plate.

As well as seeing to things he had to do in Berkeley, Soren reassured himself that a trip back west would also serve to put a distance between himself and the formidable phalanx of women who now appeared to be demanding a hearing. He would leave Brad and Craig to go on down to Mississippi together and would join them in a few days' time. Whilst on the West Coast, he would also make good on his promise to talk to Burdon, the CEO of Genotech.

During the flight his thoughts came to rest on Virginia and memories of her bed. Seizing upon the chance to forget Wilson and the Zenotech fiasco for a moment, he sensed a reawakening of old spirits he'd long thought dead. It was not so much a feeling of smugness, rather a buoyancy borne of the contemplation of Virginia's form and the possibilities their meeting had opened up. It was a thing he still couldn't quite bring himself to believe. He was fast approaching his fortieth year and he was again experiencing a marvellous infatuation and the rediscovery of familiar certainties he'd feared had long been lost. What was more, they appeared to be shared by Virginia herself.

He remembered how the seduction had been mutual and passionate, if a little unimaginative. Between love-making, they had talked with a knowing familiarity that couples do when they are at ease with each other. A little nervously at first but, by the early light, more knowledgeably energetic and enjoyably engaged. Her body, unlike his, still possessed a compellingly youthful firmness. She'd been demanding and sensitive, beckoning and reproachful, sure as to her desire for him and his memory of her now brought forth the dread realisation that this was true care. Shockingly so. Here, in one moment of pristine clarity, was the uncontrolled urge to commit – a resolution that fairly threw him. He was alive to the immediacy of her presence and the overwhelming warmth and the smell of her. And he was shocked at the unformed and dissolute nature of his previous attitude, with its casual indifference and immaturity. Silently, subconsciously, he let out a wail.

There had also been indications of a forced, even desperate, contentment from her. She had talked of others and how there had even been proposals of marriage. Elizabeth had been right; this was someone racing against time. It stirred within Soren memories of when this fragility had last surfaced, at the time of his engagement to Geraldine. Memories of Virginia's vulnerable, crumpled form, and how it had induced within him an overwhelming feeling of sadness and loss. They had also talked about her police work and how it had changed her; the way it seemed to change almost all who entered its ranks. There were the coarsened manners and the suspicious, aggressively assertive, attitudes. The uniformed people had this in spades. They were the people the public turned to whenever there was trouble. When people's instincts were to run, they were the ones expected to be headed in the other direction, towards the fray, determined to prove that their gang was bigger and better. With Virginia's crowd – the detectives – that attitude was still there, although subtly changed. And corrupted. Whereas the 'uniforms' were driven deeper into the solidarity of the blue brotherhood, the detectives liked to think of themselves as an elite breed, set apart. They were the late arrivals at any crime scene, the showmen in snazzy suits, who wanted respect when they turned up. It was something that only went to heighten their own sense of importance. Theirs was a world in which everything was viewed through the prism of corruption, be it corrupted morals, corrupted expectations, or corrupted relationships. And it forced people to make bad decisions. Something from which Virginia was not immune. Soren knew Virginia's take on life; he'd seen it on the hockey field. 'Just get stuck in!' she would scream. 'Don't think, just put yourself out there. Have a run with the stick and expect to get whacked. But just do it!' It was a philosophy that had more recently been applied to her personal life, with disastrous consequences.

So last night she'd told him about that 'bad decision'; how a relationship at work had recently blown up in her face. It was something that had been compounded by her naivety – or decency – in allowing herself to be cast as the villain of the piece. In truth she was already having problems accommodating colleagues who seemed to rate success by the number of poor saps they could get on trumped-up charges, rather than engaging in proper, painstaking, investigative work. Soren had an inkling the police work had put a lot of pressure on her, but he'd not been aware of how much, and how it had demoralised and perturbed her. That the job demanded ruinously long hours was only to be expected; what she hadn't counted upon, was the degree to which the daily grind of seeing people at their worst would become so dispiriting. There was also the trial of having to engage with the less than cerebral conversation of colleagues, or worse, their barely concealed misogyny and racism. The stress of being just one step ahead of the next fiasco, and being at the beck and call of divisional commanders at all hours of the day and night. And to cap it all, Virginia had started out on that ill-conceived affair with the son of one of her fellow detectives. Following a very messy denouement, she knew the die was cast.

There was now a more persistent and open hostility on the part of some of her colleagues, with even some of the Divisional commanders pitching in. They were now less forgiving about the problems Virginia had with her parents and the time she needed to be off work in assisting them. Some had been waiting years for her to screw up. They were the ones who'd had their noses put out by this 'wunderkind' from the DA's office and her 'rules'. Now they were joined by those who saw her as that badass bitch who'd screwed over Lou's boy. In their eyes, the wide eyed and innocent Bradley girl, the folks of Charlottesville had found so engaging, had long gone. And, in return, Virginia had fallen out of love with people who so blatantly turned a blind eye to corruption. It was a cancer she now believed would never be defeated. And there had been threats and nuisance calls, with the suspicion that one of her colleagues had given her number to a local hood. She knew her behaviour had been unconscionable, mimicking some of the worst she'd seen when she'd first set foot in the department. The whole sordid experience had gone some way to reminding her of just how lonely she had become. How it might be time to move on. So, five months ago, just before the onset of summer, she began to let go. Leave had been owing and this time she'd taken it; hence the development of that summer tan. New cases that would have been grist for the mill, were now delegated to others. And, above all, there was the irrational obsessive care she felt for Soren. Always Soren. She'd told him how it had felt like a curse: an inhibitive, unfathomable curse, that would mock her loneliness and at times drive her to depressive despair. Her honesty had been shocking, the more so for the blackness at its heart. It had left Soren fearful that here again was something where he might be found wanting.

33

West Portal, San Francisco

Soren was looking down at tangerine-coloured roofs nestling upon hills surrounding a dark expanse of bay. Around its edge was spun an arterial network of roads, along which flowed a corpuscular ribbon of traffic. He'd failed to get the usual flight to SFO, and had to settle for American Airlines, flying into Oakland. Now, with an assortment of other bemused travellers, Soren found himself circling aimlessly above that former blue collar city, smiling at the thought that some flight-control wag had managed to compose a flight path that had them circling above Lawrence Livermore, the nuclear weapons laboratory. Then came the rapid descent, the ground rush and the shudder, as the plane made contact with *terra firma,* followed by a frantic rush to collect bags and thoughts together, under the sullen gaze of security guards and checkout attendants. In no time at all he was seated aboard a BART train, gliding past the myriad array of shapes and greys that make up the Oakland container port and rail terminus, before a plunge beneath the bay and a change at Van Ness for West Portal.

At the apartment there was a succession of answer machine messages, including some from Pariche, increasingly pleading and intemperate in tone. The machine, sitting atop a smoke stained glass coffee table, proceeded to beep out further messages from colleagues and students, one asking for a last look at a dissertation, another asking for a re-mark, others wishing him bon voyage, and a call from Berthe of the *Deutsche Gessellschaft fur Soziologie,* wondering if he would be available for a conference in Madrid the following year. The idea of participating in a debate about modernist kitsch and the rise of German authoritarianism did momentarily appeal, but then his attention was drawn to a message that made him stop, just as the noise from a passing L train threatened to drown out its import. It was Cindi, somewhat plaintively wondering if they might meet up again. Settling himself upon the sofa, he remembered Virginia's injunction about the dangers of skateboarding. The final message was indeed from Virginia herself, trusting that he'd arrived safely and expressing the hope that they would be able to speak again soon. Her voice was soft, unhurried and mellifluous. It brought forth a smile and a temporary uplifting of spirits, before he turned again to the more prosaic task of calling the Departmental Office.

'Ah, Soren, we were just about to call you.' It was Maureen, Wilson's personal secretary. 'Charles was hoping to bring the meeting forward. Would this evening be OK? He had the Faculty Club at seven fifteen in mind. He's already booked for a function there later on. Is that OK? Hope we've left you enough time?'

Oh well, nothing untoward there, he thought, putting the phone down; Wilson was always having to reschedule, very much the man in demand. And the meeting with Denis Tsui would be finished by then. Still, he was aware of being knocked off guard again. An ambush by Wilson was what he had feared and was one of the reasons he'd deliberately avoided going to his office at Wheeler. It wasn't as if there hadn't been business to attend to; you could always count on a few students hanging around, hoping for that one last chat. Don't give in, he'd muttered to himself. Resist. They'll be alright. Far better this, than the possibility of bumping into Wilson or, just as likely, one of his acolytes.

The apartment was way too small for all the books, clothes and detritus that had been accrued. Maybe he should have rented it out; it would have, at least, made him clear the place up. Now, as he looked around at all the mess, he felt just a little tired and resistant to going the whole distance with Wilson later tonight. Then he thought of Denis Tsui. There was still that meeting at the Triple Rock Brewery to confirm. But, before he could do anything, the phone rang out.

'Ah, girl, you're back in town.' It was Chumley, a cross-dressing post doc from Austria; high camp and very concerned. His English was flawless. 'Heard you were having problems with our dear Fuehrer,' he continued. 'Thought you might just be in need of a little help.'

Soren let out a slow whistle and, under his breath, cursed Pariche, for he knew that he would have been the one to have put him up to it. 'No,' Soren replied, resisting the need to go down the line of conversation Chumley was suggesting. 'There's no need for that. But while you're on the phone, we could talk about the progress of the book. I trust you've finally given up trying to give Benjamin a pink twist?'

'Now, girl, don't go changing the subject on me. I feel you need looking after. You know I'm here for you!' Soren let out a barely suppressed chuckle. He guessed that Chumley was in one of his favourite hangouts, probably Eli's in West Oakland, or Larry Blake's; he'd always been a sucker for the blues scene. Soren could imagine him now, all panty hose and frocks, with one of his Jackie Kennedy wigs, chatting with the regulars and fighting off the attentions of the drunk and the more amorous. And Chumley could get away with it. He had a figure most women would die for, along with a pristine, almost translucent complexion that might have just stepped out of a Van Meer painting. Unnervingly for Soren, when Chumley did wear that Kennedy wig, his appearance looked something between a young Priscilla Presley and Mary Tyler Moore. The only other person Soren knew who could pull off a look like that, prior to her most recent transformation, was a certain lady detective from Pittsburgh. It was time to pull rank.

'I mean it, Chumley. The present direction you're taking could totally derail your main thesis.'

'I know, girl. I know. But don't you go all naughty on me again. I hear you're meeting Denis later. Yes he told me all about it. Well, I thought I might just tag along. He's expecting you at six. We could get a bite to eat before you go and do battle with that awful man!'

Soren didn't try to resist. So it had been Denis all along, although Chumley would have probably browbeaten him into it.

34

On the way back to Berkeley, Soren took time out at Powell and Market to take in a little of the city and collect his thoughts. The place was crawling with tourists and late afternoon shoppers. He looked up at the deepening contours of Powell Street, ascending all the way up to Nob Hill and Chinatown. He knew the walk would take its toll, but he was determined to get away from the crowd, the bells and whistles, the clacking sound of the cable cars and the harsh tones of their operators barking orders at errant tourists. Added to the mix were the panhandlers and street hawkers and the bible thumpers berating Catholics and whores. He walked on, beyond the Union Square storefronts; the glow from their windows, all oranges and yellows, fading into the enveloping darkness. Then it was head down, past even more beggars; fierce looking souls alert for something, or someone, to scream and holler at. He ignored their pleas for money and the howls and the expletives that followed when none was forthcoming. To paraphrase T.S. Eliot, he'd not realised the recession had undone so many. He stopped for a breather; he'd forgotten the toll the hills could take on even the shortest of walks. Then he continued; on past the few remaining open-air cafés, with their patrons attempting to deny the chill brought on by the dying of the year.

He was now above the noise and hubbub of Union Square and he felt calmer and more in tune with his thoughts. Out of habit, he brought an evening edition of the Chronicle from the kiosk outside the Holiday Inn, at the intersection of Sutter and Powell. The seller, an elderly Chinaman, gave him a nod of recognition. It was a walk he'd often made with Pariche; turn west, along Sutter, and he would be headed towards Pariche's usual haunt of O'Gradys. Instead, he continued on up towards the intersection with California. He found himself falling back into a routine he knew only too well; thinking of work and how best to resist the demands of Charlie Wilson. Ah, the (acting) dean! He smiled at the mock reverence and coruscating disdain with which Pariche usually bestowed this title, whenever he and Wilson had the misfortune to bump into each other. He paused for a moment again and looked back towards Union Square and the newly opened Nordstrom Shopping complex beyond. He remembered that this was where Wilson had taken to buying his new suits, always funereally black, and where staff had already taken to calling him 'the undertaker'.

In the lobby of the Fairmont, amidst its reflective marble and glittering crystal, Soren had time to think further about his adversary and the forthcoming meeting. It was not going to be pleasant. His mood wasn't helped by the attitude of the attendant, who served his coffee as if he wanted to be somewhere else. Soren glanced at the paper he'd bought, but his concentration was shot, the print just a blur. He knew that Wilson, with all his contacts, would have planned ahead and brought in favours. Soren wouldn't even know the half of it. A political animal to the bone, Wilson would be using every moment to plot and scheme. That was the way the man was. Most of the time he could be found in his office, on the phone to all and sundry, and, when he wasn't, he would be issuing Maureen with a list of people to be contacted and things to be expedited by the time he returned, on the dot, at seven thirty each morning. Such an approach did little to endear him either to Maureen or to his colleagues. The professors very quickly came to regard him as some kind of bureaucratic apparatchik, albeit of the all-seeing, all-powerful kind. Had his bearing been more aesthetic, and his output more academic and profuse, he might just have fitted in. If only he'd done some research and written something other than those damned interminable reports. Yes, those reports, they were the true indication of the man; someone better suited to one of the more technical divisions of the federal government, than the (acting) dean of faculty at a place like Berkeley. 'How could this have happened?' was the often heard and exasperated refrain from colleagues. The truth of the matter was not hard to fathom, for here was someone blindingly ruthless in their ambition. And worryingly for Soren, this ambition was of a type that was hardly ever satisfied.

Just what did you do after you've got to the top of your particular pile? The Chancellorship at Berkeley was far too elevated for someone like Charlie Wilson; even he knew that. There was the possibility of a headship at some lesser institution, a state university perhaps, or a second tier private college, but that wouldn't have the prestige that Wilson craved. No, he was stuck here, fighting above his weight, frustrated and becalmed, unable to give vent to the neuroses and drives he'd employed in the process of getting here in the first place. Wilson's usually calm exterior hid a private subterranean world of neurotic hatreds and it was grist to his sadomasochist mill that he was always seeking out situations that would foment such thoughts and anxieties, after which he would retreat to the privacy of his office, or his North Berkeley home, to give vent to his spleen. Of late, Maureen had been hearing whelps and cries of anguish coming from his office; sounds that did not augur well for anyone who was, as she put it, caught in the crosshairs. A certain Jedemiah Pariche had been the most recent cause of distress, but, worryingly, so had his friend, a certain Professor Soren Karlsson.

Grunwalt, over at Haas, had said that Wilson fitted the type he'd increasingly seen at his executive seminars. They were ambitious thrusting types who, on personality tests, were irredeemably psychopathic. And Wilson did very much seem to fit the bill. As Pariche had said, paraphrasing what Zwicky, the eminent astrophysicist, had said about his Caltech colleagues in the thirties; 'There was something of the spherical bastard about Wilson. A thorough-going bastard from whatever direction you cared to approach him.' A case in point was how he was able to work his way into his current position. To do so he'd started a whispering campaign against the former incumbent, Wallace Mitford, a mild-mannered soul who enjoyed nothing better than singing in the choir at his local church and being a stalwart of the neighbourhood Audubon Society. For Charlie Wilson, though, that had been the problem. Life under Mitford had become far too cosy. If the school was to maintain its position of academic pre-eminence, then it would require a dean who could give greater attention to the kind of detail that would satisfy the agencies responsible for research rankings and the distribution of government grants. There was also the health of Mitford's wife to consider, who was, at the time, suffering from pancreatic cancer. The demands this was making on Mitford's abilities to perform the administrative aspects of his job must have been considerable. So Wilson suggested that it would be better for the sake of the departments that made up the school and, just as importantly, Mitford's good health, that the burden on him was reduced. The result was to see the chorister relieved successively of his duties and then of his position as dean.

Wilson was still married to his old sweetheart, Marion, who he both bullied and doted upon in good measure. She had dutifully supported her husband over the years, something he'd never appreciated, and he would often criticise her for what he saw as her lack of interest in anything to do with his career ambitions. So they had an accord, living their lives as agreeably separate as possible, she with her party friends in the North Oakland Hills and he, doing what he believed to be his calling, protecting the good name of the department. And Wilson did believe that this was indeed his job; how because of his good works the department had been able to continue in the Berkeley tradition of having a distinguished profile, up there with the best. People in the Department couldn't hope to compete with the likes of Harvard or Stanford on salaries, but what they could do was fundraise. And fundraising was a thing that Wilson was sure he did better than anyone else. A million dollars last year, and now the Genotech deal would ensure that professorial salaries would continue to be paid. And yes, you did hear that right; Wilson really did think the Genotech deal was down to him, just like everything else that came through the department's doors. By proxy or not, Wilson was want to claim it all, with Maureen and her secretarial network providing the intelligence. Some hapless prof would have a deal in the offing and, just when it was coming to fruition, Wilson would swoop, to claim it all as his own, along with the surrounding publicity. His current, somewhat ambiguous, status as (acting) dean, seemed to instil in Wilson an even greater need to get himself noticed. More recently this had taken a rather bizarre twist with his launching himself as a man of the street. In doing this he'd successfully inveigled himself into the chairmanship of the Governor's Task Force on urban discontent and crime, something that appeared to confer on him a degree of celebrity and what Pariche mockingly referred to as rock star status. Pariche would also remind anyone who would listen, that such a role wasn't worth a row of beans nowadays. How when he'd been advising the Pat Brown administration in Sacramento, during the fifties and sixties; that was when they were really doing great things – making monuments that would last. More worryingly, though, for the present enterprise, Wilson's raised status now made him an even more formidable opponent.

35

The journey onto Berkeley was relatively trouble free, leaving ample time for the meeting with Denis Tsui. As could be expected of a Friday night, Triple Rock was heaving with the usual university crowd. Soren would have preferred one of the bars or restaurants up on Bancroft or Telegraph, as they would have been more convenient for the meeting with Wilson later, but at least he'd avoided the possibility of bumping into the likes of Jerry Friesson at the *Caffe Strada*, ostensibly looking out for his master's interests, but in reality ogling the young law students and wealthy debutantes from International House.

The last few days had obviously been something of a trial for Denis, so his greeting was effusive; the kind given by someone who's had a temporary reprieve.

'Ah, Soren, over here!' he cried, waving vigorously. 'Chumley's in the washroom freshening himself up. I'm sorry, but he was very insistent.'

Although the place was packed, Denis had still managed to get them a side table seat, set against a wall covered in cheap wood chip. The lamp on the table didn't work, so what lighting there was was cast by a series of brightly lit chandeliers, perched perilously above slow swishing fans. They gave the place the look and feel of a rather commodious washroom.

Denis was very much the James Dean clone, with a squint in one eye, as if he was constantly peering into bright sunlight. He was clean shaven, with medium-length swept-back hair. He was wearing blue jeans, a white T-shirt and a brown flying jacket. Without delay, Soren mentioned the phone call he'd had a couple of days ago with Kurst and his concern that Denis had now become the object of Wilson's gaze. He attempted to reassure. 'There is no way,' he said, 'I will be leaving for Mississippi while you're being subject to all of this!' What could be done, though, he had very little idea. But, in the back of his mind, he knew that he was in a fight and that he would be in need of calling on the help of a certain gentleman from Mono County; someone who was well known for their cantankerousness and unpredictability. The preliminaries over, Denis smiled, leant forward, and reached for a bag under the table. He was eager to show Soren its contents. 'Mustn't forget this,' he said, as he made a quick shuffle inside, before producing a small, thin package. 'Had to go all the way to Portland to get them.' He handed the package to Soren who proceeded to open it. Inside were three vinyl disks, tightly wrapped in plastic. They were original recordings, totally flawless, of The Channels, *The Closer You Are*, *Memories of El Monte* by The Penguins and *Love of My Life* by Ron Roman.

'They look so pristine!' cooed Soren, appreciatively, as he held one of the disks up to the light. 'It would be such a shame to risk scratching it.'

'Too bad,' replied Denis, dismissively, 'The whole point is to play them.'

It could be fair to say that Denis's sense of self had been very much informed by stories he'd learned about his family's journey to America; one half Japanese, the other Chinese. They were a mixture of old country myth and west coast injustice; stories about the Truckee expulsions and more recent ones of how his grandparents had been interned during the war. Denis's parents seemed to conform to the San Franciscan Asian stereotypes; hardworking supporters of liberal causes, who'd taken an almost perverse delight in their son's infatuation in all things African-American, of which 1950s Doo Wop was one of the most obvious manifestations. Denis swam easily in diverse cultural currents, as if they were his own, and in ways some might find objectionable. It was a thing that Soren had never sought to question.

The examination complete, Soren was about to call one of the servers over when Chumley made his entrance, carrying some Bratwurst he'd managed to inveigle, with the help of a friendly waiter, from Petrouchka's. Soren had been almost correct in predicting what he'd be wearing; a pleated brown skirt this time, blue pantyhose, a white blouse and a Kennedy-esque wig. His face wore a subtly masked white foundation, over which had been applied a pale powder. Around his eyes was dark eyeshadow. A somewhat sober ensemble this time, rounded off by the wearing of flat sensible shoes.

'Ah, you noticed those,' said Chumley, his voice a masculine whimsy, 'they're so much better for walking. How do I look?' He pulled up the hem of his skirt and did a rather flamboyant twirl, before stooping to invite a peck on the cheek. Smiling, Soren obliged.

Once Chumley was seated, Denis picked up the conversation again, this time about Pariche and the groundbreaking.

'No, honestly,' he said, 'Pariche didn't strike out once. He just wasn't prepared to put up with what Wilson was doing. And it *was* Wilson. Flaxel was just a bit player.'

'Tell it how it is, girl,' said Chumley, joining the fray. 'Poor Jedemiah was sorely provoked by that *awful* man.'

Despite what might be gleaned from his manner and appearance, Chumley could be relied upon to be discrete and was more clued up than most about what was going on in the department. Still, Soren felt it would be wise to keep the conversation safe and pedagogical. Chumley sat down, his left leg strung across his knee, swinging to and fro, quite happy for the moment to nod in agreement with what was being said. Denis, doing his usual trick of balancing perilously on his chair, did his best to reassure; the program was on track, and Summer, one of the teaching assistants, was doing an excellent job. There had been a good response to the request for next semester's titles, and a paper by Drexler, on aesthetics, was almost certainly publishable. Yale had also been in touch, saying that Neumann would be a definite for next year, but there had been a few problems, not least regarding the seminar attendances of some of the fellowship students.

'I can't put my finger on it, but I think they might have been got at,' he said. 'You know, with all the stuff that went down last week.' Here we go again, thought Soren, his face a look of resigned despair. 'It's just a gut feeling. I've noticed it for some time now. When they do turn up, they appear disconnected.'

'Hell, Denis, they're good students. Would you like me to talk to them?'

Denis nodded, before indicating another situation that could do with their attention.

'I would also be really grateful for your input on what's going down over at City.' He was referring to a local community college; one which Soren's program had an informal admissions arrangement with. 'They've been getting resignations all round. Folks don't seem to be able to hack it with the new broom they've got down there. Some stiletto heeled sociopath who appears to be getting it on with a member of the Board. Even Lucy Teager has thrown in the towel. We need to rescue the situation quickly.'

'Nothing wrong with stilettos, love!' chipped in Chumley, unable to resist.

'Do you think a phone call would do the trick?' asked Soren.

Denis shook his head. 'No, I think it will require a visit.'

Soren looked beseechingly. 'I really don't have time myself.'

'Way ahead of you,' Denis replied. 'I've already arranged to meet Luce next week.'

'Excellent. See if we can get something worked out. Let them know how much we value their work.' There were shrugs and nods of intent, but all knew there was precious little they could do. 'And don't forget about my elective over at UCSF,' Soren continued, 'I've left instructions with Collins.'

'Yes, as always, there's quite a strong interest.'

'And the graduate applications, how are they going?'

'A little slow. You being away hasn't helped.' Denis shot a glance at Chumley, who, in response, modestly began to preen himself. 'I've run a few past Chumley, but I think some of the better ones are being poached.'

Soren arched his left brow. 'It was ever thus,' he said. 'Well, I trust your judgement, whatever you decide.' He then proceeded to give them both the precise limitations of that assessment. 'Make sure you interview the research students with Pariche. If he isn't available, then Kurst's your man. I've spoken with him and he's only too happy to give a hand. Stop at five, and take your time. If you have any doubts, then get in touch with me. As it is, keep the letters of application and transcripts coming, and I still want to see all the dissertations. Get them to me in Mississippi, if you can and, if needs be, the proposals as well. Remember, the bottom line is that all of them must have a proven track record. No hoppers. Also, keep Rostenkowski at Harvard on message; he's one of the good guys. Let's lock everything down and, for God's sake, keep Friesson away from Progress. He and Wilson will be looking for any opportunity to trip us up.'

With the business end of the meeting coming to an end, Chumley sensed that this might be the right moment to revisit the concerns he'd raised earlier about Soren's forthcoming trip to Mississippi.

'This is no picnic you're on, girl. Couldn't we just pop down now and again, you know, just to give you a hand?' He was leaning forward, his posture languid, elbows on knees, his hands clasped together in prayer. He noted the chuckle and the incredulous look on Soren's face and drew the obvious conclusion. 'Oh, well,' he said, turning his gaze towards Denis. 'I guess I'll just have to stay with you darling and protect you from that *awful* man.'

Afterwards Soren made the lone walk to do battle with that awful man, along Wickson and University, to the Faculty Club, where he soon found himself seated in the club's panelled surrounds, on a firm, somewhat austere looking bench. The food and drink had worked their balm, leaving him relaxed and just a little too at ease with himself. It was a sensation that was to prove all too fleeting.

36

Boston, Massachusetts

Albert Constanze leant back in his chair and gazed at a couple of TV sets in front of him. On one of them was a freeze frame of Christina coming out of her Boston office. When it came to the state senator, Albert just couldn't help himself; the whore on the hill had become an obsession. He would find ways of getting at and subduing her, ways of showing her who was boss. Albert had done what he'd been asked of, attending her hearings to answer foolish questions from the serried ranks of clerks and lawyers; all martinets, with their fancy customs and titles and their airs and graces. And then there were the politicians, the real crooks of the piece in Albert's mind. That he controlled a couple of them only served to heighten his contempt for the rest.

If Christina was worried about the reputation of the man seated before her, and his appetite for violence, she never showed it. Her demeanour was always a model of calm dismissive scrutiny. Yes, she knew about Mr Constanze and the hoodlums he controlled. Her informants had told her of how this sweaty, usually unshaven, man had killed or ordered the killings of well over twenty people, and how he was given to severe bouts of depression and violent rage. She also knew that some of her colleagues in the Massachusetts state legislature would be on his payroll. But proving it would be difficult.

The uninitiated might be taken in by his sober and respectable outward appearance, dressed for the occasion in his dapper suit, silver cufflinks and yacht club tie; someone who could easily be mistaken for an alumnus of Harvard.

And it wasn't for the want of trying, as Albert had been doing his best to erase memories of his hoodlum past. But now all of that had been undone by The Bitch and her investigation, who'd been content to remind people that here was an unreconstructed thug who, not long ago, could be seen on videotape screaming a stream of expletives down a payphone, outside an establishment that was definitely not a faculty or yacht club.

What had started as an enquiry into a little local corruption had now mushroomed into a full-scale investigation into Albert's affairs. Furthermore, The Bitch had proceeded to trawl through evidence that would only renew the interest that had been shown by the Federal authorities, especially the IRS. Already, Marti, Albert's lawyer, was advising him to get his affairs in order in the event of a stretch in the pen. It could only be a matter of time. Someone, somewhere, was providing Christina's committee with very good, accurate information and it had to stop. It had led Albert to suspect all manner of people he used to count as friends and associates. She knew about the pimping, the money laundering, the numbers, the building contracts and the kickbacks, the influence peddling, the drug smuggling, and now, even where one of the bodies had been buried. It had been dug up, to much fanfare from the mayor's office, with the inevitable pledges to drive the gangs out of town.

But now he was before her again and he just couldn't help himself. He just had to ask her about the health of her boy. Yes, he wanted her to know that Albert Constanze had been taking an interest and was only too willing to deliver on the promissory note.

'Mr Constanze, this is no good,' his counsel whispered, his complexion turning sickly white. 'You're going places we agreed beforehand were no good to us.' But Albert took no notice; besides, the Bitch's reply indicated that he'd managed to get a rise.

'If that's a crude attempt at intimidation, Mr Constanze,' she said, 'I can assure you it won't work.' The idea of someone like Albert Constanze even knowing of Soren's existence was worrying; that he was now showing a malevolent interest was appalling. Still, Christina did her best not to show any alarm. 'Any more remarks along those lines, Mr Constanze and I will have the committee find you in contempt.'

But Albert was having none of it. 'Contempt!' he mouthed, snarling and just a little foolish. His grimace, though, slowly turned to horrified fascination as Christina moved the proceedings back to her original interest in the priest and his particular habit of frequenting a local brothel run by one of Albert's associates. Christina wanted to know if Albert had been pimping the priest some of the local girls?

'Were these especially young girls, Mr Constanze?'

Albert sensed danger. Now the Bitch was turning the focus towards probable child abuse. Did he, Albert Constanze, know that the girls were underage? Did he not know that he was pimping young, underage girls for the purpose of satisfying a paedophile?

Now Albert was building towards one of his rages again.

'What the fuck is this? How dare you call me one of those!'

Christina said nothing as those around took a collective deep breath. Albert now had a queasy feeling in the pit of his stomach, to go with his smoldering hatred for this bitch from hell. He'd miscalculated. His attempt at intimidation had backfired, only forcing Christina to dig her heels in further. Already he could feel the noose tightening around his neck. This one just kept on coming, just like some form of Nordic steamroller.

'Do you remember, Mr Constanze, that on June 6th 1986 you gave Mr O'Malley a birthday gift?'

'I can't recall ever knowing the guy.'

'Did you know that on February 8th of this year Mr O'Malley was arraigned on child abuse charges arising from this generosity?'

'Now wait here, what the hell are you trying to say? You can't pin that kinda stuff on me!'

'Then why was it that in a phone call you made on the 10th of April 1986, you were overheard saying that you wanted payment for services rendered?'

Albert sat there lost, his forced smile hiding a million hatreds. His counsel took over.

'This is an unconscionable slur on my client's character and I demand you withdraw that accusation. Where's the evidence?'

From her position overlooking the proceedings, Christina smiled and said nothing. She could have come up with some witticism, or some reasoning to justify her line of questioning, but she didn't. Too many of her colleagues loved to grandstand, or might get caught up in the heat of the moment, but not Christina. She was a seasoned campaigner; someone who knew when to keep quiet and let things ride. She was sure the abuse had taken place and that the priest had been procured young girls, but she had no direct evidence. Albert didn't know that of course, so she was willing to let him sweat a little. Let him feel the consequences of consorting with perverts and scum.

It had only been a brief exchange, but in just a couple of sentences, Christina had done more to violate Albert's sense of worth than a whole month's worth of testimony. In Albert's mind, had it been anyone other than the ice maiden, they would have had a contract put on them there and then. As it was, Albert knew of other ways to get at her. She did, after all, have a son.

37

'Ah, there you are!'

Soren had succumbed to the inevitable and dozed off. So it was a shock to see Wilson standing over him, florid complexion, sickly grin and with those Draculaesque protruding side teeth. Worryingly he was not alone.

'Jerry, we're over here. Bring Mr Boeteng.'

The shock soon turned into brooding anger. Soren wasn't surprised by Wilson bringing along his usual sidekick, Jerry Friesson, but the presence of Flaxel Boateng was something he did not expect. Soren chided himself. He should have known better. Outnumbered, he would have to be on his guard.

Once seated, and without ordering drinks, Wilson got straight to the point. 'We appear to have brought you here under false pretences, Soren. This should not take long.' Wilson was on top form, very much in control, with that manufactured expression of piety that, as Pariche had often said, just made you want to give him a slap. 'We feel that Pariche has furnished us with enough ammunition to see him on his way.'

Wilson's usually squat posture was this time quite erect, his back smack against the bench support. The light from one of wall lamps above his head cast a shadow that gave a slightly demonic twist to the glint in his eye. It contrasted somewhat, to the cocky and expressive smile on the face of his companion. Flaxel, Wilson's man of the streets, was a Sly Stone lookalike, with thin feminine lips and big teeth, who was capable of putting on a good pout. He looked younger than his thirty-five years, with a body that was slim, lithe and firm. His hands had long, delicate, concert player's fingers, whilst on his head was set a woolen cap, from under which protruded the beginnings of dreadlocks. He had obviously dressed for the occasion, his appearance resembling that of a card shark, rather than the usual huckster or pimp that was witnessed by most of his clients. At one stage he had been with the Nation of Islam, dressed in one of those sharp snazzy black suits, but the street hustler within had wanted out. The Nation of Islam never had a chance. For starters, Flaxel could never get use to their strict embargo on the cheap whisky he drank and the pot he smoked, and they could never get past the wide-eyed look of someone who looked as if he was perpetually on uppers. It was a distracted edgy sideways look that always gave the game away. The perceptive would soon pick up on the idea that here was someone eminently suited to the murky waters in which he swam, albeit as a representative of the bottom-feeder variety, always on the lookout for the next meal ticket. But how had all of this managed to get past Wilson?

The answer was the day Flaxel came across a woman who was just a little different from the usual customers he dealt with on the street. This player would drive down from her plush home in the surrounding hills, in the hope of scoring some cocaine, her face loosely camouflaged by the dark glasses and the headscarf she wore. At first Flaxel had no idea who she was, although he was intrigued by this out-of-place North Berkeley housewife, who had a regular order; just enough to tied her over for a few weeks. She was obviously too respectable to be caught trying to score a hit in her own neighbourhood or at one of those parties they had up in the hills, so she'd drive to the corner of San Pablo and Mead, roll down the car window and make a purchase. He guessed that she'd probably been driven to it by her husband. Then, one day, Flaxel attended a community meeting called on behalf of someone who just happened to be the Governor's favorite academic and anointed leader of the Golden State's latest attempt to placate the great dispossessed and urban poor. He couldn't believe his luck when he noticed that the self-same woman he'd been selling cocaine to, sitting next to the man on the platform, was also the great man's wife. Wilson, the great manipulator, had fallen into the arms of someone equally disposed towards the black arts of threats and blackmail.

There was an attempt on Soren's part to warm to the man seated before him, to applaud his aplomb in shaping the world to his own ends. But there was too much at stake. This bum had gatecrashed his party and, with Wilson's prompting, was now laying claim to something that wasn't his. Soren could sense his unease being returned. As always, with Flaxel, it was a scrutiny that was far from disinterested, informed by a certain indeterminacy that veered between the fraudulent and the brutally honest. A look that betrayed moments of genuine witness, menace and farce.

No, this was not good. Soren had been too easily ambushed and he knew he wasn't operating at his best. How foolish to think that he'd breeze through a meeting with Wilson with so little preparation. On his own, Wilson would still have had him bouncing off the walls, but with Flaxel in tow, things could become very uncomfortable indeed.

'Just what was supposed to have happened?' Soren asked, fighting for time.

'That does not really concern us,' Wilson replied, 'save for the fact that Mr Boeteng here was most upset by Pariche's ill-considered remarks. We almost lost the Zenotech contract.'

'We?' Soren's incredulity was palpable. 'I have...' he paused to catch his breath, 'I have already been on the phone to Burdon. He appears to have a very different take on things.'

'Are you suggesting there might be some doubt about the facts of the case?' Wilson's manner was fraudulently imperious, as he raised a hand to silence any repost. 'As I've already indicated, this whole business needs to be called to an end.'

He then turned to Friesson who, taking his cue, added: 'And one thing that might help us is Pariche being from outside of the department. It should be easy to get one of our guys in to do the work.'

'Yes,' echoed Wilson, 'our people should be the ones to get the call on this one.' He looked back at Soren and added, 'I hope you're not going to fight me on this?'

'It just wouldn't work. Pariche's contribution to the program is vital. He gives the program a scientific dimension that is practically unheard of elsewhere.'

'You appear to be missing the point, my man.' Flaxel had obviously decided that it was time to make his first contribution. 'The man has to go! Just what are the kids learning from this dude? Can he really be trusted?'

'Of course he can,' replied Soren. 'Like Socrates, he'd be continuing in a very fine tradition.'

There were knowing smiles amongst the academics, but the classical allusion was lost on Flaxel. Once again Soren found himself toying with the question as to why Wilson was here with this man. It was so utterly perplexing. Yes, he could see that Flaxel appeared to have done away with the Mohamed moniker, in an attempt to swim back towards the mainstream, but there was still so little to connect the lives of them both. If Wilson was the kind of person who'd probably be more at home running an audit at the local bank, then Flaxel would be the one hosting street parties on the proceeds that had been made from robbing it.

Flaxel was someone who'd always lived by his wits, combining a sometimes personable charm with more than just a hint of menace, to make his way in the world. His view was that everyone had a price. If that failed, there would always be weaknesses to exploit. He'd learnt this when starting out as a street hustler, before graduating to peddling dope and cocaine. He had dreams of stashing away enough money to make that move up into the Hills and at first he couldn't believe how easy it all was. But he soon began to realise that this was just nickel and dime stuff; he just wasn't ruthless or violent enough to take things to a higher level. He also tended to get too much enjoyment smoking and popping a lot of the proceeds. Factor in the cost if he ever got caught, or the risk of meeting an untimely end at the hands of clients or the gangs that were rife in the city, and he soon began to figure that his prospects didn't look good. And, to cap it all, the whole atmosphere had been poisoned with the rise of crack cocaine. The punks around today wouldn't think twice about casually doing away with anyone, let alone a lone dealer encroaching on their turf. And then there were the police shakedowns and the increasing likelihood of being sent to one of the state's correctional facilities. So, somewhere along the line, there had been a turn. The younger Flaxel knew the value of money, the power it could wield and the doors it could open, with the prospect of a good night out with a girl on each arm. The older, wiser Flaxel, outwardly at least, came to reject much of this. Now there was a different aesthetic, one that would be devoted to the faith of Islam. Well, that was the official version; the one that Flaxel kidded himself into believing. In truth, most of those who knew him still saw the same old street hustler at work, angling for a deal; so there had been an inevitability about Flaxel's return, as partial as it was, to the streets. Sure, the folks in the Nation of Islam had their own scams going on, but they could never compete with what Flaxel could make in west Oakland. And then this nice little earner had come along, courtesy of the gentleman now seated beside him and who was now sensing that things had become needlessly antagonistic and needed to be returned to the point at issue.

'Problems, Soren, do appear to be multiplying at an alarming rate,' said Wilson, as he coursed into full threat mode. 'Mr Boeteng informs me that some of his people are unhappy.' Flaxel nodded his agreement. 'There are some,' Wilson continued, 'shall we say, more vexed members who might cause us real difficulty. It's something that might rebound upon the program, not least because of the people we have teaching on it.'

'I should be very careful, Charlie,' said Soren, trying to spike Wilson's attempt at gravitas, with his first intonation of real anger.

'Well, we've already touched upon the problems associated with Mr. Pariche,' Wilson replied, with another attempt at smoothing over things. His efforts were thwarted, though, by an interruption from Flaxel that was anything but helpful.

'Why have you got a Chinaman teaching about African-American history?' he asked. If Flaxel's face was a picture of puzzled hurt, then Soren's was one of disbelief.

'His proper title is Dr Denis Tsui, and the course he is teaching is called Racial Narratives and Diaspora. There is no African American monopoly on that.' He shook his head and looked imploringly at Wilson. 'You have to be joking, Charlie. Surely you can't be going along with this?'

Wilson was clearly embarrassed. 'Mr Flaxel is just passing on some legitimate fears he has about what could happen if things were allowed to drift.' He rose to his feet and suggested to Soren that he should join him. They walked over to the bar. Once out of earshot, Wilson's tone became more pleading. 'We've had far too many experiences of programs becoming unmanageable due to their lack of credibility, Soren. Have a think. Is Denis Tsui really the most qualified person to be teaching on the program?'

'Charlie, I can't believe you're actually suggesting this! Of course he is the most qualified. He's been doing the job perfectly well for the past two years.'

'Be that as it may,' countered Wilson, his tone becoming a little more menacing. 'I well remember when there were a few whispers raised following your appointment. Some people thought that I might be pushing you a little too fervently. Where did it all go wrong? Why have you been doing your best to oppose me at every opportunity? This business regarding the Diaspora Project; can you see the position this puts me in? We need to be sure that all proprieties are adhered to. Some of your friends over at Boalt might not be so accommodating if questions were to be raised about the program's integrity.'

Wilson had overstepped the mark, totally misjudging Soren's sense of outrage. 'Is that a threat, Charlie? I'm the one who's been driving this thing forward and I fully intend to see it through.' Soren checked himself, with a swift look around to see if his discomfiture had been noticed. It had. 'Anyway, I'm not too sure that this is the right forum for such a discussion.' He gestured towards Flaxel, who was now watching attentively. 'Something I do know, is that this guy should have nothing to do with the appointment of faculty or the running of my program.'

'Congratulations, Soren, exactly what I would have said!'

The voice came from behind and it was both familiar and booming. It produced in Wilson a look that was a mixture of fear and stupefied anger. Soren spun round. It was Pariche; standing before them with two hands clasped around a cane he was using for support. He was a big, shambolic figure of a man, over two hundred pounds and well over six feet in his stockinged feet. Although veering towards the portly, his physique still exuded a compelling athleticism. As always, there was that look of incredulous mirth on his face, as if the proceedings he'd interrupted, like the rest of life, was a source of grotesque amusement. He pointedly refused to take off the sage gabardine overcoat he was wearing. He was in full combat readiness, with an Old Brigade Cavalry hat, that had been worn by a distant relative who'd ridden with the Vermonters, set on his head. For a moment there was silence as he examined Wilson and the others. He wore a stubbly two-day growth of beard and his eyes were as sharp and as impenetrable as those of the weathered buzzards he'd been brought up with on the Cocos. When he spoke, it was once again with a voice that boomed.

'What's this, Mr 'ACTING' dean?' he said, looking around him. 'A bit different from your usual audience over at the Chancellor's office!' He looked again at Soren. 'Say nothing, Solly. You have nothing to say to this shower.' He then turned again to face Wilson. 'You have been very naughty, Charlie. The nonsense you allowed those people down at Zenotech to believe had been said in my name.' He paused briefly, then continued: 'Mmm, I do believe, Charlie that you might just be suffering from some kind of mid-life crisis.' It was vintage chutzpah from someone who, it could be said, had been living a midlife crisis most of his life. He then cast an eye towards Wilson's man of the streets. 'You need to be more careful about who you mix with.' There was a squirm of embarrassment and just the hint of protest from Flaxel, as Pariche continued to look at him. 'Listen, young man,' said Pariche, pausing for very deliberately effect. 'If you persist with this we will bury you. You are not wanted here.' With that, he turned again to face Wilson. 'Charlie, if you need to contact us, Miss Hathaway over in Molecular Sciences will be happy to oblige.' He then shot Soren a smile that was both barking and oddly reassuring. Leave all this nonsense behind, it seemed to say. We have bigger fish to fry.

Soren was left wondering just how one might frame the theatre that Pariche invariably brought to any situation. He gave Wilson hardly as much as a glance as he found himself saying, 'Charlie, let's leave things as they are for the moment. We need to clarify our thoughts a little. As it is, I have this business in Mississippi to attend to.' His tone was hardly convincing, his demeanour something of a fumble, but the entreaty by Pariche had been compelling.

'But, Soren,' protested Wilson, 'we still have things to discuss. Are you really aligning yourself with *this*?'

'It will keep,' said Soren, 'it will keep.'

And with that, he and Pariche made their apologies and left, leaving the others in stunned silence, save for one exasperated and, dare one say, practised cry of 'Extraordinary!' from Wilson.

Afterwards, Wilson turned to the others and told them how insulted and embarrassed he felt on their behalf. He would very much appreciate the help Flaxel and his friends in the community might be able to provide. If only they could avail themselves of the opportunity to make their feelings known a little more keenly; especially regarding the question of whether it would be desirable to have Dr Tsui teaching a program they, the local community, held in such high esteem. And it would be very useful if Jerry could expedite the bureaucratic side of things. Pariche would be back soon and it would be a good idea to get the question of his role within the department clarified before then. He might want to look at the status of his tenure while he was about it. As for Soren, had they been a little premature in approving this sabbatical? One would hate to think that people, in the department and elsewhere, might someday feel the need to question the efficacy of the program he'd taken such pains to develop. On the conclusion of their business the looks that Wilson and Flaxel exchanged with each other were ones of a pure and knowing corruption.

38

Once they were outside Soren was summoned by Pariche to join him for a drive to June Lake. The journey would be made in Pariche's old Studebaker and would afford the older man the opportunity to inform Soren of 'the plan'. Ah, yes, the plan. It was something Pariche assured him would do for Wilson and the 'committee people'. Firstly, though, there would need to be a drive to West Portal, where Soren would be able to pick up whatever belongings he needed before the drive to the mountains. In the mountains there would be time enough to strengthen the younger man's resolve for the coming battle. Afterwards, they would go their separate ways; Pariche back to Berkeley and Soren on to Mississippi.

As they drove, Pariche maintained an animated, but mostly rhetorical, conversation that defied rebuke or interruption. Soren had often driven in this car, but still, he never ceased to be amazed at how expert a driver Pariche was, something he marveled at now as he navigated the junctions and stops in a manner that was truly to be applauded. The alternating, strobed, effect of light and shadow, combined with a vehicle driven with deliberate speed through narrow, enclosed streets, would usually have provoked within Soren alarm, but with Pariche at the helm the journey appeared effortlessly sedate, almost hearse-like. Pariche was obviously at home here, as befits somebody who would think nothing of making a weekly round trip of well over six hundred miles to June Lake when the Tioga Pass was closed. Soren wondered if his friend sometimes slept overnight in the car; there were certainly times when he looked as if he had.

It was now raining heavily. They passed the Southern perimeter of the university, through streets that were vividly lit in preparation for one of the city's many festival processions. Pariche sat hunched behind the steering wheel, as if he were wrapped around it, his body at one with the machine. His beard was a grey stubble and his eyes now had a brooding bloodhound quality. He would fleetingly breeze into laughter, quixotically enthused and despairing at the things around him. His arms would wave and gesticulate wildly, his eyes gleaming and his eyebrows arched, as if he was constantly being surprised at the incredulity of it all.

They were on College Avenue now, going south towards Oakland. As he drove, Pariche continued to speak with a voice that boomed; that unlit cigar continuing to protrude from his lips. He appeared to be never happier than when he was describing failed, but valiant, attempts to run rings around anyone or anything that smacked of authority.

'You come on up and stay with us for the weekend,' he barked. 'We'll get Mildred to put on a spread. Get things sorted before you go to Mississippi.' Soren let the mention of Mildred go. This was not the time to re-open old wounds. 'Glad to see you've finally had done with that son of a bitch, Solly. I've been thinking about the ways we can take the battle to this pestilence.' Ah, there it was. If Wilson had become something of an obsession for Soren then, in Pariche's eyes, he'd become something of an Antichrist; prime exhibit in a gallery of villainy and everything that was wrong with Berkeley, made flesh. Pariche reached into the dashboard, from which he retrieved a large pale brown envelope.

'Here! Have a look.'

Soren recognised it immediately. 'The Genotech contract?'

'A copy. It's been given a little tweak.' He noted Soren's concerned expression. 'Oh, don't worry, it's not major. We won't need to go back to committee. Brewster, over at Projects, has already given his approval. It names you as the lead. That wasn't clear in the old one.' Soren soon had the document open, but the darkness made reading it impossible.

'Something just didn't seem quite right,' continued Pariche. 'I figured that Burdon wouldn't give up like that. You know the guy, Solly, you've spent the past two years negotiating with the man. Managed to track him down in Mountain View. First thing he said was how surprised he was that you hadn't been at the ground breaking. Says he was beginning to smell a rat way before the ceremony had started. The way Friesson was all over him like a rash, pressurising him to reconsider the lead on the project. That's what alarmed him. Wilson wanted a contract that gave him, as Chair of the Department, overall say in who could be employed once the thing was up and running. Burdon didn't like that. That's why he kicked up such a fuss. He was already annoyed by the way Friesson was going about pitching things to him and he positively got the jeepers when he found out that Flaxel was in on it too. Burdon wants you, Solly, to fully integrate the whole thing into the Diaspora program. And he needs you as the named person to sell it to his people. You'll have to see this thing through, or nobody will! Any change and his people will want the option to withdraw.'

'But surely Wilson knew all of this. Knew that I'd be getting in touch with Burdon at some point?'

'That's why he wanted to get to you before you and Burdon had a chance to talk.'

'Well, he's lucked out there!'

'Yes, thank God. Honest, Solly, Wilson engineered the whole thing, between Flaxel and myself. He knew I'd rise to the bait. And that business back there! He wanted you to keep Burdon sweet. Talk him around and get rid of me.

Soren now relaxed enough to let go with a long deep exhale of breath. They were now navigating the MacArthur maze, just south of Emeryville, on the approaches to the Bay Bridge. Of course neither of them could have known they were so near to the place where Flaxel had started selling deals to a certain acting dean's wife. As he listened, Soren found himself returning to the outrageous thought he'd had the other evening; that Pariche really was the one who could be trusted with the stewardship of the program. Now the idea didn't seem all that outlandish. And he knew that Pariche would be straining at the leash, raring to be given another crack at Wilson and the committee people.

Yes, Pariche would be an excellent defender of the faith, guaranteed to give as good as he got. The time for pussy-footing was long gone. Wilson had shown his hand and it appeared to involve wresting control of the whole program. And he wouldn't be beyond using Flaxel, and the threat he posed, to help in achieving this. That was the real worry. Rubbing Wilson up the wrong way was bad enough, but Flaxel was a different proposition altogether.

Flaxel Boateng, with the contacts he had on the streets and the ones he still maintained with the Nation of Islam, would be able to make things very difficult for a program that depended so much on the goodwill of the community. And might Flaxel and his accomplices, having been promised a little of the action, feel just a little peeved if it was now taken away? Soren tried not to dwell on this for too long; something that was assisted by the diversionary company that Pariche invariably provided. As they continued in their serene glide towards the glittering lights of the city, Pariche proceeded to entertain, discourse and pontificate on topics as diverse as cheating in the academic marketplace and the impact of the wayside diner on American culture and diet. In doing so he drew upon his impressive knowledge of science and genetics in order to make hilarious, and often spurious, observations about society and what he fancifully thought was humanity's place in it. Much to his passenger's amused embarrassment, he also talked of the debt he owed Soren, for having been there for him after he'd lost his wife, Mildred. Hardly a moment would pass, he told Soren, when he wasn't giving thanks for having been given the opportunity to continue the good fight by his dear and valued friend. Yes, a cult indeed. And so the soliloquy continued; how fast food symbolised the ultimate betrayal of that original pioneering attitude and how truth had been hijacked by the petty nastiness of the herd and its need to be fed and entertained. It was a picture of America as being somewhat smaller than its original promise.

Reflections born more out of sorrow than bitterness. As if it was to be expected.

Throughout the brief stopover at West Portal, Pariche continued to paint his rather graphic portrait of what was wrong with any place that allowed the likes of Wilson and Flaxel to thrive. Pariche had also decided that he and Soren needed a little bit of a diversion; something that would be provided by a detour to O'Grady's, before that drive to the mountains. If they had loitered a little and delayed their departure, they would have still been at the apartment when Christina called. Instead, she left a message on the answer machine. Had Soren been there to hear it, he would have immediately picked up on the concern in her voice. It had a quiet desperate quality to it that failed to conceal real hurt. Something had clearly upset her.

39

O'Grady's was a bar located off Sutter, between Nob Hill and the Theatre District. It was Pariche's regular haunt. The place was also familiar to Soren, as the two men would often decamp here after they'd finished helping out at that nearby homeless shelter. Composed of a series of narrow darkly lit rooms, with alcoves that looked up towards the often fog-obscured view of Nob Hill, the charm of O'Grady's was the vibrancy and diversity of the crowd that sought sanctuary here. Tonight was about par for the course, with a good cross section of San Francisco's alternative bohemia, co-mingling with a few who looked as if they might be escapees from the Tenderloin district just down the road. The atmosphere veered between the eccentrically colourful and the downright derelict. There were a scattering of art students and players from the local rep – Pariche had always been a sap for actors – along with some of their hangers-on. There were also a few of what Pariche euphemistically called 'industry girls' and the usual Friday night revellers. At the end of the room was a small stage where a couple, bizarrely dressed in dinner suit and ball gown, were beating out a rather laid-back rendition of a traditional jazz standard. Part of the reason why Pariche so enjoyed O'Grady's was the enhanced sense of grandeur it seemed to bestow on him. Here was a place where he could pontificate, engage and entertain, as well as plan those future raids across the bay to do battle with the committee people. Where he would counsel all and sundry, make calls to the Mayor's office and bombard the city desk of the Chronicle with whatever happened to be his latest preoccupation. He was an inveterate letter writer. From his seat in O'Grady's he could regularly be seen writing things down on a pad, offering his views on all manner of things, ranging from the need to do more to protect the Bay Area's wetlands to his annual petitioning of the Northern District Federal Court in an attempt to indict Henry Kissinger for war crimes. Here at O'Grady's, Pariche would also host regular meetings of the Responsible Genetics Group he chaired, and there had even been a royal connection. To this day, folks down at the British consulate would still talk in admiring disbelief about the man with the big hat, who'd upbraided an aide to a visiting royal who'd thought it de rigueur to racially abuse one of his junior staff members.

'I couldn't believe my ears, Solly. This pompous ass shouting such filth at this lovely treasure.' Women in Pariche's parlance were nearly always lovely treasures. 'Beat the scoundrel with this cane, I did. Beat him to a pulp.'

Pariche's entrance into O'Grady's was grand and well received and their progress through the tables a stately one, assisted by Pariche's unerring ability to naturally clear a space before them. Only when they were seated, did Pariche at last take off his coat, to reveal, what Soren recognised as his usual attire; a pair of sandy-coloured pants, a crumpled yellow linen jacket, a blue cotton shirt and pencil-thin black tie. With a glass of whisky and water in hand, he thrust his jaw towards a pretty young waif of a girl sitting at a nearby table. She looked to be in her late teens, white faced, with dark eyeshadow, stud in her nose, and a big smile.

'Hi, Bonny, how's the drama?' She shrugged and gestured a wide-eyed innocence. 'But Bonny, you had plans!' His expression was one of disappointment. Hers was an embarrassed blush of silence, an adjustment to her short black ballet skirt, followed by a nervous look down at the air-cushioned boots on her feet. 'A lovely girl, Soren. Up from the valley. Giving her folks the run around. But we'll see her right. Won't we, Bonny?' A bashful flirtatious smile had returned. 'Ah, that's more like it!' She was obviously a girl who loved to please.

'I did have a bit part in one of those off-theatre productions.' Her voice was a little squeaky, her words delivered in a somnolent stream.

'So, you've dropped out of school?'

'Whatever. The money didn't come through. Neither did my folks. They've cut me loose. Say I've got to come home or else.'

'They might be right,' said Pariche. 'If it's money, I can lend you a couple of bucks. I could easily pick up the phone and give Simmonds a ring down at the Conservatory. You could call your folks.'

Bonny smiled. Yes, she could always do with a couple of bucks. Pariche caught a glimpse of Soren shooting a look at her two companions. They were young, tattooed, with one of them sporting tell-tale puncture marks on his wrists. Both looked unkempt, disinterested and removed from the proceedings. They offered a dispiriting and deadening counterpoint to Bonny's sunny disposition. The two professors shared a rather queasy feeling that there would be a price to pay for any floor that Bonnie chose to sleep on tonight.

'We're off to the mountains for a few days' continued Pariche, 'you're always welcome to tag along.' Bonny smiled again, looked nervously at her two companions, and shrugged. 'Well, you think about it,' he said. 'The offer's always open.' He then turned again to Soren; the recent incident at the Faculty Club was still playing on his mind.

'Can you credit it, Solly, bringing Flaxel along to a meeting like that? Reminds me of the things we had to deal with some time ago at the NAACP.' He paused and gazed into his glass. 'Good things can go bad very quickly.'

Soren sat and watched as his friend continued to ponder the hand they'd been dealt. It was easy to forget that Pariche was a biologist of some repute, someone who'd first started his love affair with the subject through the usual route of dissecting frogs at school and the not so usual one of de-fanging rattlers on the local trails he walked near his home. Later, whilst a researcher at the University of Chicago, Pariche had tethered his ambitions to one of the professors who'd the misfortune to come a distant nowhere to Crick and Watson in the quest to unravel the mysteries of the double helix. Still, Pariche had been thought well enough of to be offered a post at Berkeley, after which he'd secured a lucrative advisory role with Pat Brown's administration in Sacramento, helping the likes of Clark Kerr implement California's Higher Education Master Plan. It was a time he would still refer to as the golden age; before the riots, the Manson murders, the anti-tax propositions and Ronald Reagan. Before it all began to go so terribly wrong. And Pariche had never forgiven the latter for his part in the trashing of it. Never forgiving the man who – like himself – had once been a New Deal Democrat, a true believer.

Now, in this post-modern age, it was time to despair. Despair at the passing of the old guard, be they the old pols Pariche had worked with in Sacramento or the veterans of the civil rights movement. The loss of the latter was particularly galling. Although he was loath to admit it, he knew that he'd become derelict and superfluous. The younger generation wouldn't tolerate the kind of interference an ornery old fool like Pariche was likely to bring. And an ornery old white fool at that. So he'd moved on. Not to do so would mean having to listen to the ever-more strident and unattractive voices of those who sought to persuade by deconstructing and devaluing language. They were a new breed who irritated, offended and betrayed in equal measure. Now, when it came to Pariche, people would notice a hardening of attitudes and a renewed belligerence; how an initially fierce assault upon injustice and inequity had matured into a cussed contrariness and, dare one say, prejudice and paranoia.

Still, his heart was in the right place and there would always be bullies to fight and committee people to rant at. Furthermore, with Soren, there was now someone new to champion. Latching onto Soren and joining in his fight with Wilson would give Pariche the solace of battle by proxy. As well as doing the right thing, the fight with Wilson and the more extreme nonsense coming from the street would also be great fun.

Thoughts of Pariche's past achievements prompted Soren to raise the question, that Wilson and Friesson had raised earlier, about Pariche not getting tenure.

'One of the best things that's ever happened,' Pariche replied. 'Had the choice of going with either Chemistry or Genetics. Trouble was, well, you know how it is. Taking Mildred away from Sentor, the prospective chair, meant that Chemistry was out of the question, and the witch hunts that were going on at the time, well that didn't help much either. Never got round to tenure after that. Never saw it as being of any consequence. Hell, it was Vietnam. We had other things to worry about. Seemed to drift from one research job to another, then a bit of teaching – you know, just enough to tide us over. The oddity of it all, is that a few years later, the people over at Genetics went and dug something up about the conditions that had been attached to that job I did for Clark Kerr and the master plan. So insignificant, I darn well forgot about it. Seems some of the folks back then seemed to think that I'd been pretty useful in helping them get the thing through. It was one of the last things Clark did before Reagan did for him. Gave me a position, you know, one of those university appointments, in the gift of the Chancellor's office, down the road in Oakland. Thought they owed the old man a favour. Pays nothing, but they obviously wanted me inside the tent, you know, pissing out rather than in. Went through on the nod, as a kind of honorarium. Gives me the right to give the odd cross-campus lecture and sit on committee. Might be able to use it in some way to rile Wilson. Anyways, the upshot is that the folks over at Biology and Genetics think my appointment with them now has the same legal standing as a fully tenured professor. Hell, they've been paying me as much for the last twenty-five years on the basis of it. Can't see that it makes any difference though, Solly, when it comes to the teaching on your program. That's in your gift. You and yours alone. Don't go forgetting that. It's not Wilson's, or any of his cronies. That's the way it is, and that's the way I like it. Been fighting the likes of Wilson all my life, Solly. It's too late to change now!'

162

'But I'm not sure if we can afford to do this, Jed.'

'Can't afford not to, Solly!'

'But Wilson could make things really difficult for us. All he has to do is get the department to drop some of the course options and the electives, and we're screwed.'

'C'mon, Soren, you're jumping at shadows. It just isn't going to happen. The course is too damn popular for them to do that. And they just love the numbers! Wilson is sure as hell not going to risk being sued by a whole bunch of irate students and their parents in the process. And the fallout in Senate could do him real damage.'

'What about next year?'

'Let's deal with this one first shall we? There are battles to be fought, Solly. We have to sort this Genotech business and we mustn't forget the threat to Denis's teaching. Them's the priorities, Solly, as I see it. You can't let Wilson and his cronies screw with us. Can't you just smell it? The scent of battle?'

And there it was; Pariche stoked up for the fight, desperate to get his hooks into Wilson and the committee people. So, at the stroke of midnight, they emerged from O'Grady's into heavy rain and protests from Soren. He'd been to the mountains and Mono Lake with Pariche many times, but surely his wish to drive there now was pure lunacy? With weather like this, it was enough for Soren to chance a taxi ride back to West Portal, let alone drive a hundred miles across the Valley, into potentially hazardous mountain terrain.

'Don't be so city,' countered Pariche, in mock disdain, before gazing towards the heavens. 'In a few moments we'll be miles from this foul stuff and in the benign embrace of the Gods.'

40

Mono Lake, California

Of course Pariche was right. As soon as they hit the skyline, the rain and cloud changed to brilliant moonlight; a light which turned the roadside aspen to alabaster. Pariche knew the terrain through which they were driving like the back of his hand. To the accompaniment of those old blues and jazz stalwarts, Eta James and Ella Fitzgerald, and blue grass country music that Soren couldn't quite put a name to, they made a quick dash through the back-roads of Modesto and Turlock. Within hours they were passing through Mariposa, into hill country, headed towards the massif formations that make up Yosemite. Ignoring Soren's pleas to stop off at his cabin on Bass Lake, Pariche drove on, up to Tuolumne Meadows, where the brilliant luminescence of the moon bathed the valley with a shimmering light, punctuated here and there with shadows thrown by the relief of the surrounding mountains. By the time they reached Mono Lake, the air had a fresh, jagged feel, and the light had a cathedral-like quality, as if filtered through crystal. Pariche looked like someone who'd gone through too many nights with the minimal amount of sleep, bleary eyes shot through with the light of the emerging dawn. They were sat in the car, just off Highway 395, gazing at Mono Lake's glistening expanse, observing the dawn's increasingly victorious shadow play with the silhouetted formations of Tufa that grew from the water's edge. The landscape was beginning to work its balm as Pariche had known it would. For Soren there was an almost giddying and vaulted sense of disbelief and awe. There was a brooding inhospitality here, a sublimely disinterested force, suggestive of human irrelevance. Time would come, it appeared to say, when the earth would shudder, as if it were adjusting its cloak – just a flick; but enough to remind humankind of its utter insignificance.

'Wow, what a moon! It's so much bigger than the ones we see down in the Valley.'

They turned to see that Bonny had emerged from underneath the pile that was her hastily retrieved belongings on the back seat. She was peering through the window, the expression on her face one of childlike wonder. 'You can almost reach out and touch it!' She'd obviously forsaken the opportunity of a Tenderloin roughhousing with her erstwhile companions back at O'Grady's. A weekend in the mountains would be a much healthier proposition.

'Snow,' said Pariche, looking up at the mountains. 'Could soon be pretty deep around these parts. Another couple of weeks and we wouldn't have been allowed through Tioga Pass.' He reached over and handed her some coffee from his flask. 'Now, Bonny, you will need to call your folks when we get to June Lake.'

'Do I have to?'

'They will be worried.'

Bonny bared her teeth a little, gave a shrug, and leant forward, resting her forehead into the back of the front seat. She was tired and just a little shivery.

'Yes, it's time to get you home,' said Pariche.

Home for Pariche was a dwelling that looked to be an homage to Frank Lloyd Wright's Fallingwater, built into a hillside at the end of a dirt track just off a particularly twisty section of Route 158. From there, Bonny made that phone call to her parents. At first Pariche was content to hover in the background, but when he sensed she was beginning to struggle, he gently took the receiver from her and proceeded to instruct her parents as to what needed to be done. As could have been predicted, with anyone dealing with Pariche, they didn't have a chance. He soon had them agreeing to the idea that Bonny should indeed take up that college offer, and that he would be monitoring all of their progresses: daughter and parents. He would drop down later next week, daughter in hand, to seal the deal. And they appeared to be grateful to him for this. Grateful that their daughter wasn't lying in a ditch somewhere. And they appeared to accept that, as far as their daughter was concerned, Pariche had now assumed the role of parental surrogate.

Whilst Bonny and Pariche were speaking to her parents, Soren made himself busy in the kitchen, where, with some eggs and leftover rice, he was able to conjure up something the others – by the way they wolfed it down – found palatable. The polished oak table they sat at, like the rest of the household's furniture, had been lovingly fashioned by Pariche. It was a skill that had served him well, especially during the lean years, immediately following the Chemistry Department imbroglio. Pariche would constantly rib Soren about how his fancy private school education had left him bereft of any practical skills such as carpentry. To the older man, it just beggared belief.

Those early years in Mono County had been hard for Mildred and Pariche as they knuckled down to the task of digging latrines, hand-washing clothes, chopping wood and mending broken down machinery. Getting through those long hard winters had been an almost unbearable struggle at times, and, for Mildred, it must have been far worse. Pariche could at least get away from the place, teaching at Berkeley and flying off to conferences. For Mildred, once the prospective wife of an ambitious high-flying academic, and with the social whirl that came with it, the experience must have been awful.

After they'd eaten, Pariche saw to it that a bed was made up for Bonny, but she didn't immediately take to it. The bright, early morning light had given her, just as it had the others, a renewed sense of vigour. Soon they were striding out again, into the wilderness, along one of the old mule tracks that criss-crossed the area. For the two men, the conversation still focused on how best to counter the malign influence of Wilson. Bonny was quick to catch on.

'It strikes me,' she said, after listening intently for a while, 'that the only person of interest is this person you have down in Mountain View.'

'You mean Burdon?' said Soren.

'He's the one controlling the money!'

The men shrugged and smiled knowingly at each other.

'And what of Wilson?' asked Soren.

'Had a dog once,' she continued. 'Kept on looking at things he oughtn't to. Gotten so as we had to move stuff out of sight.'

'You mean move the program? I think Wilson will be a little more tenacious.'

'The principle's the same though, surely? Why does the program have to be stuck with him? You know, in his department?'

Now there were guffaws as the two men stopped in their tracks. Finally, Pariche, in a hushed slightly astonished voice, said, 'Solly, it might just work!'

Soren was unsure. 'As you said, Jed, we have to get through this year first.'

'Still, we in Genetics would be only too willing to give you a hand. Hell, you could even get your folks over at UCSF to help out.'

'But, Jed, the logistics of getting a thing like that through committee doesn't bear thinking about.'

'Screw the committees! They're all mobbed up anyway. Let's wind the thing up and see how it flies. Wilson's already shown his hand. We know he's hostile. The best way for us to protect ourselves is to keep things away from prying eyes.'

Soren stroked his chin and thought about it for a moment. Hadn't he just been saying the same thing, to Denis and Chumley, a few hours earlier? He looked at Pariche and chuckled to himself. Then, in consort, they both extended a congratulatory hand to Bonny.

Later, Soren gave Burdon a call. He told him of the rather outlandish idea he'd been mulling over for the last couple of days. How Pariche would be ideal as the Berkeley lead. To Soren's surprise, Burdon had already factored the possibility in and didn't find it at all disagreeable. Sure, there would be need for constraints. His people would want to see Soren remain as co signori, for example. But, for all intents and purposes, Pariche would now be in charge.

'Hell, Solly, this is wonderful,' a beaming Pariche declared, on being told the news. 'Something we can really get our teeth into. Wilson is going to have kittens when he hears about this!'

And there it was, the whole awful spectacle of it all. A man who'd been cited by, amongst others, his co-confederate, as the original catalyst for communal and academic discord, and with antennae demonstrably ill-tuned to the sensitivities of the street, would now be in charge of a centre that had a need for both. Wilson and Flaxel had better watch out. Here was a man who intended humiliation and hurt to be inflicted upon the aforesaid gentlemen – and with extreme prejudice.

41

The following Monday, after making calls to various airfields around Bishop and Mammoth Lakes, Soren managed to get a short-haul charter to San Francisco, from where he was able to fly east. His aim, to join up with Brad and Craig, who would be arriving in Memphis later that same afternoon.

Between moments of snatched sleep, Soren found himself cursing the fact that events had conspired to deny him that most American of rites, the road trip. He thought about Brad and Craig and how they would now be coming to the end of a journey that would have taken them down the spine of the East Coast that was the Appalachians. It pained him to think that it was something he'd missed. He figured they might have travelled with Virginia as far as Pittsburgh, then, after stopping over, they'd be on their way south, circumnavigating the Shenandoahs and the Alleghenies, before breaking through the Cumberland gap at Chattanooga. He found himself smiling at the thought of how Brad would have been moaning, straight from the word go; complaining about the proliferation of all things rural and how he would probably need to be chemically inoculated against the forested vistas to come. He wouldn't be able to smoke around Virginia, of course, a fully formed representative of the Pittsburgh's finest, but confronted with the horrors of the Appalachians, he would need the comfort of the odd joint, along with a regular supply of liquor. Some of the dry counties would pose a challenge, but good planning would see them through. Throughout the drive south they would relish the challenge of unearthing those out-of-the-way stills, where they could interrogate the owners as to the processes and ingredients they'd employed. Their progress would be further delayed by Craig's need to assuage his love of Country and Blue Grass music, and the lure of mountain medicine would also be hard to resist. The prospect of encountering some shaman experience, be it spiritual possession or ritual emersion, would be too tempting to pass up. All of those back roads and detours, with each stop providing the opportunity to sniff the breeze and take on board the changes in culture, slowly acclimatising to what might be in store for them in Mississippi. It was something that Soren was acutely aware of having missed.

On the flight Soren noted the preponderance of Southern accents and the premium placed on good manners. In past lives these people would surely have taken part in the most politest of lynchings. Even the children were a picture of civility, all courteous smiles and on their best behavior. There were a few black faces which reassured, along with a surfeit of cowboy hats which didn't. Apart from a conference in Atlanta and the occasional visit with Virginia to Charlottesville, Soren had long given the states of the old confederacy a wide berth. The possibility of embarrassment and the insinuation of threat just didn't appeal.

On the flight Soren found conversation with the passenger sat next to him. An inveterate smoker, Harvey Wilks had a withered left arm and a bad leg. He introduced himself as a sometime reporter with *Rolling Stone Magazine* and looked the part of someone you might expect to see taking in a show at the Fillmore, or bar hopping along Telegraph, hoping to catch the next best thing since *Moby Grape*. Harvey liked to think of himself as a better class of journalist, steeped in the music of the blues. He regularly travelled the route between San Francisco and Memphis and had, in search of the old blues legends of the South, trod the ground where Soren was now headed, in Mississippi. It soon became clear that Harvey could barely tolerate the A&R and music industry people he usually had to put up with, or the chumps hell bent on going to that circus still being played out in Nashville, a decade after Elvis Presley's death. Aided by considerable quantities of complementary bourbon, he provided amusing company, with tales of crooked agents and deals gone bad, the egos and the squabbling, the parties and the girls.

At Memphis, Soren's first tentative steps onto southern soil involved escorting a somewhat tipsy and enervated Harvey to a waiting taxi. On parting, he gave Soren a long studied look and said how much he would have loved to have been going on with him. His parting words were a plea to take care. He'd heard so many bad things about Mississippi.

Shortly afterwards Soren was reunited with Brad and Craig, delighted to see they'd managed to purloin Virginia's refurbished Saab. Following a brief and decidedly forgettable acquaintance with the somewhat seedy offerings of Beale Street, they made a call on the motel where Martin Luther King had been murdered twenty years before. The place was closed. A passer-by, a black woman cradling her shopping, told them there were plans for a memorial. The last tenant had been evicted only the other week. Soren's thoughts and emotions were decidedly mixed. He remembered the black and white mugshot of James Earle Ray and the people pointing to where they believed the shots had come from. And there was the image of a certain Rhyming Man, stooped with his arms in the great man's blood. He found himself cursing the fact that this picture, of Jesse Jackson at Martin Luther King's side, was the most pervasive of the memories coursing through his jet-lagged mind.

42

Christina did, after a few more attempts, manage to get through to Soren's West Portal apartment. The person who answered was some waif of a lass who stopped a tearful Christina in mid-sentence with a 'Hi there, Soren's marm!' It was Bonny, who now went on to give Christina a daughterly peroration so enthused, it brooked neither interruption nor dissent.

'Now, don't you go worrying yourself, Soren's marm,' she continued in a flood. 'I'm just babysitting here while your son's in Mississippi and I'm so impressed with you, Soren's marm, at the way you've been dealing with those bad people over there and...'

The older woman smiled, but she could feel herself beginning to shake and the tears beginning flow again.

'I'll look after this place, honest; Mr Pariche will make sure of that. I've already given the whole place the once over. You should have seen the dust, Soren's marm, with all those books...'

An audible chuckle now, all the way down the line from Boston.

'No, Soren's good, he and Mr Pariche have a plan and I thought you was Cindi; she's called a couple of times, seemed quite upset, goodness knows what your son was doing with an airhead like that...'

Now Christina let out a real laugh.

'...you need to give him a right talking to!'

'Believe me, I've tried!'

'I know, Soren's marm, he says you can be a bit of a dragon at times.'

Now a real guffaw.

'Anyway, Pariche is around to keep an eye on things. He's out at the moment. I could get him to call you back if you like?'

'No Bonny, that won't be necessary. But would you thank him all the same?' There was a pause, then a heartfelt, 'Thank you. You've been a great help. Both of you have.'

43

Toshoba County, Mississippi

Soon they were on the road driving south. On the way Soren was told about the journey the others had had to endure; it had been far from the ethnographically tinged delight that Soren had been so convinced he'd missed out upon. As soon as they'd crossed the Mason-Dixon line, Brad and Craig had been at each other's throats and generally unimpressed by the prospect of being cooped up together for the next two days. In truth, both had been envious of Soren and his decision to fly, so, after delivering Virginia to her home in Pittsburgh, they settled upon the fastest journey possible south along Interstate 71. For most of the trip, while one of them drove, the other, if not asleep, would have his nose deep in some reading matter, be it *Cell Magazine* or the *Journal of Mathematical Physics*. Towards the end of their journey, a rapprochement of sorts had been made, just in time for a bemused hitchhiker, picked up south of Louisville, to find himself witness to an often heated exchange about the feasibility of visualising prions and the modelling of algorithms needed to fight HIV.

But now it was mid-afternoon on the third day, and, with Soren on board, all the scientific discourse in the world couldn't hide the fact that they were more than just a little fed up. So it was with welcome relief that, under an unseasonably hot winter sun, they finally arrived in Toshoba County. It felt like another country. Soren couldn't put his finger on it, but something just didn't feel right. The small town rural life he was familiar with, in upstate New York and New England, was here transformed into something strange and alien. The South was like that, requiring the conversant to have an understanding that had been filtered through a particular historical scope. Virginia would have immediately felt at home here, breathing in the feint whiff of pine and burnt hickory and enjoying the warmth of the sun as it stridently worked its fingers into the lush vegetation. For Soren though, it all felt unnaturally out of season. There was also that seemingly oppressive presence of threat, of something lurking in the darkened recesses of the forested wayside. Either way, he had an awareness of things cast out of time and place.

Adding to the confusion was the fact that they were now lost. The road out of Memphis had seemed the right one, but now they weren't so sure. The mixture of wooded hillside and farm scenery did little to offer clues as to where they were. Having voted unanimously to take the left hand fork in the road, they now felt an urgency to ask if this was indeed the correct choice, as Brad was hopelessly lost by the map. After a while they came across a group of semi-derelict farm buildings. On a makeshift-looking porch, sat an old man, white haired, with patched trousers and dowdy checked shirt. Soren, who'd taken over the driving, manoeuvred the car to a halt and, along with Brad, watched as Craig opened the window.

'Hold on a minute,' said Soren, 'as this is the land of hospitality and good manners, perhaps you'd better get out and speak to him.'

In full agreement, Craig clambered out of the car. With his legs still suffering the effects of being cooped up for hours, he walked over to where the old man sat. The lump of saliva expelled by the gentleman did little to suggest that any good would come of it. If hospitality was a southern trait, it certainly appeared to be lacking here.

'Excuse me sir, me and my friends are trying to get to Hampton Academy in Coulee. We wondered if you might direct us there?'

The scowl the man wore had now turned to something of a puzzle as he noted Craig's ponytail. There was no answer, with all further entreaties from Craig, tentative at best, drifting off into nothing. Another expulsion of saliva brought the Montanan to conclude that any further attempts would be fruitless. He thanked the old man and informed the others of the outcome. For Brad, though, hours of pent-up anger suddenly came forth in fit of rage.

'Ignorant old fool,' he howled. 'Still sulking over the civil war!'

His outburst was met with knowing looks of disbelief from the others. More worryingly, the old man was now on his feet and disappearing inside.

'Well,' said Brad, indignant, 'where does he get off with behaviour like that?'

They turned to see that the man had returned, carrying a shotgun, prompting Craig to think there was real cause for alarm.

'Come on, Soren,' he cried, urgently. 'Let's get the hell out of here!'

Before Soren had time to act, though, a gunshot blast shattered the rear window, lacing the three of them with a blanket of glass. Now convinced of the emergency, Soren stabbed the accelerator, sending the car lurching forward. Once out of sight and out of range, he halted the vehicle, and they checked for damage, both to persons and property. Apart from a slight graze to Brad's neck, all were unhurt.

'Where the hell did that come from?' Craig was almost screaming at Brad.

'Yes, I thought the guy's reaction was a little extreme,' he replied, deliberately ignoring the intent of Craig's concern.

'I mean you, you son of a bitch. What the hell were you thinking? I've been waiting to see just how long it would be before you managed to get a rise from one of the locals.'

'Don't go taking that tone with me!' cried Brad defensively, shooting a glance at Soren, who was having none of it.

'You just can't go around doing things like that,' he said, siding with Craig, before getting out of the driver's seat and walking around to the back of the car. 'That's the way it is down here.' He let out a slow whistle as he took stock of the damage. The back windscreen had been totally shot out. 'I suspect there aren't too many places down here that will be able to fix that.'

After taking time out for a little physical and emotional recuperation, the three of them continued on their way, a little tremulous, fearful even, half expecting a visit from whatever passed for the law down here. That blast had gone some way to confirming the worst fears Soren had about the land they were now driving through. So those statistics about this region's general lawlessness were painfully true. Toshoba appeared to be setting a very formidable picture of what might be in store. And with this, there came a renewed acquaintance with doubt. That here indeed was the true dark heart of this country.

44

It wasn't until they came across Coulee's suburbs that the visitors felt confident enough again to ask for directions. Soren once again brought the car to a halt, this time alongside a middle-aged man cutting his roadside hedge. This time, deciding to dispense with Southern manners, Craig called out to him without bothering to get out of the car. The man had started up on first registering their presence. Now he stood there staring at the shattered back windscreen. In a high pitched and slightly intemperate voice, he asked if they'd had some trouble.

'You could say that,' replied Craig.

The man's facial muscles appeared to visibly tighten as his gaze settled upon Soren. It was hard not to conclude that the man's complaint might just be racial. His face remained expressionless as he continued in his study of the others.

'You from those parts?' He pointed to the car's Pennsylvania license plates.

'No, California.'

'What you here for?'

'I wonder if you could direct us to Hampton House? We're going to be doing some work at the institute they're planning up there.'

The man's demeanour changed, his lips quivering into a scowl. 'Can't say that I can.'

This was met with only a resigned shrug from Brad this time. Soren though, was beginning to show signs of irritation. 'So much for Southern hospitality,' he said, by way of conclusion.

'Don't you go knocking this here place, boy.'

The words and the delivery of the man's drawl was deliberate and contemptuous. 'The only place where true American values exist.'

For a brief moment there was silence, while the visitors considered the veracity of the man's argument. Brad took up the cudgels.

'Would you like to expand on that statement please?'

'History, boy; a history based on good Christian values.'

'You're proud of your history down here, are you?'

The man could feel himself being set up.

'Ah!' sighed Soren. 'Mr Sweeney amongst the nightingales.' The game was very much afoot.

'You outsiders always think you know best, meddling in things you don't understand.'

'Meddling? We're just here to do some work.'

'You're tearing this nation apart.'

'I would have thought that is something you secessionists have been doing for years,' interjected Craig. The man was clearly beginning to irritate him too.

'Don't you use that language with me, boy. If only we'd had somebody like Governor Wallace in the White House, then you'd have respect for the law!'

'Respect for the law! What do you people down here know about that? You were the first to start killing members of our armed forces, you have the nation's highest crime rate, and your elders in Washington have been telling you to desegregate your schools for years.'

'No commie judge is going to tell me to send my kids to school with nigras.'

'Now, really! Why did you have to go and lower the tone of the conversation like that? Honestly, have you ever come across a Supreme Court justice fully versed in the writings of Karl Marx? I thought you were a person of intellect.'

'Don't you go calling me one of those damned liberals!' he cried, his stance moving towards the pugilistic. His temper was not helped by Brad's rendering of the old battle hymn of the republic, *John Brown's Body*, much to the others' amusement. Soon, Craig and Soren were out of the

179

car, freewheeling, arm in arm, engaged in something they fancied to be a Scottish reel.

Glory, glory, hallelujah!
Glory, glory, hallelujah!
Glory, glory, hallelujah!
His soul goes marching on!

A young woman, probably the man's daughter, had now appeared. On noticing her, Soren and Craig stopped and bowed, as she enquired, in a rich Southern accent, what the problem was.

'Troublemakers, Bridget, troublemakers!'

The woman quickly deduced that the people before her were not from these parts and were probably deserving of better treatment than they were presently getting. There were apologies, as she quickly ushered the man towards the house. 'Come on, Pappy, this is no way to treat visitors.'

All watched as he somewhat reluctantly shuffled off in the direction of the house. Soren was quick to proffer his thanks.

'Oh, that's alright. Pappy's bark's much worse than his bite. You folks visiting?'

There were admiring, almost disbelieving, expressions, as she extended her hand. In response to Soren's gaze she looked nervously at the ground and danced from foot to foot, her manner just a little flirtatious.

'We're trying to get to Hampton House.'

A momentary look of anxiety crossed her face.

'Is that a problem?' he asked.

'For a few folks, maybe. Anyways, you're a bit out of your way. You've got to go through town and hang a right out towards the state line, up past Halton.'

'Well, thanks very much... and you are?'

'Bridget.' She gave a quick glance at the others and then back to Soren. 'You be sure to come over and visit, whenever you get the chance. Don't go taking what Pappy says to heart. He's really quite harmless.'

Soren looked apprehensively towards the house, smiled and shrugged. 'We just might,' he said.

45

Feeling more confident about their bearings, they continued on their way. The manicured lawns of suburbia gave way to the enclosed sidewalks and the white clapboard storefronts of the town centre. There was a proliferation of old glories and flags from the old confederacy. They turned left, as Bridget had told them, and were soon skirting the blighted district of 'Flashlight'. As they did so, they kept an eye out for any bar or eating establishment able to offer some refreshment; they were determined that the first such establishment they tried, here in the state of Mississippi, would be a black-owned one.

One was soon forthcoming, which they entered under the watchful gaze of a few bemused locals. They soon realised they'd made a mistake; the place was grubbily spartan and the smell of home-grown cooking noticeable by its absence. Had it been anywhere else, it would have been a place they would normally have avoided. Brad, of course, loved it, although his enthusiasm was not returned by any of the locals. He asked for three beers as a precursor to seeing what there was to eat.

'Sorry, no alcohol.' The barman replied warily.

Brad looked around at the other patrons, some of them furnished with glasses of beer. Soren waited for the explosion; thankfully it never came. Instead Brad asked if there was any food.

'I suppose I could do you some sandwiches.'

Brad took on board the spirit of the man's offer and declined. Instead, he ordered coffees, after which they drifted towards an empty table at the back of the room. An old woman, big and broad of beam, went around the room collecting glasses and wiping the tops of tables. She took one look at Soren, arched her eyebrows and, with a sniff of the nose, was gone. Soren continued to study the woman as she made her progress round the tables. She, and the men she moved amongst, content to continue in their conversation and card playing, were a closed book.

'Do you think anywhere down here will be able to fix that back windshield?' Soren was still somewhat fixated by the damage done to the car.

'Well, this is the home of NASCAR,' replied Craig, 'there's bound to be somewhere...' He stopped, aware that the others were now peering over his shoulder, at something that had quietened the bar. He turned around, to see an officer of the law walking towards them. Wearing sunglasses and looking ridiculously youthful, he pulled up a chair.

'You don't mind if I join you now, do you?' he said, drawing a fat stubby cigar from his breast pocket. The gaze of the visitors was interestedly bemused; were they about to witness something out of the Bull Connor handbook of policing, or one that was more akin to the Dukes of Hazard? Thankfully, it was the latter. Gazing around him, the deputy waved an arm and shouted across to the man behind the bar. 'Don't mind me, Earl. You folks carry on about your business.'

As the noise in the bar began to pick up again, the deputy turned his attention back to his guests. His awkwardness and slightly defensive smile, gave off a mixture of callowness and decency, and with this, as far as the professors were concerned, all the attempted pretence of mystery and awe dissipated. Here was a man-child whose cigar chomping now looked just a little foolish.

'Looking at your car back there, you appear to have had a little trouble!'

'Yes, Officer...'

'Deputy, sir, Deputy Cranston, but most folks round here just call me plain Cyrus. I hear you're looking to go to the Institute?'

They nodded. News seemed to travel fast around these parts.

'Real fine gentleman, Mr Doleson, if a little "out there", if you get my drift. Decent man, all the same. Anyways, when you've finished here, I'd be only too pleased to take you over there. Can't have you getting into any more trouble, can we!' The broken windshield, and the altercations they'd encountered were left unsaid. That he was so keen to help them on their way, was indicative of the fact that the deputy didn't want anything further untoward happening on his watch. The sheriff would be away for the next couple of days, fishing down on the Delta, and the idea of letting 'the boss' down was something Cyrus daren't contemplate. There was also the complication that came in the form of Mr Doleson. These people were most certainly his and he and the Sheriff were very close. So, until the Sheriff got back, Cyrus would have to keep a lid on things, even if that meant babysitting a bunch of big city liberal types a large number of the locals would rather see the back of. The Deputy got to his feet and, doffing his hat, told them to take their time; he'd be waiting outside to take them when they were ready.

On the way to the Institute, Cyrus took them through the district of Flashlight. It was only a glimpse, but the visitors were still shocked by what they saw. Soren counselled himself in the knowledge he had always known this kind of poverty existed, he'd even chaired a conference panel on the subject, but this had a rooted permanence to it. Flashlight, he fancied, was a place that most of the town's population, black or white, would strive to avoid. Most of the men appeared to be in various states of immobility and indolence, hanging around in small groups on street corners and in lean-tos, while kids played in the street, dodging the uncollected garbage. It was easy to see why such a place would give rise to mortality rates that would shame a third-world country. The roads were unpaved and what cars there were, were burnt-out shells. Sometimes, through the open car window, would come a pungent and stale smell, saturated with the stench of burning charcoal. The smoky haze intimated that anything eaten here would, by necessity, have to be slowly cooked over an open fire. Every now and then voices would be heard, raised voices, which died to silence as the visitors passed by. Had Cyrus been in the car with them, he would have told the visitors that here were the lowest of low, from which the good people of Toshoba needed to be protected. Where self-hatred, immorality and social depravity had left its mark, resulting in a litany of murders, rapes and beatings that would make your heart weep. Where the drug addled and the unhealthy, with their extremes of emaciation and obesity, would ensure lives were ended prematurely. All the visitors could see was an ugliness that bore the defective marks of cumulative self-loathing and the diminution of spirit. A spiral of squalor that ultimately went back to a suffering inflicted long ago, at the crack of a whip.

In the late 1970s a pastor's wife, Darlene Phillips, had gone into Flashlight with the aim of setting up a self-help group. She enlisted the support of some of her friends who, for a while, successfully drove Flashlight's pimps and abusers out of town. After time, though, the rest of Toshoba went back to thinking and talking about Flashlight as it had always done. As a warning that could all too easily befall them all.

46

At the Institute an expansive Doleson, half gentleman, half pitbull, greeted his visitors, whilst examining the damage done to the car, his face a picture of fascinated disbelief.

'I heard about what happened,' he said, twirling his moustache and stroking his chin. 'The Sheriff's been threatening to take Willard's shotgun away from him for years. Can't work out how's he never got round to it.'

It took no time at all to register that Doleson was a very driven man. He had an alert expectant expression and his speech had the cadence of a machine gun, constantly challenging and probing. His was a sustained monologue, with a teasing delivery, fast curved, always expecting a response, but scarcely leaving an opening for one. One could only imagine what a conversation between him and Pariche would be like.

'Cyrus took you through Flashlight, did he? Guess he had his reasons. Most folks think it got its name on account of not ever having any street lighting. Here, look at this!' He lifted up his shirt sleeve, to reveal a scar. 'Tripped and fell there some years back. I was probably drunk at the time.'

What he'd been doing there, his visitors could only guess. Soren speculated that he would probably have been up all hours, shooting the breeze with one of the locals, but, with Doleson, it could all so easily have been a woman. The call to go south had come from Doleson. He and Pariche went some way back together, mostly through their support for the NAACP. More recently there had been Doleson's plan to set up 'the Institute', something that had resulted in Soren and the others being here. They should have known better than to trust someone who, in the madness stakes, would give even Pariche a run for his money. Something of an oddity in these parts, Doleson was a social liberal with an evangelical gift for oratory, lazily delivered. The product of Vanderbilt, Doleson could easily strike the uninitiated as being just a little deranged. Looking much like a lofty version of Groucho Marx, with the wit to match, he could cuss and swear with the best of them, yet still manage to convey the stately bearing that one usually associates with southern aristocracy. A family sense of *noblesse oblige* had ensured that Doleson had felt the need to find a 'calling', but the role of squire, especially in a backwater like Mississippi, would have been far too constraining, and a life in the church too hilarious to contemplate. There had been talk of a career in the military, but, in the end, the study of agriculture and land management had won out, with the unintended consequence of Doleson developing a lifelong interest in education and rural poverty.

Some people observed a dereliction about Doleson, a quality that invariably led to confrontation and disaster. Where the locals might find an amiable eccentricity, numerous employers and prospective funding agencies found conflict, irascibility, and inevitable complaint. At 'Old Miss', just down the road in Oxford, Doleson had form. There were tales of wheeling and dealing that often sailed close to the legal wind, or whatever counted for that in the state of Mississippi, along with bouts of illicit drinking and the odd night spent in jail. There had also been numerous liaisons, including a very public one with a local black woman. Nothing much had been made of it though, with most accepting that it was 'just Doleson being Doleson!' Of course, there were a few people, mainly of the hooded variety, who didn't go along with this somewhat quaint interpretation. Family money meant that Doleson was in a position to pursue his own demons with scant regard for the opinions of others. This, along with his championing of improved race relations, hardly endeared himself to some of the more extreme representatives of the community. That he hadn't been on the receiving end of a beating or worse, was down to a certain amount of luck; not least the enduring friendship he had with Toshoba's chief law enforcement officer, a certain Sheriff Harper.

The Sheriff had been promoted, from the rank of deputy, some twenty years ago, by a county board that had become increasingly exasperated by the lazy corruption of his predecessor, Hollis White. The final straw had been when an innocent man had been set up for a series of child sex crimes. Usually this would have been par for the course in this neck of the woods, excepting that the perpetrator had struck again and had been shown to be none other than one of the Sheriff's own hunting partners. He'd even been let in on the frame-up, so that all along he'd been privy to information that had allowed him to keep one step ahead of the investigation. To add insult to injury, both he and Hollis White had been skimming funds from the County Tax Office, where the abuser had been employed.

So Harper, newly installed as Sheriff for the county, and with the help of Doleson and a largely sympathetic council, had set about refashioning the county's image. The Klan soon all but disappeared, with its membership down to a few 'race-hate perverts and losers,' as Doleson liked to call them; people who were now just as likely to pop up on cross filings the FBI had on the various neo-Nazi and survivalist groups operating across the country. Under Sheriff Harper's stewardship, the Jim Crow ugliness had gone. No longer were there signs that said that if you were coloured or negro, you'd better be prepared at some stage to beg and crawl. This did not mean that the county's white population had suddenly become wonderfully enlightened. They might not have liked the Klan, but that didn't mean that they were about to extend a hand across the colour divide either. Toshoba still had its own White Citizens' Council and many still held views and sentiments that harked back to the era of segregation.

As far as Soren knew, Doleson had neither brothers nor sisters and had never married. That last detail was the one thing all locals did agree was a blemish; something that wasn't helped by the string of mistresses and girlfriends that Doleson seemed happy to parade around. The last time

Soren had met him, Doleson had been complaining about a woman who'd been bombarding him with demands for maintenance payments for her daughter's child.

Doleson continued in his scatter-gun like cadence. He was grandstanding now, his chest protruding proudly and his eyes enthused. Didn't they realise that this was where they were going to build a new Athens? Where they could revel in the coming together of like minds, all in the pursuit of excellence. With over twenty rooms, the mansion, and the grounds in which it stood, would be ideally suited for such a venture. Pride of place would be the library, a truly sumptuous collection that ran to over thirty thousand volumes. It had been started by a distant relative who'd been 'bequeathed' the bulk of the works from a family whose heir had run up gambling debts. Doleson's upbringing had been one of almost total immersion in its contents. Besides being the local chronicler of Toshoba County history, he'd amassed all of the classics, on European art and literature, and almost everything written on the subject of poverty, from the Webbs and Frederick Engels, through to W.E.B Du Bois and yes, a certain Patrick P. Moynihan.

'And the old ballroom's already earmarked for a couple of classrooms,' he said, showing them around the rest of the house. 'Some of those rooms across the way, the old staff quarters; they can be made into seminar-study rooms. We've also plans for a theatre.' Ah, yes, just like Pariche, Doleson had a predilection for actors and the theatre. He led them into a large, sparse and rather antiquated kitchen, where some food had been prepared. 'Help yourself,' he said, 'bring it out onto the veranda.' With food gratefully gathered, they were soon outside again, gazing up at a darkening sky. 'This is an opportunity to make a real contribution,' he continued. 'Already Vanderbilt and Memphis have promised a couple of graduates and student interns; they should be able to help with some of the grunt work over the spring break.'

Doleson had obviously given things a great deal of thought. In this very much downscale Chautauqua Institution, students and fellows would do research and produce works that would fancifully become items of national record. At the same time, in the wooded grounds in which the Institute stood, beneath the old hickory and pine trees, the local kids would enjoy summer science camps whilst, out in the community, others would be collecting audio and video histories, modelled on those carried out by Studs Terkel up in Chicago. They would even try to get some of the old bigots on board; get them to open up and admit to the error of their ways. It would be Toshoba's own take on those reconciliation committees people had been going on about in the media. As he continued, there were also repeated and pained remonstrations on his part about the outrage he felt about the greeting his visitors had received on their arrival.

From Doleson's viewpoint, Toshoba County was a decent enough place, now awakening to the idea that it was about to lose its battle with the seemingly irresistible march of Memphis's urban sprawl. Being close to the state border, there was a real ambivalence about how the locals identified themselves. To the west of the county the land was mostly flatland, sloping down gently into Clancy and the Mississippi River, where it was prone to flooding. To the east and to the north, there was mainly farmland and wooded countryside, beyond which was forested hill country. At Toshoba's heart lay the county town of Coulee. With just over five thousand souls, it was a place where Doleson still appeared to command respect; in both communities, black and white.

When not entertaining up at the house, Doleson was more likely to be seen out and about, glad handing and talking to folks face to face. He was never happier than when he was at the farmers' market every Thursday morning pressing the flesh and talking the talk with the small business owners and farmers who'd come into town to do business. The market in Coulee was more accepting than most other parts of the Deep South. Long gone were the days when dealers had been allowed to rig the market with a crooked and unfair black sharecropper price. Now, on each weekend, the townsfolk would rub shoulders with workers from the county's only paper mill, along with the growing numbers employed at the newly opened GM engine plant just across the border in Tennessee. As Doleson repeatedly said, the place wasn't up to much, but then again, people tended to like it that way. This rather upbeat rendition was met with hardly suppressed wariness from the visitors; after all, they *had* just had the back windshield of their car shot out.

'Honestly,' pleaded Doleson, 'I wouldn't have invited you down if I'd thought there'd be trouble!'

But hadn't it been the case, countered Soren, that for the last forty years the district has been represented in Congress by that arch segregationist, Jamie Whitten?

Doleson was having none of it. 'A few months ago, Congressman Witten was sat just where you're sitting right now. Much of what he did and said those years ago he's long done apologised for. Hell, he's even got black staffers and is still, if my memory serves me correct, a registered Democrat.'

Soren was not content to back down.

'Whitten might have been civilized by his tenure in Washington, but what about his constituents?'

Doleson leant across and gave his knee a squeeze. 'Of course you're right. We in the South haven't always acquitted ourselves well. The whole business is a running sore and a shame on us all. Hell, I couldn't even guarantee that you'd get a fair shake in one of the bars or restaurants up on Main. But things have changed. Jim Crow was still alive and well in these parts well up to fifteen or so years ago.'

'And what about now?' asked Brad. 'What's the black experience today? What kind of voice do they have?'

'Well, there's Garv; Garvey Horsemead. He has a law practice over on Tucker. He might just go and get himself elected the town's first black councilman anytime soon. You'll be meeting him tomorrow. But no, you're right, the council have the place carved up so as to make sure that the black vote doesn't get as much as a piss in the breeze when it comes to representation. One third of the town's population is black and they still don't have a black councilman.'

'And what about the schools?' asked Craig. 'Are we still dealing with a segregated system.'

'Well not exactly,' Doleson replied. 'Most of the kids go to Toshoba County High, which is both integrated and keen to get on board. The Cedars, is all white and private; that will be a much different proposition. A large number of the kids who go there have parents fleeing Clancy, the mainly black county to the west of here.'

'So there's still some way to go?'

'Well, I never said it was going to be easy!'

47

Next morning, memories of the previous night were rendered somewhat indistinct by the haziness of drink-fueled hangovers. Leaving Doleson behind, who had a certain vexatious ex-partner to placate, the visitors set out to obtain provisions and take in the town. Brad, who'd drunk more than the others, still felt the need to sleep things off. So, whilst Soren and Craig discovered the relative delights of the local Winn-Dixie, he stayed put, asleep in the car. The store they entered was just like any other, with the same slightly down-at-heel clientele, bored staff, and wall to wall formica. Some of the locals did look at them a little quizzically, but, in the main, they were no big deal and their mission to purchase supplies was expedited relatively painlessly.

They returned to the car to find Brad still somewhat comatose, a condition to which, after a perfunctory acknowledgement of their presence, he returned. Soon they were back on the road. After a while Craig's attention was drawn to something moving in one of the car's side pockets, against which Brad was resting. A cold sweat began to form as he realised what it was; the up-reared head of a snake. Already it was beginning to pour onto Brad's lap. Soren noticed the alarm on Craig's face and immediately registered its cause. In a purely academic sense, what he could see was a beautiful example of an Eastern Diamondback. Olive green in colour, it had obviously been jolted into life by the car's movement. After a while it came to a rest, in a bulbous bundle, still on Brad's lap. Without further ado Soren brought the car gently to a halt and, very slowly, he and Craig got out.

'What the hell can we do?' asked Soren. 'We can't risk waking him!'

Craig raised a finger. The Montanan in him now appeared to assert control. 'I've an idea.' Slowly he reached into the car's front glove pocket, from which he retrieved a couple of Brad's cigars. He handed one to Soren and they both lit up, blowing the smoke into one of the open windows. The effect on the snake was almost immediate. It appeared to sense from where the threat was coming, and began to slither in the opposite direction, towards the shattered windscreen. Its progress was steady, but then, just as all appeared to be going well, a stir from Brad seemed to alarm it. Instinctively the snake raised its head, ready to strike. Just as instinctively, a now fully awake Brad struck out with his left hand, hitting the reptile on the side of its head with a blow of such ferocity that it sent the reptile flying out of the car. There was now a feeling of ecstatic relief, as Brad staggered from the car while the others watched the snake disappear into the underbrush. Their relief was short lived, though, as Brad soon began to complain about a numbing ache in the hand he'd used to strike the snake. On closer examination there could be seen a bloodied puncture mark.

'Jesus,' cried Soren, 'we're going to have to get you to a hospital.' In desperation they looked around for someone to ask directions. They were in luck as one, a middle-aged woman, was soon forthcoming.

'Snakebite! Can you help? Our friend's been bitten by a rattlesnake!'

The woman looked Brad up and down. 'Canst say that he looks too good,' she said, concerned. 'You'll need to be getting over to McClaren.' Without further ado, she got into the car and took her place up front with Soren, whilst Craig did his best to console Brad.

'Now remember,' he said, 'the answer is to relax. Just pretend it's something like a bad trip.' He was worried, though. Brad was looking increasingly sick and appeared to be entering a state of stupefied trauma, a lone figure of moist sweaty calm being driven at high speed through unfamiliar streets. Now he was beginning to shiver and his gaze had become fixated. His arm was now swollen and he was having trouble breathing.

At the hospital, the on-call medic, a short stubby figure of a man, soon had the situation under control; they were obviously used to this kind of occurrence here. His authoritative command did wonders for the visitors' moral, although he did show some concern that no attempt had been made to clean the wound immediately after the incident. A quick blood sample indicated that the dose had been big, but the doctor was intent on playing down the risks. He obviously wanted everybody calm.

'The danger posed would usually be quite minimal,' he told them, 'but there are complications. The readings indicate much more tissue damage than we would normally expect.' It was at this point that Soren felt it might be pertinent to mention Brad's cocaine habit. He watched as the doctor's countenance turned from one of concern to one that was unmistakably grave.

48

'Basil, why does shit always happen when you're around?'
The sheriff was standing with Doleson and Cyrus before a
pathologist's slab upon which lay a half-covered corpse. The
sheriff found himself distractedly tugging at the shroud, as
he attempted to make sense of what he was seeing. Had the
whole debacle been some monstrous trick of the mind?
Eventually though, reality did begin to kick in. 'This one just
has to be one of yours!'

The Sheriff's words, directed at Doleson, were more a
resigned statement of fact, rather than anything more
pointed. When Cyrus had got the call from the hospital just
twenty-four hours ago, he'd instructed some of the locals to
hunt the sheriff down and get him back from his fishing trip
with all due speed. He'd also given Doleson a call. Now the
three of them stood side by side, immobile and momentarily
silenced. The Sheriff shot his friend another weary look of
disbelief. In their long collaboration they'd never come
across anything like this. Whatever the motives for this
young man coming down to Mississippi, it was surely over
now. The Sheriff continued to shake his head in disbelief.
Yet again Doleson had given him another mess to clear up
and, as always, Doleson was mortified.

'Now come on, Harold. Do you really think I would have
given the go ahead if I'd known?'

The Sheriff smiled and said nothing. Doleson had
managed to shock and amaze in many ways and the Sheriff
had always known that this Institute the fool was planning,
would be yet another headache he would have to deal with;
but this could not have been predicted. A visitor from out of
state, and a physician from one of the nation's top hospitals

to boot, had most likely been murdered. Such an event would have every state and federal agency crawling from out of the woodwork.

As he surveyed the scene, the sheriff knew that he and the 'Queen' would soon have a lot of explaining to do. The sobriquet 'Queen' had been bestowed upon Doleson more in recognition of his regal bearing than any regard to his sexuality. Although both men were mirror opposites physically, they shared a mannered and easygoing charm, arising from a familiar and contented involvement with the locality and its affairs. Harper was small, rotund and hound-dog gruff, whereas Doleson was very much Southern aristocracy personified; tall and lean and with a countenance that was affected and slightly camp. The two men had history, with the newly installed Sheriff very much reliant upon the support his friend had been able to give when the county's schools had been ordered to de-segregate in the early seventies. Doleson in turn had been grateful for the assistance he'd been given by the sheriff in the face of his many social and legal transgressions. That the 'Queen' had liberal tendencies had not been too much of a concern for a man who'd always thought it better to keep a semblance of civility in the way the county was policed, being only too aware of the problems that could arise from giving too much sway to the more extreme elements in their midst. Counties and parishes that had gone down that route, with their shootings, whippings and hangings, had all ended up having to deal with the filth that inevitably rose to the surface along with it.

'God awful business, Harold, God awful.' Doleson was uncharacteristically subdued. 'If there's anything I can do!'

The sheriff nodded. He knew that over the coming days and weeks he would be making good on that call. He turned again to his deputy.

'Cyrus, what happened? I only left you in charge for a couple of days.'

'Well, sir...' For a moment the deputy's expression was one of horror, like a deer caught in a car's headlights, before registering the wink Doleson and the sheriff shared with each other. The last thing Sheriff Harper was going to do was lay this at the feet of one of his own. Cyrus composed himself and continued; 'Well, Sheriff, as you can see, he's been shot. Shot and poisoned that is.' The sheriff tempered his look of incredulity and nodded for him to carry on. 'Couldn't believe it myself at first,' the deputy said, mirroring the sheriff's look of surprise. 'The deceased was already in hospital with snakebite when he was shot. We're still not sure when all this happened. We'll get a better idea when Sam gets here.'

'Has the room over at McClaren been sealed off?' His deputy's expression of rueful forgetfulness quickly turned again to one of fear. 'Oh hell, Cyrus, the place is supposed to be a crime scene.'

'I'll get onto it straight away.' The deputy moved to make his exit. He was stopped by the sheriff motioning towards a man who'd just entered the room. The man acknowledged the sheriff's presence with a perfunctory nod, before leaving again to take a seat in an adjacent waiting area.

'A friend of the deceased,' the deputy said. 'Not from these parts. Haven't had time to question him much. And there is this...'

'OK, Cyrus,' said the sheriff, cutting him off, 'leave this with me. Let's look as if we know what we're doing.'

The sheriff followed the man out and walked over to where he was sitting. He immediately surmised that the stranger was big city, not from these parts. Before he could say anything though, he was stopped by Doleson, who now pointed towards something or someone standing behind him. The sheriff turned to set eyes upon a woman carrying a tray of refreshments. With her was a squat, but distinguished looking gentleman, florid faced, with jowls as pronounced as a bulldog's.

'I trust it's OK if we have these?' The woman's voice was assertive, with a soft, almost lyrical, quality to it. She handed one of the coffees to the stranger, before offering the sheriff her hand.

'Let me introduce you to Miss Christina,' Doleson said, taking over formalities, 'she's come all the way from New England.'

They shook hands. The sheriff could see she was a woman of real elegance and sophistication, of a worldly kind you didn't come across too often in Toshoba County. He noticed her narrow mouth and slender neck. He could also see that she needed feeding up, something that definitely could not be said of the gentleman with her, who Doleson now introduced as a Mr Dyson. Dressed in tweeds, bow tied and cloth capped, he looked for all the world as if he'd just stepped out of a production of Toad of Toad Hall.

'Yes, Senator Christina Karlsson,' the woman said, peering down at the Sheriff. 'I sit in the state legislature, up in Massachusetts.' She was in full professional mode, punching her weight, knowing how to make just the right impression. 'Mr Dyson is here as a friend. He represents Dyson, Freeman and Palme. He used to be with the Justice Department.

The sheriff's expression appeared to be one of genuine interest and admiration, but Christina could also detect a feint wariness, suggestive of someone who might be a good poker player. She smiled and offered him her drink. As always, she had an expression that, with her eyebrows slightly arched, hovered between one of benign interest and disgust. It was a ploy that appeared to be playing well here, just as it did with the folks back home in Boston, where people very much appreciated the idea of having State Senator Christina Karlsson scowl in their best interests. As for the sheriff; all he could see was someone capable of causing a lot of mischief.

Doleson appeared to be getting enjoyment from his friend's discomfort, as he watched him struggling with the hand he'd been given. Initially the Sheriff had been the epitome of calm collectedness, but his retreat into a more mannered rectitude revealed someone who was beginning to struggle. Already events seemed to be overwhelming him. He'd been given a dead body and two Yankee interlopers to deal with; one an ornery, and potentially meddlesome, politician and the other a lawyer who'd once been with the US Justice Department. Both were things that most white Southerners loathed with a passion.

The Sheriff could feel the heat of their scrutiny; a struggling small-time law officer in a hick town, out his depth. He wasn't far wrong, although Dyson's take on the proceedings was more charitable than Christina's. He'd seen it all before; not here, in Mississippi, but across the way in Georgia. He had a certain understanding of what the folks down here might be going through and had immediately concluded that Doleson and the Sheriff were decent people. As a Lincoln Republican, Dyson had fought the good fight in the 1960s for civil rights. Then he had railed against the inequity of it all, where a few white politicians, at the heart of the old Democratic Party machine, could maintain their power by disenfranchising an entire people. He was certain that the men he was talking to now were no part of that. He knew this because Dyson was the kind of person who loved to do his homework; someone who had, in the past, had constitutional and backwoods lawyers, deep in the heart of Georgia, flummoxed about their own state's constitution. No detail was too small to be perused and tallied as a guide for future actions. And to this end, Dyson had researched the town of Coulee and the county in which it sat. And he knew that the folks here, next Tuesday, would cast their votes overwhelmingly for George Herbert Walker Bush, just like the rest of the South. He often thought about the irony of it all: how the party of Abraham Lincoln, the one that he'd grown up with in Massachusetts, had become the party of Southern evangelicals, Dixiecrats and erstwhile segregationists. Some of these sentiments had been playing on the sheriff's mind too. He remembered how, eight years ago, Ronald Reagan had kicked off his presidential campaign downstate, not far from where those three civil rights workers had been murdered in 1963. The message was obvious: at last they had someone in the White House who was one of their own. When those kids had died the FBI had been all over the place like a rash, but not now. All he ever got now was an enquiring phone call from one of the regional offices in Jackson or Memphis, regarding reports about accidents to out-of-staters and a wish to be kept informed. Yes, all dark suits and sunglasses, and the odd courtesy call.

But with this murder, the sheriff sensed that all of this was about to change. He would have to inform the state and federal authorities as to what had happened and he would have to fight damnably hard to make sure he had a say in how they went about their business. He knew he needed their help, as well as the assistance he could get from the state police down in Jackson, but, more than anything, he wanted to make sure that his department was seen as being competent. But, boy, did he need help. He needed help, period! Presently, though, Sheriff Harper was concerned with moving to a more congenial setting. 'Good to see you have refreshments,' he said, as he began to steer them away from the corridor and into the pathologist's office. 'As you can appreciate ma'am, we need to allow the folks here to get on with their work. The pathologist will be here soon. Would you and...' He gave his deputy a pleading glance.

'Professor Ginnsberg, Sir.'

'Would you and the professor and, of course, you, Mr Dyson, would you like to come along with me? I've a few questions I'd like to ask. Cyrus, would you please get on to that thing we discussed earlier, you know, about the hospital?'

In the pathologist's office the sheriff solicitously drew up some chairs and Dyson informed them of the senator's wishes.

'We're not here to make an already difficult position any worse, Sheriff; the senator is here to take the deceased home.'

Sheriff Harper looked back towards the corridor. 'I'm sorry, ma'am, but was that your boy?'

'No, thank God,' said Christina hesitantly, her face turning to one of distracted agitation as she sought to reproach herself for expressing relief at the fact.

Dyson helped her out. 'The deceased's name is Brad Hemlin.'

'Yes,' said Christina, taking over, 'my son is still freshening himself up in the washroom.' She shot Dyson a look of gratitude. She was beginning to struggle. 'He and Brad were very close. His family have asked me to bring him home.'

'Yes, and they will want to be kept informed,' added Dyson, perhaps a little unnecessarily.

'Wouldn't have it any other way,' replied the sheriff. 'I'd like to give them a call as soon as possible.'

'That would be most appreciated.'

The sheriff turned to Craig;

'I hear you and the deceased came down together. Do you feel up to telling us about what you remember? What happened when you first hit these parts? Anything that might help in clearing up this dreadful business.'

Craig was wary at first, his tone tentative, but some of the old confidence did begin to return as he went on. Later, they were joined by a visibly shaken Soren, his entrance met with a smiling nod of acknowledgment from the sheriff, followed by a warm handshake. Christina made a mental note; something more to admire about the man. When the pathologist arrived to reclaim his office, the sheriff called proceedings to a halt. Before Christina acceded to his wished though, she ventured the suggestion that, if he so wished, she could get someone down to assist him with his investigations. He smiled. 'That won't be necessary, ma'am. We can handle it ourselves. Believe me, we will get to the bottom of this.'

Christina wasn't buying any of it. She and Dyson would let them go through the motions, and they would respect a little of the protocol, but then they would be back. It was a sentiment that appeared to be shared by Doleson, who, once they were outside, took his friend aside.

'You don't fool me, Harold.'

The sheriff shrugged. He had a wintery, almost tearful, expression. 'Jesus, Basil, I thought we were beyond all this.'

'C'mon, Harold, you'll get whoever did this!'

'That's not the point, Basil, you know it!'

'It's the only thing we can do, Harold. Pick ourselves up and get on with clearing this mess up. And don't be too quick to ditch what the senator was offering. We could do with all the help we can get. Besides, it's not going to cost us anything.'

'I know, Basil, I know,' the sheriff replied, cursing the situation he found himself in. Doleson gave his friend another hard look, before squinting into the early morning sun.

'Yes, we could all do with a little help,' he ventured in an almost oratorical tone of voice, as if he were summoning them all to prayer. The sheriff could see, by the glint in Doleson's eye, that the old coot was planning something. And indeed he was. His blessed Institute trumped all. If the sheriff had known how his plans would involve the visit of yet another outsider – someone well known for his cantankerous and meddlesome ways – then he might have been even less sanguine about the way things were moving.

Afterwards, Doleson caught up with Christina and the others as they got into their car. Now out of earshot of his friend, he counselled her to go ahead and give this person a call. The sheriff was a stubborn old fool but he'd soon come round.

For much of the journey back to the Institute, they sat in silence, save for Doleson's oft repeated – hardly audible – mumblings of regret. Christina found herself studying this strange exotic relic of man, noting again the number of times he attempted to apologise and reassure. All impotence, she thought, masquerading as good manners. Oddly enough, though, it was something that did indeed reassure.

49

When Christina first heard of Brad's death she panicked and caught the first plane out of Boston's Logan Airport. This was not like her. Usually she was the picture of calm calculated rationality, taking in all the angles in order to determine her next move. But this had been different. She'd been spooked by her run-in with Constanze, so when the call from Mississippi came, there had been an overwhelming urge to be with her son. She'd even thought of doing her best to get him to come home, even if this meant he'd be a thousand miles nearer to Constanze's baleful gaze.

More crucially, she'd made a tearful phone call to Pariche, whose influence she wanted to harness in her attempts to get Soren home for good. The call changed everything. Pariche listened sympathetically, with contriteness of heart and the best of bedside manners, but he was having none of it. He had a tendency to see Soren as a trainer might his prize fighter and it was quite obvious that in this case he wanted his champion back. The Soren he knew was someone who'd echoed the older man's uncertainties and misgivings, but was also possessed of a mind that could usually be relied upon to make the correct call and see things through. Now Pariche was fearful that there might be a chastened aspect to this quality; one that would be capable of raising all manner of obstacles to the continuance of the voyage. He needed Christina's assistance in stopping the rot before it was too late.

'We all have our duties to perform, girl, and yours is to stand by your son.' Of course Christina had attempted to resist, but it had been useless. Pariche had been like a force of nature. 'Get on down there,' he thundered in a manner that made her jump. 'Go and be with your boy. I've seen you in action, girl. In front of those clowns at the committee you've been chairing. You were a tower of strength. A woman who knows how to get things done. This is no time to go wimp. I know the folks down there, Christina, they're decent folks. But they need licking into shape. And, whilst you're about it, why don't you get Soren's friend, you know, the lady detective, to do some poking around down there too?'

And deep down she knew that he was right. Correct to snap her out of her stupor. The most important thing in her life was her son. So, as she drove back to the Institute with the others, her thoughts harked back to that call from Pariche. How she'd been surprised by his sensitivity and how he'd gone some way in drawing her out of her Nordic reticence. They had talked for a long time about the Constanze investigation and also the situation she found herself in at work. How Diane, one of her young investigators, had been on the receiving end of threats from one Constanze's goons, forcing her to call in sick. And how Christina herself had been neglecting her own work at the law partnership; how she'd taken her eye off the ball. Worries about her son's safety and the grueling hours she'd put in as chair of the Commonwealth hearings, had all gone some way in distracting her from the job she was supposed to be doing as a senior partner of a very busy law firm. Some of her colleagues had made their move. It was innocent enough; a feasibility study about joining forces with another outfit, the better to bid for some of the contracts that would be coming up, preparing for the land acquisitions needed for Boston's Big Dig. But then the proceedings had somehow taken a left turn, with a vote to formalise the deal.

'C'mon, Christina!' one of them had said. 'You should have seen that coming. Some of the partners have been angling for this for years. They want more clout with New York.' Christina knew the 'boys in New York', as everyone in the office called them, were playing a much bigger and bolder game. They were out to consolidate and grow, chasing the big bad world of mergers and acquisitions and leveraged buyouts. Where Christina had sensed danger, they saw big profits and the prelude to a feeding frenzy. And with the proposed merger, the firm would be facing a major reorganisation. New York would have marked Christina as being very much out of it, out of her depth. The Christina of old wouldn't have let this happen. She would have got word to them and made sure that she herself was in on the deal. And she would never had opened herself up to the attacks that were now being made, *sotto vocco*, about poor earnings and loss of profits. How had this been allowed to happen? Healthy margins had always been her mantra. But then she'd started playing to the wrong crowd. She'd allowed the investigation and her love of the public stage to get the better of her. Now some of her old allies felt embarrassed and short changed. Just who was in charge up there in Boston? It certainly wasn't Christina Karlsson. She'd well and truly been left out of the loop; exposed as someone who wasn't pulling her weight. She smiled at the irony of it all. Just over twenty years ago she'd done the same thing when she'd shaken up the cosy little world of her predecessors. Now it was her time to feel the effects of the wheel turning, the subtle shift of the ground under her feet, shaking up a world that had become too predictable and cosy. If Albert Constanze had known, he would have no doubt have raised a glass, pleased that his actions had added to her distress.

As she rode with the others back to the Institute, Christina could feel the initial shock and fear that she'd felt on hearing of Brad's death, slipping away, to be replaced by the need for answers. What was more, she was resolved to act on Pariche's last injunction and get Ginny down here as quickly as possible, if only to keep tabs on what the various policing agencies would be up to after Christina had returned to Boston. So, for the moment, there was no inner voice of panic telling her to get the hell out as quickly as possible. There were dangers of course, and as the scenery rolled by, she thought about some of them, real and imagined. Part of the problem was personified by the man sitting next to her. Notwithstanding the warning Pariche have given her, about the roving eye and wandering hands, there was something about Doleson that only reinforced the worries she had about the South. He and the Sheriff were part of a landscape where half of the population appeared to be in a state of denial, as if they were inhabitants of some disconnected and dysfunctional charm school. Now she was here, she could see for herself that this was only partially the case. She thought about the meeting she'd just had and how the civility and courteous manner of her hosts had carried with it a calm dignity and hurt. It revealed itself as both decent and real, conveying the undeniable fact that here were people who appeared to be just as shocked and troubled by the events as she was. Had she and rest of America been wrong about the South? That a whole country – another country – was being judged by the actions of an unrepresentative few. But then she thought again. Hadn't it always been the way of things down here: thuggery and violence, gloved in the veneer of politeness and good manners?

Christina allowed Doleson time, then with the assistance of Dyson, she began a gentle, but deliberate, debrief. The questioning soon coursed into a plan of action. She would keep to herself the more substantial concerns she had regarding her son. Both he and Craig still appeared to be in various states of shock. They would be of little use in considering what needed to be done. And the loss of Brad would have hit her son especially hard. So Christina had resolved to take him back north as soon as possible. Meanwhile, she would wait for what she knew would be coming; the dissolution of her son's resolve. Later that evening, Christina went to investigate his whereabouts, after he'd gone missing for over an hour. She eventually found him in the shower, head bowed, drenched to the skin and still fully clothed. The process had begun.

50

Berkeley, California

At ten a.m., the day of Soren's flight to Memphis, Pariche and Denis Tsui began preparations for the departmental meeting Wilson had called. Their first call was on Eddie Richards over at Sociology, Berkeley's resident expert on all issues to do with race. He could be relied upon to offer good counsel and advice regarding their little 'local difficulty'; if he was so minded. Pariche knew that any meeting with his old friend and sparring partner could be a daunting experience, so, on the way over, he took Denis through the do's and don'ts, whilst at the same time doing his best to reassure. Most importantly Tsui was to let the old bruisers go through their initial shadow-dance. 'By all means chip in whenever you feel the need, but remember, this has to be serenade.'

Pariche and Richards had known each other a long time, ever since the days when Pariche had been the lone voice raised in support of the latter's application for tenure. The friendship – if that was not stretching it a little too far – had been a strained one, not least over Pariche's desire to fight issues that would have his liberal colleagues running for the hills. The rumpus over that doctoral student had been a case in point, with Richards at one stage accusing Pariche of doing his utmost to help further the survivalist cause. But things had eventually blown over and now Pariche was back, asking for his friend's help in the coming battle.

A negative appraisal from Richards would pose a real obstacle for them both. Richards had celebrity status here, where he'd gained a reputation as a wonderfully prescient writer and commentator on sports and contemporary culture, treating them as if they were his alone to frame. He'd also managed to soar above much of the sordidness that passed for political infighting and intrigue at Berkeley. It only seemed to enhance the esteem in which he was held, and Wilson, for one, knew better than to take him on. Richards's roots within the black and sporting community ran deep, and his adroitness in using the media was legendary. One could always count on the national press making a beeline to his door, following whatever happened to be the latest outrage the country had to offer in the field of race relations. He also had a direct line to the Chancellor's office.

Richards was an imposing figure, something that suited the grandeur of the office that Pariche and Denis now entered. He was tall, shaven headed, and wearing a tracksuit that looked as if it had never been used in anger. The two older men greeted each other with an assortment of rigorous handshakes, backslaps and mutual ribbing.

'Sorry if I sound a little hyper,' Richards said, in a tone that was anything but, 'I've just come from doing battle with some of the deconstructionists over in Wheeler. They seem to think watching Kevin McHale on the box is just as "real" as watching him in person. They really appear to believe that shit!' There were knowing chortles, before Richards's tone turned decisively cooler. He was now looking at Denis, who remained standing on the fringes.

'Ah,' said Pariche, picking up on his cue, 'let me introduce Dr Tsui.' He beckoned the young man forward to receive a decidedly cautious handshake. It wasn't anything personal, Richards was like this with everyone; especially if he thought he was being 'played', as he most definitely was, this time, by Pariche.

'Yes, Charles has been in touch,' Richards said, in a haltingly slow drawl that threatened at times to come to a premature stop.

'Wilson been getting at you already, Eddie?'

'What do you expect, Jed? This is a sensitive matter. He's invited me along to a meeting later today.'

'Is that the one we're going to?'

'No, he's lined me up for something later. I don't know what you've been getting up to, Jed, but you sure appear to have a way of pissing people off!' Richards's pretence at ignorance was just a little disingenuous. Indeed, as he continued, it became increasingly clear that he had a sneaking admiration for what Wilson had got himself into. The (acting) dean actually appeared to be getting his hands dirty at last. Going into areas that were a world away from his usual haunts in and around the echelons of power.

'Well,' said Pariche, finally broaching the subject, 'we're a little apprehensive as to what Wilson is trying to do to the Diaspora Program. You do know that Soren Karlsson's away this year?'

'Yes, I heard. I sense an ongoing process of rediscovery! At least he doesn't appear to be helping out another set of white folks, like those Czech dudes he seems to be so keen on at present.' His last point was reference to the support Soren had been giving to Vaclav Havel's Charter 77 group.

'Well, be that as it may,' Pariche was becoming just a little irritated by his friend's evasiveness, 'what it means is that I've taken over the running of the Program. In that capacity I fully intend to keep Denis on. He will be doing most of the instruction.'

'I see.' Richards laughed and cupped his hands to his chin. He then pointed his two forefingers at the young man before him. 'And I suppose Flaxel's objection is to...' They both nodded. 'Then there's not much I can do. I'm surprised Soren left you in this position.'

'What, you're not going to do anything?' Pariche's tone was one of disbelief.

'Don't come that with me, Jed. This is the wrong time to be fixing to have a fight. I wish I could help, but Wilson does have a hell of a lot of reach.'

'Look here, Eddie, you remember when you were just starting out...' Pariche paused as he noted Richards's expression harden.

'Please don't lay this particular one on me, Jed. You're the one who's playing politics!'

'Hell, Eddie, this isn't like you. We didn't come over here to ask you to fight our battles. We just want a fair shake, along with some advice as to how to deal with this. We need to be protecting the likes of Denis here. Doing the right thing. Surely you're *not* saying that Denis shouldn't be teaching?'

'No, I'm not saying that.'

'Then what are you saying, Eddie?'

Richards looked up and at last gave Denis his full attention.

'Do you really think you can teach black history?'

'It's not just black history, Sir,' Denis replied, calmly and forcibly. 'The issue is about race and diaspora. Surely no one group has a monopoly on that!'

Richards let out a laugh at his directness and Pariche swore that he detected just the semblance of a wink.

'Please do drop the "Sir",' Richards said, feigning embarrassment. He shot a quick glance towards Pariche who was also laughing, before returning his attention back to Denis. 'Do you think you can handle what they're going to throw at you? Do you know what it's like to have your vitals squeezed inside a vice?'

'I trust it won't come to that.'

'Trust!' Richards guffaw was loud and raucous. 'Don't get me wrong, Denis, I do wish you well, but they're going to come at you from all angles.'

'They already have,' he replied.

'Yes,' joined in Pariche, 'don't worry on that score. I can testify to the fact that this young man really has what it takes. He's not easily put off.'

Richards looked at his watch and rose to his feet, signalling that the meeting had come to an end. 'Then be prepared,' he said, as he showed them the door. 'We had a run-in with some of Flaxel's friends some time ago, out in Richmond. The whole thing had to be abandoned.'

'Then why are you going with this, Eddie?'

'I'm not,' Richards replied somewhat defensively. 'Look, I'll help you with what intelligence I can get and I won't brief against you, but that's about as much as I can do.'

On leaving the office Pariche felt just a little slighted by the limited help that Richards had proffered, although he was relieved he wasn't going to be siding with the opposition. Hell, he'd even got off his butt and showed them to the door. That was an honour usually reserved only for the most exalted.

51

Typically, Wilson had not missed a trick. The meeting he'd called, would, in his own words, be 'informally formal' and would involve the hijacking of a departmental meeting already planned. The numbers expected would mean moving to a more conveniently sized seminar room, just along the corridor from his office. Unofficial feelers had been put out to the department's usual power brokers and this would mean that some of the awkward squad would be in attendance. Wilson knew, though, that it would be nigh impossible for most to attend at such short notice, something that had always served his interests well in the past. Most of the professors were quite happy to leave the details of running the department to him, along with the recording of any decisions or non-decisions that might be made. It would be no different this time. Maureen, the secretary, would dutifully collate a sense of what the meeting had decided and Wilson would decide which items to progress.

The first to arrive was Kurst, accompanied by Marjorie Forster from Rhetoric. Kurst, as always, wore an old tweed jacket and green trousers, whilst Forster's full-length pleated dress, with short puffed sleeves, harkened back to a time she'd been an undergraduate at Oberlin in the sixties. When so inclined, she could pull a lot of weight with the powers that be in Senate, and, more importantly, in the Chancellor's Office. Colleagues tended to view her pronouncements as having the veracity of a sermon on the Mount. She was someone Wilson had always striven to keep on board and had commanded Friesson to keep her well supplied with cake and drink. It was clear that Kurst and Forster got on well together. In their different ways they exuded a certain old world authority, something that Wilson and Friesson now feigned due reverence to, as they fussed around them. Once seated, Kurst leant back in his seat, stretched his arms above his head and gazed heavenwards. 'This had better be good, Charles!' he said, in that same camp, slightly distracted manner that Soren had witnessed earlier on the phone. Wilson gave him a slightly apprehensive, willowy smile in return.

'I think you will warm to what I have to propose, Larry. I think we might have just saved the day.'

Other tried and trusted souls were now making their entrance. They were colleagues carefully vetted by Wilson so as to keep dissent to a minimum. Kurst – very club-able, but also unfortunately still on friendly terms with Soren – and Margaret Forster were the only ones Wilson couldn't be sure of. That was until Pariche and Denis Tsui made their entrance. It would be an understatement to say that Wilson was a little put out at the sight of them.

'Oh, Jedemiah, I wasn't expecting...' Wilson's voice trailed off as he watched Pariche and Tsui ignore his protestations and take their seats opposite. Kurst smiled and surreptitiously flashed them both a wink.

'Pariche,' continued Wilson, now back in harness. 'You do know this meeting was really supposed to be for department members only?'

'We know exactly what this meeting's for Mr "acting" dean,' replied Pariche, a smile fixed firmly on his face. 'Let's just get on with it!'

'Yes, Charles, I trust that this is not going to take too long!' It was Professor Forster, her voice deep and her delivery ponderously manufactured.

Pariche could see Wilson's handiwork in the people seated around him. One just had to admire the sheer nerve of the man. There was Seymour; bow tied and full of reaction. He'd been brought over from the History Department and still appeared to be yearning for an America that harked back to the era of Teddy Roosevelt. All smiles and oily charm, Pariche knew him to be no friend. More likely Seymour would be relishing the ironic deliciousness of it all; his role in employing someone like Flaxel Boateng, so inimical to his own sense of fine breeding, in the curtailing of such a wantonly heinous project as the Diaspora Program. The others present would already be of the mind to let Wilson have his way, full of admiration for someone who was that rare breed: a person in authority, fully conversant and at ease with the labyrinthine bureaucracy of university administration at Berkeley and able to play it to their best advantage.

And Wilson did get things done. This fact, along with his ability to bully and ruthlessly deal with those who got in his way, made his position almost unassailable. It had never ceased to amaze Pariche, as an interloper from another department, just how easily cowed his fellow colleagues could become in the face of an onslaught from Wilson. Here were people supremely confident in their field, including a past chair of the Western Division of the American Philosophical Association, two fellows of the National Academy of Sciences and a corresponding fellow with the Royal Society; yet all could so easily be bullied into silence by this advisor to the Governor's task force on urban planning and inner city deprivation. The distinguished gentlemen found it difficult to compete with a man who seemed so ready to use forces from beyond the narrow confines of the department, be it the rarefied structures of the university administration, or, as was now the case, with moves more usually associated with the street. Pariche knew that if Wilson could intimidate people like this, he would have little difficulty dealing with the likes of Soren and Denis. Here was someone who could change the general course catalogue so that a person's teaching mysteriously disappeared, arrange for teaching rooms to suddenly become unavailable, or see to it that instructor and support services were cut. Before the poor fools knew what was happening to them they would be out on their heels, heading for some dead-end post as somebody's TA at a lesser university or worse. Yes, Wilson was in a position to make life very difficult indeed. And now, not for the first time, Pariche was the one holding things up. Only the novelty, this time, would be that he was the one enslaved to committee room ritual and protocol, protesting why Wilson hadn't seen fit to call a full departmental meeting. Pariche though did have a trump card: he was the only person present, outside of Kurst and Forster, Wilson couldn't really get at. Not only was Pariche's position, as a university-wide professor, within the gift of the Chancellor's Office down the road in Oakland, most of his teaching and research was over in Genetics and equally beyond Wilson's reach. In full knowledge of this, and before the self-regarding and smug expressions of Wilson and Friesson, Pariche sat and brooded. With Denis obediently at his side, he waited for the moment when they could execute the plan he'd hatched with Soren two nights before.

Now though, Pariche's begrudging admiration of his foe's skills moved to an altogether new level as Flaxel and his entourage made their entrance. Wilson remained completely unfazed by the disruption; he'd obviously been expecting them and now sat back and enjoyed the unsettling effect their presence had on the rest of the room. Amongst the group was one of Denis's more promising students who attempted to manufacture a brooding attitude that in truth came across as somewhat childish. Apart from Flaxel, Pariche had not seen any of them before; in truth, the only time he was ever likely to set eyes on an undergraduate was at the odd lectures he gave over at Genetics and the very occasional mass rallies he conducted, by way of university lectures.

With the group was an older man; an exotically dressed individual who was introduced by Flaxel, only half-jokingly, as his personal Iman. His name was Ismail and in reality he was a graduate student over at GTU. Pariche surmised that he was either of South Asian Indian or Pakistani origin. Eventually the man found himself a spot to squat, cross-legged on the floor, from where he proceeded to open a burlap, inside of which he busied himself in search of something. His was a picture of pure distracted eccentricity which Pariche, at some other time, might have readily identified with. To this spectacle was added the growing realisation that the fellow had some kind of speaking disorder that made him cry out at intermittent intervals. Apparently it was a form of Tourettes, mercifully conveyed in something akin to Hindi. Every now and then, the meeting would resound to the noise of some foreign imprecation piercing the air. One could only guess what young Constance, a Sanskrit scholar, would have made of it had she been in attendance. Pariche found himself warming to the pure absurdity of it all, a moment redolent of more than anything he could knowingly construct. Just how had Wilson managed all of this?

Flaxel's presence obviously had Wilson's full support and the gathering remained suitably acquiescent. All, that is, apart from Pariche, whose pained expression became more evident as he witnessed the enthusiastic way Professor Forster registered the group's arrival. There were stifled murmurs from the other academics present, along with the odd bewildered look and, for some, a keen anticipation of the fun that might be in store. Wilson had been very busy indeed, and Flaxel, for one, appeared to be enjoying what he fancifully interpreted as the audience's expectant admiration. He was cocky, his body a preening swagger amidst the giggles and brooding intent of his entourage. Pariche knew the type. He'd had to deal with a growing number of these proverbial man-children of late in his beloved NAACP. This one though, was out of his depth. Surely his colleagues must be thinking the same? Pariche was incredulous that they were even prepared to give the fellow an audience, let alone contemplate his involvement in the running of one of their programs. Just *what* did this guy have on Wilson?

'Yes, Jedemiah,' added Professor Forster, 'it is so important that we are seen to be working with the community.'

'And what community is that, Marjorie?' Pariche replied, as Flaxel continued to play to the non-existent gallery around him.

'The one represented here, of course.' Professor Forster's expansive embrace of those present was greeted with another self-preening beam from Flaxel and a knowing nod of acknowledgment from Wilson. 'These people are fine examples of the diversity that Berkeley should seek to aspire to.'

Fighting for composure, Pariche let out a despairing gasp and slowly looked around the room. 'I take it you've shared this observation with the folks down at the city council?' he said, before turning to face Wilson. 'Denis and myself have been speaking to some of the people down there. It appears they might not share your assessment.' Some of the academics were now peering interestedly over spectacle rims and down noses as Flaxel and company began to shuffle awkwardly in their seats. Their discomfiture was mirrored by Wilson who was now becoming alarmed at the prospect of the meeting showing Pariche even the modicum of respect. Pariche though, couldn't resist spreading more fuel on the fire that were Wilson's anxieties. 'Hell, Charlie, you don't normally bring this amount of colour to these proceedings. I sure hope you're not having a midlife crisis?'

'I trust, Jedemiah, that you will show our visitors a degree of civility. You won't allow things to get too out of hand!' Wilson's plea, although issued with a placatory smile, still had a threatening edge to it, something which Flaxel quickly sought to emulate.

'Yes, I thought we'd been invited to this meeting as guests!' Flaxel's earlier attempt to win over the audience with a winning smile had now been replaced by a look that invited rebuke only from the foolish. Pariche duly obliged.

'You weren't invited by any of us,' he shot back.

'Oh Jedemiah, Jedemiah! This is not the way we do things here!' Wilson's tone was one of exasperation. He was also worried by Professor Forster's segue into silence.

'Yes,' echoed Flaxel, getting his cue once again from Wilson, 'just why have you never seen right to do the right thing by us?'

'What does that mean exactly?' Pariche's lip was a dismissive curl, the look on his face withering. Flaxel, in response, heaved in his narrow shoulders and leaned back in his seat, again looking towards Wilson for help.

'Jedemiah, this is intolerable. This is hardly the place to carry out this kind of character assassination. You are being exceedingly rude.' Wilson had obviously figured that if the insinuation of threat wasn't working, then a touch of sanctimonious upset would do. Pariche smiled gamely, before assuming a posture that might have invited the uninitiated to conclude that he'd acquiesced. Kurst knew better. Sitting across the table from Pariche, he knew the signals well; Pariche was going to ensure that an already stressful occasion would become increasingly so as the afternoon progressed.

Wilson carried on regardless. 'I'm sorry to have called this meeting at such short notice. We find ourselves in a rather delicate situation regarding the delivery of one of our programs. It is unfortunate that this has arisen at a time when that program's architect cannot be here with us. I speak of course of GW800, the Modernism and World Diasporas Program, one of our more popular courses, and one that has recently accrued a few question marks as to its funding and teaching.' Pariche began to stir, but said nothing. 'Furthermore, these not unwarranted and not insubstantial problems appear to have come along at the same time as we've had questions raised about the program's acceptability to the local community. That is why we have invited Mr Boeteng and his friends along.'

'Why don't you invite every sundry waif and stray?' said Pariche, his patience finally exhausted. Wilson though, was determined not to be deflected.

'He is only here to observe, may I add. To see that all is decided in an open and fully democratic manner.' Pariche harrumphed grumpily and mumbled something barely comprehensible to himself. 'I'm sure that all of us here appreciate the need to fully involve people from the immediate community and to that end, in Professor Karlsson's absence, we propose that Jerry Friesson takes over the program's day to day running. At some time in the future we would seek to enlist the help of Mr Boateng here. It is something that would allow for greater community involvement.'

Pleasantries now a distant memory, Pariche let out another guffaw. He was not going to let that one pass. To his credit Denis was in there too, arguing the absurdity of it all, and conveying the unmistakable message that the two of them were inseparable on this issue. Leaning back in his seat and gazing down his nose at Wilson, who was still attempting to maintain an aloof calm, Pariche spoke with a voice that was as thunderous as his pleas were impassioned. How dare they even contemplate this course of action. Why were they threatening the integrity of such a thriving program and doing their best to dispense with the goodwill and provenance of an association with the likes of Zenotech and the research facility they were planning? Why was all of this being put in jeopardy? And, if that was not all, now the acting dean was looking to deliver the program into the grasping hands of those who would seek to pervert its original premise and, in the process, destroy. They were placing it with the very people the program needed protecting against.

And there was more. To the consternation of Wilson, Pariche went on to inform the meeting of how he'd been asked, by the CEO at Zenotech and Professor Karlsson, to head the Diaspora Program. They wanted him to ensure that it was fit for the facility they were building. And this is what he, Professor Jedemiah Pariche, fully intended to do. He would protect it from those who had their own hidden political agendas or were set on personal aggrandisement. There was a brief pause, with Pariche striking a rather ironic tone, as he pointedly chided the "acting" dean about how they did things so differently in his own department over at Genetics. Then he went for the throat. He wondered why they were welcoming on-board a person of such dubious character; the type who should never have been invited onto university premises in the first place. One could only gaze in incredulity at the criminality of it all. He and Denis would welcome the support of everyone, especially from Marjorie and her friends over at Senate, but the fight would go on regardless.

It was clear that Pariche's words had hit a nerve and were beginning to win over some of the waverers. Wilson had clearly miscalculated. A meeting with Pariche present would always be anything but a formality, and now Kurst was showing signs of restlessness. What stuck in his throat was having to answer to the likes of Flaxel when discussing course requirements. A further worry for Wilson was that Marjorie Forster was also beginning to question the meeting's purpose, feeling that she might have been misled as to its legitimacy. Yes, the mood of the meeting had changed and with it the smile on Wilson's face became ever more fake and obsequious. The meeting was in danger of being totally derailed and for Wilson this was indeed unconscionable. It was time to let the dogs loose.

Prompted by Wilson, Flaxel now stared around him with an exaggerated menace that bemused and in some cases alarmed those present. Pariche was not fooled, finding the whole act rather amusing. Struggling to keep the laughter to himself, he watched as Flaxel, in tones both menacing and absurd, proceeded to state his case. Flaxel's demeanour was never predictable at the best of times and now it veered between that of a wayward teenager and the worldly wise man of the street. His facial features had a limp, insouciant quality that would, with a flick, turn into one of exaggerated shock and disbelief. And always present was the threat of explosive violence. Some of the scholars present were obviously uncomfortable with such a turn of events.

'We in the community have grown used to white people ignoring us and the issues that we think are most important.' His voice was now raised almost to a shout. 'For years we've been planning to do something that would honor the people who'd been scattered to the far-flung shores of this earth by those who would enslave and rob us of our heritage.'

Once again, Pariche wasn't fooled and his tone scarcely concealed his contempt. 'That's news to us!' he declared. 'You weren't at any of the planning sessions!'

'We were never invited!'

Pariche sniffed and with a look of mock disbelief, said, 'No wonder!'

'There you go again, insulting us, belittling us, ignoring our community!'

'I wish you wouldn't keep on saying that! Confusing yourself with the community. All you ever do is hustle and rob from it. The community can look after itself.'

Flaxel, now visibly shaking with anger, was now looking at Denis. 'Yes, I'm sure we can,' he scowled, now in full threat mode, as some of the academics showed signs of growing concern and apprehension.

'I hope that is not a threat?' interjected Pariche.

'I'm sure, Jedemiah, that was not what was intended,' said Wilson, trying to rein Flaxel in. In response, the man of the street pulled in his shoulders and quickly attempted to express a contrite disbelief. Of course he'd been completely misunderstood, his show of remorse followed by an embarrassed silence as all strove to reacquaint themselves with the original purpose of the meeting. It was something that was now given an additional steer by Denis, who'd been quietly monitoring proceedings and, as yet, had hardly broken sweat. He now took over. The assembled gathering were told of the plans he and Pariche had for the program and how they would be only too willing to listen to what people had to say. There was that screwed-up James Dean smile on his face again as he went on to give a presentation that was, even for the academics present, a somewhat forbidding and in-depth analysis of the statistical methodology that would be employed; something that would involve the ideas of palimpsest, grand narrative and the problem of forgetting. It was quite a winning performance. Unless, of course, you were Charlie Wilson or Flaxel Boateng. After which, it was Pariche's turn to add to their discomfort.

'Yes, we will be making quite a few demands on the maths department over the course of the coming year,' he said, with a beaming smile on his face and a proud arm around Denis. 'And we fully expect there to be a run on that old standby of mine, *The Statistical Provenance of the Mitochondria Gene,* available in the Doe this coming semester.'

Marjorie Forster had had enough. Where she had been given assurances by Wilson, she could now only see problems. Her friends in Senate would find the whole exercise rather baffling. Wilson would have to come up with something much more clear-cut and less contentious if he was to count on their support. Then, as the meeting was showing signs of running out of steam, the gentleman who'd been introduced as Flaxel's religious mentor, much to the amused and growing interest of Pariche, began to exhibit signs of increasing distress, as he fidgeted on the floor. Leaning slightly to one side, he raised his right buttock and let rip with a slow, cleansing, fart.

'A perfect commentary upon the proceedings,' said Pariche, as people attempted to escape what was now an airless, increasingly ripe, and eminently unpleasant atmosphere. Later, when they got to the departmental office, Maureen passed on news of an incident that had occurred in Mississippi. Its nature was still rather vague, but alarmingly, it appeared to have involved the use of a shotgun.

52

New York City

Soren had begun to see again. The dissolution that had begun on the evening of his mother's arrival in Mississippi, had been replaced by a certain healing. The pain of Brad's death had been almost intolerable, followed by an inevitable feeling of guilt. The person he turned to was Virginia. It had been in the early hours; a primeval howl of a call where, amidst the tears and silences, there had been an honest meeting of souls, a moment that mined an ecstatic despair within her. For both, it had been a moment of blinding clarity and coruscating release.

Soren couldn't remember Craig's departure, back to California, and he had no recollection of what had facilitated his own presence here in New York. In trying to fathom out what had happened, days had become a blur of disjointed, half-flickering images of southern gargoyles and a sickening in the pit of his stomach. Nothing appeared to make sense, save for an overriding sense of guilt at being implicated in the cause of his friend's death. And it was this that had taken him back to Virginia. Of course he'd been sensitive and prudent enough to keep his calls to a minimum, but the two of them had been complicit in their enjoyment of each other's concern; a source of reassurance to them both.

Virginia had listened and gently counselled him, mirroring his disquiet and providing him with the space and time to think. And after that initial call, she'd wept and rapturously punched the air with her fists, revelling in the knowledge that she'd been his first port of call. It was an almost too perfect and splendid antidote to what had been

224

going awry in her personal life. Something so delicious in its timing.

It was the eve of Brad's funeral and Soren found himself in the Italian House at Columbia, sitting in on a graduate seminar. Earlier that day, he'd awoken in the half light of a November morning and it was as if a spell had been broken. Five days after Brad's death, Soren had been struck with a renewed urge to create. It was something he'd not felt since he was last here, in New York, under Professor Rosen's tutelage. Now he had that sensation again; the first exhilarating glimpse, amidst bewitching calm, of lived immediacy, when the spirit promises to be in true accord with the mind's resolve. He didn't know how the city, with its constant bustle and striving to be heard, had managed to achieve this, but it had given him space to think. The vision was still somewhat hazy, with the sharpness of line and form not yet fully resolved, but there were definite tell-tale signs of renewal. A willingness once again to believe that life had purpose and worth.

This morning he'd risen early, before the muggers and rapists, so that he could take in the emerging beauty of Morningside Park. There he sat, under trees, with their blackened and silver hides, callused and peeling, where he'd felt a tranquility of thought, as if he were experiencing a true sense of care. He was beginning to give thanks for his continued involvement with life, and this gave him hope.

Afterwards he walked the corridors of the Italian House, on the way to see Rosen, only to be stopped in his tracks by the slow and sparse tone of a piano being played in the distance. It was Mozart's *Piano Concerto Number 12*, and its simple economy almost reduced him to tears. By the time he arrived at Rosen's seminar, his outlook was one of an almost charmed serenity. The session was well underway and, on seeing who it was, Professor Rosen rose to her feet and hurried over to him. Their embrace was warm. This was a keenly felt affection. She was a short woman, with long dark flowing hair that appeared to exaggerate the size of her head. She was a lot thinner than he remembered, but sprightly for someone in her late sixties. There was a twinkle in her eye and a smile that appeared to drive away the years. He was surprised at the power of her arms as she swivelled him around, in order to present him to the assembled students.

'Ladies and gentleman, we are indeed honoured. May I introduce Professor Karlsson. Yes, the self-same author of one of your required texts. This *is* indeed an honour.' Soren blushed a little, though in truth he found himself quite enjoying the praise and the attention. Rosen continued. 'Just fifteen years ago, Professor Karlsson was sitting where you are today. Now he's a full professor at the University of California.' Soren didn't feel this was the time or place to correct her. She turned to him again. 'Take a seat. We've not long to go. I'm sure you'd be interested in what we have to say.' She beckoned one of them to continue.

Soren took his place under an assortment of youthful and approving gazes, before they all turned their attention to a rather pale looking redhead, wearing a sleeveless tank top, and a stud protruding from the side of her nose. On her forearm was a small mark or blemish, or it might just have been a tattoo. She was also caressing a glass of wine, provided by Rosen for the occasion. Some things, Soren thought, never change. When the woman spoke, it was with a conviction that belied her fragile appearance, as she gave vent to an opinion of how the Saudis, through their guardianship of Islam, were trying to brand the faith as their own. Every now and then, Rosen would interrupt, in that enthused, confidently clipped, tone, Soren remembered so well. They were left pondering the significance of the protests currently being staged against Salman Rushdie's *Satanic Verses,* along with a rather novel interpretation of Theodore Adorno's *Jargon of Authenticity*. To Soren, it felt just like old times. Good to be back. Then, as the session drew to a close, Rosen distractedly dug deep into her handbag and produced some keys. 'Same old place, 202A,' she said, handing the keys to him. 'Make yourself at home. I'll be along in a minute.'

When he got to Rosen's office, Soren sat himself down on a small settee, under a precariously stacked wall of books.

The large mahogany desk before him was cluttered with first editions, journals and student papers, all waiting to be read. Soren knew the room well. Wonderful memories, he thought, and it hadn't changed a bit. Christina had been right in believing that New York, and the subsequent years spent at Columbia, had, as she phrased it, 'turned' her son. There was the New York intellectual scene, of course, and access to all that literature and art. The chance to revisit those teen summers, immersed in whatever had been exhibiting at MOMA or the Met. There had even been the emergence of a good friendship and correspondence with the author, Mary McCarthy. Above all, there had been Professor Rosen. The room was testament to the influence and scope of her interests in philosophy, art and musicology. He remembered the photographs: Rosen being honoured by the American Philosophical Society, another with Jimmy Carter at the White House, and then again with friends and literary luminaries at her Park Slope home. All around was evidence of someone who really was worthy of being called one of the greats; the artistic equivalent of an Oppenheimer or a Feynman, whose genius would have been felt in any field she'd chosen to contribute.

Soren remembered his first interview here, all of sixteen years ago. It had been more a homage, and duet of praise, to a TV show they'd both seen on some obscure Marxist philosopher, rather than the usual run of the mill admissions interview. She'd been scarcely able to contain herself at seeing someone both knowledgeable and sympathetic to ideas she held so dear, and from someone so young. Rosen had never been one to warm much to the young men at Columbia College, disliking what she saw as their presumptive arrogance at being the chosen heirs of those who felt entitled to be there as of right. Soren, though, was different; an outsider, like herself. He was also possessed of an intellect that she felt she could fashion; a talent that needed to be nurtured and protected from itself.

'I've not heard enough from you lately!' Was the first thing Rosen said when she finally got back, carrying a bottle of wine she'd rescued from the seminar.

'I've been a little busy I guess, but I have tried to keep in touch...'

'Is Wilson still giving you the run around? I should have counselled you against allowing him to bully you into taking that position out there. It's been such an impediment to your work. And *where* is that work, Soren? Where's the writing?' He smiled, but said nothing, embarrassed. 'As I said at the time,' she continued, 'the time you spent with the dark forces over at the law faculty, before you went out there, totally mystified me. I can see now, how it might have been preparation for the ethical stuff you ended up doing at the medical school. But I suspect it might have been at too great a cost.'

'I know, I know.' Soren was still feeling defensive.

'I think I detect just a little trouble in paradise?'

'You might say that. I'm taking a year's sabbatical. Doing some research down in Mississippi. I've been meaning to do it for some time.'

'There's a lot to be said for taking time off.' He could see her mind going through the gears. 'But how does this play with your research interests?'

'It doesn't really, I suppose.'

'Mmmm, and what brings you back here?'

'A funeral.'

'Oh.'

'You remember Brad?'

'Oh, how... how utterly dreadful!'

'Yes. He was killed down there. Murdered.' Soren was shocked at how easily the words came out. Up to now, apart from when he'd spoken to Virginia, he'd hardly spoken of Brad's death to anyone, and this was definitely the first time he'd uttered the word murder. 'Yes, murdered,' he repeated.

Briefly, Rosen was nonplussed, then, collecting her thoughts, she said: 'I do remember you were very close.' Soren nodded. 'It's really hard to know what to say. How do you feel?'

'Guilty I guess. It was me who urged him to go there in the first place.'

'But surely he would have had some part in the decision? You can't go blaming yourself for having an impact upon someone.'

'Perhaps. But I feel such a fraud.' Yes, Soren had been in shock and had felt pain, but he wasn't sure if it had been out of any real concern for Brad. It had all felt a little indulgent.

'But this is only natural, Soren. Grief hits us all in different and, dare I say, very similar ways.' With this, she got to her feet and, demonstrating surprising agility for someone her age, clambered onto a chair. Reaching for something on an upper shelf, she called down to him; 'Remember this?' She handed him a small tightly bound package. He recognised it immediately. It was a paper he'd delivered all those years ago; a rather dry piece on Hegel's treatment of natural law. He was surprised the old girl had kept it. 'I still maintain that this was exceptional, Soren. One of the finest papers on the subject I've read. It's something you might like to revisit after the dust has settled. You need to be clear about what you want to do and stick to it. Might I suggest that your trip to Mississippi smacks somewhat of a distraction!'

Soren felt conflicting forces at work. He'd enjoyed the praise, but now one the most pre-eminent minds on the planet was telling him that his present endeavours, in California and now, in Mississippi, might be something of a bust.

53

Later, after making promises to return, Soren found himself walking along Amsterdam Avenue, a couple of blocks south of the university. From a payphone, he gave his mother a call, who informed him that she'd called the realtors who'd said that the buyers for the Morningside apartment had pulled out. The wife, in her final trimester, had seemed very set on the deal, but now they'd withdrawn. A total mystery. The woman at the office said it was almost as if they'd been pressured not to complete. So, as he continued his walk, Soren was left to reflect on the lost sale. He was stuck with a house he didn't want, smack in the middle of a property slump. In addition the brownstone hadn't been rented during the time it had been up for sale and the agent's fees, as well as the interest run up on the loan, would now be in the thousands.

A real money pit, Soren thought, as he stood outside, in the Morningside gloom, gazing up at the house that was now adding to his many anxieties. For just a moment there was that feeling of dread again, quickly followed by a forceful intake of breath and a renewed focus on what needed to be done. The meeting with Rosen had left him with an almost sanguine regard for what lay ahead. Bracing himself against the chill, he climbed the steps and tried the key. A push at the reinforced mahogany door revealed the blood red tiles of the hallway, from which rose a rather sturdy looking staircase. Ahead, he could see that a light had been left on in the kitchen. A quick reconnoitre revealed nothing untoward. There was, though, that deathly chill; the house had been left empty for far too long. Was it too much to ask for the realtors to have kept some semblance of heating on, if only to prevent the pipes from freezing? Mercifully, the water had been turned off. He tried the phone; it was still connected. He called Christina again, just to tell her that the cold was conspiring to drive him into the warm embrace of McGinty's, a bar he and Brad used to frequent nearby. From the front room he looked out onto a street that was the divide between the old Bloomingdales district and Riverside. Walk a few blocks south and east and you were in, what local people were attempting to rebrand as, Manhattan Valley. When Soren and Brad had been at Columbia, this had been bandit country and, apart from the odd party, a place they rarely had need to venture into. The 1 train from Cathedral Parkway, with its umbilical connection to all points south, was their preferred route through this part of the city. He didn't know why, perhaps it was because he was younger then, but the seventies felt a lot safer than today. Now the papers were screaming blue murder about the threat of an emerging underclass strung out on crack.

He moved onto the lounge, where there was a different chill; a ghostly stillness that still seemed to reverberate with Brad's presence. He could picture him, in pride of place, settled upon the now vanished sedan, joint in hand, holding forth on the likes of Balzac and Proust. It had been errant nonsense, of course, delivered with a wise-cracking, jack hammer delivery; a stoned erudition, wrapped in a stream of invective that was a true wonder to behold.

The room was large, with a vaulted ceiling. It had been this that had first sold the place to him. He remembered how the people over at Student Housing had urged him to gut the place and make it into separate apartments. But he'd resisted. What he wanted was for a succession of young professional couples to rent and look after the place. But now he was barely covering the property taxes and the cost of utilities. Hence his decision to sell. A property like this would be ideal for those city workers downtown, seeking to get a foot on the property escalator. But then the property crash had happened.

The more Soren looked around, the more he could see the need for costly repairs. He wondered if any of them stemmed from the parties they'd had back in the seventies. Brad had always insisted that any rooms Soren wanted to rent should always go to art students or architects, as they always had the best parties. Now, some fifteen years later, the bills would be coming in. There were dirt marks all around the ornamental fireplace and the gas fire grills were rusted and warped. The paint on the windowsills was beginning to flake and the windows were dirty. Some of the tenants must have kept dogs as the hardwood floors were badly scuffed. Much of the wallpaper had now begun to fade and there were black marks forming around the ceiling's moldings and cornices. How did he ever think he could sell the place? Especially with the price he'd been asking.

The memories of Brad were now beginning to have a distant vanished feel to them and for the first time Soren found himself wanting to move on. There was still the funeral to endure but, thankfully, due to worries about the fragile state of Soren's mind, Christina had worked with Brad's parents to ensure that he'd been spared any involvement in its planning. And now it couldn't even be said that he was the most significant of Brad's friends; that mantle had long been passed onto Brad's partner, Martin, and Soren half expected trouble from that quarter at the funeral tomorrow. Martin would blame him for taking Brad away, and at a time when there were more important battles to be fought closer to home, in San Francisco. Soren could see the retribution coming, and, in all honesty, he knew he probably deserved it. He had been the one responsible for luring Brad away from those who were now much closer to him. The Brad he would be paying his respects to tomorrow was different to the one he remembered here all those years ago.

Soon he was back in the street, staring up at the house's exterior. As he did so, he noticed something move out of the corner of his eye. Someone was standing, partially hidden, in the shadows. He made to say something, to make towards the figure, but then stopped himself. What the hell was he thinking? That was not the thing to do, in the descending darkness, up here in the hundreds, in New York. The tension

232

was broken though, and further thoughts on the matter banished, when a young couple, walking arm in arm, came into view. As they passed by Soren turned and followed them, at a discrete distance, along 110th Street towards McGinty's.

In McGinty's Soren presented himself to a somewhat disinterested barman who continued his flirtatious conversion with a colleague as he took his order. The walk had given him time to recapture some composure, but there was still a certain wariness. It didn't help that the place he'd entered had changed out of all recognition. McGinty's used to market itself as the only really Irish bar experience on Morningside. Then it'd had a student feel, a little down at heel perhaps, but a place where Columbia faculty and their students would come to rub shoulders with the people who rented and cooped together in the neighbourhood. Now it had a more gentrified look and feel, a place now frequented by those young professionals Soren had been so keen to sell the Brownstone to. Folks who'd been priced out of the sixties and eighties and were prepared to take a chance on an area that – at a stretch – could still be called the Upper West Side.

Soren watched and listened and noted the changes. Discussions about society, philosophy and protest, and the parties people might move onto, were now replaced by talk of work, property prices and family vacations. He guessed that the politics would have changed too, with a liberal tone replacing the radicalism he remembered. Perhaps a little self-consciously, he could see in these people something of what he'd become himself. People who were perhaps just a little too comfortable and at ease with themselves. Suddenly though, through the throng, he noticed a face he did remember. Yes, sitting alone, at one of the side tables, was Terry Steuben, from the English department at Columbia. He was no longer bearded, but it was definitely him, with that shocking white mane of hair. Soren walked over and made his introduction.

'Terry! It is you, isn't it? How long has it been?' The figure's baffled and slightly fearful expression should have been a warning, but Soren didn't pick up on it. 'My, this place has changed, hasn't it? It was the English department, wasn't it?'

The man smiled nervously. 'I think you might have got me confused with someone else!'

'Oh, I'm dreadfully sorry...' It was Soren's turn to feel fearful. He looked at the man again. No, Soren couldn't remember Steuben ever having such a noticeable birthmark on his left cheek.

'Not to worry, it's an easy mistake to make,' said the man, now more composed.

'I really am sorry, I thought you were someone I used to know at Columbia!'

'No, just passing through.' The man seemed relaxed and friendly enough. He looked to be a good ten years older than Soren, perhaps in his mid to late forties. 'I take it you're back revisiting?' he said, offering his hand.

'You could say that. Thought I'd check out a property I've been letting while I was at it.'

'There seems to be a lot of that. People moving in with an aim to rent. Lots of bucks to be made, I suppose.'

'Barely.' Soren shrugged and smiled weakly. 'Got the property when I was studying here. Seemed too good an opportunity to miss.'

As he spoke, Soren could feel the man's scorn behind a well-crafted smile. A judgement that said that here was yet another poor little rich kid, being bankrolled by his parents. But still, Soren couldn't help himself. Shut up you fool, he heard himself saying, as he answered a seemingly primeval need to expurgate his guilt, and this quiet, and now apparently willing, stranger, seemed to be the ideal sounding board. Then, picking up on the direction of the man's gaze, Soren became aware of someone standing over him. He turned smartly to see that it was his mother. She was with Elizabeth, who appeared to be distractedly tugging at something caught in her pashmina. If Soren's erstwhile interlocutor needed further proof, here it was; two women dressed to the nines, in evening gowns, mohair and cashmere coats, straight out of Saks. As much as it would have pained them both to admit it, the look was very Upper East Side; very much the other side of the park.

54

'Ah, you made it!' Soren was quite overjoyed. 'And you too Elizabeth; what a lovely surprise!' They embraced. 'I was just talking to...' He turned, but the man had gone.

'Yes, he did appear to be in a bit of a hurry to get away,' said Christina.

'Didn't even get his name.'

'Oh, well, he's just going to have to remain a mystery then, isn't he?' She was showing no signs of wishing to remove her coat. 'We have a taxi waiting outside. I don't think the driver wants to be left hanging around up here too long. I'm sure you could do with something to eat.'

Once in the taxi, with Soren seated between the two of them, Christina continued. 'Elizabeth thought we might like to join her at Le Cirque.'

'Le Cirque?'

'Yes,' interjected Elizabeth. 'The thought of banging around in that mausoleum (the name she always gave to her Upper East Side apartment) all evening, just fills me with dread.' She put a comforting arm around him and said: 'We were getting a bit worried about you.' She squeezed his hand and gave him a peck on the side of his temple. He could feel tears beginning to flow again. Not here, he reproached himself, not now!

'At some time you're going to have to let yourself go,' said his mother, somewhat irritated. 'It will do you good. In Brad, we have both lost someone close.' She ignored the questioning look he gave in response. 'Yes, I feel wretched too. Wretched and just a little frightened I guess.'

'Frightened?'

'Yes, Soren, if anything were ever to happen to you...' Her voice trailed off for a moment, before returning with a renewed vigour and a change of subject. 'I remember all those years ago when you were studying here.' She gestured at the darkness outside, as the taxi sped along Cathedral Parkway and past South Harlem. 'When you first wanted to get out of student housing and move into that flophouse. Wasn't that awful, Lizzie?'

'Yes, I remember. That's why we helped you with the apartment!'

Soren chortled at the word 'helped'. The two women seated beside him had provided almost every penny. 'This ghastly business,' sighed Christina, to nobody in particular, before a return of her gaze to Soren. 'If anything were to happen to you.'

'It won't, Mother, it won't!' It was his turn to give the two women a reassuring hug.

'But how can you be sure?' demanded Christina. 'We need more facts. We need to hear from Virginia!'

'Ah, yes, Ginny!' replied Soren, feigning ignorance. 'Just how is she getting on down there?'

'We thought you would have been able to tell us! You do seem to have been talking to her a lot of late' He didn't respond and the two women let it go. Soon the taxi was turning into Park Avenue, headed south towards 65th Street. The two women continued with their conversation, albeit in a more consciously upbeat way, about what they could expect at tomorrow's funeral.

'Julia, – Brad's mother – says that Father O'Brien will be officiating. I remember you used to get on well with him.'

This was true; the blessed priest was indeed a rarity for Soren, a staunch defender of the Catholic faith prepared to indulge in a knowledgeable discussion about Karl Marx. A good man, even if he was known to be a little combustible at times, especially when confronted with issues about the relative merits of the priesthood, as was so often the case when he came across members of the Hemlin household. Also at the funeral would be Rabbi Schulz, representing Julia's half of the family. Soren gave a rather stoical smile;

the last thing he could remember the rabbi saying to Brad's father, Paisley, was a rather peremptory 'fuck you!', after they'd had words. It was a dead certainty that the rabbi would also be bringing his congregation with him, the whole of the Upper East Side mob, if only to spite those dumb schmucks Julia had had the misfortune of marrying into. Indeed, some of her more orthodox relatives, on hearing of her marriage to Paisley, had even attempted to 'sit shiva'.

They should have known that Paisley, a short muscular man who knew how to look after himself, would, like his son, find inevitable complaint. He'd made a fortune in futures, a business that had, in turn, fed into the rough and tumble of Paisley's personal life. He and Julia were always fighting and had been on the brink of separation for well-nigh thirty years. And this is what finally had come to pass, with Paisley rewarding himself with, what most of the family saw as, a trophy wife. Tanya was beautiful, tall and curvaceous, and being twenty years younger than either Paisley or Julia, was roughly the same age as the son they were about to bury. She repaid Paisley, for the good life she now had, with total obeisance; a thing that Julia would never have countenanced. Even after the break-up, Paisley would look to Julia for guidance on most things. Very garrulous, she was built like a mini pocket battleship, with an attitude to match; someone who'd treat any setback as an affront that would need to be overcome. When stirred into action, Julia was a force that would just keep on coming, and when she and Paisley were together, the result was often explosively toxic. Poor Brad didn't stand a chance; banishment to Exeter, and a budding friendship with Soren, had been the result.

'And Martin will be coming' added Christina. Ah, Martin! Soren had forgotten him. Yet another element to be added to the mix. Soren knew that he would be only too keen to blame him for tempting Brad to Mississippi. Martin's presence at the funeral tomorrow, along with the friends he would be bringing from San Francisco, would also be a reminder of Brad's homosexuality. Soren wondered what the congregation would make of that. He knew his own behaviour in this regard had not always been above reproach, his comportment not as aware as it could have been; something that had been aided by a certain blindness, even indifference. Soren's self-flagellation though, on this regard, was short lived as he found himself chuckling at the thought of what Paisley would make of it all. How would this combustible and staunch adherent to the Catholic faith accommodate the entourage that this representative of the Castro District was bound to bring with him? If the past was anything to go by, this was yet another thing that did not bode well. The funeral tomorrow, in the words used earlier by Virginia, promised to be a hoot.

55

They were now turning into 58th Street, not far from their destination. Elizabeth now produced a blue and red striped tie which she proceeded to fasten around Soren's neck; she had pulled rank to get a table at such short notice, and she was sure as hell not going to allow the Van Buren name to be associated with anything other than proper decorum. She was funny that way. As they made their entrance, it soon became clear that Elizabeth's fastidiousness, regarding good taste and etiquette, didn't necessarily extend to the flashiness and glitz that was Le Cirque. As he looked around the room, with its vast awnings and canopy, Soren was aware of how it was all such a surreal contrast to where he'd been just a few moments before. And Mississippi? Well, that might as well have been another country.

'The best time to come is lunchtime,' said Elizabeth, as she wove a path through the tables past a luminary being interviewed before the glare of TV lights. 'You just can't move for all the tiaras.' Heads were now turning towards them, along with greetings and nods and the due supplication that Elizabeth's presence demanded.

The food might be superior, but Che Panisse in Berkeley couldn't hold a candle to the kind of clientele this place seemed to attract, and this evening was no exception. There were the usual assortment of TV celebrities, art dealers, UN diplomats, bankers and financiers, along with the odd dowager, and a physician from Sloan. At a nearby table, a group of women appeared to have extended their ladies-who-lunch routine into the evening; all high heels and plunging necklines, shimmering lamé and chutzpah, dripping with pearls and squeezed into the tightest of off-the-shoulder dresses. Soren laughed as he returned their waves. Melanie Griffith and Demi Moore had a lot to answer for.

'I think they might just come at a too-high price, Soren, even for you.' Said Elizabeth giving him a wink, under the watchful gaze of Christina, who, in truth, was thankful for the leavening tone her friend always gave to the proceedings. It was something her son desperately needed, being just the type to go and do something destructive like bottling it all up. It still rankled somewhat, with Christina, that it had been Virginia to whom he had turned and not her, so for the moment she was content to sit back and let Elizabeth make the running. Much of the initial conversation between the two women was pure gossip, which passed Soren by, as did their forensic examination of the latest episode of *Thirtysomething*. Sensing this, Elizabeth brought the conversation back to a subject that she thought would appeal to Soren's sense of fun. It involved the women at the next table, who were now even more voluble, periodically stooping together into a conspiratorial huddle, as if they were in some kind of papal conclave.

'Okey, then,' Elizabeth said, tugging at Soren's sleeve, 'what do you make of the one nearest us?' Soren, eyebrows raised, was just a little unsure as to what was expected. 'Yes,' continued Elizabeth, urging him on, 'the one that's all tattoos and ankle bracelets?'

'Well, I don't know...'

Elizabeth helped him out. 'Oh, her name will be Saffron – not her real name of course – and she finds it almost impossible to get through the day without bitching about the "friends" she's out with tonight.'

'Is she married?'

'Of course,' said Elizabeth. 'He'll be a cosmetic surgeon who gives her friends discounts although they don't know he's already factored them into his tax plans for the year.'

'What about lovers?' He was now getting up to speed.

'Oh, Soren dear, look at her!'

'Yes,' interjected Christina, at last, who, much to Soren's surprise, seemed to be as well clued up on the subject as Elizabeth. 'Who from her entourage gets to do the honours?'

'Well,' replied Elizabeth, 'I guess there are quite a number of possible suspects: hairstylists, dieticians, dog walkers, maids...'

'Maids?' Christina was shocked.

'Why not?' Elizabeth replied, in a wickedly superior tone. 'She might just have that AC-DC thing going for her. Now let me see, there will be an interior designer, and she's bound to be into that alternative therapy stuff, so she'll have a psychic and spiritual guidance counsellor, you know the score! And then there'll be a tax adviser, personal trainer, a shopper, a publicist – just in case – and a driver, a pool attendant...'

'Ah, stop, it's always the pool attendant!'

'And, of course, one of her friends over there, perhaps the one who's listening so attentively, is her paid social escort. None of the others know this of course, but they have their suspicions.'

With the restaurant service in full swing, it was left to Elizabeth to anticipate and expedite things in accordance with what she perceived to be her guests' best wishes. It wasn't long before she was buttonholing a tall, rather severe-looking gentleman, who'd managed to tear himself away from the TV scrum they'd witnessed on their arrival. He was introduced as Reginald Perry, a TV personality and one-time fashion designer. Not missing a beat, Elizabeth beckoned him into the chair he was leaning against. 'Reginald,' she said in a voice that hinted of mischievous possibilities, 'you will join us, won't you?' She'd obviously decided that Reginald, with his mastery of the gossiped tale, wittily told, would add something to the conversation that might keep any anxieties about tomorrow's funeral at bay. 'We can't have you missing out, can we?'

Reginald, although apologetic, elected to remain standing, as he gave a rather worried look towards the scrum he'd left behind. 'I'm sorry, but I might have to rescue someone. One of the Valentino girls has been rather let down

242

and we have a TV crew filming at the next table. They've been giving her hell.'

'Go and get her then,' urged Elizabeth, 'the more, the merrier. Go on, bring her over!' Acceding to her wishes, Reginald walked back to the mass of lights, where he could be seen beseeching a woman, dressed in a slimline off the shoulder number, to come over. They watched as she poured out of her seat and followed him, camera crew in train, back to their table. This woman was staggeringly beautiful and her stately progress keenly observed by everyone, including the women at the neighbouring table, one of whom, with the prodded encouragement of her friends, was now getting to her feet, intent on coming over.

'Is it, it is, Reginald Perry?' she gushed, caught between gaping in turn at him and the Valentino girl. They in turn had a look of utter dismay etched on their faces.

'Oh dear, must I?'

Soren watched with bemused fascination as Reginald composed himself and assumed the countenance of a rather put-upon mastiff. The princess though, was not to be denied. In full TV presenter mode, Reginald rose from his seat and gently, with placatory cooing and promises to see what he could do about getting them tickets for the show, walked the woman back to her seat. Eventually, farewell hugs were exchanged and a triumphant princess – 'that's Miralda with an 'a'– returned to the bosom of her friends.

'Miralda with an 'a',' Elizabeth mouthed to the others, scarcely believing her ears. 'Not Saffron then.'

The Valentino girl looked nonplussed.

'Don't worry,' said Soren, 'just a game we were playing earlier.'

Relieved to have extricated himself from his gaggle of admirers, Reginald was now free to turn to the purpose of his capture. He and Elizabeth had an understanding; she would give him her undivided attention and entrée into the rarified heights of old monied New York, and he would provide the gossip, in all its uncensored, un-expurgated glory, as long as it went no further. As for now, Reginald and his rather glamorous companion would serve as an exquisite

243

antidote to the past week's events. And the therapy appeared to work, as Elizabeth and Reginald delivered on that promise, with Christina and Soren content, just for the moment, to let things go.

56

Later, after they had savoured the paté, lobster bisque and roasted sea bass, and after Reginald and the Valentino girl had moved onto a reception at the French Consulate, they walked the short distance back to the 'mausoleum' that was the Van-Buren's apartment. On their arrival, they were greeted by the sight of a recumbent Pariche, slumped in front of the gas fire. It was something the two women had obviously thought best not to worry Soren about. Furthermore, noises could be heard coming from the kitchen. It was Doleson. 'Anyone for a nightcap?' he asked, that mischievous glint in his eye a seemingly permanent fixture. Then, with a spluttering of coughs and snorts, Pariche was awake.

'Ah, Doleson, make mine a large one.' He said getting to his feet. He walked over to Soren, arms outstretched. 'Good to see you, my boy.' He gave him a hug, and, with a comforting arm around the younger man, added, 'I bet you could do with a drink too, Solly. We have much to discuss.'

Doleson immediately ducked back into the kitchen to make good on Pariche's injunction. As shocked as Soren was by this vision of double trouble, Elizabeth could only admire how quickly the pair of them had adapted to Upper East Side living. The tell-tale signs were everywhere; the games room had been investigated, the multi-channelled video stream to the New York Stock Exchange was in full flow and the minibar had been well and truly sampled.

'How the other half lives...' boomed Pariche. 'Your good mother and her esteemed companion have been most kind in welcoming us into their humble abode.' Soren looked at his mother imploringly. 'Don't reproach your mother,' Pariche continued, 'she had no part in my presence here.'

This was a lie of course. After that first phone call, when Pariche had urged Christina to go to Mississippi, there had been a regular flow of calls between the two; calls that, in all honesty, Christina had come to look forward to. Pariche talked sense in a way that appeared to belie all what she'd been led to believe about the man. Indeed, in the support Pariche had given to Soren, in his battles with Wilson, Christina had always held the view that he had a judgement she could trust. In those late-night calls she'd also discovered a warmth and maturity that contrasted with the irascibility and madness she'd been led to expect. That here was someone she was even beginning to warm to. So there had been a certain inevitability about the call from Pariche when it finally came, inviting himself to Brad's funeral. Where the two of them, he and Christina, could work together in stiffening Soren's resolve. So here he was, in Elizabeth's Manhattan apartment, taking Soren's coat, as if he were the proprietor of the place.

'We thought you might need a bit of support in your quest.' Soren blanched a little as he handed over his coat to Pariche and accepted Doleson's offer of a whisky. 'We've been talking about how we can fix this.' Pariche was about to continue when he noted Christina screwing up her eyes. 'Sorry,' he said, correcting himself, 'we thought we'd see how we could help you through this.'

'Jed, it is late!' It was Christina again. 'I'm sure that you have much to discuss, but I for one would like to turn in.' The knowing and familiar use of Pariche's first name came as a surprise to her son. 'I suggest you do so too,' continued Christina, shooting a glance at Elizabeth, hoping for support. She, though, was far too captivated by thoughts of continued conviviality to be of any help. 'Then you are not to keep my son up too late. Hopefully you will be a force for moderation!' Yes, there would be the need for someone with Elizabeth's level-headedness to counter the lunacy that the combined forces of Pariche and Doleson would be bound to come up with. 'Remember, Soren,' his mother added, before

246

finally retiring, 'I've seen to most of the things you'll need for tomorrow. All you have to do is get yourself into the suit I've brought down from Ashleighs, and be ready by ten.'

With Christina gone, Pariche resumed his seat, joined by Doleson and a gleefully conspiratorial Elizabeth. He immediately picked up on Soren's caution. 'Solly, my boy, you'll get over this. Can't say that I know what you're going through. I found the counsel of Mildred to be a great source of comfort when I went through a similar thing some times back.'

'Mildred?' asked Elizabeth.

Soren raised a finger to his lips in a way that suggested to her that this was a known issue. With a smile, Pariche continued.

'I won't beat about the bush, Solly, we need you back on the job. Sure, it could be said that Basil here is more worried about his blessed Institute, and you know I'm concerned as to how we're going to take the fight to a certain acting dean, but it's all part of the same battle. I would be lying if I said different. The vultures are hovering, Solly, and we need you back in saddle. More to the point, I think you need it too.' He looked across at Elizabeth, who nodded her agreement.

Their deliberations continued into the early hours, during which Soren was told about the faculty meeting and how Pariche fully expected the forces of darkness, in the form of Wilson and Flaxel Boateng, to be coming for them anytime soon. He also spoke of Kurst and how he'd agreed to babysit Denis whilst he was away, and yes, Pariche would be away for a few days, as he was fully intent on joining Soren down in Mississippi. 'Hell, yes, Solly. Haven't been there for years,' he said, before gazing across the room at Doleson, now soundly asleep. 'Basil dropped me a line about you needing a little help.'

What he didn't say was how this might just provide him with the opportunity for a little more mischief, and he kept to himself the news that Doleson had brought with him from Mississippi; about what he and 'Miss Ginny' had discovered down there, and how it had moved Soren into the line of fire.

57

Toshoba County, Mississippi

For the trip to Mississippi, in acknowledgment of southern sensibilities, Virginia packed a series of no-nonsense business suits. It was a world away from the attire she'd worn to the Star Inn. Her response to Christina's summons, to drop everything and go south, had been immediate, even if she had been somewhat peeved at being denied the opportunity of being with Soren. The assistance she could offer in finding Brad's killer would act as partial recompense. The taxi ride from Memphis was costly, but she comforted herself in the knowledge that it would prove useful in getting a feel for the lay of the land. She didn't expect to find much. She was arriving long after the suspects had flown the coop and she knew the local sheriff's office and the state police would have already contaminated whatever forensics there were to hand. As for the FBI, heaven knows what they would be doing.

The taxi driver, a stringy middle-aged white man with a luxuriant crop of hair, spent most of the journey sizing her up in the rear-view mirror.

'You down on business?' he asked, the pitch of his voice as sharp as a pencil.

'Visiting a friend,' she replied. A lie, of course, and he wasn't fooled.

'You here regarding that dead boy?' She smiled, shrugged and nodded her head. 'Shame about what happened,' he continued, 'but they had no business coming down here, poking their noses around. Folks down here just don't like people doing that.'

'You think that's how most of people see it?'

'Sure, even the nigras.'

And there it was. That ability the Old South had to catch you off guard.

'You at least must have appreciated all the business that's come with all the media interest.'

'So, you with the papers?

Virginia smiled. 'You caught me out again. What have you heard?'

For a moment there was a pause as he thought the question through. 'Not much,' he drawled.

She sensed that she might have transgressed some invisible boundary, but soon she was listening to a steady stream of complaint, her smile becoming just a little forced as she listened to the driver bemoaning the South's fate of having been lumbered with a people incapable of pulling themselves up by their own bootstraps. She found herself looking out of the window, just like Soren had done a few days earlier, but, unlike him, she did feel more at home. Although this was very much the black belt, a place with a sultry down-at-heel feel, there were signs that were still familiar to her. She recognised the odd Tupelo gum protruding from a terrain that had for an age succumbed to a blanket of laurel, spruce and longleaf pine. Gaining height, they began to move through a landscape of small farms and encroaching forest. This was a place where most of the wildlife would be fearful of imminent violent death, as owning a shotgun or a fishing rod in these parts was seen very much as a rite of passage. She also noted the numerous times she saw the state flag flying from flagpoles and rooftops, with its rebellious confederate saltire at its heart. More than just a state of mind, she thought, more than just a state of mind.

On arrival at the Institute, Virginia made her first acquaintance with an especially spruced-up Doleson who'd just come from a meeting with the bank. Mutual felicitations were soon brought to an end, as Virginia informed her host of a busy day ahead; there was indeed a long list of people to talk to and places to see. Before they set off, Virginia examined the car meticulously, intent on carrying out a little initial forensic work on the results of that gunshot blast.

Leaning forward, she reached into the shattered rear window and picked something from out of the shelf. She let forth a hardly suppressed laugh. 'Yes, a real pee-shooter,' she said, as she held it to the light. Doleson could see that she was holding a tiny pellet, so small he could hardly make it out. 'Surprised it was able to smash anything, let alone this,' she said, as she removed a shard of protruding glass.

Doleson was suitably impressed. There were things about Virginia that Soren had already prepared him for, but as always, it didn't match up to what he was seeing in the flesh. This was one hell of class act. She in return noted the roving eye, the touch of the debonair gone to seed, along with that flicker of Parichean madness, all wrapped up in light-coloured trousers and flayed linen jacket. Doleson was very much back to his garrulous self, so much so, that Virginia was soon finding it difficult to get a word in edgeways. With everything that had gone on, it was still all about his blessed Institute. And in Virginia, Doleson could see someone who was probably key to keeping Soren on board. Without him, his organisational skills and the Californian connection, Doleson knew his plans for the Institute would be dust.

'But, Miss Ginny, you've seen what he's like,' said Doleson, about Soren. 'He seems to be in such a fragile state. You know how important it is to get him back with the project?'

Although a little suspicious as to the angle of Doleson's pitch, Virginia knew he was right. That early morning phone call had shown just how brittle Soren's state of mind had become. 'I fear that it might not be as easy as you seem to think.'

'I didn't say that it would be, ma'am. But at some point he's going to have to get back into the saddle.'

'Might I remind you that someone has just died!'

'Yes, I know.' For just a moment his mood appeared to deflate, then, just as quickly, he burst back into life. 'Don't you think I'd change things if I could, Miss Ginny? It just don't make sense.' There was another silence, before he was straining at the leash again. 'The snakebite, Miss Ginny, I can just about stomach that as a kind of fool thing that some folks around here might do, but the shooting!'

This was something that was playing on Virginia's mind too as they made their first port of call, at the pathologist's office. Here, the clerk responded somewhat sniffily to their inquiries. She'd obviously had enough of being at the receiving end of Christina's questions and, via the telephone, one of Paisley's tirades. Now she informed them that the FBI and the state police had finished with their enquiries and that the sheriff had OK'd the body's release. Virginia thanked her and said she would arrange for the funeral service people to collect the body, after she herself had examined it.

In the morgue much of what Virginia saw agreed with what the pathologist had already found. His report, fetched by a still rather disgruntled-looking clerk, confirmed a puzzle that Virginia had noticed immediately on seeing the body. The entry point of the bullet was at the back of the top-frontal part of the skull, as if the gun had been fired from above and behind the head. And the wound was far too small for the .45 ACP cartridge that had been found in the ceiling of the hospital room where Brad had been shot. Only a small fragment of the bullet had done the damage, coming to rest inside the brain. It also pointed to the possible use of an M1911 pistol; something far removed from the run of the mill weaponry usually associated with the hunting and hooded fraternity in this neck of the woods. The bullet had grazed the mettle support of a ceiling light and it was a splinter from this impact that was thought to have killed the deceased. It also pointed to the possibility of a struggle, something supported by further examinations carried out by the pathologist, which revealed bruising to the victim's right arm and the presence of foreign human tissue under his fingernails.

Virginia was an experienced detective, with an acute sensitivity to protocol. In Pittsburgh, this would usually involve a subtle, but obvious, insistence on rank. Here, in Mississippi though, she would have to make sure she was seen to be doing things in a businesslike, no-nonsense, fashion, whilst trying not to tread on too many toes. On meeting Sheriff Harper this didn't change. Like Christina before her, Virginia soon surmised that the Sheriff was someone who could do with a little help. Yes, she would need to be careful, but she wanted him to get the message that here was someone with real expertise and experience to offer. So, courteous to a fault, she waited, biding her time.

The Sheriff did indeed seem to be impressed with what he saw, but, to begin with, this didn't seem to get past his mannered bewitchment with this woman's obvious grace and beauty. As for the investigation, there was still resistance.

'Ma'am, I'm thankful to you for taking all the trouble to come down here, and I'm sure that you're very capable, but miss, this is not Pittsburgh.'

Yes, a proud man, she thought, and she would play along with the dance, just like Christina had done before her.

'Now, now, Sheriff,' said Doleson, coming to the rescue, 'I'm sure we could all do with a little help.'

The sheriff gave a distracted smile, before pausing to look at Virginia again. Like so many of those who'd gone before, he was having trouble trying to square what he was looking at. This was not the kind of law enforcement officer you usually saw down here in Toshoba County, Mississippi. Could someone this striking really be the kind who'd enjoy being up to their armpits in the filth and detritus of murder? Still somewhat reluctant, the sheriff shrugged his shoulders and leaned back in his chair. The events of the past few days had shaken him. 'We're only a small department, ma'am, in a small town.'

Virginia gave him an acknowledging smile, as she surveyed the rows of mugshots that surrounded a picture of the sheriff engaged in his favourite pastime. He proudly followed her gaze. 'Yes, that's a largemouth,' he said. 'A fifteen pounder. Took almost an hour to reel it in.'

'I've known one to clean up an entire stretch back home,' she replied.

He tipped his hat and nodded his approval. 'I'm impressed. You fish yourself?'

'No, but some of my friends do.' She turned and took a long look at the two gentlemen before her. 'You folks look as if you've been under a lot of pressure.'

'We pride ourselves on being able to handle most things, ma'am.' The Sheriff's smile, if a little forced, was still there. 'But this business had been a real challenge.'

Again, like Christina before her, Virginia was beginning to be won over. This was a decent man, she thought. She guessed that during his stewardship he'd always attempted to be one step ahead of the community he represented. Looking at him, she correctly deduced that the sheriff had never married, although he was known to step out now and again with a spinster who was the local librarian. No one dared suggest that it was anything other than platonic. Virginia wondered if she could ask a few questions. The sheriff had no objections, so she went ahead. Firstly she was concerned as to what tests might have been carried out, along with the whereabouts of the documentation.

'We don't go much for paperwork, I guess. We've had a lot on our plate. A lot of ground to cover since this dreadful business broke. I hear you're going to be taking the body back home?'

'Well, not exactly. I've arranged for a funeral firm to pick it up later today. I myself will be staying on for a couple of days until the end of the week.'

'You seem to be in a bit of a hurry!' The Sheriff gave Doleson one of his mockingly surprised looks. It cut no ice with Virginia.

'You *do* understand that it needs to be done quickly?' she replied.

'Yes, I understand that some of the deceased's relations are Jewish. They have been in touch.'

Yes, Virginia could see the sheriff had obviously had a time of it. Days of fielding enquiries from relatives and friends from across the country. Martin would have been a handful and Brad's parents would have been no pushover. Paisley would have been barely off the phone, and would probably have been all for making the journey south himself.

'About the murder, Sheriff,' Virginia had had enough of the prevarications, 'do we have any witnesses?'

'Well, there's Bridget, Bridget Harrelson, who came in the other day. Her father was the one they had the argument with the day they arrived. Lovely kid, was real cut up about the whole business. Didn't know anything. Just didn't want us to think that her dad had anything to do with it.'

Virginia had now produced a notebook. Already her enquiries were beginning to morph into a gentle, but definite, interrogation. Doleson didn't have a clue as to how she had accomplished this but, nonetheless, he marveled at the ease at which she appeared to be eliciting information from his friend. It was like being at confessional.

Her questioning was becoming more direct now; uncomfortably so. The type of gun used, and the calibre of bullet, was soon established, but it soon became clear, as far as forensics were concerned, that there were certain limitations. The sheriff knew that there had been deficiencies in the way he and his department had gone about things, but this was painful. Forensics, forensics, forensics, was the mantra of Virginia's work in Pittsburgh. Down here she suspected that this would be seen as just another big city affectation; required only to keep up the pretence that the police knew what they were doing. 'Besides, Sam the pathologist, could usually be relied upon to do a competent job.' Virginia was left wondering what the FBI would have made of it. And so the interrogation continued.

'What did the crime scene look like? In what position was the body found?'

'I'll get Cyrus to check out the photos we took.'

'What technical resources were there to hand?'

Blank.

'Had ballistics matched the bullet?'

Another blank.

'What was the time of death? The pathologist's report had indicated a time somewhere between ten p.m. and five a.m.'

'We got news of the death at about four a.m., and we think it happened sometime up to two hours before then.'

'Who discovered the body, and who reported it?'

'Nurse Rosa, down at the hospital.'

'How many people had access to the room and how many have had access since the murder?'

Ah, the blanks had returned.

'What security did the hospital have?'

'What kind of security did you have in mind?'

'Personnel, cameras.'

Blank

'Was the crime scene still accessible?'

'I'll get Cyrus on to it.'

'What blood and tissue samples have been taken?'

The sheriff raised an eyebrow and this time Virginia filled in the blanks. 'Might I suggest, Cyrus?' She'd had enough and, partially out of regard for the sheriff's sensibilities, called the litany of woes to a halt. She would find answers to the rest of the questions she had later. The Sheriff did though, have a few ideas about the snakebite. He didn't think that was linked to the shooting at all.

'Yes,' interrupted Doleson, 'Miss Ginny was saying as much to me on the way over.'

The Sheriff continued. 'We've had a few leads, but I would be most obliged if you would leave that part of the investigation to us, ma'am. I'd hate for you to have to have dealings with the lowlifes we'll be talking to.'

Virginia smiled; just what did they think she got up to on the streets of Pittsburgh? Before she left, though, she did venture an interest about what the other agencies might have been up to. 'Just what have the state police and the FBI been doing?' Now that was something the Sheriff did know. 'Nothing,' he replied. 'The FBI knew shoot.'

58

Virginia, Doleson and the deputy drove to McClaren Hospital together. The drive was a brief one and they soon found themselves in a reception area whose design owed much to the era of FDR and the National Recovery Act. From here they were escorted by Cyrus to the crime scene. Virginia was relieved to see the room had not been put back into circulation.

'I take it you still have all the original bedding?'

Cyrus looked downcast. 'I guess we could ask.'

Virginia shot him a look of resigned disbelief. Only when it changed into a deliberately maintained glare, did the penny drop. He made his apologies and departed to chase things up, leaving Virginia and Doleson alone to mull things over. The room had been made up, but there were still bits of detritus scattered around, and this served as a prompt for a question from a baffled Doleson.

'Why is the bedding so important?

'There might be something left on it from the killer and, just as importantly, there might still be bits of it on him. It's a long shot, but if we do get a suspect, then we're into a different ball game.' Doleson smiled appreciatively, but still looked none the wiser. She tried to enlighten him. 'If there was a struggle, and I think there definitely was, then there could be sweat and hand impressions. There might even be a wound.'

'How do you know there was a struggle?'

Virginia lifted herself onto the bed and lay down. She pointed to the top of her head and the entry point of the bullet. 'It seems odd to me that the killer could have gone through all the trouble of walking over to the victim, lifting his head, and shooting, with the gun pointed down, through the top and back of his head. You see, it's impossible.' She gave the wall a tap. 'This would be in the way.'

'Well, he might have been lying on his side, with his head bent down.'

There was a genuine look of surprise on her face. 'That is a possibility. But I don't think someone suffering from an arm swollen with snake bite is going to lie on it, and I think you will find that it was his left arm. He would have been sleeping on his back, with his head propped up on the pillows. Or he could have been lying on his right hand side. Either way, the angle of the shot is a little odd. That's why I want to see those photos. Besides, the sheriff said that the bed had looked a mess. The shot would have killed him instantly, so why the mess?'

'Might the killer have deliberately messed things up, to make it look that way?'

'Why? Why risk leaving evidence?'

'Then, here's another question, you said you don't think the snakebite and this are linked?'

'The snakebite was probably not even a murder attempt.'

'How do you figure that?'

'It's a bit of a longwinded way to go about committing a murder. No, whoever did that was probably thinking of just sending a message, although not a very nice one. No, this has all the markings of someone who does this regularly. Someone usually much more professional and efficient. They probably even used a silencer.'

'How do you figure that out?'

'Just a hunch. But something did go very wrong here. The killer didn't expect to be in a fight. I guess he didn't even know Brad!'

'But who the hell would want to kill him in the first place?'

Virginia gave a puzzled shrug, then, commandeering a bedside chair, stepped up to examine the metal base of the light fitting above their heads. Just as the pathologist report had said, there was a small blackened impression and a dent in the metal, right next to the hole where the bullet was found. Virginia had seen many ricochet marks before, and this definitely looked like one. She turned to look at the bed again and, before long, was soon examining a metal handrail, set against the wall, above it. A small mark had caught her attention. She now produced a small penknife from her pocket, which she used to scrape some residue into a small plastic bag. There was a shake of the head, then a sigh. 'Brad was so unlucky,' she said, looking up at Doleson, 'so very unlucky.'

On the way back to the reception area, Virginia reflected on what Doleson had asked earlier. Just who could have done this? It certainly wasn't the people responsible for the snake. Virginia just couldn't get herself to accept the idea of local rednecks going around with silencers. And yes, a silencer must have been used. There had been no reported hearings of a gunshot, and a .45 makes an awful lot of noise. On their return to the reception area, Virginia asked the clerk on duty if she could see the duty roster for the night of the shooting. Without needing to check, the woman informed her that it had been a Nurse Rosario and she would be back on duty later this afternoon. So they waited, Virginia and Doleson, for Nurse Rosario to return. Their sojourn was interrupted by a red-faced Cyrus, informing them that the bed linen they were looking for had indeed been sent for cleaning. He promised that he would salvage what he could, and that the photos they'd asked for would be waiting for them back at the office.

Over coffee and sandwiches Virginia listened as Doleson and the deputy went through a list of people they thought might be capable of the rattlesnake stunt. They were the usual suspects; 'Losers, all of them,' said the deputy, but it didn't make the exercise any more palatable. The list of potential candidates, the various hate groups and people who might wish them harm, was a long one, and it was not lost on Doleson and Virginia that if anyone had been at risk, from people such as these, it would probably be Soren.

When Nurse Rosario did finally turn up for her shift she was understandably defensive and only marginally reassured by the presence of Doleson, who she immediately recognised.

'Yes, Miss Rosario,' said the deputy, taking the lead, 'this is Miss Ginny. She has some questions for you.'

Not sure whether to thank him or not, Virginia smiled and asked her question.

'The other evening, when you were on duty, can you remember what you heard?'

Nurse Rosario was still leery at yet another person prying into what she'd been doing that night and making judgments about her performance. 'Honestly, miss, I don't know how that man got past me.'

'Don't worry, Rosario, nobody here is questioning how you do your job,' interrupted Cyrus again, 'just answer this lady's questions.'

'Didn't hear a thing,' she reiterated. The shutters had come down.

'Nothing?' said Virginia.

'Nothing.'

'And you finally found the deceased...'

'As I said, when I was on one of my rounds. Must have been about four in the morning. It was awful!'

'Yes, I'm sure it was. And when was the last time you checked in on him, before you found him?'

'About two.'

'That's how we can pinpoint it so precisely,' added the deputy. 'Fits in with what Sam says.'

Now Virginia was annoyed. She walked around to where Nurse Rosario was sitting and invited her to join her in a small back-office area, out of earshot from the other two. As she did so, she shot a pleading glance towards Doleson, who, getting the message, immediately took Cyrus by the arm. 'Come,' he said, 'tell me how Harold is bearing up, what with all this going on.'

Virginia and Nurse Rosario were now alone.

'Now, Rosario, don't you go worrying about the deputy. Everything you tell me here is strictly between us.'

'I heard nothing, miss,' she replied, repeating the mantra, 'honestly, I heard nothing!'

'I know, but if you could go through everything you do remember that night.'

So Virginia talked Nurse Rosario through the night's events and it soon became apparent that she did indeed have nothing more to add than was already on record. Virginia thanked her and gave her one of her cards.

'If you do think of anything, give me a call. That's the number I've written at the top. I'll be there for the next couple of days.'

Nurse Rosario studied the card and let out a soft sigh. 'My my, all the way from Pittsburgh? Ain't that a thing!' For the first time she appeared to drop her guard, giving Virginia an engaging smile. 'I'm sorry I've not been much use. But I do hope you catch Professor Karlsson's killer.'

Virginia stopped dead in her tracks. 'Pardon, what did you say?'

'Professor Karlsson! The gentleman who was killed.'

'The deceased was a Professor Hemlin,' replied Virginia, now intensely interested.

'That's not what was written on the sheet,' said Nurse Rosario, getting up and going over to retrieve the case records from a nearby drawer. Virginia made after her, waving Doleson over as she did so, just in time to see Nurse Rosario produce a tag with Soren's name on it. The nurse who'd been attending on Brad's reception to the hospital had entered the wrong name. The realisation of what Virginia was looking at struck home immediately, as it did with Doleson, who was beginning to mirror her look of anxiety. For Virginia, there was now a moment of extreme internal panic, followed by frantic attempts to counter and reassure.

'Would these notes be visible?' she asked.

'Sure, they're the ones we put at the foot of the bed.'

Now her mind was working overtime. No, this just couldn't be. Surely someone, hell bent on murder, doesn't stop in the moment of the act, and in pitch darkness, to look through a medical sheet. But there again, that's the first thing he would do. Think girl, the very fact that he was in darkness would have meant the need for some reassurance that this was indeed the correct target.

'And if anyone had phoned the hospital, would he have been told that it was a Professor Karlsson who'd been hospitalised?'

'Sure,' replied Nurse Rosario, 'that was the name we had on the sheet.'

As they walked away, Doleson ventured a thought about something he remembered when Christina had visited earlier. How the sheriff had thought that the deceased had been her boy.

'We appear to have discovered another line of enquiry,' said Virginia. Still very much shaken, she forced herself a smile as she indicated her wish to leave. She needed time to think and compose herself. Their exit, though, was halted, by Nurse Rosario, who called out after them, buoyant and very voluble. 'Now, I remember. I did hear something. Sounded like a pop. Or was it a crash.'

'Hell, Nurse Rosario, why didn't you say something about this before?' interjected the deputy, hurt.

'Don't worry about that,' said Virginia, irritated. 'Concentrate on what you think you heard. When was this?'

'I don't know. Maybe about ten minutes before I went to check I guess. Just didn't think much of it at the time.'

'And you're absolutely sure?' continued Virginia, determined to cut off any further interruptions from Cyrus. 'You're sure it sounded like a pop?'

'Well, more of a crash actually, sounded like something heavy, glass maybe, being whacked against something.'

'Where did you think it came from?' Virginia was back in control.

'Well, that's the thing, it didn't come from the direction of the, you know, the room, but from outside.'

'And you're certain of this?'

'As sure as you're sitting there now.'

Virginia thanked her, then was off, purposely striding towards the hospital entrance. At the door, she stopped and looked towards the gate at the end of the drive that served as the hospital's main port of entry and exit. Without saying a word, and with the others in tow, she strode off towards it. At the gate she stopped, looked around, then stooped to peer at something lying in the gutter. The others watched, entranced, as she bent down, balancing on one leg, while she splayed the other to one side, as if she were a gymnast balancing on a beam. One moment she would be hovering, the next squatting squaw like, before balletically assuming another pose; all urgent examination and enquiry. Cyrus, for one, couldn't help but marvel at the efficiency and grace of it all. It troubled him to think, that this almost flawless movement was effortlessly combined with the kind of police work he'd hardly envisaged before. What's more, he'd never seen Sheriff Harper move like this.

'There you go, Cyrus,' she said handing him a fragment of glass to look at. 'Probably came from a parking light. Hit the kerb, or a stone, I guess. Takes an age for something like that to get swept away. Someone was in a hurry.' She quickly pocketed a couple of fragments for herself before giving him instructions to bag the rest as soon as possible. She fully intended to take one of the fragments back home with her to Pittsburgh. Another would be sent to Craig and his people at Berkeley. She didn't hope for much, but maybe they had at last come up with something.

59

Morristown, New Jersey

It was one of those crisp November mornings when New Yorkers are reminded of the first portents of winter. The drive across the Hudson, through the urban wastes of Newark had been, for Soren, something of a numb slow-motion blur, albeit one that had managed to elude the taught prism that usually accompanies a Pariche-induced hangover. It wasn't until they were well into the frosted stillness of the New Jersey countryside that Soren felt able to take in the scenery around him with any tangible form of coherence. In less than an hour the car was turning into a driveway at a cemetery just outside the town of Morristown. Paisley had insisted on an open-air ceremony with seating provided for some. There were about one hundred mourners present, before an open burial plot, with everybody on their best behaviour, truces firmly in place. Soren found himself seated once again between Elizabeth and his mother, near the front, with Pariche and Doleson banished to the outer fringes. At the front were five figures, centre stage, at the graveside's edge. Alongside Paisley and Julia, were Brad's partner Martin, Father O'Brien and Rabbi Schulz. Julia had seen to it that Tanya, the trophy wife, had also been banished to the back, where she could pout under the admiring gazes of Pariche and Doleson. When Soren arrived, both Paisley and Julia had risen to their feet, intent on coming across. He waved for them to stop and, instead, went over to where they were seated. There were embraces and promises to speak at the wake afterwards.

'Don't be a stranger, Soren,' Paisley said, 'you've always been family to us.'

Christina had felt increasingly superfluous since she'd been able, with Virginia's help, to facilitate the release of Brad's body and have it brought home. Now the Hemlins were in charge and the funeral arrangements had been all theirs. They sat, stiff-backed and mostly silent, save for the acknowledgement of various mourners, and the occasional word with Martin, who was clearly struggling. The two clerics were in deep discussion with each other, seemingly oblivious to what was going on. Soren relaxed a little, grateful that others had assumed centre stage. Some of the mourners from California were clearly ill prepared for the near-freezing temperatures and sat shivering in their lightweight suits. They were colleagues of Brad's from San Francisco General and UCSF, along with some friends from Castro. Dean Unsworth, the medical school's official representative, looked suitably grave, solemnly doing his duty, but with half a mind on the performance he would be attending, of *Il Trovatore*, at the Met later that evening. Apart from Elizabeth, upholding the secular episcopal tradition, and Soren and Christina the lapsed Lutheran one, the congregants were overwhelmingly Catholic and Jewish. Christina had been right in her prediction that there would be a large turnout from Julia's side of the family. Soren knew some of them very well, from the many times he'd stayed over with the Hemlins during school vacations, when Julia had given him over to a string of Brad's uncles and aunts. And if Paisley had had problems getting to grips with his son's sexuality, it was something that appeared to pose few problems for the folks at Julia's synagogue on Fifth. Despite this, and the Hemlin family's somewhat precarious relationship with the synagogue, the old hands from the *chevra kadisha* had done a fine job preparing the body. Soren found himself chuckling at the thought that they'd even tried to have the casket shrouded with an Israeli flag. The mind positively boggled as to what nerves had been frayed in the ceremony's planning. He also found himself smiling at the disapproving looks now being given by some of the older mourners to the skimpy outfits worn by some of the women. There was also a late arrival, surely a kindred spirit of the princesses that Soren had observed at Le Cirque the night before, who made a grand, and somewhat, theatrical entrance, with full entourage in tow, blaming her lateness on the hapless man, her husband, trailing in her wake. Yes, Brad would have loved that.

When it came to the eulogy, there were kind words from Father O'Brien. He could have made a fuss; Brad after all had hardly been the model communicant. But no, the good reverend stood the memory of him proud, using a couple of stories Soren had provided, whilst at the same time glossing over the more colourful ones. Then he did something Soren had not anticipated. He looked up and asked if anyone had anything to say. Soren could see the eyes of everyone following the gaze of Martin, as it, horror of horrors, settled on him, importuning him, Professor Soren Karlsson, and Brad's oldest friend, to answer Father O'Brien's call and say a few words. Of course, he chided himself, this is what they do at funerals! He should have been better prepared. Should have known this would happen. He felt the hand of his mother tugging at his arm. 'Go on,' he heard her say, 'it will do you good.' He rose to his feet, shakily at first, and as he did so, he caught a glimpse of Pariche sitting at the back, beaming forth with what was, dare one say, an almost fatherly smile. So he began to speak, hesitantly at first, but then the words began to flow. He didn't know from where it came, but he found himself talking about Brad in a very calm and collected way, as if he were reliving those moments he'd spent the day before in Morningside. The memories came flooding back; the Exeter days, followed by their time together at Columbia. He spoke of Brad's energy and how he'd been such a force for change. The Brad he knew then had been the one to get his retaliation in first, organising rent strikes and fighting curriculum battles. How it had been around this time that he'd first became aware of Brad's homosexuality and his first tentative steps into the gay scene. Soren looked at Martin and said, 'In this you were a truer friend.' He then went on to talk about Brad's medical career and his contribution to the fight against AIDs. This brought forth a loud 'hear, hear' from Pariche, and a slow deliberate hand clap that sent a ripple of sympathy through the part of the audience that included Martin's entourage from San Francisco. The rest of the congregation remained impassive, torn between admiration, bemused intrigue and sullen hostility. Soren could see that Martin was struggling. Apart from the last few years in San Francisco, he was being exposed to a world that, in the main, he would have been shielded from and, dare one say, excluded. And, of course, Soren knew that he, himself, would be resented, by Martin, for being centre stage now, no matter how brief.

Soren's sense of unease about Martin's fragile state was confirmed when, after leading the filling in of the grave, he did finally break down. It needed all the efforts of both communities, familial and spiritual, to prevent an extravagant embrace of the casket, leaving Soren a little leery and somewhat jealous of the spectacle. Jealous that here again was true emotion being displayed; something in which he, himself, would be found wanting.

60

Afterwards people drifted back to the old Hemlin home, now in Julia's name, set amidst the forested foothills that rolled into the Appalachians. About half the congregation had made it back, and they were soon scattered throughout the abode's assortment of rooms and annexes. The buffet was barely tolerable and not partaken of by Soren. Over dried pastrami and soggy rolls, people were beginning to prize themselves free of the constraints imposed by the protocols of mourning, and were soon talking of work, golf handicaps, fitness tips and school fees, and finding out what had become of long lost relatives. Their children, also liberated from the need to be on their best behaviour, now ran amuck, darting between legs and trying the patience of all – all, that is, with the exception of Pariche. Presently this big, broad-shouldered specimen of pioneer spirit, and still wearing that white Stetson, was telling a tall western tale, with a group of youngsters at his feet, hooked on every word.

Julia's side of the family could be divided into two. There were the wealthy Fifth Avenue set that she lived alongside, and her more orthodox immediate family who mostly hailed from Brooklyn. Paisley's brood had mainly driven in from Queens and Nassau. They were third and fourth generation Italian-Irish, split between Fenian insurrectionists from Dublin, communist revolutionaries from Bologna, and primitivist Catholics from Calabria. When not fighting amongst themselves, they would find ample opportunities to continue the conflict with everyone else. In this, Julia's family were the perfect foil. Both sides knew that the sources of any discontent and conflict would be likely to come from their own, and with Dukakis's resounding defeat in the presidential election still fresh in the air, they knew there would be many well-rehearsed opportunities for blame to be apportioned. Added to the mix would be the unpredictable counsel that might be offered from those members of the west coast contingent still present. And there was always Pariche and Doleson to add to the mix.

Having forsaken his storytelling duties, Pariche now saw it as his job to drop not so subtle hints to Soren about the need to get back to Mississippi. As he did so, elsewhere amongst the assembled guests, conversations took a more predictable turn as certain tensions began to work their way to the surface. It started with a perceived sleight from Paisley about the house they were in and how it had become somewhat neglected. This was quickly followed by another from Tanya, about how this diagnosis might also be applied to Julia herself. This did not go down well, leading one of Julia's brothers to wonder aloud as to why his sister had risked apostasy for this shmuck. Soon everyone was shouting, with arguments breaking out all over the place. Doleson, not wanting to miss out on the fun, was soon upbraiding one of Paisley's Wall Street clients over the latter's dismissal of poverty, as two of Paisley's brothers nearby squared up to each other over the running sore that was their father's legacy. Then everyone's attention was drawn to yet another cry of distress. Julia had overheard one of her more distant relatives glorying in the one-upmanship of having such an exotic funeral to go to.

'Why,' the woman had declared, 'I might have done the deed myself if I'd known there'd be a send-off like this!'

Within seconds Julia was up and at her, wagging her finger, her face a picture of rage. The relative, reinforced by a few of her bejeweled and drunken friends, gave as good as she got. On hearing the commotion, Paisley sailed into the fray. 'You fucks, you fat fucks!' he screamed. 'How dare you talk to my wife like that,' much to the chagrin of the young woman he'd bourn on his arm to the funeral. To give Tanya her due, she too was up for the fight, defending both

Paisley's and Julia's honour, as well as giving her new husband a good ear-wigging in the process.

And Soren wasn't to be spared, as he finally got the full assault he'd been dreading. Martin, now stood before him, the sober attire of his dark suit contrasting with the fire in his eyes. He had an alcohol-induced list of grievances and Soren knew that he would just have to take what was coming. He didn't know much about Martin, save for the fact that he was a graphic designer and had been a drag on Brad's full participation in the trip to Mississippi. He was also a member of a gay activist network, and it had been this that had brought him into contact with Brad. Theirs was a relationship that had withstood a series of harrowing assaults as they witnessed many of their friends succumb to an ailment that appeared to be so monstrously vengeful. And it was this that was used against Soren now. How he'd managed to drag Brad off in pursuit of such an arcane and dead issue as civil rights, when he could have been fighting the good fight against AIDS back home in San Francisco. Soren knew the charge was unanswerable and he found his attempts to mollify falling on stony ground. Now he was being accused of being responsible for Brad's death. Why had he taken him to that hate-filled place? Had there not been more than enough to do at home? It had wreaked of betrayal. Always, in the background, there had been, between Soren and Brad, that boyhood friendship that had trumped everything else. In the end it was left to Julia to put a gentle arm around Martin and lead him away.

Soren felt both wretched and guilty about his failure to reach out to him. Martin still looked the child: lost, and not yet out of his twenties. Apart from a couple of old friends from the Harlem Co-op, and Soren, of course, Martin's had been one of the few black faces visible at the funeral, and one that was subject to a very visible and public anguish. Soren felt culpable in adding to his distress. His comments had cut in other ways too, testing Soren's thoughts about his true relationship to Brad. Here was someone, very important to Brad, who'd been kept at a distance, unattended to and denied. Once again, it left Soren wondering if he'd really been such a true friend.

Later, as was so often the case, Christina took it upon herself to draw things to a close as far as the Karlsson-Van Buren entourage were concerned. It ended a conversation she and Elizabeth had about a call they'd received from Virginia. More than anything, the detective was now convinced that Soren had been the intended victim of what had happened in Mississippi; something that had been confirmed by Doleson when he'd arrived yesterday. Christina wasn't sure whether Soren was still in danger, but she immediately recognised the need for action. He would have to lay low for a while. If Pariche and Doleson were hell bent on returning to Mississippi, then so be it; but Christina would do her best to keep Soren safe, something that would be facilitated by having him stay with Virginia in Pittsburgh. Not surprisingly this was something that had met with Virginia's approval.

'Yes,' Christina had said, 'Virginia had been most insistent.'

61

Albert and Tank were mulling over the latest disaster. Not long after his boss's most recent appearance at the committee hearings, before the bitch from hell, Tank had contacted Felix in order to get the latest intelligence. By various means, mostly foul, Felix had been able to establish that Christina had a son teaching at Berkeley; could they get one of the boys in Vegas to take a look? The people there reported back that the kid had flown the coop, apparently embarked on some kind of trip to Mississippi.

But perhaps things weren't so bad after all. New Orleans was conveniently close, and the people down there owed Albert a favour. Could they take a ride into the sticks and deliver a warning; something that would send just the right message to the bitch. Besides, nobody would be able to trace anything back to Albert, sitting, as he was, fifteen hundred miles away in Boston. But things had gone terribly wrong and for some reason the boys in New Orleans had whacked the guy. So Albert and Tank waited. Waited for the flack. But for some reason, it never came. The reason was soon forthcoming, for Tank was now in receipt of a photo. He showed it to Albert. 'Felix got this to us from New York, just a couple of days ago.'

'Well, I'll be...!' Albert studied the picture carefully. 'Wasn't he the guy we saw out at her place?'

'Yes. He's the guy we were after.'

'You mean...'

'Yes, Boss, he's the son.'

'My, my, who'd have figured that she'd have a nigger for a son. So who did they whack down there?'

'Dunno, Boss, one of his friends I guess. Case of mistaken identity.'

Albert thought for a moment, before turning again to face Tank. 'OK,' he said, 'Keep Felix on standby, we might have to deal with this ourselves.'

'You sure, Boss?'

Albert gave one of his cold, dead-eyed stares. 'Just make sure he's on standby,' he repeated. 'Just make sure.'

62

All along Virginia had been intent on making a call on
Bridget. She didn't know why, but there appeared to be an
inner voice telling her that this person would be worth
following up. Soon she found herself outside the nondescript
suburban house and garden that had been the setting for that
original altercation. Bridget saw the car pull up and, putting
down the cups she'd been washing, came out.

'Well, hi,' she said, in that drawl that had had such a
winning effect on Soren. 'Now isn't that just the self-same
car them folks from up North were driving?' She walked
round to the back and looked at the rear window. 'I guess
you're that fancy detective; the Sheriff said you might be
dropping by.' She paused for a while, as Virginia clambered
out of the car and made her greetings. They shook hands. 'I
said then there wasn't much I could add. Pappy would never
had done anything like that.'

Virginia watched as Bridget walked back and sat herself
down on a swing seat in the porch. She looked the kind of
girl who, anywhere else, would be planning to go to college.
Here though, in small-town Mississippi, one suspected that
she'd be content to settle down and keep her horizons local.
She sat there swinging her legs and kicking her feet. Virginia
asked if she could join her.

'Sure.'

Virginia sat down next to her, mirroring her gaze into the
far distance as she did so.

'I was sorry to hear about what happened to your
friends,' said Bridget, chancing a slightly bashful glance at
her companion. The smart sophistication of the older woman

273

obviously impressed her. 'You must have really cared to have come all this way!'

Virginia smiled; the youngster had her taped. Bridget was of slight build, a couple of inches shorter than herself, with straight shoulder-length hair which curled up at the edges. Virginia leant forward in an attempt to capture the younger woman's gaze. She wanted to reassure. 'Bridget, it is Bridget isn't it? I don't want you to go worrying about your father. He's not even on the radar.'

'Then why are you here?'

'Because you had the good manners to go and see the sheriff and I thought I'd return the compliment.' The younger woman looked unconvinced. 'Look, Bridget, I honestly have no desire to get at your folks. Call it casting pebbles. You're one of the few people down here who've come forward.'

The younger woman heaved a sigh. Whether it was relief or not, Virginia wasn't sure. 'Folks can be a little defensive, I guess.' She stopped for a moment and then, a little more relaxed, continued. 'When I heard, you know, about your friends, well, I thought I'd better get in touch with the sheriff.' She paused again and then repeated the mantra; 'There's no way that Papi would do a thing like that.'

'I know, Bridget, I know. It sounds to me that you acted out of concern. No, as I said, I'm not interested in your father, only anyone you or he might have spoken to since.'

'I keep saying, Papi just wouldn't be involved.'

'But he might have mentioned something to someone. He'd have no control over what they or their friends might make of it.'

At this point both women caught a glimpse of a curtain twitching in the window behind them.

'Yes, he's in there. He's been too scared to come out since...'

Bridget's smile was infectious and Virginia found herself being caught up in a conspiratorial chuckle. The two Southerners were beginning to mirror their assessments of each other.

'C'mon then, which one was it?'

This question from Bridget blindsided Virginia completely.

'You know I can't tell you anything about the investigation, Bridget.'

'No, not that. I meant which one was responsible for bringing you all the way down here? The one you're obviously very close to.'

'Which one?' Virginia was embarrassed.

Bridget let forth a cry of exasperation. 'C'mon, Miss big shot northern detective; you didn't come all the way down here on no accord!'

Virginia stood up, still somewhat off-putted, but the smile soon returned. 'You know, Bridget, you'd make a very good poker player,' she said, as she took out another of her cards, and scribbled some numbers on it. 'Here's the local number where I can be reached if you think of anything.'

'Well, my my,' she said, giving the card a long hard look as they walked over to the car. 'Virginia Bradley-Moore Van Buren. Well, isn't that a barrel full! Whoever it is you came down fuh, I sure hope he's worth it.'

Virginia smiled and shrugged her shoulders.

'He is.'

63

While Virginia was interviewing Bridget, the sheriff resolved to make a call on one of the county's less salubrious establishments located just outside of town. Before he did so, he called on Mayor Dickinson's office, to give him the low down on how things were going. The mayor and his friends on the County Board wanted reassurances that everything was under control. 'We've got to show them, Harold,' the mayor said, 'that we're open for business. Go and get those you think who did this.' The subtext was clear. Let's *not* do this the old Hollis White way. And to that end, with one of his deputies in tow, the sheriff entered a place that, at an extreme push, could be called a lounge bar. No bigger than someone's front room, it was darkly lit, with a rank smelling pool table standing in the corner, its cloth ripped and festering. A pair of frayed curtains, oiled and grubby, shielded what rudimentary furniture there was from the light of day. It was a kind of place where it was only too easy to imagine depraved things having taken place. Besides the sheriff and his deputy, there were four other people present. The sheriff declined the offer of a seat; the last thing he wanted was to give the impression he was comfortable in this company.

A fat man, with sweat marks on the underarms of his stained T-shirt, appeared to be in charge. Sheriff Harper shot a glance at someone who'd chosen to stay in the background, partially hidden from view. The fat man responded by motioning him to come forward, revealing a poor wretch of a man, skinny, with sunken, hollowed-out eyes, who appeared to flinch in the face of the sheriff's grimace. It was barely mid-morning and all of them had drinks in their hands. Well, the sheriff was prepared to forgive that, but what he could not abide, was the varying degrees of nonchalance etched into their faces.

'Randolph, I don't know how you did it,' the sheriff said, addressing his remarks towards the fat man, 'but that rattler stunt you pulled has given me one hell of a headache.' There were nervous laughs and sniggers all round. 'But murder?' Suddenly they were no longer smiling. The sheriff, not before giving the chair a wipe, chose finally to take up the offer of a seat. 'Hell, I really don't like doing this,' he said, 'sitting with you bums. Just makes my flesh crawl.'

'What the...' Randolph's complaint was cut short by the sheriff, who now drew closer so that their faces were only a few inches apart. The former klansman looked visibly unnerved, something that was swiftly conveyed to the others; their sniggering becoming just a little self-conscious. The sheriff though, remained outwardly calm, as he gave a nod back at his deputy, who'd remained standing in the background.

'You see,' he continued, 'I don't really think you have the brains between you to...' He paused and left the deed unsaid. 'But I can see how you might leave a rattler as a calling card. But here's the rub, to warm the cockles of your paranoid hearts. Toshoba County is washing its hands of you. So we're looking for someone to take the fall.'

'Hell, it was only meant to scare them some,' exclaimed the skinny man.

'Shut up, Luke!' cried one of the others.

The sheriff let out a laugh and rose to his feet. 'Cretins, absolute cretins. Tell me, Randolph, how does it feel to be hanging out with filth like this?' The sheriff was now looking a little more deliberately at the skinny man. 'Someone whose been getting just a little too close to his younger kith and kin. Is that what the Klan gets up to these days?'

'You mean...' Spooked, Randolph joined the sheriff in his now contemptuous gaze at the skinny man. The sheriff nodded. Soon the two of them, Randolph and the skinny man, were rolling around, fighting in the dirt, much to the amusement of the lawmen. After a few moments the truth dawned upon the two protagonists and they stopped, dishevelled and embarrassed.

'Boy oh boy! You really don't have a clue, do you? I've no wish to repeat myself and extend this stay longer than I have to, so you'd better listen carefully. If I hear you have so much as taken a dump in this neck of the woods, I will have you up on every charge we, in the county of Toshoba, can think of. Do I make myself clear?'

There was no response. But the sheriff did notice the skinny man, who was still lying on the floor, moving to take something out of his pocket. As quick as a flash, he stepped forward and met the man's jaw with his boot. The squeal of pain and the sound of the splintered crack was awful. All knew that the man's jaw would be wired up for months.

Afterwards they were all brought in for questioning. When they were released, the sheriff ordered his deputies to keep an eye on their movements; after all, they were just dumb enough to go and do something stupid. He was also concerned about what might happen if one of these animals happened across a certain lady detective who just happened to be visiting from up north. What they would make of her he dared not think about.

64

Virginia continued with her exploration of Coulee. She noted that the white population still appeared to possess the town's grazing rights, as they went about their business. Most were middle-aged to elderly, their pace pedestrian. There were a few black faces, one of them a woman coming from out of a Methodist Church, across the road from where she was now sitting. She briefly met Virginia's gaze and 'hello'd acknowledgment, smiled, and then, just as quickly, was gone. Virginia had chosen to park the car on what appeared to be Coulee's main street. She counted a post office, a library, the County Court building, a couple of clothes stores, and a bank she'd not heard of before. They were set opposite a grill, a restaurant called the *Cactus Buell Inn*, a craft shop, and Paterson's, a general store. Once again, they all appeared to be patronised by whites only, as did the Pemberton Tea Rooms further along the road. This last establishment looked particularly inviting. She was about to disembark and enter the place, when she thought of Soren. She was witnessing a scene shaped by Toshoba's segregated past. The library had probably been whites only well into the sixties and as for the Tea Rooms, well, she had an inkling of what would happen if she ever attempted to enter such a place with Soren on her arm. 'Sorry, madam,' would have been the response, 'but we're fully booked, but there is another restaurant further on down, across the street.'

For a moment she sat in her car, underneath a willow tree, undecided as to what to do next. Then she noticed them. Across the road, between a park and the old theatre; a group of black youngsters, chatting and joshing with each other. They were in an establishment that appeared to be a cross

279

between a lunch counter and record store. She let out a slow sigh of disbelief. On the main street, in small-town Mississippi, a group of black kids were relaxed, going about their business unmolested.

She got out of the car, crossed the road, and entered the store. Her entrance did not go unnoticed, as the lads ribbed each other, desperate to point her out. The record collection appeared to be surprisingly good, she thought, as she perused the jazz section, near to where one of the youths was standing. It wasn't long before he summoned up the courage to come over and introduce himself. The manner of his expression was obvious. What was such a foxy lady doing here in Toshoba County? Wouldn't she like to check out the stuff he was looking at? And, of course, he was beside himself when, peering over her Ray Ban glasses, she said yes. She followed her new found host over to the R&B section and asked after his name.

'Nathanial, but most people call me Nat, and yours?'

'Ginny.'

'Like in Virginia the state?'

'Yes, that's the one.' Soon they were joined by his friends. 'So, Nat,' she continued, 'what's the current hot ticket?' As soon as the words came out, she felt a spasm of embarrassment. Nat ignored her clumsy attempt at street credibility and pushed a record sleeve, he was flicking through, towards her.

'*Express Yourself,*' he said, 'the real deal!'

'What does N.W.A. mean?' The boys looked incredulous and giggled to each other. 'I guess I'm more used to people like Tom Waits and Gil Scott-Heron.' Yes, a white lie, she thought, but what would it matter if she'd borrowed something from Soren in an effort to restore a little of that lost credibility?

'*The Revolution Will Not Be Televised.* Respect!' said Nat, impressed.

Pleased that her standing had been somewhat restored, Virginia moved the conversation on. 'I'm really quite surprised that the people around here listen to this kind of stuff.'

'Not many do. If some of the folks around here were to seriously check this place out, then...' His voice trailed off.

'And what do *those* kinds of people listen to?'

'They tend to go for that stuff over there.' He pointed towards the rock, country, and pop sections. 'None of them like this.'

'What, not even your school friends?'

Nat looked at her with a puzzled expression.

'Doesn't do to know too many white kids,' chipped in one of his friends, by way of clarification, while another added, 'We know a few white girls though!'

'Nah, no way man.' There was a cacophony of guffaws and ribbing.

'People don't mix too much around here then?'

Before they could respond though, their attention was caught by the sight of a police car pulling up alongside Virginia's Saab. Deputy Cyrus gave the car a long hard look before looking around, searching for the car's elusive owner.

'Oh dear, I guess I'd better go and put him out of his misery. Don't worry, he's looking for me. I won't mention our little chat.' She waved to get his attention, but by the time she'd turned to wish her erstwhile companions goodbye, they'd long gone. Once back outside she was confronted by a deputy who was in serious need of mollification.

'Ma'am, I wish you wouldn't go off on your own like that.' His tone was pleading and anxious.

'Why, Deputy, I'm touched by your concern.'

'I hope those boys weren't giving you any trouble?'

'No, they were real gentlemen.'

'The sheriff says that I'm to keep an eye on you.'

She looked up, all wide eyed and innocent, that Cheshire cat grin employed, again. 'Well, I am honoured!'

'Ma'am, it's just not safe to...'

'I know.' She gave him a reassuring smile. 'I'll be over at the Institute if you need me.'

'Where did you go, miss? If you don't mind me asking.'

'Oh, you know, around. You do have such a nice little town down here.'

65

When she arrived back at the Academy, Virginia found a visitor waiting to see her. It was Harvey Wilks, and already she was busily calibrating what the authorities down here would arrest him for first. It was just as likely to be for his – not too convincing – portrayal of a wired Dennis Hopper, in any film you cared to mention, as it was for his attire; something that pointed to that self-same actor's role, as a drug dealer in *Easy Rider*. Either way, his impact on Virginia was less than underwhelming.

'Hi, ma'am, Harvey Wilks of *Rolling Stone* magazine at your service. Your friend, Soren, said that I might find you here.'

Virginia felt the twin sensations of caution and intrigue.

'Soren! How do you know Soren?'

The man rose and offered his 'good' hand.

'We flew out from San Francisco together. Said I might be of help. Sure as hell am sorry about what went down here the other day.'

'You've been talking to Soren?' Virginia was obviously having trouble turning the page.

'Aye, he said you'd be ultra fly. Cautious. Said you could do with some help.'

Inwardly, Virginia was livid, her anger directed northwards. What the hell, Soren, do you mean by foisting this on me? The man standing before her reminded her of the ten-bucks-a-shot pimps that she came across on the streets in Pittsburgh.

Harvey Wilks didn't look like a journalist. With long, unkempt hair, tied down by a red bandana, he was a slight figure who smelt of stale tobacco and cheap bourbon. He also had deformities of arm and tooth, and a deep basso voice that Virginia got the impression had been deliberately cultivated in the mistaken belief that it was somehow attractive. There was, at a stretch, a winning smile and an honest eye, but all in all, this was someone who, in an earlier age, could have been a snake oil salesman. Despite this, Virginia could see something about him that might be useful. If her judgement of him was right, here was someone who could, withered arm and all, do some of the legwork. His journalistic skills might just be put to a little investigative use. Her face broke into that beckoning Cheshire cat grin again, and Harvey duly took the bait.

'Yes, ma'am. You're limited in the amount of time you have down here, and that's a commodity I sure as hell have a lot of.'

'And, of course,' she interjected, 'you might just get a good story.'

'Well, yes, there is that angle I suppose, but I wouldn't divulge anything you wouldn't want me to. I want to see whoever did this put behind bars just as much as you do. I could maybe get into places and ask a few questions.'

Virginia gave it some thought. Of course Soren was right. Why not leave Harvey to poke around a little and see what else he could dig up? Besides, she had precious little time herself! She had forensic samples that needed to be returned to Pittsburgh and she needed to talk to Dyson. She had a sneaking feeling that the latter, with all the contacts he had in the Justice Department, would be of help. More importantly, she desperately wanted to be with Soren. That mistaken hospital chart had changed everything. Christina would have to be told, but telling Soren that he'd probably been the killer's intended target would be of an entirely different order. The last time she'd spoken to him, he'd sounded so fragile. This could push him over the edge. She looked again at the man standing before her. Perhaps she was looking at something that indicated that Soren was back on the mend and had been thinking things through; thinking of her. She felt that tug again. That urgent impulse to be gone. To drop everything and be with him.

66

Berkeley, California

After the departmental meeting he'd attended with Pariche, Denis had felt emboldened by the seemingly free hand he'd been given to get on with things back in Berkeley. And, with this invigorated sense of purpose, he set about making that visit, he and Soren had talked about at Triple Rock, to the local community college. It would involve an audience with a certain Miss Phyllida Truss, a Betty Boo figure who seemed to be relishing her newfound status as the college's local power broker, a privileged position she owed to an ongoing liaison she had with the Chair of the Board of Governors.

Before he went, Denis gave Lucy Teager a call, the unfortunate teacher who'd had the misfortune to be in post at the time of the new broom's arrival. He wanted to reassure her and, if possible, get her back the position she'd walked away from. He also wanted to show her he had influence and authority. That here was someone from the University of California, with all its lustre and prestige, prepared to fight her corner. Miss Teager was far from sanguine about his chances.

'You'll need to be careful,' she said. 'You'll be dealing with a thorough-going sociopath who's very much mobbed up. She can guarantee the Board's interest in everything she says and does. They're only too willing to give her everything she wants.' Denis listened as she continued to paint a portrait of someone brazenly flouting her newly elevated status, terrorising senior managers and the college principal, and getting the Board to approve spending on her pet projects. Poor Lucy Teager would be just a footnote;

anything she had the gall to put her name to just didn't stand a cat in hell's chance.

So it was with this rather dispiriting conversation still playing on his mind, that Denis made his way along a rather featureless corridor towards Miss Truss's office. He was prepared for battle and was sure he had a few cards up his sleeve, not least the illustrious name of the institution he represented. He'd hardly had time to sit down, though, before this illusion was well and truly shattered. Just what was Denis's position at the university exactly? Miss Truss asked, not making any entreaties as to his health. 'Teaching assistant? I'm afraid, Mr Tsui, that doesn't carry much weight around here. It would have been so much better if we'd had someone with a little more authority to deal with.' He ignored the calculated snub and the low-cut cleavage. Her voice was low, sonorous and seductive. It was also dismissive. He was confused; the ambiguous tone and negative message was in sharp contrast to the closeness of her bosom and the hand placed reassuringly on his arm.

'But I can assure you, Phyllida, I do have Professor Karlsson's full backing!'

'I hear that might not be enough!' she replied. 'That he might not be running things next year.' This last missive was delivered with a delicious, almost gleeful deliberateness. Denis felt the pit of his stomach churning. Just what did she know? What was her source? Now he really was on his guard. As Phyllida continued, Denis began to wonder if Lucy Teager had somewhat understated the warning she'd given, for here was someone most adept at formulating the congenial lie and dissembling the truth; fronting the most egregious of deceits. As their meeting progressed, Phyllida's insincerity became ever more pronounced, as did the continuous head nodding and nervous foot trembling. It took great effort, on Denis's part, not to show any discomfort at being witness to such a collection of neuroses.

'Lucy was a most valued member of the team,' she swooned. The past tense was a worry. 'But what we do is so much driven by what the students demand.'

'And just what have they been demanding?' he enquired, wondering just what the hook was going to be.

'We so much value our partnership with you at the university, but we feel our students need something a little extra, like a guarantee.'

Ah, there is was.

'Phyllida, you know that's not going to happen. Indeed, there might be occasions when no one reaches the standard we would like, although,' he quickly added, 'that's not likely to happen with the program as it is. What is important is that you continue to give your students the opportunity.' He could see the nodding and foot trembling were now becoming more pronounced. In an attempt to control the latter, Phyllida hitched up her already very mini skirt, and tightly crossed her legs. She then leant forward, the more to display that ample cleavage, leaving Denis to form the impression that here was someone who might be auditioning for a spot on one of those programmes you only found on cable.

'So that avenue isn't open to us then, is it?' she said, leaning forward so closely that he could feel the warmth of her breath.

'C'mon, Phyllida, you know we can't offer that!'

What was in danger of coursing into something more intimate was brought to a sudden halt by Denis's better judgement and a knock at the door. It opened and to Denis's shocked amazement, there was Flaxel. By the look on her face, Phyllida had obviously been expecting him. Rather than making his apologies and leaving, Flaxel strolled in and took his seat next to Phyllida, whose greeting was, to say the least, effusive. Denis soon got the message: his presence was no longer required. Rising to his feet, he made towards the door. There was nothing more to be done here.

'So that's it? You're leaving?' asked Flaxel. Denis smiled, but said nothing. 'Ain't that just like a Chinaman!'

This did bring a response.

'Is this the kind of person you're associating with now, Phyllida?' To her credit, Phyllida did appear to be embarrassed, as she half-heartedly moved to admonish her companion. Flaxel, though, just found the whole business amusing.

'Anyway,' she said, standing up and directing her full attention, once again, towards Denis, 'we've been exploring the opportunity of a tie-in with one of the state colleges. That at least would enable us to provide the guarantees we want.' This time, against his better judgement, Denis lingered, intent on giving her one last chance.

'I would ask you to think again,' he said, 'before you do that.' His face was a picture of concern. 'Think about the strengths of what you already have, Phyllida, with the program you have here, and the variety of choices your students have. Think of the diversity.'

'Diversity!' It was Flaxel's turn to pitch in. 'What do you people at Berkeley know about diversity? What do you know about life down here in the flatlands?' Denis recoiled a little and returned his gaze to Phyllida, hoping that she might call the pitbull off. But her expression had hardened.

'Is that what you think too, Phyllida?' Denis raised an eyebrow and let out a resigned sigh. Yes, she was burning her bridges as irrevocably as she could. Any further pleas would be wasted. He wanted to say more; to say how short-sighted it was to put all their eggs into one basket. How this program, in a good year, could place a dozen students at Berkeley and the other California divisions. While others would get into Stanford and, further afield, those east coast Ivy League schools. And now they were throwing it all away for the dubious pleasure of a guarantee that limited their horizons to the local state college. As he stepped back outside, into the sunlight, Denis reflected on what had just happened and how he was beginning to see the hidden hand of Flaxel and Wilson everywhere. They seemed to be investigating almost all the possible ways to get at Soren and the Diaspora Program. One of the program's strengths had been its outreach work, and now that also looked as if it was in ruins. And, as he drove out of the parking lot, Denis noticed something else. He saw Flaxel and Phyllida emerging from the college reception; their parting embrace was anything but platonic.

287

67

Pittsburgh, Pennsylvania

It was an early Thanksgiving morning. Virginia was sitting up in bed, reading glasses perched on the end of her nose, looking through reports with the aid of a bedside lamp. She was also connected by earpiece to a large TV, mounted in an oak-panelled frame at the foot of the bed. It was still dark outside and the morning broadcast was relaying the news that the inhabitants of some of Pittsburgh's remoter neighborhoods, perched high up on hills, would soon be emerging to a sizeable dumping of snow. Then it was onto the usual mayhem: an attempted bank robbery in the business district, a body found in a disused warehouse in the Strip and a shooting on Polish Hill. Added to this was the routine litany of assaults and beatings. She was pleased to be away from it all. Her thoughts drifted to poor old Buzz Johnstone, one of the few commanders she was still on speaking terms with, who would, at this very moment, be geeing up the poor saps who would have to go out and deal with it all.

Gazing down at the sleeping form of Soren next to her, she thought of the time Christina had first pitched the idea to her that he should lie low at her Shadyside home. That Soren had agreed with such alacrity had given her great joy; hell, he'd even agreed to help out for a few days with her parents down in Charlottesville. He'd not seen them for some time and both knew the meeting would be something of a trial. But then again, it might just provide the creative tension he needed to get over Brad's death.

Virginia had always known that she could do no wrong as far as her father was concerned. It was a view that had been challenged by some of her old friends and, a little nearer to home, her mother. Because of her relationship with Soren Virginia was seen as hopelessly dissolute and fallen. So be it. Their reaction, though, only served to strengthen Virginia's belief that her behaviour had been both honourable and necessary. She did have some nagging doubts though, about the revisiting of old times and old loves. Was she pushing too hard? Elizabeth had been right; her actions did smack just a little of desperation; someone who was very much racing against time. Still, it did comfort her to know that she was being true to her emotions. That lying beside her was someone she felt a deep well of affection and care for. And with this, came the realisation of a simple truth: she'd fallen once again for this man. Fallen badly.

The visit to Charlottesville had actually gone very well, with her father saying all the right things; as conciliatory and entertaining as Virginia had always known he would be. On their re-acquaintance, Wendall had, once again, been most impressed by Soren's intelligence and seeming authority. The young man's relationship with his daughter might have got off to a rather inauspicious start, but it did appear to have an enduring quality to it. He appeared to be much better than the disasters Wendell had witnessed Virginia struggle with of late. Soren might not have been what the family had expected, but Wendall, at least, found himself warming again to someone who hadn't fallen victim to some of the more barmy trends that seemed so *de rigueur* these days. Someone who could also converse knowledgeably about both Elliots, Thomas Sterns and George. Of course his politics were far too liberal, but that was about par for the course these days for anyone interested in academic life. Charlottesville was full of them.

Wendall Bradley had been born in Omaha, Nebraska, where he still had extensive family ties. After studying at Princeton, he'd obtained a post at the University of Virginia, in Charlottesville, where he had remained. Born High

Church Episcopalian Wendall had brought with him his family's Republican Party allegiance. He tended to keep the local Democrats at arms' length, although he did once entertain Harry F Bird Jr at his home, in an attempt to counsel the senator against his continued support for his father's stance on civil rights and his call for massive resistance. With Wendall, one got the distinct impression that the whole question of race, and Southern attitudes to it, was a thing that was perhaps a little too embarrassing for polite conversation; someone who'd never felt comfortable with the segregation he'd found at the university when he'd first arrived during the 1950s. By instinct, he was a country club Republican, who, whenever possible, would still ride to hounds with the Farmington & Keswick Hunts. Otherwise, there was nothing he would like more than to go scouring the country's libraries and byways, looking for obscure manuscripts and literary gems.

The last few years, though, had been difficult for Wendell and it showed. He looked shrunken and diminished by his wife's illness; much thinner and frailer than Soren had remembered, his eyes milky and his face more heavily creased. This was a man who'd once sculled for Princeton; a point of shared interest with Soren that had come to the aid of those first tentative, and dangerously flagging, conversations. This time the older man's spirits had momentarily been lifted on their arrival, his voice still possessing that euphonious mid-Atlantic quality that had been inherited by his daughter, but Soren had seen through the mask; seen that he was struggling. There was still some of the aloof distain he'd remembered, but this was now suffused with more than just a hint of fear and circumspection.

When it came to Virginia's mother, Elspeth, and her relationship with Wendall, there was now very little by way of agreement or shared interests. She was someone who'd been raised by her parents 'for Society' and the putative standing of the Bradley clan just didn't make the grade. Her marriage to Wendall, as patrician as his demeanour was, posed few of what a Moore would consider as *real* prospects.

University life in Charlottesville was decidedly dull and provincial compared to what was possible, just up the road in Washington. Feeling let down, and living in a social void considered way too small for a Moore, Elspeth's life had veered towards one of indolence and drink. Wendall began to tire of the pretentiousness and snobbery of it all and would do his utmost to avoid what he considered the ghastly crowd Elspeth would attract to her 'soirées'. That original spark though, that had attracted him to her in the first place, had never died. It had very much given her the upper hand.

Virginia was to become the surrogate for her mother's thwarted desires and it was this that was finally to prove most devastating to Elspeth's fragile health. All that investment in nannies, fine schools, and social jamborees, along with Wendell's plans for Virginia to go to Princeton, all of this had been subverted by that 'monstrous plot' that had seen Virginia take flight and be led a merry dance around the dives of New York and Berkeley. Perversely, Elspeth had been triumphant.

'There you are!' she'd cried, 'a typical Bradley child. Just like your father. And all over that Karlsson boy! Don't you wish you'd listened to me now?'

It was clear that a major thrust of Elspeth's complaint was racial. Wendall would have been mortified if he'd thought such a charge could have been levelled at himself, but there were no such qualms when it came to his wife. Soren still remembered with dread the moment when he'd happened across Elspeth after she'd been dozing in the conservatory. She'd awoken from her slumbers and, looking up, had said, 'Oh, you've come for *her,* have you?' with ill-disguised contempt. 'I thought you were the help.' She'd hardly uttered a word to him since. Now, with the dementia taking its toll, the hostility had been replaced by a glacial smile. Soren was quite certain which one he preferred.

Elspeth had visited her rage upon Wendall's head for what she saw as his failure to keep a tight rein on Virginia, and it was at this time they first noticed the signs of illness. It was something the doctors had first diagnosed as depression, as Elspeth disappeared into her own private world of derangement and paranoia. Her daughter had always been 'daddy's girl'; that was the nub of Elspeth's complaint, and the distance between the two women soon became something of a chasm. That original dislike by Elspeth of academia, and Wendall's role in it, grew fiercer as it became a bond that tied father and daughter together. Elspeth's exclusion was total and its effects cruelly felt. Many times, into that distant night, she would rage against the injustice of it all and the wicked calumny that she saw as transpiring between the two of them. Increasingly, those moments of lucidity became few and far between, with Wendall's role reduced to that of nursemaid, witness to his wife's regression into an immobile and counterfeit childhood. Sometimes there would be the odd glimpse of the old Elspeth, and this would stir within him a warmth that was almost transcendent; proof that she was still there struggling to connect. Then there would be a return to that dialogue of non-recognition; as if he were holding a séance in a fog.

So now Virginia found herself in bed, at her Pittsburgh home, watching the sleeping form of Soren beside her. She was thinking of that night two weeks ago when she and Soren had been together at the Van Buren's. Soren had pointed at the position they'd found themselves in, entwined and in bed together, and had asked 'How did *this* happen?' Yes, just how did that happen? Before that night they'd hardly spoken in over a year. When they had, it had only been through snatched phone conversations, or via channels of communication that were the work of, or channelled through, Christina. The year had coincided with Virginia's mother's health taking a turn for the worse, something that had become increasingly burdensome for Wendall. So Virginia had given him support; something that had involved regular gruelling five-hour drives, before she'd finally succumbed to the dubious charms of US Air and the shuttle service flying out of the cramped South East Dock Terminal at Pittsburgh's airport. All of this contributed to the strain that Virginia herself was under and she too began to sense that she needed help. The strain had taken its toll, coming as it did at the same time as that ill-fated affair with that colleague's son and having to cope with the demands of a high-maintenance twenty-something man-child. In the end it forced her to reappraise her position within the Pittsburgh Police Bureau, in the knowledge that she had very few places left to turn. It therefore seemed inevitable that she should seek out the one person she knew she could confide in: Christina. Both women had been only too willing to continue the close friendship they'd forged, with Christina being quite shameless in her attempts to get Virginia and Soren back together again. In no uncertain terms she'd told them they needed their heads banging together, and, just for good measure, had employed the same ruse that Elizabeth had used earlier with Soren.

'Ticking clocks, Virginia. Ticking clocks!'

So last night Virginia had told Soren about her feelings for him and her decision to quit her job. She'd received an offer of some teaching at Carnegie Mellon, an approach that had come at the same time she'd heard the news of Brad's death. Finding his killer would be more or less her last case. As well as the teaching, there would also be the opportunity to reactivate her bar membership, with the aim of one day returning to the practice of law. All of this would assist her in wresting back some control over her life. Considering what had just happened to Brad, it was something of a perverse and tragic irony that Virginia would be doing what he had attempted to do; putting some time in, down there in Mississippi, between jobs.

For the rest of the time they were in Pittsburgh, Soren and Virginia continued the discussion that had started two weeks ago at the Van Buren's. There had always been a knowing engagement, but here was signalled a growing awareness of the need for commitment. It was time for all those discussions about past concerns and shared experiences to expedite something more tangible than the mere promise of new beginnings. Her spirits were lifted by what appeared to be Soren's willing acquiescence in this, as if something from within, in all its clarity, had been seized upon. Deliberately, irresistibly, compellingly so.

68

Toshoba County, Mississippi

'Might I remind you, Jed, that we're not here to relive the Civil War!'

Each time Pariche visited Doleson in Mississippi, he would treat it as if it were a spiritual homecoming. The South was the place where much of the original seed corn for Pariche's life-long concern about racial injustice had been sown. Where so many good men and women had gone before; Medgar Evers, Rosa Parks, and the three boys who'd been killed in Philadelphia. And of course there had been the great man himself, Martin Luther King. But there was still a great deal to do, particularly here in the state of Mississippi. So many minds to change, especially amidst a populace that had shown so little sign of remorse.

Whenever Pariche and Doleson got together, they were trouble just waiting to happen. There's was an object lesson in how two individuals, with energy to burn, could coax each other to new heights of lunacy. A meeting between the two was something to behold. Once the conversation had begun, the frantic hand shaking and arm flapping would start, like two old roosters attempting to take flight. As the conversation became more heated, as those involving these two gentleman invariably did, the shaking and the flapping of arms would become more frantic and dance like, as they both, in an exceedingly animated fashion, sought to outdo each other in what they could suggest. And this is what was presently happening, as both of them talked up their ideas for the Institute. After a while though, Doleson began to urge caution, worried that Pariche's deranged take on enthusiasm might derail his carefully laid plans. Pariche of course was having none of it.

'Don't talk so much phooey, Basil. You're beginning to sound like one of those management technology clones I keep bumping into, in and around Haas. Used to be that you could just roll up your sleeves and get stuck in. Now you have to 'strategise' and have focus groups in place, and maybe some poor chump with a calculator doing the metrics.' Doleson kept his counsel, content to let his friend's ire run its course. 'It's becoming more difficult, Basil,' Pariche continued, with just a hint of melancholy. 'The rubbish we're having to deal with back on the Coast, what with the Bakke case and Proposition 13. Don't see as we need to put up with that kind of nonsense down here as well!'

'Come on, Jed, that's not the way to play this thing.'

'You're beginning to sound like a committee person!'

'If that's the way you feel, Jed, you can always get back on the plane!' Pariche smiled, took another sip of his whiskey, and chortled to himself. 'Listen, Jed,' continued Doleson, determined to make his point. 'I suspect we'll be lucky to have this place up and running this side of Easter. But I'm determined as hell going to make sure it does happen!'

'I know, Basil, I know.'

'This thing started when we got Soren to agree to come down here, that night in Denver, and it *will* definitely happen. You heard what he had to say then; we've got to get it into the minds of the folks down here that this is a done deal. Get them used to the idea that the Institute is already here amongst them and here to stay.' He paused for a moment, gave Pariche a placatory smile, and then added; 'And it isn't going to be helped by you going around fighting the Civil War all over again!' Pariche held up his hands in mock surrender as Doleson paused for a while. Both men knew that this place had certain perils; where a sizeable number of people might not be too adverse to making their views known in more direct and unpleasant ways. Pariche picked up on his friend's disquiet.

'You still getting those nuisance calls, Basil?'

'The odd one, you know, the usual race-hate perverts. It was ever thus. We appear to be getting some of those survivalist types you get out west. Can't always predict what they might do next. Sheriff Harper does his best to keep tabs on them. Tries to drain the pool from which they feed.'

The conversation between the two men continued into the night, until the well of whisky ran dry. There were reminiscences and regrets, interrupted by a call from one of Doleson's women, and promises to take the struggle, the next day, to a certain sheriff who'd just been attempting to get over a particularly trying couple of weeks.

Come the morning, a somewhat bemused Toshoba County had a re-energised Pariche to contend with. It was a Sunday and the first thing to do was to attend a black Pentecostal Church, where his booming voice could be heard amidst the whoops and hollers of the saved. Afterwards, following a long chat with the pastor, and ignoring his friend's pleas to remove his Vermont regular's Stetson, Pariche joined Doleson on his rounds. First port of call was the lawyer, Garvey Wilkes, who Pariche knew from previous visits and was now considered an old friend.

Garvey and his wife, Cecilia, lived in a three-bedroom bungalow, fronted by a covered porch, set in a neighbourhood that was home to most of Coulee's black population. There was a basketball hoop fixed to the front of the garage and the rear lawn was bounded by well-attended flowerbeds. One of the Horsemeads was obviously an avid gardener and Pariche, by long association, knew that it wasn't Garvey. Soon they were swapping stories, comparing scars, and wondering where it had all gone wrong, just like Pariche and Doleson had done the night before. Garvey could see that Pariche still appeared to be very much in rude health. All Pariche could see, was an old friend who, at best, was still alive.

Garvey was bemused by the recent course of events. 'Reminds me of the good old days,' he said mischievously, 'when white folks came down here, hell bent on getting themselves killed. Ain't seen nothing like it since the days when Hollis White and his cronies were in charge.'

He was obviously pleased to see his old drinking partner, something that was not entirely acceded to by his wife, who'd not had this many white people in her front room since the time Doleson had been pursued here by two of his mistresses. Still, Cecilia was somewhat cheered at seeing someone who was representative of the world beyond the narrow confines of Toshoba County. Maybe Pariche would be just the person to prod her fool of a husband into actions that didn't involve him looking down the bottom of a bottle. So she watched, suspiciously at first, then with a little more enthusiasm as the evening progressed; that was until Garvey, urged on by Pariche, started to show interest in causing mischief at the Cedars, the all-white private school.

In the past, as assuredly cranky as her husband was, when it came to agitating white folk of an excessively illiberal frame of mind, Garvey would usually be the first to urge caution – it would, after all, always be black people who'd be left feeling the consequences. Now her husband was at it again, being egged on by a white man, into doing something that would surely end badly. And, yes, they were drinking again, on the Sabbath, with the afternoon not yet done. Time to turf them out. Garvey Wilkes was something of a legend around these parts. Not on account of his being something of a troublemaker, nor for the prodigious amounts of liquor he was known to drink. Not even his atheism. No, what took the biscuit was that he was all of these things and a black man to boot, and still alive to tell the tale. At another, more unforgiving time, in the manner of that old Billy Holliday song, Garvey Wilkes might been different, strange fruit. Like Pariche, Garvey could drink. Unlike Pariche, he was always the worse for it. At times, because of his drinking, Cecilia had moved out, to stay with her mother in Shreveport, from where she would rail against this 'drunken no-good fool'. And because of his drinking, his law practice had suffered. He'd never been abusive, but bills went unpaid and the arguments had been fierce. What Cecilia could not stand was being witness to the decline of someone who could still, on occasions, be so vibrant, intense and loving.

After a rather inauspicious start at a historically black college along the road in Clancy, fortune did indeed smile on Garvey in the form of a grant from a northern Quaker charity. This gave him just enough to see him through a law degree at Carbondale, after which he moved back to Toshoba and a single-handed practice that, during the good years, barely broke even. Doleson had helped out on occasions, doing his best to send business their way, but Garvey and Cecilia mostly had to pull in their horns and ride out the bad times as best they could. Garvey would readily tell anyone who'd care to listen about the good times, when, as a young man, he'd marched, protested and boycotted with the SNCC and the civil rights movement in the fifties and early sixties. When the Klan had threatened to come calling, with mortal hurt only a shotgun blast away. And the bad times? Most could see that these were more recent. Where a poor diet and drink, compounded by financial insecurity, had taken its toll, with both Horsemeads possessed of fragile health and Garvey just one coronary away from calamity. That they had survived said much for their good standing amongst Toshoba's black community and Garvey's ability to tenaciously fight their corner. The legal practice, although financially shaky, had at least provided a degree of independence, something that had helped in his civil rights and political work. In election years, he'd advised and assisted the women getting folks registered and at other times he would counsel those threatened with losing their jobs or their homes or worse.

Sheriff Harper and his deputies didn't really know what to make of Garvey Horsemead. At times there had been a sore desire to lock him up; at least then they would know that he was safe. In the end though, they'd figured that if anything was going to happen to Garvey, it would probably be by way of some hot head after a session of hard liquor, or someone Garvey had crossed within the black community itself. Nothing much could done about that. How could you keep tabs on someone who saw drunken fights with neighbours as nothing out of the ordinary, and a black eye as a badge of honour?

So, with Garvey now in tow, Pariche and Doleson made their next stop the county courthouse. Of course, being a Sunday, like everything else in this god-fearing part of the country, it was shut. But a Mr Dexter, of *The Toshoba Democrat*, the local newspaper, was able to inform them that a certain 'long-haired hippy type, with a withered arm' had been poking around, 'asking damned fool questions.' At the end of the tour, Pariche gazed along Main Street and declared that the town, still hopelessly segregated, now needed their help more than ever. 'The answer,' he declared, stabbing his finger at his companions, 'lies with the young. That's where we'll start when Soren gets back.'

69

It was late afternoon when they did finally get to see the sheriff. Under the gentle swish of a rotating fan, he sat the three of them down, a veritable regiment of potential discord, before attempting to inform them of what progress had been made. The greetings and the words between the men were friendly but businesslike. The sheriff had a feeling that Garvey and the madman from California would soon be demanding answers, but, for the moment, the latter did appear to be successfully tempering his usual visceral dislike of being in the presence of anything that smacked of authority. He even commandeered the semblance of a smile which, in itself, went some way towards stoking the sheriff's sense of unease; an unease that harked back to an earlier visit, when Pariche had roped poor old Garv into one of his hair-brain schemes. Then it had been a campaign to ban the White Citizens Council from using the Town Council for its meetings. 'Let them discuss such filth in the gutter,' Pariche had howled, 'right where they belong.' Of course, at the time, he'd been unsuccessful, but the seeds had been sown that would eventually lead to the authorities putting a stop to it. It also had the additional effect of adding to the already considerable list of those who would wish Pariche harm.

On the sheriff's desk lay various bundles of papers and objects, pride of place being a blue folder containing the report that had been written by Virginia. The sheriff looked at it and let forth a chuckle. He just hadn't expected anything like it. A report, and not only that, it was damn good. 'I must say,' he said, as he proceeded to open it for the benefit of his visitors, 'that Miss Ginny did a very thorough job. Even managed to turn up a few things we hadn't considered.'

He watched as his visitors made themselves at home. Once again he was looking at the usual suspects, learned gentlemen with letters after, and before, their names, and yet more questions. More people with opinions on everything. All wanting answers. At least the TV and newspapers had come and gone. Now, to cap it all, the mad man from California was here, reading the report and compounding the offence by wearing that ridiculous hat.

'Mr Pariche, sir!' He pointed to the offending item. 'Some folks might just take offence.' Courteous to a fault, Pariche took it off. 'Now, let's see what we have here. The progress we've made so far. Of course we are dealing with murder. The decisive trauma was inflicted by a .44 bullet fired from a gun, by an assailant as yet unknown. Miss Ginny seems to think that it might have been accidental, with the shot going off during a struggle. The folks from the FBI have nothing to add, but they still wish to be kept abreast of things. The state police have been cordial, but they don't know much either, which is a shame. I usually get very good intel from them, but on this occasion... well, zilch. The medical evidence suggests that the snake bite, of itself, should not have been fatal. We think we have those responsible for that. One of them is currently locked up out back for his own good. The District Attorney is considering the option to charge him on something else that's cropped up. The others are out on bail. Don't think any of them would have the capacity to have been involved in anything like that, you know, the shooting. Whether it was a professional job or not, and Miss Ginny seems to think it was, those gentleman couldn't conduct a crap shoot in a hay barn. Her report very much bears that out. She also thinks that your boy might be in danger.'

'Boy!' repeated Pariche, sniffily.

'Hell, Jed,' said Doleson, jumping to the sheriff's defence. 'Calm down. He doesn't mean nothing by it!'

The sheriff shrugged and continued, obviously untroubled by any thoughts of prissy outsiders taking unnecessary offence. 'She seems to think that the shooter might have been after Professor Karlsson.'

Pariche, who'd spent the last couple of days counselling a rather distraught Christina, sat silently for a moment. Then he seemed to wake up.

'Well, hopefully, Soren's tucked up safe somewhere. Now about that snake bite; can we be certain that those wretches you bailed, and the man back there, are the right ones?'

'Yes, Sheriff,' interrupted Garvey, seizing on the opportunity of scratching a long-running sore. 'It sure seems to have taken an age getting that scum off the streets!'

'Now, now, Garv, you know we can't pick folks up willy-nilly, just because you don't like the look of them. We're doing the best we can. I know we've not always seen eye to eye, but you know I've always attempted to be even-handed.'

Garvey didn't like being put on the spot, especially when it came to dishing out praise to southern law enforcement officials, and he wasn't about to let this one go. 'If we're talking about treating people fairly, what about my client, Tyler James? Was that fair?'

Pariche and Doleson looked at each other, bemused. Garvey and the sheriff seemed to be coursing into one of their private quarrels.

'Now come on, Garv. I'm really sorry about that. I know your client didn't have any priors, and we were wrong to pass him on to the county prosecutors. That was an honest mistake!'

'The amount of weed on him was nothing!'

'Yes. We could have handled it differently and I've given instructions to my people to do so in future. But it's done now. That's the way they do things down in Jackson these days. I'll keep pressing Bill over at the prosecutors, but they'll only repeat that it's out of their hands.'

This time Garvey did let it go, knowing the damage had already been done. A young kid from Flashlight who'd flagged down a passing patrol car, because he feared for the life of his mother, who was being abused by her boyfriend, was now looking at spending the rest of his school days in juvenile prison. A more experienced officer would have overlooked the smell of dope and helped the boy out; but this officer was new to the job, inexperienced, and the boy's misdemeanour had come to light in front of others. Sheriff Harper gave an apologetic shrug and continued. There was much he didn't tell them of course. How the agents of the FBI had visited two days of condescension upon his department and how they'd briefed against him to the local media. How they wanted everything to go through their offices in either Memphis or Jackson. Only they had the resources and the professionalism to do justice to the case. And yes, as this was an interstate crime, it was in their jurisdiction. After a while, the fuss had died down and, to no one's surprise, the FBI had left, promising and delivering nothing. Certainly not the stuff that Miss Ginny had found when she'd got to work; and the sheriff wasn't going to give the FBI any of that.

Before the visitors left the sheriff asked what he could expect from them over the coming weeks. He soon wished he hadn't, as Pariche informed him of their plans 'to take the Cedars down.' Not with anything as crude as protests or boycotts, but with love. They were going to show, through their work at the Institute, and in the community, just what the kids at the Cedars were missing. 'Give them time,' he said, 'and they will come begging.' So, through gritted teeth, the sheriff wished them well and, after they'd gone, immediately detailed one of his deputies to keep an eye on them, just in case.

70

Berkeley, California

Denis and his assistant, Summer, strode purposely into Lecture Hall One and took up their places on the stage. From there they gazed out at the massed ranks who'd come to hear their take on Eugene Genoves's and Frank Tanenbaum's interpretation of the ante-bellum South. The place could hold up to three hundred, but today the numbers seemed much greater, swelled by elective students and tutors from other departments. This was Berkeley, of course, so there were also a few itinerants; locals, drifters and ex-students who'd been lost to the streets years ago. All waited expectantly. As always, there were the usual faces at the front, with the black and Asian study groups, as always, keeping a healthy distance from each other. Professor Stubbs, from History, was also in attendance; here to see if these Johnny-come-latelys would be taking too many liberties with what he regarded as his territory. Denis gave him a wave and a smile, which was returned with a scowl and a thunderous 'hurumph!'

As Denis looked out across the auditorium he had the inkling of something not quite right. Some of the students he couldn't place; nothing new there, except that he could not remember people having their faces covered before. Then he noticed him. Sitting quietly, near the front was Flaxel. Since that outing, to see Betty Boo at the local community college, there had been a steady stream of calls from Flaxel's associates. They were stupid nuisance calls from idiots with nothing more to do than harass an easy target. But now their instigator was here in the hall, sitting in front of him, and

Denis was intrigued. He'd hardly had time to collect his thoughts, though, when there was a slight stirring from some members of the audience. He looked up to see that Chumley had made his entrance, this time more soberly dressed in slacks, matching pearls and high heels. With profuse apologies he made his way to the front and joined Denis and Summer on the stage.

Denis started his address. Every now and then his gaze would catch that of Flaxel's, who gave away not a flicker of emotion. Denis was momentarily unnerved. Just what was he doing here? He collected himself and continued. Then, from the rear of the hall, came the noise of a disturbance; a thunderous rumble, as people surged forwards. A fight had broken out. Exactly why, wasn't immediately clear. Amidst the shouting and the hollering and the screams, Denis made his way up the aisle towards the point where the disturbance was coming from: a patterned wave of movement pointing to a bloodied focus of student bodies, and where a group of men, dressed in black, and with their faces covered, were standing, one shouting 'Boycott the carpet baggers,', and another, 'Black history for black people.' Some of the students, having got over the initial shock, were now rushing back, determined to see what was happening, whilst others came to the aid of the fallen. There was more shoving and pushing and more punches as some of the students began to show signs of wanting to fight back. Denis didn't know how he'd managed it, but Chumley was there too, wielding his heels at one of the attackers like a club. It all looked as if things were about to turn spectacularly ugly when, just as quickly, it was over. By the time Denis had managed to get a handle on the situation, and security had been summoned, the assailants had gone, dissolving into the lunchtime crowds on Sproul.

For the next few minutes Denis assisted Chumley and the paramedics in treating the wounded who thankfully had only superficial cuts and bruises. The police were here too, taking statements, so that by the time things were returned to a semblance of normality a full thirty minutes had elapsed. But a return to normality there would be, Denis was determined about that. Back at the front of the hall, Denis was faced with an audience that was between the throes of shock and bemusement. It quickly became clear that what had just transpired had been Flaxel's work. Rather like a craftsmen taking in his own handiwork, he'd chosen to stay behind, all the better to bathe in the discord he'd sown, his face a mocking smile. Denis, by contrast, was strangely unmoved. Deflecting Chumley's pleas to exact some form of summary justice, he remained still, his gaze firmly fixed on his adversary. After a few moments had passed, he lifted a hand and pointed to one of the side doors. Flaxel's smile turned to one of embarrassed unease as he felt the gaze of the audience settle upon him. With one last attempt at a swagger and accompanied by two of the security staff, he rose to his feet and left the building.

Later that evening, Denis made a call to Soren. In Pittsburgh it was night-time and Soren and Virginia had already retired to bed. The call had a cathartic effect, as if all Soren had needed was just one more shock to bring him out of his torpor. 'Well done, Denis, it sounds like you handled the situation brilliantly. I'm glad to hear that you are alright.' His concern for Denis's wellbeing was tempered somewhat by the relief he felt at seeing the enemy at last showing their hand. And what a crude hand it was.

'Leave it to me, Denis. You might just have saved the day, or dare I say, Flaxel has.' After he'd put the receiver down, Soren turned to Virginia and punched the air with his fist. 'We've got the bastard, Ginny,' he declared, 'Wilson, we've got him!'

Now very much awake, Soren gave his erstwhile nemesis a call. It was, for Soren, a moment of unadulterated pleasure; words that were very rarely deployed when describing conversations with Wilson. The news of what had happened had obviously reached him too; after all, some students, innocently attending a university lecture, had just been beaten up by a group of people the (acting) dean had chosen to associate with. So he was now extremely receptive to what Soren had to say and listened politely as he was informed of the consequences of being identified too closely with the likes of people who violently disrupt proceedings of the university. One just wondered what Senate and the Chancellor's Office would make of it all? Did the (acting) dean, with his supposedly caring vocation, really want to be seen as being party to extortion and intimidation? By the strained protestations of innocence and the contrition in his voice, Soren could sense that Wilson was already on the run, trying to put as much distance between himself and Flaxel as possible. How his only crimes had been the extending of a hand to the less fortunate and being a poor judge of character. But Soren wasn't interested. Wilson was guilty of a far greater charge of not stopping to think about how this hoodlum, 'This known peddler of drugs and beatings, might just be capable of actions that were inimical to what a great university should stand for!'

Yes, Soren sensed that he had him now. The least Wilson could do was to make sure that Denis and his students were safe. And what would happen if some of the students were to take things into their own hands? After all, this was Berkeley! One could imagine the usual suspects jumping on board, disrupting the proceedings of Senate and boycotting the Chancellor's Office. With hot heads on both sides, you couldn't guarantee what would happen next. And, of course, there was always the press. The mind just boggled as to what they would make of a story like this, especially with Pariche supplying the ammunition. Also, Wilson didn't need reminding of what his friends in Sacramento would be thinking; that one of the Governor's pet projects was in the hands of someone so compromised! Soren knew that it would be this last point that would make the most telling impression on Wilson's well-honed political antennae. And there were other worries, such as the question of Denis's safety. Even if Flaxel did attempt to reign in his friends from the Nation of Islam, his credit rating with some of the more extreme elements would be spent; their blood was up and they'd have ideological reasons for wanting to escalate things further. The fight would need to be taken to the white establishment, with Denis, poor Denis, becoming the symbol of their hatred and resentment. Denis's safety was now of real concern. Soren wanted assurances that he would be protected; that Denis would be left to go about his work unmolested. So later that night, a university black and white was seen to pull up outside Denis's apartment on Ridge Street, and over the next few days uniformed officers were detailed to shadow his movement at every turn.

There were further attempts at disruption, but, in the main, Soren had been correct in his belief that Flaxel had over-played his hand. Some of Flaxel's associates did indeed see the need to take the fight to the 'white colonial oppressors' and this meant, for a brief moment, that Denis did indeed become a target. A token picket was placed outside his lectures and there was a drop off in the attendance of some of the students. But there was also a positive outcome. The events seemed to provide Denis with the context in which to start a debate, on his own terms, about the purpose of the course and how the students perceived it. A workshop was started and those two study groups – black and Asian – at last began a dialogue.

Soon Denis was getting messages of support from all quarters, from Pariche in Mississippi, as well as from Soren and Craig. There was also the collective resource of the more senior faculty to draw upon; advice on how best to handle the nuisance calls and how to accommodate and adjust to the noise, drifting in on the breeze, from the loud hailers being used by the protesters on Sproul. It was not lost on the acting dean that Kurst and the symbolically powerful figure of Marjorie Foster were also now involved, providing Denis with excellent counsel and taking it in turns to sit in on the lectures and seminars he gave. They had been outraged by Flaxel's antics and wanted to demonstrate that they were resistant to anything that smacked of an attempt to debase academic enquiry. That these two names were now acting in concert against his interests was, for Wilson, a cause for real alarm. He desperately needed to cut Flaxel loose and, God forbid, there would soon be Pariche to contend with, when the old fool got back from Mississippi.

Things were also looking decidedly grim for Flaxel. As soon as he and his associates had returned from their disruptive activities, he was counselling caution. They'd gone too far. They should never have bloodied the noses of those students. As it was, his associates were not content to just bathe in the afterglow of what had been for them a good day's work; they wanted to take things further. This was not good, thought Flaxel, who still had hopes of inveigling a good pay-out from the day's proceedings.

At the Nation of Islam, Brother Michael had been onto Flaxel from day one. In his eyes, Flaxel was definitely not a person to be trusted; rather he was someone who would probably have to be smitten at some point in the future. Brother Michael was lean, deep voiced, and, at six foot six, towered over Flaxel and the others. He had a shaven head of hair and looked sharp in his black suit. He also had a laconic turn of phrase that was a match for any of the quips that Flaxel cared to try. He was also very suspicious of the true nature of Flaxel's calling; that the wisecracking 'former' street hustler might not be all that committed to combating the evils perpetrated by the 'white devil'. When he spoke with Flaxel, it was always with a deep distrust, with Flaxel always just one step ahead of a good beating, or worse. Brother Michael and his associates, in their dealings with what they thought of as 'low life', were not averse to dishing out a quite severe form of retribution.

Although no longer a part of the Nation of Islam, Flaxel had seen Brother Michael as a means to make some money. How Flaxel had come across this deal with Wilson and the university, Brother Michael had no idea, but he'd been keen to get in on the act. Flaxel had promised that there would be plenty of money to go round, even enough to employ some of their own. So they'd stumped up the cash, five thousand bucks and counting, so that Flaxel could go and do what he did best: hustle. And he was near to delivering on his promise. He'd only gone and hustled those fat cats, up there in their cathedral of learning, into giving them a million bucks! And he'd been able to do this because he had this dude, this fat cat professor who sits on all those committees, who owed him; owed him big. Five grand was a small ask. Just think of the prestige they'd get, he'd told them, and they'd lapped it up. And he couldn't resist tapping them for some money into the bargain. Just five thousand bucks; that would do nicely.

The day after the 'incident', Flaxel called Wilson's office, only to be told that the acting dean wasn't available to take his call. After a few more attempts, Flaxel sensed that he was being shut out. 'Whitey' was closing ranks, with Mr Blue Chip disappearing over the horizon. And Brother Michael would soon be asking for his money back. So the next time Flaxel attended a rundown former pizza parlour, that was now the local mosque, he was aware of a distinct chill in the air. This might have been, in part, because of his plea for some members to go easy on the Chinaman; more likely it was because they were also beginning to see through his protestations of having a close working relationship with the dean. Hadn't they just heard, on local radio, the self same gentleman denouncing them in no uncertain terms? Added to this were the actions of the police, shaking folks down and making life difficult. And there was still the question of that five thousand bucks.

Later, Brother Michael pulled Flaxel to one side. 'Brother,' he said, 'we need to talk. I've a feeling you've not been straight with us.'

'How was I to know you'd go and blood those students?' cried Flaxel, all innocence. 'Man, that's just not the done thing in those circles. You really queered my pitch.'

'The man appears to be cutting you off,' replied Brother Michael. 'But that's no matter. It's you, Flaxel. You're beginning to pose us a few problems.' As the brother spoke these words, Flaxel sensed one of the others moving to block his exit. Besides being built like a concrete outhouse, this one had a reputation for enjoying the dishing out of one of the Nation's more physically demanding punishment regimes.

'Are you prepared to join with us in striking a victory for the Good Lord?' asked Brother Michael.

'You know me, bro, I'm game for anything.'

'Yeah,' Brother Michael replied, with a laboured sigh, barely convinced. 'I do believe you are. Think you can blood someone proper?'

Flaxel was momentarily wrong footed, relieved that he wasn't himself the object of this 'blooding', but still slightly alarmed, none the less, at what Brother Michael seemed to be suggesting. His fears were confirmed when Brother Michael produced a gun and placed it on the table before him.

'Go on, go and get yourself a Chinaman.'

To his credit, Flaxel resisted, quickly attempting to turn the table on his host and bluffing a chuckle as he did so. 'Surely you can't be serious? You want me to waste a prof? On a campus crawling with cops?' There was a pause, as he considered his options. Then, he said, 'No, leave the Chinaman to me. I've got a handle on how best to deal with him.'

Leaving the gun on the table, Flaxel made to make his exit. He was stopped by Brother Michael's final retort. 'Remember, we want him gone. And you still owe me ten thousand bucks.'

'Ten thousand?'

'Yes, the rate just went up.'

Flaxel knew exactly what he had to do. The ante had been raised way beyond his comfort zone; his nimbleness of thought was already working on other priorities that needed to be addressed. His first port of call was to his ex-girlfriend's condo, from where he made a call to a somewhat bemused Denis Tsui. 'Keep yourself holed up for a while,' Flaxel told him, attempting to reassure, 'but believe me you're safe. I'm the one who's going to have to take the heat for this one.'

A couple of days later, the police, acting on a tip off, raided Brother Michael's apartment. At the same time, in what passed for the Nation of Islam's headquarters, they found, hidden in a safe, evidence of graft and influence peddling down the road in Oakland. There was also an unregistered gun and, just to make sure, (and the detectives really loved this one) two ounces of cocaine, sealed inside a couple of plastic sachets, usually used for the carrying of coin. They were exactly the same as the ones Brother Michael used in his day job as a teller at the local branch of Bank of America. And when police scanned the bags for fingerprints, his were the only ones on it.

71

Toshoba County, Mississippi

The buoyancy of the mood at the Institute was lifted by the return of Soren, who'd flown in from Pittsburgh with renewed resolve as to how the project should proceed. Spirits had also been raised by events on the West Coast, the most recent of which heralded the news that Craig was on his way back, having overcome, what Pariche referred to as, 'The mystifying objections of his good wife, Alice.' At this very moment he was being conveyed to them, via Delta Airlines, across the great expanse of the American south west. And he was bringing with him a large computer workstation he'd managed to liberate from his place of work.

Looking around, Soren could see that Pariche had been no slouch in making his mark. The builders, making good on Doleson's plans for the seminar rooms, were all black; the result of Pariche's demands that all the firms tendering for work should accord with his ideas regarding affirmative action. He also appeared to have made good on his promise to cause mischief with the Cedars; something that had been accomplished by way of leaflets, posted in and around the school, asking for anyone, interested in contributing to the work of the Institute, to get in touch. Names were also required for a planned oral history project. Pariche had this vision of black and white kids being trained to carry out interviews and then going around the county together, conducting ethnographic surveys to all and sundry. Of course, nothing had come of it, but Pariche had enjoyed stirring the pot.

On hearing of this, Soren was mortified; mortified as much as Doleson had been by Pariche's seemingly innate

313

ability to needlessly antagonise the locals. Why, Soren asked, had the old fool failed to keep to his original injunction of making it all about the kids at Toshoba County High? Where there was already a sympathetic ear to the project's aims, alive to the enrichment opportunities available and the possibility of enhancing those grade profiles. 'Instead, you were going around stirring up a hornet's nest at the last white bastion in the county!' Rather than looking bruised by this encounter, Pariche was positively beaming, very much relieved to see his old friend back on form. Without taking so much as a breath, he dragooned Soren into joining him on a visit to Garvey and Cecilia at their home in Asheville.

Soren could see that Garvey was a proud – some would say vain – man. He looked a lot older than someone supposedly in their mid-fifties. After their greeting, Garvey set himself centre stage, while Cecilia saw to things in the kitchen. A diet of Southern fried excess, complemented by generous amounts of liquor, had caught up with Garvey; his stomach was pot bellied, his nose bulbous, and his socks had slipped to reveal blotches on his ankles. Cecilia gave the impression of someone in perennial complaint of having to do her best to work around his tendency to leave papers and documents strewn wherever he'd been working on them last. Although Garvey's filing system had a degree of coherence, all knew that here was another reason, besides the ingrained racism of the place, why he'd failed to rise up the legal food chain. But there had been developments.

'Well, I'll be darned,' sighed Pariche incredulously, picking up on what Garvey had said, 'you're getting white clients?'

'Yes, can't believe it myself. A couple of years back, this old gal marches in and says she wants to divorce her husband. Been married to him for well nigh thirty years. I says to her that there are plenty of white firms that could do the job. Shoots right back that she wants the shock to be terminal.'

'Yes,' chipped in Cecilia, 'it almost was.'

'Got me to thinking if there was any more of where that came from, when, darn, out pops another one, this time a small claims case. Just can't figure it out myself.'

Pariche shot a glance at Doleson, whose smile looked just a little forced. Both knew that Doleson had tried to help as much as he could, but there were limits. Doleson's preference was to keep the family's business with the blue bloods of Jackson and Atlanta. It wasn't so much a matter of race, well, not directly anyway, more a matter of family connections and, looking at the state of Garvey's filing system, competence. Pariche was still concerned about his friend's health.

'Don't mind me, Jed. Don't fuss. I told you when you were here the other day, Cez and me are doing just fine. Just fine.' A rather wan smile from Pariche conveyed a mild rebuke to this observation. 'And this young man?' Garvey had at last got around to addressing Soren. 'I presume this is *the* Professor Karlsson?' His deliberate emphasis spoke volumes; this whipper snapper might have been dressed up as being from some prestigious seat of learning, but that didn't cut much ice down here. Soren's offered hand wasn't taken; instead Garvey chose to rib him about his name. 'Karlsson! Just what kind of handle is that?' His tone was off-hand and suspicious.

'Swedish. On my mother's side,' the younger man replied; his words a fumble.

Garvey huffed a little and gave a rather wistful look out of the window. 'So, you've come down here to help us change our ways have you?'

'Well, I wouldn't say that.'

'Just joshing with you, son, just joshing.' There was a smile and a proffered hand. 'It is good to see you. I guess things down here are changing.' He gave a look to somewhere beyond the window. 'Can't say so much for Clancy, though.' Another pause, then; 'So you've done buried your friend?

Soren nodded.

'A damn shame. They had no right to do what they did.'
He turned to Pariche. 'I take it, Jed, you'll soon be taking
your leave of us?'

'Guess I will. There are a few things that Basil and
myself have a mind to do first, but this here is your man.'

'Yes, I guess you are,' replied Garvey, sizing Soren up
and down. 'Have you met the sheriff yet?'

'Only briefly,' Soren replied, 'after Brad's death. He
appears to be a decent enough man.'

'Decency doesn't always do it!' replied Cecilia, finally
deciding to join the conversation. 'What else can you do in
a place where most folks round here would still vote for the
likes of George Wallace and Bull Connors if they had the
chance?'

'You're being unfair, Cez,' said Garvey. 'I'd say...'

'Anyways,' she continued, cutting him off, 'the girls will
be over here soon.' She was referring to a couple of high
school students who would be helping out at the Institute.

'Yes, Angela and Busby,' said Garvey. 'They're good
kids, from Toshoba County High.'

'And church!' added Cecilia, sharply.

'Yes, church,' repeated Garvey, with a sigh. 'They're
going to help us out.'

'You still fighting the church, Garv?' asked Pariche.

Garvey shrugged and, looking across at his wife, let out
a weary, sigh-laden, laugh.

'Stubborn old fool,' said Cecilia. 'He could have signed
them all up years ago. If only he'd keep his big mouth shut.'

'But Cecilia, he would no longer be the Garv you've
come to love and obey.'

'Dream on. Dream on.'

Later they were indeed joined by Angela and Busby, the
two ladies Cecilia had spoken of earlier, who took their seats
under the appreciative gazes of the men. From the off, their
presence added a certain vitality and youthfulness to what
had now become a very crowded lounge. It was time for
Garvey to preen and glow. These were his girls, his
contribution to the program. The city slickers from out west
might sit and talk and plan, but it was plain old Garv who'd

gone ahead and got things done. These were merit students who'd already been busily engaged in mapping out their visitors' itinerary for the next day few days; something that would start first thing tomorrow with a visit to their school, Toshoba County High.

Both girls were assured and full of confidence. Angela, a cousin of Cecilia's, was the shorter of the two. Like Cecilia, her nose, which she tended to look down a lot, was narrow and long. Her eyes had a limpid brightness to them and her long dark hair was drawn back into a tight ponytail. Her appearance tended to hint at a current infatuation with a certain Morten Harket. The pork pie hat on her head and the Salt'n Pepper T-shirt said that this interest in all things new romantic had its limits. In contrast to the somewhat reserved countenance of Angela, Busby was a lanky, gawky girl, all gestures and waves, who seemed to delight in all that she did. As far as the Institute was concerned, she was excited to be on board and full of eagerness to get on with things. Within seconds she'd ribbed Pariche with such force that it was hard to say whether his howl was a wince of pain or a whoop of delight. The others were just content to have a big sisterly arm around their shoulders. The girls were not shy about expounding their wishes, whether it was about being considered for one of those 'fancy schools up north' or casting an opinion about how the Institute should be run, and both wanted their visitors to know that they were accomplished and hardworking, and, in Angela's case, 'saved'.

And what did they think of Brad's death?

'Some folks think you brought that down on yourselves,' said Angela.

'And some feel ashamed,' added Busby.

'Not many of those,' was Angela's reply.

72

The next morning Angela and Busby took over. Under no circumstances would the visitors be allowed to venture into town on their own. Pariche, of course, would have to be left out of the equation and allowed to do his own thing; he was, after all, a known problem. So, with Soren, and a newly returned Craig, in tow, the two girls set out on foot for Toshoba County High, a brisk forty minute walk away. For the first time since their foreshortened arrival, just over three weeks ago, Soren and Craig were to get a leisurely, and hopefully more peaceable, introduction to the county. The sun was again high in the sky, but this time, in the two girls, the visitors had the most knowledgeable and welcoming of hosts. It was a refreshing antidote to the apprehension both had felt prior to their return.

As they walked along together the two men were subject to a thorough interrogation. Busby, tall and gangly, aimed questions at them scatter gun fashion, whereas Angela was more deliberate and controlled, just like a cruiser weight, probing for weaknesses and revelling in the professors' ignorance. Sensing the need to show clemency, Angela changed tack, asking about the possibility of study on the West Coast. Busby quickly caught on, eager for advice about the preparation of testimonials and the prioritising of majors. Both appeared to be well informed about the AIDS situation, although their knowledge was tempered somewhat by Angela's insistence that it must, in some way, have all been ordained by God. Seeking to deflect, Soren asked about the school they were on their way to visit. Once again, it was Angela, the more serious and reflective of the two, who took up the reins.

'There are two schools in the county,' she said. 'The one that we're going to now is Toshoba County High. That's our school,' she added proudly. 'The Cedars is white and private. Set up by parents who don't want to send their kids to school with the likes of us. Happened after they were ordered to desegregate. There's no way they're going to send their kids to school in a district that's poor and black.' They were now walking four abreast, the two girls flanked by the visitors, who listened quietly and dutifully. Angela continued with her peroration, telling them of how the Cedars was now widely believed to be struggling. A significant minority of Toshoba County's whites never joined their Clancy counterparts, choosing instead to stay with the integrated Toshoba County High. Three people had been instrumental in all of this; Doleson, Garvey and the person they were now on their way to see, school principal, Seacombe Sweeting. All three had had trouble for their pains, with Principal Sweeting even having to deal with a cross burning on his lawn.

'Dumb fools,' said Busby, 'Couldn't even get that right. They could have at least used wood that burned.'

The plain truth though was that Principal Sweeting had indeed achieved a minor miracle at Toshoba County High. Together with Doleson, he'd quickly established the need to get to grips with the county's poor taxpayer base. A school bond had been floated and monies raised, with the newly established GM plant to the north of the town contributing towards a new science block. Slowly things had been turned around, so that most of the county's white kids now studied at Toshoba County High, rather than the Cedars. Test scores had also improved and now the school could boast an assortment of clubs and societies and an extensive track and field program. With such progress, some people had even mooted the possibility of merging Toshoba County's school system with neighbouring Clancy's. But the school board wouldn't hear of it. The not so often unsaid observation was still one of race; such a system would be overwhelmingly black.

The road they were now walking along was shaded from the midmorning sun by towering cedars that lined the banks on either side. For Soren, there was still that element of strangeness that hinted at the possibility of danger. It was chastening to think that he was walking along a road that had probably witnessed murders and lynchings; and, if it hadn't, then it had almost certainly conveyed people hell bent on as much. The question he now asked reflected this strangeness he felt; of feeling like a fish out of water.

'Is it safe to be walking around like this?' he asked, much to the girls' amusement.

'Man, you are way too nervous!'

'Well, I did notice that you were a little reluctant to let us come down here on our own. Just what are the chances of coming across elements of the Klan? Do you have any fears yourself?'

At this the girls put aside their joshing, their demeanour becoming just a little more measured.

'I guess there are a few scary people out there,' said Busby. 'It pays not to get too cosy with some folks. There's good and bad in all, I guess. You just need to be careful.'

Soon they were gazing upon a collection of redbrick buildings that harkened back to the 1950s. Toshoba County High catered for both junior and senior age ranges and had seen numerous refurbishment and extensions over the years. As they entered the main foyer they couldn't help but notice that the student traffic appeared to be in one direction; a steady stream of humanity flowing through darkened corridors towards what appeared to be the main hall. The students marched in discrete groups, black and white, boys and girls. Every now and then, the professors noticed a friendship that appeared to cross the racial divide, but these were few and far between. Their progress was regularly checked, as their guides exchanged pleasantries and made promises to meet up with friends. Most looked reassuringly familiar; the kind of kids you would see back home, if a little more soberly dressed. There were no goths or grunge types, although some of the older white kids appeared to be well on the way to becoming *Breakfast Club* or *Brat Pack* clones.

Amongst the black kids, there was the odd Michael Jackson T-shirt, but none of the MC Hammer baggy trouser types you found in abundance on the streets and in the classrooms back in Oakland. And, for some reason, everyone appeared to be excited and pumped up.

73

Principal Sweeting was a small, balding man, with glasses that reflected the light streaming in from the expanse of office glass. His face had the anticipation of a smile, as if he were a bank manager possessed of just one more reason not to give a loan. He rose and extended a hearty handshake to them all before ushering his secretary out to hasten upon some refreshments.

'We are really honoured, gentleman. Mr Doleson has told me so much about you. Let me first say how sad we all are, here at Toshoba High, to hear of your loss. The whole school extends its sympathy. The tragedy was felt by us all. We're very much looking forward to working with you.' He leant back in his chair and, with his chin tucked into his chest, gazed at a TV monitor placed on a cabinet to his right. 'My, my, they are getting a little exited!' He turned to face his visitors again. 'You couldn't have come at a better time; we've just qualified for the play-offs. The football team has been a great success this fall.' He stopped for a moment. A thought had obviously just occurred to him. 'I guess you being here has been somewhat providential. Might you want to say a few words? Now that we have such a fine assembly at your disposal. It would be a shame to waste such an opportunity.' He turned again to give a brief glance back towards the monitor and the heaving masses, chuckling to himself as he did so. Having second thoughts, he added: 'Then again, perhaps not.'

'An excellent idea, Sweeting!' They swung round to see that Doleson had arrived. 'Of course they would love to. What a golden opportunity!' He'd brought Pariche and

Garvey along with him. 'You know Garv, but may I introduce you to Professor Jedemiah Pariche.'

They shook hands and Sweeting sent for more chairs.

'So, I get to meet you at long last, Mr Pariche; your reputation goes before you.'

'You're too kind. I trust it's not all bad!'

'But of course. You all come highly recommended. I was telling your colleagues how fortunate they are to be here at the time when we've got everyone together to celebrate our football team getting to the play-offs.' There was a brief interruption as the swiftly requisitioned chairs made their entrance.

'We would be delighted to accept your invitation to the party,' Doleson replied, as he took his seat. He chose to sit strategically at Sweeting's side, from where he proceeded to make his pitch. 'Sweeting,' he said, earnestly looking at the gentleman sitting next to him. 'We are so grateful for what you've done already. We're also alive to some of the risks you've taken, being so closely associated with what we aim to do.'

'We've dealt with problems in the past, Basil. Problems that were much scarier than this.' The deal had long been sealed as far as Sweeting was concerned; he was one of the good guys. But he did have one concern. He smiled, rested his face in his hands and pointed a forefinger in the direction of the man from June Lake. 'I do have one worry,' he said. 'That you and your colleagues might be aiming to stir things up just a little *too* much. Don't get me wrong, I want to see our school associated with people of your calibre, and the school you represent. My, my, the mighty University of California, and little old Toshoba High; how could anyone possibly object?'

His look of resigned incredulity indicated that there was probably a long list of people who could and would find such complaint. Just for good measure, he filled in the blanks. 'Four years ago we first put forward the idea of having a mixed prom night here. As you can imagine that bought out all manner of complaint from the usual suspects; flat-earthers and the born again crowd, and Millicent Pierce and her people down at the White Citizens Council. They were all here, threatening all manner of things with the School Board. Hadn't there always been separate black and white homecomings? Why spoil it all by getting people agitated on no good account? They said there would be problems, such as the drinking of alcohol and youngsters getting drunk! Think of the liabilities and insurance claims that would bring. Of course, the real issue was race. What would the rednecks make of black boys and white girls serenading each other at a prom? And believe you me, we do have our fair share of rednecks here at Toshoba High. By the time everyone had had their say, the whole idea had been shot down in flames. I suspect the county still isn't ready for such a move. But this Institute of yours is different! This time I won't be dismissed as an old fool having one of my turns. The School Board knows that there are real benefits to be had. That you appear to be promising an extra-curricular largesse that will benefit everyone in the long run. It's all about horizons, folks, opening up horizons. But it's got to be done right!' He was looking at Pariche again. 'We can't have people getting folks agitated on no account!'

'I wouldn't want it any other way,' replied Pariche, his face a picture of innocence.

'I want to get away from people saying, "Thank God for Mississippi; always at the bottom of the heap".' But now, as he gazed at his monitor, Sweeting began to show signs of concern at what he was witnessing. He rose quickly to his feet. 'Gentlemen, I can see things are getting just a little boisterous down there. I think you'll get a kick out of what you're about to see. Who's up for giving us a few words?'

Pariche, once again, all innocence and charm, smiled and pointed towards Soren. 'That's your man,' he said; 'Professor Karlsson will do an excellent job.'

Of course Soren could have swung for him, but before anything more could be said, he and the others were being ushered along that darkened corridor again, towards the main hall, from where there could already be heard the increasing crescendo of student cheers and a cacophony of trumpets. When they did finally emerge, into an almost blinding light, they were met with a wall of noise that crippled the knees and stymied the senses. Principal Sweeting's entrance appeared to drive the students into even a greater frenzy. Soren caught a glimpse, over his shoulder, of a student holding aloft a trophy – the real focus of all the veneration – that was almost as big as himself. Half the hall was a sea of brown, with ripples of white, the other half its mirror opposite. It appeared to be that Toshoba High still had some way to go in its fight against self-imposed segregation.

Sweeting was in his element. He not only had the joy of footballing success to celebrate, something that had always been very dear to his heart, but here, in his beloved Toshoba County High, he had a real live big school professor to exhibit, and a black one to boot. Someone who was going to show his students what they could all aspire to if they applied themselves to the basic principles of hard work and sacrifice. How learning, with its gift of true insight, could be the vehicle to facilitate this. It was the kind of argument that got Sweeting into trouble, especially with the more conservative and religious elements of the school's governing body. But, as he was always the first point out, most of the complainants seemed to be folks who'd already decided to have their kids educated at 'the other place'; the sobriquet Sweeting chose to apply to the Cedars.

After a while the hall went quiet. Craig and Soren watched transfixed as the student body swayed slowly and rhythmically from side to side. The principal now produced from his pocket a paper plane, which he proceeded to launch into flight. Amidst a rising crescendo, the plane did a graceful circuit of the lower reaches of the hall. When it finally came to rest, the audience let forth an ear-splitting, thunderous clap, like the crack of a whip. This was followed by the continuous chant of 'T.C.H., T.C.H., T.C.H., T.C.H.' Soren could see that everyone on stage had joined in, including Pariche, who was now waving his cane above his head. Sweeting now slowly raised his left hand. As he lowered it, the noise subsided. It was a perfect model of control.

'Ladies and gentlemen, this is truly an historic day for Toshoba High.'

More chants of 'T.C.H.'

'Last Friday our brave boys, for the first time in our school's history, qualified for the playoffs. I'm so proud of them. Let's get them up here. Let's have them take a bow.'

Amidst more chanting, a procession of young men, about thirty in number, equally divided between black and white, took to the stage. They were escorted by a throng of whooping and dancing cheerleaders, swirling their batons and dressed in bright green dresses. Soren was left marvelling as to how this was done without anyone being brained in the process.

'Come on, Coach,' called Sweeting, this time with a roar. 'Coach Madeley! Come on up and bring your people with you. You all deserve to take a bow.'

With this, a small muscular man, in his late fifties, came forward. The crowd were now ecstatic. It was not lost on any of the visitors that the person getting this adoration from this young, mixed, but mostly white, Southern audience, just happened to be black.

Now there were chants of, 'MADELEY, MADELEY, MADELEY.'

Sweeting milked the occasion for all it was worth, savouring every moment as the jamboree continued for what appeared, to the Californians, to be an eternity. Afterwards, when the dust had settled, Sweeting finally got around to introducing his visitors.

'If I can have your attention again, ladies and gentlemen. You could hardly have failed to have noticed that we have some visitors here with us today. Really distinguished visitors. All the way from the University of California. Would you please extend a warm Toshoba County High welcome to Professors Karlsson, Pariche and Ginnsberg.'

Soren, amidst all the excitement, had forgotten that he was due to make an address and was visibly surprised at this turn of events. The crowd went quiet. Soren knew that talking to this lot would be a different proposition to the lectures he usually delivered in Berkeley. Speaking in public was always liable to induce trepidation and that sinking feeling in the pit of his stomach and, as he looked at the audience before him now, he knew that many of them had the potential to be hostile. Still, being a Southern audience, maybe good manners would kick in, and there was always the football success to keep them in a relatively receptive mood. He remembered the words he'd said at Brad's funeral. As Sweeting had already indicated, the students would have heard of Brad's death and would be expecting some mention of it. So Soren talked about his friend and how the audience assembled before him had no need to reproach itself for his death. He then went on, as Sweeting had suggested, to explain the work of the Institute and how its main purpose was to work with the students now sitting before him.

'We aim to broaden the opportunities that you have to study at college. We hope that this might be extended to, at some later stage, to those studying at another place... you know where I mean. Just down the road.'

This was immediately met with more chants of 'T.C.H., T.C.H.'

From there on, his address was set fair, with Craig adding a few words and telling the students about one last thing he'd brought along to show them. Doleson, who'd been missing for some time, now reappeared on stage, directing some students who were carrying a packaged item. It was the BSD workstation that Craig had liberated from the Lawrence Berkeley Lab. Something, he informed them, that would be for the sole use of students from Toshoba County High. More chants of 'T.C.H., T.C.H.'

Long after the students had beaten paths to their respective homes, the general euphoria of the occasion assisted in the conveyance of the visitors back to the Institute. Pariche was his usual expansive self, telling them how they would now be able to take the battle to the whole of the community. Their feeling of wellbeing was soon to be dampened though, when, on their arrival back at the Institute, they found the driveway blocked by a tractor load of foul-smelling pigs' swill.

'Oh, well,' sighed Doleson, 'it could have been worse.'

They were words that were to prove prophetic, for before them lay an odoriferous trail that led all the way the library. Here they found the shelves and many of Doleson's precious books sprayed with the stuff. Intriguingly, there was someone standing aloft a set of sliding steps, busily trying to rescue what they could. Doleson looked up and called out. The figure, dressed in overalls, wearing rubber gloves and wielding a cloth, paused, removed the scarf protecting her face and her nose from the stench, and turned to face him.

'Oh, hi, I thought you might need some help!'

Soren now entered the room and looking up, called out: 'Bridget, is that you?'

'Ah, you remembered!' she cried with an impish expression on her face. 'So you're the reason why that nice lady detective came all the way down here! Mmm, yes, definitely worth it.'

74

Georgetown, Washington DC

Virginia desperately needed answers. She was now more than ever of the opinion that Soren was in danger and, following his departure, had gone through all the information she had, and it frightened her. There was still much that was sparse and mockingly inconclusive, but the strands that she'd been able to piece together all pointed towards the involvement of something more threatening than just a couple of hicks from some small Southern backwater. So that night she'd lain awake enduring the extremes of emotion, between soaring flights of fancy and moments of stultifying paralysis. Christina had told her of the threats that had been made by Constanze and immediately she'd sensed that they were into an entirely different ballgame. She knew this from experience, having watched the FBI at work on her own turf in Pittsburgh. They were, at that very moment, attempting to build a case against Pittsburgh's own mafia kingpins, the Genovese family. Virginia had good contacts with the local field office and they were usually quite forthcoming. But when it came to Albert Constanze, she was met with nothing; save for a long embarrassed silence. Something was very wrong in Boston, but what it was they weren't prepared to say.

So Virginia gave Dyson a call. He was, perhaps, the only person able to give the answers she craved and he immediately invited her to join him in Washington. Although he ostensibly listed his Berkshire home in Lennox, just down the road from the Karlsson's, as his main residence, he still liked to spend most of his time at his apartment in

Georgetown. From there he would work his old Justice Department contacts, incidentally feeding bits of financial intelligence to his friend, Peter Van Buren, as he did so: all the better to aid the latter's banking interests.

The club in which Dyson usually dined, and where he and Virginia were to meet, was small and unpretentious. It had formerly been a tavern and was situated in the historic heart of old Georgetown. The club's bars and smoke rooms had once been home to the political elite, but they now catered mainly for lawyers from State and Judiciary departments. It was a place where Dyson felt naturally at home. Dyson had been upset to hear of Brad's death; as disagreeable as his company had been at the Van Buren's, no one deserved a thing like that. He was relieved that Soren had not been hurt and like Virginia was very much concerned for his old walking companion's safety. In asking Dyson for help, Virginia knew she'd be pushing at an open door. Any threat to Soren would be taken by Dyson as a personal affront.

'Yes,' said Dyson, taking a sip of his wine and ignoring the fish on his plate, 'I agree with your assessment that it was probably a professional killing. It's enough to have to deal with the unreconstructed bigotry of some of the locals down there, but this smacks of something completely different.' Virginia nodded, her smile withheld. 'But if you're right,' he continued, 'then why? Why was Soren targeted?'

'I'm beginning to suspect that it's all to do with what Christina has been doing in Boston,' replied Virginia. Dyson looked unconvinced, rubbing his chin thoughtfully and laughing just a little weakly. 'It does make sense,' she persisted, 'if you think it through!'

'I suppose it could pose a plausible line of enquiry.' He paused, as if he'd just become aware of how pompous he sounded. 'Sorry, Ginny, of course you're right. When I was down there with Christina, I got the distinct impression that the Sheriff and his people didn't know what to think. That the whole thing was a little outside of their compass.' He sat back in his chair and cupped the back of his head with his hands.

'Well, well, Mr Constanze! The department's had quite a lot of dealings with that gentleman!' His manner was assured, very much suggestive of a certain confidence and mannered rectitude of the kind that Virginia, herself, would recognise, having been brought up in an environment that seemed to breed them. She knew that Dyson, as a man of his word, would do his utmost to find out what the federal authorities had on Constanze and she had faith that he would deliver.

A telephone call from Dyson, after the Thanksgiving weekend, confirmed everything that Virginia had feared. Various leads had been found in Mississippi, pointing to the possible involvement of Constanze. They told of an increase in the communications traffic between the Boston and New Orleans' crime families, including phone transcripts that pointed towards heated exchanges about something having gone very wrong. These had been forwarded by the FBI in New Orleans to the agency's office in Boston. They had not been followed up. One of their agents up there had been hopelessly compromised by his involvement with another well-known gang leader.

75

Toshoba County, Mississippi

'Jesus, what the hell is all this?' Pariche was standing motionless, shocked into a freeze, his face a picture of incredulity. Standing before him, as sure as life, was Flaxel Boateng. 'You sure have a nerve!' He walked over to the stairs and called up to the landing. 'Solly, you're not going to believe this. You have a visitor.'

'Sorry, Prof,' was, a somewhat contrite, Flaxel's first words. 'Ain't no cause for alarm. We come in peace.'

'We?'

A figure appeared in the doorway; a slight figure, carrying a burlap. He was of South Indian origin, with bright, somewhat sunken, eyes. Everything about this man, his facial features, his legs, and his torso was skeletal, sharp and hard. Pariche smiled a smile of surprised recollection. 'Ah, Ismail! I remember your rather telling contribution to our last meeting.' As heartwarming as it was to gaze upon the incongruity of this man's presence here, in the heart of Mississippi, Pariche still wasn't buying any of it. He turned again to Flaxel. 'I'm sorry, but this will not do. I want you both gone!'

'Hear me out, Prof; as I said, we come in peace.' Flaxel's protestations were echoed by his companion, but Pariche was insistent, his response indicating that he was suspicious of anything these two had the temerity to offer. 'Honest, man,' Flaxel tried again, 'I'm not here to cause you trouble.'

'Yes, we heard you'd gone missing,' Pariche muttered to himself, seeming to be accept that they weren't going to be going anywhere soon.

'I thought it might be good for my health to get away for a while.' Flaxel's voice was calmer now; low and matter of fact. 'A few of the Brothers might not be too keen to see me for a while.' Sizing the two of them up again, Pariche's immediate thoughts were still for them to be gone. 'Believe me, I've taken a lot of heat to save your friend,' Flaxel continued, his tone pleading and hurt.

'Yes, I heard; most magnanimous!' There was more than just a note of sarcasm in Pariche's reply.

'I needed to give them a fresh target.'

'Target? Who?'

'Some of the Brothers in the Nation.'

'So, you're running from your friends?'

'Hoodlums!' interjected Ismail, in a thick Indian accent. 'I do not believe myself, but no true Muslim would do what they do,' he said, before adding a quick 'Fuck it.'

Pariche chuckled at the man's progress; at least he was now swearing in English. Resisting the temptation to debate the relative merits of authenticity, religious or otherwise, and forgoing the wish to congratulate Ismail on his progress in language acquisition, Pariche was about to proffer further suggestions as to what the pair of them might do when Doleson and Soren appeared, their faces a picture of befuddled astonishment. 'You just couldn't make it up,' Pariche sighed, his eyebrows raised and his teeth gritted.

'Well, this just won't do,' said Doleson, in full proprietorial mode. 'You must leave immediately!'

Pariche, though, was beginning to have second thoughts. 'I suppose we can't just throw them out,' he said, still with a total look of disdain on his face. 'Besides, we've got to think of the safety of the animals out there!'

Whilst ignoring Pariche's attempt at humour, Soren was in full agreement. 'They're going to have to stay awhile,' he said, in a tone that was somewhat lacking in enthusiasm, 'while we work something out.'

'Exactly, my man,' said Flaxel, sensing the change in the tone.

'Don't push it, Flaxel,' Soren cautioned, looking distractedly at his watch, subconsciously registering that the

333

clock was ticking. Just how long would it be before the sheriff found out they were here, not to mention the rest of the community? He hadn't forgotten where they were; the locals would have a field day with the two of them, something that also appeared to be playing on the mind of Doleson too, although his thoughts were tinged by what their presence would be doing for the reputation of the Institute.

'I think they might be just a little too exotic for these parts,' he said. 'Just like that fellow with the withered arm.'

'You mean Harvey?' Soren stopped for a moment, deep in thought. Something had just occurred to him. Of course, Harvey! If there was a way of getting these two out of their hair, then Harvey might just be the person to do it. 'I will have to make a call, but I think I might just have the solution.'

For the moment though, they still had Flaxel and his companion to contend with. Ismail, currently prey to baser priorities, was now talking of the need for food and was soon being led by Doleson, with Pariche in tow, to the kitchen, leaving Soren and Flaxel alone together. The two of them could, as Doleson put it, "have a heart-to-heart". Of course this was the last thing Soren had wanted. Something that wasn't helped by Flaxel who, having invited himself into one of the side rooms, was now scrutinising a journal that Soren had been reading.

'Jeez, Bros, you do read some mind-boggling shit.'

Soren smiled, but he was still very much torn. With the help he'd given Denis, Flaxel might just have done one of the few decent things in his short hustling life, but that didn't change the fact that this was still someone he didn't trust. He watched as Flaxel feigned a languid, 'indulge me' pose, that was meant to be superior, but even he must have known came across as something laughable and wreaking of defeat. All Soren could think of was the question, why? Why was Flaxel here? And what was he angling for? Was he still after money or whatever passed for action in his sordid little world? Or had he become so obsessed with Soren and the Diaspora Program that he just couldn't let go? Whatever it was, it was troubling.

As Ismail continued in his discovery of English profanities in the kitchen, Flaxel persevered in his attempt to win over a reluctant and suspicious Soren. With shoulders slightly hunched, he leant forward, his elbows firmly placed on the table before him. His demeanour was no longer threatening, but now came across as rather tired; the look of someone who'd spent far too long trying to think of ways of avoiding the retribution that was surely going to be coming his way. He was also desperately trying to fathom out why the 'prof' seemed to be so lacking in grace, forgiveness and respect. After all, hadn't he just given up a lucrative business opportunity to help him out? Of course, it hadn't occurred to him that the 'prof' might just find the idea of talking to him somewhat distasteful, even distressing; the overweening belief that everything he did, no matter how outrageous, could in some way be smoothed over with a few words. For Soren, it begged the question as to how someone like this had ever managed to hook up with Wilson in the first place.

'Let's just say,' Flaxel said, by way of illumination, 'that I was able to remind the man of just how naughty he'd been.'

'Go on!' Against his better judgement, Soren was beginning to show signs of interest.

'Ah, I thought that would get your attention.'

'Well?'

'Charlie, my man; his wife just loves the white stuff.'

'No!'

'Yes siree, as sure as you're sitting there.'

'Well, well!' Soren was nonplussed. Whatever he'd expected, it hadn't been anything like that. He let forth a self-conscious chuckle, before returning to the more familiar terrain of terra anxiety. 'I think I ought to warn you,' he continued. 'The whole of the sheriff's department will be descending on this place anytime soon. You see, this is still technically a crime scene in a murder investigation.' Now it was Soren's turn to have his interlocutor's full attention. 'Also, as the crime was interstate, the FBI have already been here and will probably be so again.'

Flaxel held up his hands in mock horror. 'OK, I get the picture.' His eyes were wide open, his mouth and lips a curl.

'You obviously don't want me around. Hell, I wouldn't want me around!'

'It would be in your best interest!'

'So, someone got killed?'

Soren nodded. 'Yes. A good friend.'

'That's bad. Seen a lot of bad shit like that myself. Known a few folks who've been wasted.'

No, that was not the response Soren had expected or wanted. He didn't want to give this man the idea that they had any shared interests, but his curiosity was beginning to get the better of him. Something about this visitor, and the story of his relationship with Wilson, was irresistibly compelling. The clattering of pots and the sound of laughter coming from the kitchen, reminded Soren of the presence of Ismail, and prompted a question as to why Flaxel had become so mixed up with the Nation of Islam.

'As I've been saying all along,' answered Flaxel, a little defensively, 'people need ways of coping, what with all this shit going down. The Nation was the only deal in town. The only ones who weren't corrupted by whitey.'

'But now you're on the run from them!'

'I know.' Flaxel's reply was accompanied by a slow exhalation, as if this had been the only thing on his mind too. He'd been on the run for well-nigh thirty hours and now he looked spent and in desperate need of sleep. The cockiness and lightness of spirit Soren had witnessed at the Faculty Club had now very much gone. 'I knew the brothers weren't spotless,' Flaxel continued. 'Hell, it *is* the flatlands! Just got in a bit too deep, I guess.'

'Too deep?'

'Yes, I owe them some dues.'

'Money?'

'You wouldn't have any on you, would you?'

Ah, there it was. Just a glimpse. The street hustler back again. Soren's raised eyebrows and slow shake of the head indicated that it would be unwise for Flaxel to continue with that line of enquiry. There was now a brief lull as they continued to size each other up. The regard they held for each other appeared to be moving towards one of grudging

336

respect, although, for Soren, this was still very grudging indeed. There might have been a temptation to succumb to a growing admiration for the streetwise smarts of his adversary and his ability to navigate an environment that had done all it could to turn, subdue, and humiliate, but the downside to it all was that the street had clearly won; Flaxel's personality and character had been irredeemably shaped by it. He would always be looking for the easy option; an attitude that Soren feared would be waiting to manifest itself in anything Flaxel chose to turn his hand to. Even now Soren had the feeling that he was being played, by a character who'd continually demonstrated an antipathy for everything he considered to be important, not least the value of education and the discipline required to succeed in it. That Flaxel had shown a willingness to abuse this, was something that, in Soren's eyes, was an irredeemable defect of character.

As for Flaxel, well he was staring across at someone who appeared almost alien in their accomplishments. "The prof" seemed to possess a certain coolness that the street hustler in Flaxel admired and he was, after all, outdoing 'Whitey' at his own game. But then again, *that* was the problem. This guy was too good, too white; perhaps even thought of himself as being white. He didn't seem to know that everything he did, all that he would ever amount to, would be measured by the colour of his skin. The prof needed to be told that they'd both been branded in a way that would mean they would always be found wanting by the society they were living in. Of course Soren disagreed; he *did* have an understanding of what it meant to be black. Only he had always resisted attempts to categorise or be categorised by it. For Flaxel, that was not good enough. Race would always be a symbol of difference; something to embrace and play upon for all its worth.

'This stuff you teach at Berkeley, what got you into all that Jew boy stuff?'

Soren gave a resigned shrug, not exactly sure of what he was being asked. 'You mean the support I've been giving to the Holocaust Centre?' Flaxel nodded. 'The subject hardly needs explaining!'

'Thought that was the whole point...'

Soren let it go. It was a point well made.

'...And this shit!' Flaxel had again picked up the journal he'd been leafing through earlier. 'What kinda school prepares you for shit like this?' Once again Soren shrugged defensively; perhaps this was not the best moment to regale Flaxel with tales of dorm life at Exeter or sculling on the Squamcott. Flaxel was beginning to show signs of annoyance. 'There you go again. Why do you always clam up like that? Is it about what went down back on the Coast? You can't blame me for trying.'

'You were trying to get your hands on something you had no right to. The stuff wasn't yours. You hadn't earned it.'

'Brother, our people have done more than enough to sit at the table with the likes of those Mr Blue Chips in their fancy mansions.'

Soren raised his eyebrows and smiled to himself; something that hinted at just a little impatience. 'But what have *you* done, Flaxel? What have *you* actually contributed?'

Ignoring Soren's question, Flaxel changed tack. 'We're getting flooded out west, man. Have you seen how many Chinamen there are on campus these days? Hardly a black face in sight!'

Gazing into the darkness off what, in all probability, had been a slavery plantation, Soren felt the urge to remind Flaxel of where they were. Instead, he said; 'Well, they did help build the place I guess.' He paused, before asking a further question. 'Have you bothered to ask yourself why there are so many Asian faces on campus?'

'Who knows? Maybe their brains are wired up differently.' Flaxel's smile soured a little on registering the somewhat admonishing and pitying expression on Soren's face. 'Well, I'm sorry. It's just that I get so mad when I hear bros like you defending them. You know, with that Chinaman you have teaching on the program.'

'OK, let's stop right there, shall we? I take it that you mean Denis? Yes, he does have a name, and he is actually both Chinese and Japanese American. His family was interned by us during the Second World War...'

'Don't include me in that "us!'

'...they come from a whole class of people who, just a century ago, were no more than serfs.'

'But teaching us our history, man!'

'"Us"?' sighed Soren, returning the compliment. 'I thought Mississippi was out there, not in here?' He pointed his finger at his temple. Flaxel took the point, but was in no mood to concede.

'Mississippi is everywhere, man. Just look at that Tawana Brawley case they had in New York!'

'But that was proved to be a fabrication!'

'There you go again, making apologies for them, making out as if you were white. Gotta call it as I sees it, prof. You really do puzzle me. You just don't seem all that black to me.'

'I think you'd find that many of the locals around here might disagree.'

'But why don't you reach out to it, you know, embrace it?'

'Embrace what exactly?'

'Your African heritage man, Africa!'

'Why just pick on that?'

''Cause that's where you're from! You're deluding yourself if you think you're not.'

'But why choose what others have decided for you? Isn't that what you've been fighting against?'

'Man, you're slippery. Ain't no flies on you. But can't you see we're going backwards. That out there,' and this time it was Flaxel's turn to point to the dark expanse of the fields and the old plantation outside, 'is where we all might one day end up.'

'Now that's a different thing all together,' replied Soren, now warming to Flaxel's argument. 'Perhaps one should never attempt to gainsay history.'

'Look at the way they're ganging up on us. The Bakke case. Stopping us from getting an education.'

'Sure, black kids do have the cards stacked against them, but does that mean they should get preferential treatment?'

'Get real, prof, we already do. Just look at what that cross-dressing faggot, J Edgar Hoover, did to Fred Hampton and Bobby Seal. If they can't enslave us, they shoot. They don't want black people around anymore. Used to be they needed us to work their land and their factories. Now that's all gone and they can't think of any ways to work us no more. We've become a luxury they can no longer afford.'

Soren was a little embarrassed, peevish even, about being on the wrong side of an argument with Flaxel, and it was now his turn to try not to show any weakness or wish to concede. Instead he talked about how Flaxel appeared to be making the survivalists' case for them. How he could see that the system was corrupt, with people seemingly being penalised for something as basic as an accident of birth, but this didn't mean that one had to tear the whole thing down.

But Flaxel wasn't finished. 'All I see, prof, is that you seem to be into all of this foreign shit? Those Jew boys at the Holocaust Centre and the help you've been giving to all those Chileans!'

'You really have been doing your homework!' Soren shrugged, once again wrong footed by an opponent he'd obviously underestimated. Seeing his opponent knocked off guard, Flaxel attempted to force home his advantage; 'The only thing "the man" understands is the bullet and the gun.'

'If you carry a gun, there's always a risk that you might have to use it.'

'And your point?'

'Well, innocent people might get hurt.'

'Always have, man, always have.'

'Then you lose the moral authority.'

'Now you're beginning to sound like my man, Ismail. He's always sprouting on about that non-violence shit.'

'Well, remember, Flaxel, it doesn't mean that you have to keep to the law; the civil rights campaigners spent their lives challenging and breaking it. But they were able to maintain a moral authority, mostly by not resorting to violence. If you're fighting people who've gone rogue, then the best course of action is to use that against them. That might mean that you have to break the law yourself; but not at the point of a gun. Look at what those people did over in Media, Pennsylvania. They broke into the offices of the FBI and dug up a whole load of dirt on what they'd been up to. But they were unarmed. Had they used violence, then they would have lost.'

Flaxel was still unconvinced. In no time at all he was giving Soren the benefits of his knowledge about another bane of his life; namely the attention being given to the AIDS epidemic raging out west. Soon the authentic man of the streets was talking about 'faggots' and 'queers' and the 'curse of San Francisco'. Soren sighed despairingly to himself. Had he come all the way to Mississippi only to find himself being regaled by another kind of prejudice?

'The friend I was talking about earlier, the friend who was killed. Well, he was also gay.'

'No, you don't say!' Flaxel paused for a moment, then pointed his finger in Soren's direction. 'And you?'

Soren, remembering the imploringly despairing look that Martin had given him at Brad's graveside, looked at Flaxel and very deliberately mouthed a 'Fuck you!'

For Flaxel's part, there was a deep intake of breath and a look of hurt. He knew he'd gone too far. His new friend, 'The Prof', was looking at him as if he was something he had accidentally trodden in. Although near to rage, Soren was thankful for Flaxel's return to type. It gave him some recompense for the blows that had been landed earlier. And Flaxel, in his untutored, street hustling style, had landed a few. It had left Soren questioning, not just his motives for coming to Mississippi, that was just the hors d'oeuvre, but also his ability to engage; that here was another person he'd failed to get through to. Soren had had these arguments many times before, with the young Turks back home who would veer between complaints of emasculation and strutting virility. He knew the type. He'd seen the way they'd come after Alice Walker and James Baldwin. They had the words

341

and the attitude, but not the insight to see that much of their posturing pointed to something that was immanently dysfunctional. Theirs was the kind of argument that could so easily lead people into the gulag. It employed a dismissal of all disputation, by having an even greater claim to hurt. It was a thoroughgoing victimhood that provided a distorted self-knowledge, shielding people from any reproach. A form of cognitive dissonance. Prejudice! They could never be accused of anything so heinous. Not so much a banality of evil; more a thoroughgoing psychosis of deluded self-righteousness.

Later, the two men were joined by the others who'd returned from the kitchen bearing gifts. Ismail had done them proud, providing them with a meal furnished with ingredients he'd been carrying in his burlap. Whilst Soren and Flaxel had been talking, he'd been directing Doleson and Pariche in the making of lassi, chapatis, naan bread, and an assortment of vegetables and spices, perfect for a dish of besan pakodas and biryani rice. Doleson had taken to the task immediately. Oh, joy of joys! Already the big house was being subjected to his original injunction that it should, amongst other things, be a place of cultural celebration.

Pariche was less convinced. Like Soren, he too was hell bent on getting the two of them – Flaxel and Ismail – out of here by next morning's early light.

76

Next morning the Institute's occupants were greeted to a re-energised Harvey determined to claim his prize. Within minutes he'd awakened a bemused Flaxel from his bed and corralled him away from the scrutiny of the others. Soon our man of the street was alive to all manner of largesse that might be forthcoming from *Rolling Stone* magazine and the prospect of making it big in the Big Apple. Soren's call had stimulated Harvey into a frenzy of activity rarely seen from him in all the fifteen years he'd been sending in copy. He had already filed a report about Brad's murder and this, with its rather incongruent setting, had indeed turned a few heads amongst the editorial staff up in the magazine's headquarters in New York. Now he had the motherlode. They'd not heard of Flaxel Boateng, of course, but they were intrigued by the Nation of Islam angle. This, along with the murder story Harvey had been planning to write, meant that his standing with the boys in New York was sky high. Now he would be able to make real demands. They'd have to look at that series he'd been planning and there would be syndication rights, even a book. Harvey wasn't sure how all this had happened, and he didn't have much of an idea as to what he was going to put down, but, boy, he could see all the angles. A street-hustling con artist on the run from the Nation of Islam, hiding out in Mississippi; just what would the natives make of that? The possibility of Flaxel meeting some of the more extreme elements that the Magnolia State had to offer was far too good to pass up. How different it had been just two weeks ago when Harvey had first called Bertholdt, his long-suffering editor. Bertholdt was wise to Harvey and the stunts he tried to pull. He'd judged quite correctly that Harvey had been at the chemical aids again, having known him from the time they'd worked together in San Francisco. Ten years ago the management of *Rolling Stone* had upped sticks and moved east, taking Bertholdt with them. Harvey, though, had decided to stay put, choosing to remain with the disparate elements that made up the Bay Area music scene; the nearest thing he had to family. Good riddance, Bertholdt had said, but for some reason he'd continued to throw Harvey the odd commission. Harvey was like that. Infectious; just like a rash. During the intervening years, Harvey had carried out his duties with the minimum of fuss, filing reports that were usually both humorous and outfield, always knowledgeable and well written, requiring very little by way of editing on Bertholdt's part. Not that Harvey could have cared. All he wanted was for the cheques to be made out to cash and wired to whatever dive he happened to be staying at the time. Only on rare occasions would he phone the office, usually to complain, and nearly always about money.

So Harvey had called Bertholdt about this story he'd come across. An old-fashioned inside scoop that seemed to have everything. Something that would make the liberal mind salivate with stories about redneck violence, race, and the murder of one of their own. What was more, he'd actually been asked, by this pretty little detective, to help out with the investigation. At this point Bertholdt did indeed ask what he'd been inhaling. All Harvey wanted was for his friend and editor to give him the go ahead. Bertholdt promised to mull it over before putting the phone down. Poor Harvey, drunk and fantasising again. And wasn't he supposed to be doing that Elvis commemorative piece across the way in Nashville?

But now, at the Institute, Harvey was watching Flaxel talk to Bertholdt over the phone. It was typical Flaxel, as fly and winning as he'd been the night before with Soren. After he'd finished, he handed the receiver back to Harvey.

'Did you hear that, Bertholdt?' shouted Harvey down the phone, 'did you hear that?' He could sense what Bertholdt was thinking. If the story was that good, then why not give it to one of his more favoured, and dare one say more talented, staff reporters?

'This is my story!'

Harvey's refrain was now almost a howl, much to the amusement of Doleson who was eavesdropping at the door. If they tried that one again, then he was walking, and taking with him one of the best scoops the paper had had for years.

Afterwards a buoyant Harvey was able to inform the others that the paper was indeed on board and raring to go with anything they'd care to suggest. Doleson, ever the one for the main chance, immediately interpreted this as meaning that *Rolling Stone* magazine, with all its street credibility, actually wanted to run a story about *him* and his blessed Institute. Harvey, of course, just wanted to lap up the adulation. How things had changed. All those fools who had doubted him and had failed to recognise his excellence. Now they would all be dancing to his tune.

By the time Busby and Angela arrived to do their weekly stint at the Institute, Harvey and his prize were about to leave. It was clear the girls found the men standing before them, both equally fascinating and repulsive. Everything about Flaxel resonated with things they'd spent the best part of their short and very Christian lives being warned against. The contrast couldn't have been more stark. Here were two straight-out-of-Sunday School Mississippi lasses, set against a couple of the East Bay's more down at heel representatives; who needed protecting from whom was not immediately apparent. Soren was just glad that their exposure to Flaxel and Harvey would be minimal, as the putative luminaries of Rolling Stone magazine and media stardom collected their things together in preparation to making their exit.

'Don't you be making him no slave now,' said Busby, on hearing of Harvey's plans, her initial reserve now coursing into the flirtatious.

'You could always hitch a ride with us,' said Flaxel, 'I know a few gentleman who...' His response trailed off to silence as he registered Soren's look of exasperation. 'No, maybe not. Best listen to the man.'

The two of them departed without Ismail, who'd decided to go back to Berkeley and his studies at GTU. During a long conversation with Doleson and the others, which had lasted well into the early hours, Ismail had impressed them with his consummate knowledge about all things spiritual. It turned out that he hailed from a family that had been heavily involved in the Naxalite tradition of communist rebellion in West Bengal and had forsaken all of this for something that approximated more to Ghandi's original injunction of non-violence. Although some might find him a little too exotic, and non-Christian, for these parts, Doleson had found himself warming to someone who might, at a future date, be someone he could use at the Institute. He was left with an open invitation to return at some time in the future. Besides, he could cook a mean biriyani.

77

New Orleans, Louisiana

Dyson's news about the New Orleans connection was enough for Virginia to immediately hightail it to the city of Mardi Gras. She went straight to the FBI's regional offices on Lafayette; a red brick edifice that was permanently shaded from the sun by the high-rise buildings surrounding it. Virginia had arrived when the office was quiet, so Agent Fuller had more than enough time to show her what they had. Anything to keep in with Pittsburgh's finest; an easy win. Within minutes of her arrival he was showing her photos of a certain Mr Gambietta, a run-of-the-mill 'soldier' and enforcer, known for the distribution of threats, beatings and worse. Gambietta had been off the radar when the mob had been last subjected to a Bureau surveillance operation, something that had occurred at precisely the same time as events were playing out in Mississippi. Virginia instinctively knew that this was their man. She asked if they had any license plate numbers. Joy of joys, they did; a record of all the cars that had been owned by the mob in New Orleans over the last fifteen years.

'Just Gambietta's would do. Any chance of taking a look?'

'Sure,' replied Agent Fuller, his look betraying just the hint of unease.

'Is that a problem? Do you need authorisation?'

'No, I don't think that will be necessary.' All the same, he did go and have a word with one of the older hands, who now rose to his feet and followed him back over. He introduced himself as Agent Parkes. In contrast to Fuller's fair-haired youthfulness, Parkes was thickset, with those unsmiling eyes that reminded Virginia of some of the colleagues she'd left behind in Pittsburgh. As if they'd witnessed a little too much of the darkness on the other side. He was both more guarded and direct than his partner.

'You want to pay a visit to Mr Gambietta?'

'Well, not exactly, I just want to check out his car.'

'Lou,' he called across the office to a man in braces and striped pants sitting in front of a computer. 'Gambietta's wheels. Am I right in thinking he's always used the same one?'

'A 78 Imperial. Wouldn't be seen dead in anything else. And probably will be.'

For the first time, Agent Parkes let forth a smile. 'Come on,' he said, 'let's go and take us a peek.'

After the most cursory of looks around the French Quarter, Agent Fuller pointed the car towards Metairie, a built-up area to the west of the city. Upfront, beside him, Agent Parkes sat half turned, so that he could give Virginia a running commentary on the FBI's love affair with the Big Easy, or NOLA as he liked to call the city and the state of Louisiana. About the times they'd gone after Bonnie and Clyde and their more recent attempts to nail the gang boss Carlos Marcello. He also knew that some of the mob, and Gambietta in particular, liked to hang out at a club called the Blue Weasel, and this was where they were now headed. The Blue Weasel was a rundown and downright seedy looking place that passed itself off as a bar-restaurant and sometime strip joint. It had surround parking and sat between a couple of car dealerships, both of which, Agent Parkes was quick to point out, had to pay their dues. 'If Gambietta so desired,' he said, slightly puzzled, 'he could have traded that old pile for a top of the range Chevy a dozen times over. We do see him sometimes in a car from the lot. Probably uses it as a freebie. Gets one of the showroom guys to give him a lift home if he's had one too many.'

At their destination Agent Fuller pulled the car to a halt and they all scanned the area for any signs of that old

Imperial. Nothing. He eased the car forward, intent on doing another circuit, when Virginia called out.

'There, does that look like our guy?' Sure enough, an old light blue-coloured Imperial had came into view. At the wheel was a silver haired gentleman who the Agents immediately recognised as Gambietta. Yet another dapper looking don, thought Virginia. Big nosed, big mouthed, with a smile for the girl sat beside him. She was one of the Blue Weasel regulars and Gambietta's mistress. The watchers were pleased she was there, providing a diverting tug on Gambietta's attention. After Gambietta and the girl had decamped and gone into the club, Virginia got out with the aim of taking a closer look at the Imperial. 'I won't be long,' she said before setting off in the car's direction. She took care to avoid being seen by any of the Blue Weasel's patrons, at one stage almost crawling on all fours. Soon she was close up, gazing at a vehicle that had been on her mind since the day she'd discovered the glass on the driveway at the hospital in Mississippi. And there it was. The smashed parking light. She bent down and gently prized free a fragment, before bagging it.

'That's hardly legal, is it?' She spun round only to see the rather welcome figure of Agent Parkes standing over her.

'You gave me a fright,' she declared, scrambling to her feet. 'Thought I'd bag me a control sample. Don't worry, it's just to compare notes.'

He wasn't convinced. 'This isn't the way we do things. What you have there wouldn't stand up in court.'

'But it can point us in the right direction. That is until you get this thing impounded!'

As they stood there, arguing the legality of presenting evidence, neither of them noticed that one the secretaries in the car sales room, had, on seeing them, picked up the phone. Suddenly, men were running towards them, a picture of angry intent. One had even drawn a gun. Both Virginia and Agent Parkes cast a resigned look towards each other. Then, without saying a word, both held up their IDs, much to the surprise and bewilderment of the lead figure, Mr Gambietta himself. Whatever disagreement Parkes had with Virginia, he was professional enough to see what needed to be done in a situation like this; brazen it out.

'Is this your car?' he asked, putting his ID away.

'You know it is, you fuck!' screamed an angry Gambietta, caught between retreat and full assault.

'And you are, sir?' he asked, shooting a wink at Virginia, who indeed was impressed.

'Don't give me that you fucking shit. You fuck, you know who I am!'

'So, it *is* Mr Gambietta I am talking to?'

'Very clever. You enjoyed that did you? You fuckwit!'

'Now, Mr Gambietta that will get you nowhere.'

'And you?' Gambietta said, directing his remarks to Virginia. 'Who the fuck are you? They have broads working with the feds these days?'

'I can't help noticing,' said Virginia, 'that you have a quite a nasty gash on your hand.'

'None of your fucking business.'

Virginia exchange glances with Agent Parkes and let out a shrug.

'Well, thank you for being so cooperative,' said Parkes, before looking at the man holding the gun. 'I hope that gun's licensed? I should be careful if I were you. One false move and my partner over there might just be tempted to act.' They spun round to see Agent Fuller standing behind them, his gun drawn. Caught off-balance, it was as if Gambietta had only just noticed that one of his company had indeed drawn a gun. In the face of another expletive-laden series of imprecations from his boss, the man hurriedly put it away. Whilst he did so, Virginia and the federal agents made their exit. Back in the car, she told them why Gambietta's Imperial was so important and why they would need to have it impounded before it miraculously disappeared. The agents must have been suitably impressed, for within the hour they were at the Blue Weasel again, with a hastily signed warrant.

78

Toshoba County, Mississippi

Before Pariche returned to Berkeley he had one small but important task to perform. Putting on his best behaviour and without the adornment of his Vermont Regulars hat, he accompanied Doleson and Garvey to a meeting of the County Board. Doleson, a member of the Board himself, did most of the speaking, with Pariche and Garvey content to chip in whenever the situation demanded it. Underneath the becalmed blades of a malfunctioning ceiling fan, and before the interested scrutiny of the public gallery, the Board listened courteously and intently; Doleson was obviously held in high regard by its members. Mayor Dickinson was there, but Sheriff Harper had sent word that he was running late. Amongst the members in the public gallery, Doleson's light shone less brightly, although there were a few friendly faces. Cecilia, Garvey's wife, sat impassively, waving a small turquoise hand fan. Pariche gave her a wave. She was sitting with a group of black women, who included Darlene Phillips, the woman who'd led those initial attempts, years ago, to empower the women of Flashlight. She, in turn, was presently cocking a snoop at one of Doleson's biggest detractors, Millicent Pierce, the one-time leader of the White Citizens Council and the two pieces of trailer trash seated next to her. It soon became clear that Miss Pierce was intent on making her feelings known about the Institute, something she saw as being akin to a den of iniquity that would bring in all of those outsiders with their godless and foreign ways. Pariche's flyers had done the trick far more effectively than anything she could have dreamt up, bringing out an even bigger crowd than would normally be expected. Most were suspicious, with some downright hostile. Anything that had

Doleson's imprimatur on it was bound to be a cause for concern and soon Miss Pierce, their most vociferous champion, was expressing her disgust at what was being suggested.

'Has the Doleson place been licensed as an educational facility?' she asked, her voice firm and far too vigorous for someone well into their seventies. Pariche, of course, thought she was magnificent. 'Do we really need another school?' she added, her face an expression of ill-disguised contempt. The attire she wore would have done the original Daughters of the Revolution proud, right up to the stern-looking bonnet atop her head. It contrasted somewhat with the two greasy haired, pot bellied trailer park specimens sat with her. Most of the Board tolerated her presence because her views still carried a certain amount of sway with many of their constituents. A few years ago she would have been more assertive, assured in her belief that hers was the majority viewpoint here; that the whole idea of negro equality was an unquestioned affront to nature. Now she was more temperate in the things she said, more defensive. Nowadays she would grumble about the need to turn back the clock. How there had been virtue in the way things were and that we threw them away at our peril. If only the meddlers would leave things be. This was indeed a change. It used to be communists in Washington and big city liberals and rants about the need to keep the nigras in their place. Now she had to watch what she said. People so easily took offence. Hell, there was even one of them on the platform. Now she would talk of the need to make sure that the sheriff was keeping a lid on Flashlight and how the Board needed to be stopped from betraying the community by going down the equal opportunities route. To her mind the sheriff and the mayor had gone over to the other side. The latter had even been elected by appealing to the 'nigra vote.' Not her. Her watchword was still an insistent 'integration... never!' Now into her twilight years, Miss Pierce had become something of a back-room lawyer. Segregation, hiding behind the phalanx of law that was the Mississippi State Constitution, was the way to go. Keep those smart lawyers from

Washington busy in the courts and make sure that everything you did was legally bomb-proof.

Mr Moxley, the Board's chairman, who'd arrived suited, was now taking off his jacket and rolling up his sleeves. He nodded in the direction of Mayor Dickinson who immediately took up the reins.

'Millicent,' he barked, 'it's good to see you and your friends from the Council in attendance.' There was just the hint of tired sarcasm as he gave the two gentlemen seated either side of her a look that positively sneered. 'As I've already pointed out, as I understand it, the house is to be turned into a charitable institution, not a school.' He looked across at Doleson, who nodded in agreement.

Pariche couldn't resist the temptation and added quite audibly: 'Just like the Cedars.'

This did not go down well with Miss Pierce who coughed her disapproval and said, 'I like to think that we already have the right number of educational establishments here in Toshoba County.'

'One too many, I would have thought.' It was Pariche again.

Moxley, the Chair, tried to sound conciliatory. 'Now, Mr Pariche. Surely you can't be seriously suggesting that the Cedars should close?'

But that was exactly what Pariche *was* suggesting. 'Sir, one can only hope that the reasoning behind the need for such a place might soon become as outdated as the views that support it!' The white trash sitting next to Miss Pierce were out of their seats now, shaking their fists, shouting complaints.

It would be fair to suggest that Pariche had already caused considerable alarm with the posters he'd been putting about. Word had gone round like wildfire that the Cedars was to close, with all the students there being sent to a new integrated complex in Clancy, where they would be outnumbered two to one. Furthermore, outside teachers were going to be hired, who'd be filling their children's minds with atheistic filth. The agitation that had so afflicted Miss Pierce and her two companions was beginning to spread to the rest of the public gallery. Things were beginning to get out of hand. By the time Sheriff Harper arrived, the talk had turned pretty ugly with some of the more sober members of the audience feeling the need to detach themselves from the rabble, signalling to Cecilia and Darlene their unalloyed apology and regret. Sheriff Harper, on his arrival, read the situation immediately. He didn't wait to be introduced and his manner – to say the least – was brusk.

'Millicent! You will not prevail!' he growled, dispensing with his usual gentlemanly greeting of her. 'Had it been some twenty years ago, then things might have been different, I guess. And I wouldn't be here. I don't have to remind you folks about who would be standing here in my place. I remember, Millicent, when you, and the people you represent, used to be able to fill this place to the rafters. Now, just what do you have? He gave a long lingering look at the two gentleman seated next to her. His expression was just a little tired. 'I'm here to warn you,' he continued, 'stay away from doing anything stupid. Stay away from the Institute. I know you have concerns, but I guess that isn't any of my business...' He was interrupted here by half-hearted cries of 'shame'. He looked again at Miss Pierce and the two gentlemen sat next to her.

'Some of you will have heard that we picked up some lowlifes the other day. Of course you do. If we hadn't, well, they might just have been with us today, seated with these two...' Now the shouts of protests and denial were more pronounced.

'Millicent, you need to be more careful about who you associate with. Following the events of two weeks back, we have made arrests. The prosecutor's office will want one of them charged for indecency with minors. You take your choice I guess.'

The sheriff knew it was a gamble; a gamble to rely upon the Millicent Pierce's sense of decency and another to think that the White Citizens Council she represented might just be a diminished influence here in Toshoba County. That the rest of the audience might have moved on. It seemed to be working. It was noted by some that there was a deliberate attempt, on the part of Miss Pierce, to create a gap between herself and the gentlemen she was with.

'We just wanted away with them posters, that's all!'

'Just as we could have done without the muck your friends enjoyed spreading up at the Institute,' countered Pariche, a broad grin etched on his face.

'For God's sake, Jed,' whispered Doleson, 'we're attempting to win friends here.' Still smiling, Pariche looked again at Miss Pierce and he could have sworn he half detected a smile. A smile of recognition perhaps. Someone like herself. Too stubborn to know better. Doleson now rose to his feet and turned to Miss Pierce, who now appeared to be showing a more contrite interest. 'Millicent, I know we are some ways apart, but I hope that one day you might be alive to coming over and taking a look at what we have planned. I think you might be impressed.' For just a moment it looked as if they were about to be rewarded with that half-formed look of contempt again, but no, not this time. Instead there was a smile. That self-same smile that Pariche had registered earlier. Then another question

'Have the Board any comments about the mess that's been visited on us by all those media people?' Ah, much better! The voice of the White Citizens Council had moved onto a subject all agreed had been a nuisance and in a tone that was more much conciliatory. Mayor Dickinson's reply was the equal to it, appealing to her sense of etiquette and what it is to be a good host. It was a ploy that was to prove only partially successful though, as Darlene Phillips now took it upon herself to throw a spanner into the works, much to the delight of a certain Jedemiah Pariche. She wanted to know if the sheriff was still considering the appointment of a black deputy and did the Board endorse such a move?

'Yes,' the sheriff answered, 'the Board has approved funding for another deputy and yes, at some stage I will be looking to appoint the best-qualified candidate.' His reply ensured that both camps were both variously content and aggrieved. Now Miss Pierce was up again, like a dog worrying a bone. Why was the Sheriff's Department playing the role of welfare queen, while all these murderers and rapists were abroad? Why was the sheriff no longer picking up all the waifs and strays and locking them up? Why was he no longer acting in the broader community's interest?

It was all to no avail. The combined forces arrayed against her were far too much for a mind that, if not in its dotage, was certainly beginning to suffer for its reliance on fading certainties. The discussion moved onto other things, such as nearby Holly Springs National Forest, and whether it was still under threat from loggers and, with this, the room seemed to heave a collective sigh of relief. But then, there she was again, on her feet, asking if congratulations had been sent to Trent Lott, for his fine senate victory over that 'communist radical' Wayne Dowdy. Pariche chuckled to himself. My God, this was a formidable woman.

By the time the meeting came to a close Pariche had formed the distinct feeling that his time in Mississippi had come to an end. Berkeley was calling, along with the chance to rub salt into the wounds of the mortally damaged reputation of a certain (acting) dean.

79

Virginia had stopped over on her way back from New Orleans, ostensibly to keep the sheriff briefed about what she'd found. Her real purpose, though, was to be with Soren. The old madness had returned and, with it, a desire to give certain issues a gentle shove. This would be no easy task; in matters of the heart Soren was too indolent, always likely to take the line of least resistance. It was a submissiveness that could all too easily translate into flight. She would need to be careful.

She noted that Pariche had gone, but the effects of his visit were everywhere. Some of those flyers were still in evidence and restorers were at work salvaging the books in the library. More intriguingly, Soren and Craig appeared to have three young women at their beck and call. She recognised Bridget immediately, who, within seconds, was dragging her away to look at something on the computer. Craig, the one who'd gone to such pains to procure it, was watching a host of figures scrolling across the screen. On noticing Virginia, he rose to his feet and gave her a welcoming hug. 'You must have a look at this!' he said, pulling up a chair so that she could sit beside him. He leant across and pulled a TV monitor towards him. It was attached to a videocassette recorder.

'I really don't know how they managed to do it' he said, somewhat vaguely, as Virginia sat down next to him. He handed her a printout, while the girls, all bubbly and giggles, hovered in the background. Virginia read on.

RECORDING OF INTERVIEW WITH MILLICENT PIERCE. DATE 11.25.88 WITH BRIDGET, ANGELA AND BUSBY.

Virginia smiled as she imagined how the girls would have inveigled their way into Miss Pierce's affections. And that *is* what they would have done. She would have been at a loss in trying to resist the combined forces of these three. Miss Pierce would have seen Bridget as one of her own and she would have been thrown on account of her being in the company of two coloured girls. Then Busby would have been all over the old girl, not letting there be no for an answer. 'But, Miss Pierce,' she would have said, as she towered over her, 'you're such a big part of the community. You owe it to set the record straight!' Yes, they would have smiled, fluttered their eyebrows and appealed to the vanity of the woman. Then the questions would come. Questions that would have been provided by Angela; subtle conversational ones. And what was this? Now there was the unmistakable sound of Millicent Pierce's voice. And more unbelievably, there she was, on film, in her own home, seated between Busby and Bridget. Virginia let out a slow whistle, her face an expression of stupefied disbelief. It could be safe to assume that this would probably have been the first time the woman had ever had a black person in her house who wasn't a maid. Angela was pointing the camera so that her every reaction was recorded. The initial look of bewilderment. A sideways glance. A suppressed scowl. Then a smile. The old girl looked her robust self, still very much attempting to retain a dignified control, as Busby and Bridget responded to her commands and fussed over her. But the undeniable truth, unfolding before their eyes, was of a woman whose universe was undergoing profound change. She spoke freely, and for some time. There was the story of her share cropper upbringing and the serious thought her folks had given to moving west. How she'd lost her father to lung disease and how she and her mother had been saved by the war when they'd both moved to New Orleans to work on the Liberty ships. 'I can still turn my hand to anything that needs welding!' she said, her chest brimming with pride. She was on her feet now, leading the interview team, with swinging camera in tow, out into her backyard. Once there, with an agility that would have done justice to someone half her age, she held up a pair of riveter's goggles in one hand and a welding torch in the other. Within moments she was hovering over an initially anxious Busby, tutoring her as to its use.

'Jesus,' signed Soren, who had just entered, 'she's out-Busby'd Busby!'

Later that day, feeling the need to get away for some time on their own, Soren and Virginia took a walk along one of the back roads not far from the Institute. It was now that Virginia told Soren of her worries for his mother's safety. How they might have got to grips with things down here, but the focus of her concerns had now moved north. Things had not been helped by what she'd learned from Dyson, about the FBI's operations up in Boston. Their colleagues in New Orleans had thought them so derelict, they'd asked for a formal review of the agents involved.

'So it's all been about Mother's investigation? It's been about her all the time? Then I need to get back!'

'To do what, Soren? Give them two targets! No, you need to carry on with what you're started here; Christina agreed that that would be the best course of action. You could, of course, call her. See how she's doing. You know, tell her how you feel. I know that's something you two find hard to do. God, you Karlssons really don't do that talking-to-each-other-thing much, do you?'

Soren let out a laugh. Apart from Elizabeth and Virginia, he knew that his mother didn't have that many confidants, but there did seem to be a growing correspondence with Pariche. She'd fallen for Pariche's irascible humour and his absurdist take on things; something that had gone some way to dispelling the worries and concerns she'd had. It was madness of course; the big bad world, with all its menaces and perils, would still be there waiting to be confronted. But, for a few precious moments, she'd been able to forget, and embrace the involvement of someone else's care. For Soren, the moment was bittersweet.

There was also something to remind them just how far Mississippi, the Magnolia State, still had to go. As they walked, they heard the chugging noise of a pick-up as it passed them. It slowed and they could see the occupants, two young boys, looking back at them through the rear window. Soon it was moving off again, but not without a defiant shout of 'Go home, nigger!' as it disappeared into the distance. And there it was: a casual, unrehearsed, and not atypical insult for these parts. Virginia smiled, squeezed Soren's hand and said, 'I guess folks down here are still not ready for this yet.'

After Virginia's departure, the next few weeks saw the clear up and development work at the Institute go on at a pace, with the seminar rooms finished just before the Christmas break. Craig oversaw the construction of the science lab and, through his contacts, Doleson came up trumps with the Rockefeller Foundation, convincing a certain Mr Bundy to travel south from his office in New York. The upshot was a decision by the Foundation to join with Zenotech in the funding of two teaching and research scholarships. And throughout all of this time, Pariche, much to the relief of all, was in Northern California looking after Denis and, as he repeatedly reminded people, 'Settling accounts.'

80

Boston, Massachusetts

In Boston, Diane, the young investigator working for Christina, finally put her fears to one side and stepped out into the winter sunshine. The weather was unseasonably mild, something she welcomed, being one of those people who always seemed to need an extra layer to keep out the cold. Now she was standing next to her boss, who gave her hand a reassuring caress as she led her to a dark sedan that had pulled up alongside. It had been a long haul, with Christina, in the end, having to more or less camp out on Diane's doorstep, not prepared to take no for an answer. It had been weeks since Diane had had the last of those calls; a vile, bloodcurdling call, where nothing had been left to the imagination. That the calls had stopped gave her hope that she might be out of danger. It was a foolish assumption. In accepting Christina's offer of help, she had only moved into the line of fire.

81

Albert Constanze knew that he was fighting for his life. On all fronts. As well as 'The Bitch', there were the Feds and the boys in New Orleans to worry about. He was also furious with himself. Furious for having lost face and for putting the boys down south in so much trouble. He knew they would be livid about getting the heat for something that appeared to be as petty as a personal grudge. Why had he allowed it to come to this? It had been a vanity project that had only drawn more interest from the authorities into his affairs. The New Orleans boys would want to know why Albert Constanze had needed to grandstand in front of the Karlsson investigation. Why had he brought all of this down on himself? Why couldn't he do his own dirty work? And what was this about a kiddy beef charge? Didn't he know they had standards? Now, as he sat in the back seat of his chauffeured limousine, his look was one of worry. Albert Constanze had never known things to look so bad.

'The boys in New Orleans are as mad as hell, Tank. They've had the Feds all over them and they've seized the car they used.'

'Can they link it to us?'

'The boys think they've got it covered, but this has gotta stop. We need to kill this thing at source!'

So later, when they were well alone, free from any possibility of being eavesdropped upon, federal or otherwise, Albert ordered a hit on The Bitch and her son. A day later, in a parking lot near Brookline, Tank could be seen sitting in his car, talking through an open window to a man who'd drawn up alongside in an old Chevrolet. A man with a shockingly white head of hair and a birthmark on his left cheek.

82

Berkeley, California

It would be fair to say that Pariche was like the proverbial pig in shit. When he got back to Berkeley there were only two things on his mind: to look after Denis and to make sure that Wilson at last got his comeuppance. It was only a question of time as to how long the (acting) dean could delay the inevitable and Pariche was determined to get in on the denouement when it came. Rumours about the real reason for Wilson's involvement with Flaxel were now doing the rounds and Pariche did his best to ensure that the flames feeding upon them would get an ample supply of fuel. Within hours of his arrival he was at the Chancellor's Office where, uncommonly for him, he received a more than sympathetic ear. Next, he was on the phone, bawling out some fool official in the Governor's Office in Sacramento who'd been a little too slow on the uptake. This was followed by detailed discussions, with Marjorie Forster and Kurst, about what needed to be done in the department. Forster's ardour for Wilson had been cooling ever since that initial departmental meeting, but the intimidation of Denis, and the disruption of his lectures, had been the last straw. Now she and Kurst set about Wilson with an affective and telling whispering campaign. And by the end of the week, Pariche had managed to get one of the shops along Telegraph to mockup a T-shirt, with a picture on it of a hand pointing at a well-known acting dean. It bore the caption, 'THIS MAN IS EVIL!' Needless to say, the students lapped it up.

Wilson for his part had chosen to brazen it out. He'd continued with his official duties, attending functions and taking an almost fatherly interest in Tsui's health. Of course he'd professed shock and ignorance of the true character of the man he'd gone into business with, and was only too willing to make amends. Nothing could be too trivial as far as Denis's welfare was concerned. Had the security added to his apartment been enough? Were there enough hours contracted for development and planning? And, of course, he'd see to it that a favourable track to tenure was set in train. Tenure not withstanding though, Denis was having none of it. Egged on by Pariche, he'd fallen into line with an entirely different agenda.

Already Pariche, and his people in Genetics, were in contact with Soren's colleagues over at UCSF, with an aim to spiriting the whole management of the Diaspora Project away from anything that could be associated with Wilson. Even Jerry Friesson was having cold feet. He'd heard reports from Marjorie, and from sources in the Chancellor's Office, about how they'd been alarmed at Wilson associating himself with those who'd seek to disrupt classes and beat up members of the Berkeley community. There had even been talk of resignations. Didn't they know that Wilson had acted alone? That Jerry Friesson had been one of the first to counsel against such an arrangement. The words 'rats' and 'sinking ship' came readily to mind. And when the denouement did indeed come it was swift and brutal, arriving in the form of a series of articles published in *Rolling Stone Magazine*. Harvey had done a sterling job, penning articles that appeared to show the blessed (acting) dean engaged in an assortment of barely legal and flagrantly illegal activities with folks from the seamier side of East Bay life. The pictures of him snorting coke and cavorting with hookers were enough, but what really did for him, in the eyes of the Chancellor's Office, and the good people on Academic Senate, was the evidence of a direct link between the dean's office and the campaign against Denis Tsui. The chump had even been foolish enough to pay monies into a checking account accessed by a certain member of the Nation of Islam in that person's alternative role as teller at the local bank. And the cherry on the cake? Well, there was a picture of Wilson, along with a certain street hustler whose face had been blacked out, in a state of undress, cavorting with Miss

Betty Boo from the local community college. Within hours the Chancellor's Office had sent out a press release to the *Daily Californian* letting its displeasure be known at the way Wilson had brought disrepute upon the university. His resignation was accepted immediately.

Of course, Wilson didn't leave the university. People at Berkeley don't allow themselves to give up tenure that easily. But as dean, he was finished. Soren's old friend Kurst was agreed in the position by acclamation and one of the first things to cross his desk was a proposal from Marjorie Foster, supported by Pariche and Soren, that Denis should be given an associate professorship. Once appointed, the first thing he asked for was that a certain Miss Teager should be hired by the university and given the task of liaising with the local community. Something that would include the rather crestfallen head of a certain local community college.

83

The Berkshires, western Massachusetts

Christmas had always been a time when Christina would try to get family and friends together. After the events of the past few months, it was something she aimed to accomplish with even greater finesse this year. She brooked no nonsense, even strong-arming Pariche into making an appearance. As far as she was concerned, he was a person who'd become an increasingly welcome figure; a true friend to her son and a provider of good counsel. So Pariche flew east, pleased to be escaping the usual contemplation of Christmas alone, stranded high up in the Eastern Sierras. Christina herself had left it late getting back to Ashleighs, as she had committee and practice work to complete in Boston. She finally arrived back on the morning of Christmas Eve, with Diane, her young investigator, in tow. That same morning, Virginia drove up from Pittsburgh.

By the time Virginia was making her last approach up the lane towards the house, it was already late afternoon. She had just one more month left to serve with the Pittsburgh Police Bureau and was looking forward to a period that would be mostly composed of leave and the opportunity to hook up with Soren. Crucially, she hadn't as yet handed in either her badge or her gun. As she drove up to the house, through a light covering of snow, she was struck by the sight of a police car and a Ford compact parked outside. Something didn't look right. Almost instinctively she went into cop mode, reaching inside the glove compartment to retrieve her hand gun as she turned off the car engine. Approaching on foot she could see that the driver's side door of the police car was open. Then she saw the body. A prone figure lying half out of the patrol car; his feet in the well of the vehicle and the rest of his torso on the driveway. She could see that he'd been shot several times. His name tag identified him as State Trooper Briand. Although she could see that he was dead, she still felt the compulsion to check his pulse. Immediately there was a realisation that the killer or killers might still be around.

She made quickly and stealthily for the house. She was beginning to sweat, beginning to panic. Something had gone terribly wrong and she sensed that the people closest to her were in grave danger. A couple of paces and she was at the back door. It was open. She did not enter, but continued to the terrace and the French windows that opened into the study. They were unlocked. This time she did go in. It took only a few moments to establish that there was nobody home. Where was everyone? Who had been responsible for this? Frantically she looked for clues; anything that could give her some idea of what had happened and where people had gone. Then she caught sight of a note on the kitchen table. It was from Christina, telling her they'd all gone for a walk on Porter's Mount. Almost immediately she was back outside. At the front of the house she noticed a pair of footprints with a zigzag thread leading from the Ford compact. She quickly deduced that they probably belonged to the killer and that he was alone. She looked up at Porter's Mount and then down at the tracks again, almost frozen in horror. The prints were tracking others that appeared to belong to a group. The certain knowledge that they belonged to Christina and her party filled her with dread. Momentarily she turned and caught sight of the stricken patrolman again. She went over to his car, reached in, and carefully picked up the radio receiver. The dispatcher at the end of the line was suspicious.

'Just who is this? How did you get hold of this frequency?'

'Sir, will you please shut the fuck up and listen very carefully. You are talking to Detective Bradley-Moore with the Pittsburgh Police Bureau. I'm at Senator Karlsson's house in East Brunswick. You have an officer down.'

'Down, did you say?'

'Yes, I'm afraid he's dead. I fear that the senator might have been the target. It is important that you get people out here quickly. I'm going to continue on foot. I believe the killer is headed for Porter's Mount. Check me out with Divisional Commander Dilks in Pittsburgh if you must, but get your people out here pronto!'

As she replaced the receiver she noticed the stricken police officer's handcuffs, and ammunition for a gun the same as hers. 'The more the merrier,' she muttered to herself as she helped herself. Before long she was setting off at an easy jog. Once again she could feel panic driving her forward. As she ran along the track all she could picture was a prone Soren laid out on a mortuary slab, just like she'd seen so many others. She sped past the reservoir and over the snow-covered links, into the barren woodlands of the valley floor. Within minutes she was at the clearing that had so enthused Soren just eight short weeks before. About a hundred yards ahead of her, she could see a lone figure. Her relief was palpable. For the first time she allowed herself hope. There was still time. The man stopped, turned and appeared to crouch. He was now raising an arm pointing towards her. PING – there was the popping sound of hot metal zipping into the snow and ice at her feet, and the distant retort of a gun. The figure was now running towards her, obviously unaware that she might be armed. Quickly she ducked behind a nearby wall and pulled out her gun. She kept perfectly still. Her gaze was fixed, her attention total, her body taut. Then she caught sight of her quarry. She tensed, took aim and quickly let off one-two-three shots. There was a cry, followed by the sound of a body slumping to the ground. Felix had attempted, and failed, his last job.

She rose to her feet and cautiously approached the prone figure. She could see that his gun had fallen from his grasp. She quickly kicked it away, then, unceremoniously, she turned the man onto his front, at the same time forcing his hands up behind his back. This brought forth a howl of pain. Ignoring this, she expertly applied a pair of handcuffs before allowing him to assume a more dignified position.

'Sorry about ripping your shirt,' she said, 'but we can't have you bleeding to death can we?' She said, before administering a makeshift dressing to a wound just below his ribs. 'Guess I don't have much legal jurisdiction in these parts,' she continued. 'Can't read you your rights. I'll leave that to these gentleman.' She pointed towards the distant flashing lights of police cars, all reds and blues, converging below, and distant figures making their way onto the mountain, up towards them.

With Felix safely in the hands of the local police, Virginia borrowed one of the officer's binoculars and pointed them towards Porter's summit. She could see the outline of nine figures set against the failing light. Christina had done an excellent job in rounding them all up. Instantly she recognised Soren and Christina, herself, the Van Burens, Dyson, and Soren's father, Harold. Next to him were two young black women, one of whom she remembered as Soren's half-sister. The other, she was later to learn was the young legal investigator, Diane. She was arm-in-arm with another mystery, a young waif of girl who herself was holding on to the man who'd assumed the mantle of her surrogate father. Of course, they just had to be Bonnie and Pariche and, like the others, they were watching the commotion below in various states of curiosity, anxiety and alarm. Virginia could see that Soren was now himself peering down at her through a pair of binoculars he'd managed to purloin from Dyson. On recognising her, his face broke into a smile, and, in no time at all, he was gesticulating excitedly to the others and pointing in her direction. After a few moments, he calmed down, and turned the focus of the binoculars on her again. He waved, and, with an ecstatic sense of relief and a welling up of tears, she waved back.

84

Christina herself saw to it that Trooper Briand's widow and their two children were taken care of. A memorial fund was set up, with executors appointed to ensure that all proceeds were set aside for the children's education. What had promised to be a welcome break over Christmas had turned into a harrowing inquest and burial, along with a renewed resolve on Christina's part to go after Constanze. People also noted the return of an inner confidence that presaged a change of appearance and a growing ambition as to how she should look and what she could wear. Rather than being teased into a taut bun, her hair was now carefully coiffured into a fashionable fringe, long and straight at the sides. Also, there were more social outings with Elizabeth and those dark funeral suits began to give way to light satin ghost and body hugging retro dresses so beloved by Mainbocher and Jacques Fath. It was not lost on colleagues that the transformation appeared to coincide with the increasingly frequent visits made by a certain gentleman from Mono County, California. There was still the political intrigue of her partners, at the law firm, to deal with, and the threat of merger, but, for the first time as long as she could remember, Christina appeared to have other, more important, priorities.

Albert Constanze never did stand trial, but he was much diminished as far as his friends in the mob were concerned. His fate had been sealed as soon as he'd taken umbrage at what was coming out of Christina's enquiry and had demanded his time in the spotlight. He'd been led by the nose into a sucker play; an act of pure hubris that had made him a marked man; the charge of child procurement had just been the icing on the cake. But as hard as Christina tried, none of the authorities in Boston, federal or otherwise, could make anything stick. Felix, of course, would serve his thirty years to life, whatever was the shortest, but he wasn't going to talk. Elsewhere, though, things were looking up. In New Orleans the FBI had been hard at work and a Mr Francis Gambietta was soon being arraigned for manslaughter. Forensic work on those glass fragments, by the FBI themselves and the labs in Pittsburgh and Berkeley, had been backed up by General Motors's own people in Lansing, Michigan. It proved conclusively that the fragments did indeed come from Gambietta's car. The FBI also found gas receipts and a hotel bill that put him in the state of Mississippi on the day of the killing. Of course he kept quiet, but it would be fair to surmise that a certain Albert Constanze would not have been exactly flavour of the month.

As for Soren, he had to cut short his sojourn in Toshoba and return to Berkeley, where he was joined by his now pregnant partner and prospective wife. It did not go unremarked that he'd greatly reduced his teaching and research commitments and was devoting more time to those of impending house husbandry, writing and shooting the breeze with Pariche, with the two of them making regular forays into the high Sierras to 're-tool', as Pariche so colourfully put it. Of course, the Genotech people saw to it that Soren was made director of the Diaspora Centre, but, in the main, he was content to take a back seat, leaving the day-to-day running of the program that fed into it to Denis. And the prospects for Virginia also looked good. She had offers for her story of how she and Christina had managed to bring the great Constanze to his knees. The blue blood publishing houses of New York were positively salivating at the thought. There would be TV appearances, along with book tours and signings. For Virginia though, things were perhaps moving a little *too* fast and she had misgivings about anything that might be seen as revelling in a mafia hoodlum's misfortune. Let sleeping dogs lie she'd counselled to herself. No, she would continue with her plans to return to law, sitting the California bar exams, and joining a firm in San Francisco. Moving to California had been a wrench and she still had her parents to think about. Her father, though, did finally bow to the inevitable and agree to place her mother in a home. It meant that there would be more time to do the things he'd always wanted to, with the promise of making regular visits out west to be with his daughter and prospective grandchild.

Back in Mississippi, the Institute never did reach the giddy heights envisaged by Doleson, although, in other ways, it positively surpassed them. Kids from all of schools in Toshoba and Clancy – yes, there were even some from the Cedars – now made use of its refurbished library and its suite of study rooms. And Craig had managed to come up trumps again, purloining a whole class set of BSD workstations for the science lab. Angela and Busby did get to go to an integrated prom, taking Bridget along with them, although a quarter of the white students stayed away, choosing to attend an unofficial 'whites only' one instead. Still, it was a victory of sorts. Garvey resolved once again to quit drinking, and for a time kept to it. But his practice began to suffer, or so he said, and he took to the bottle again. So Cecilia carried out her threat to move out. Doleson tried to help as best he could, but had to sorrowfully conclude that this was one broken promise too many. With Cecelia gone, Garvey quickly fell into immobility and depression again, although he did perk up on learning that the Californians would be returning for the Easter break.

And Pariche himself? Well, in addition to the frissons and joys of his emerging friendship with Christina, he'd found a new mission in life, something that would really make the committee people look up and take notice. Except that there was just one fly in the ointment. Up in the foothills, about thirty miles from his June Lake home, late heavy rains and a mudslide had washed away part of a mountainside to reveal the skeletal remains of a woman. It was Pariche's late wife, Mildred, and an ambitious district attorney, down the road in Bishop, had quickly decided that Pariche might be the one responsible for her death. After all, as Pariche had so often said, Mildred Hildegaarth Neuman was someone a good man could so easily kill for.